# NIGHT OF TH...

In the dark, the earth spoke to Big Oak, the white man who could see the future, who would, if he could, save the men who were coming to kill him.

To Sam's front there was motion, then faint shapes, six of them, ten yards apart. Sam laid his sights on one blurry shape, troubled, his mind astir. They began to move forward again and it was then, as he pulled the trigger, that he knew.

"To your front, Thad!" he cried, and when his son looked he saw that overnight the seven who had pursued them had become three times that many.

Everywhere there were shrieking, screaming Mohawks, flourishing tomahawks. A muzzle flashed so close that Thad could feel the powder burns on his cheek, but somehow the bullet failed to find its mark. A tomahawk whizzed by his ear. The enemy was making horrifying noises. There were so many of them, and the night was so dark . . .

*The First Frontier Series by Mike Roarke*
*from St. Martin's Paperbacks*

# THUNDER IN THE EAST

## MIKE ROARKE

ST. MARTIN'S PAPERBACKS

First published 1993 by St Martin's Press, Inc., New York

First published in Great Britain 1994 by Pan Books Limited
a division of Pan Macmillan Publishers Limited
Cavaye Place London SW10 9PG
and Basingstoke

Associated companies throughout the world

ISBN 0 330 33446 8

A CIP catalogue record for this book is available from
the British Library

Printed and bound in Great Britain by
Mackays of Chatham Ltd, Chatham Kent

# For Shirley, Ken and B.J.

coat now and then he would continue with the task at

# ❧ I ❧

"SOME FOLKS ARE JUST NATURALLY HAPPY," Big Oak would tell his son Little Oak in soft tones as they sat by the campfire. "Other folks walk through life like a rainstorm was meant just to get *them* wet. Of course, now, if you let yourself get *too* happy, your mind might wander a bit when it should be tendin' to business. And that could get you killed."

Big Oak always spoke in soft tones when he and his son were in the woods, under the tall green canopy of oaks, maples, elms, birches, and hemlocks that stretched from the Hudson River clear out to the big lakes.

Big Oak's ears were tuned to the song of the forest. He knew every note of that song and he knew when the song was being sung right. If just one of the players was out of tune, he would freeze in the middle of whatever he was doing for the split second it would take him to identify the sour note, and then he would continue with the task at hand.

Otherwise Big Oak was forever in motion. Little Oak, his eighteen-year-old son, was part of that motion, and had been since his mother had died seven years before. Motion was survival in the woods, whether it was a careful journey to check their traps on the nearest beaver creek, or the careful cleaning of their Friedrich Deutschmann Pennsylvania long rifles, or a visit to a far Seneca village to repair some ancient muskets in return for a bit of peltry.

Little Oak could not imagine what it was like to be the kind of person who blamed the Great Spirit for sending a rain shower on a personal quest to soak him. In fact, it was hard for him to understand why anyone would mind getting wet on a warm summer's day. Like his father, his spirit soared from the first moment he opened his honest eyes to the cry of the morning bird song, till he pulled his blanket around him at the end of the day and let the nighttime serenade sing him to sleep.

The man and the boy were of a type so often found among American frontiersmen—conditioned by a life of constant movement, they had not an ounce of fat on their bodies but were well-muscled in their shoulders, their chests, and most of all, their long legs, which swung effortlessly, one step after the other, in their journey across the English colony of New York. Their faces bore a look of open honesty and tolerance that hid the shrewd calculating mind common to all successful traders.

Their Christian names were not, of course, Little Oak and Big Oak, those names having been applied to them by their Seneca associates. Their surname was Watley, their given names Sam and Thad, although they called each other, naturally enough, Pa and son. Sam, the older, sometimes bearded and nearly always red from wind burn, had fair hair and bright blue eyes, while the younger was beardless, with black hair and dark eyes. His bronze skin defied the sun, for his mother had been a full-blooded Seneca.

Sam had lived for many years with the Seneca in their western New York village of Tonowaugh. The Seneca were the most populous nation of the six member Iroquois Confederacy, which for more than two hundred years had terrorized Indians and intimidated whites hundreds of miles from their council fire in Onondaga.

Dozens of tribes, nations, and confederacies surrounded the huge territory that fewer than fifteen thousand Iroquois held as their birthright. Their names included such stalwart, warlike groups as the Abnaki, Algonquin, Huron, Delaware, Mohican, Twightwee (Miami), Ottawa, Chippewa, Shawnee, Caughnawaga, Erie, Susquehannock, and many others, but the five, and later six, nations of the Iroquois Confederation held fast against them all, and in fact reached out to control lands far beyond their borders.

Thanks to their fearsome reputation, there were Seneca villages in the west like Tonowaugh, which managed to live in peace and security for many years. No matter how hated were the Iroquois, even their most fanatical enemies shied away from revenge raids, knowing that if their warriors harmed a hair on the head of an Iroquois child, then the scalps of many of their own people would soon be drying in the longhouses of the Iroquois.

Among the Seneca, Sam had settled as a trapper and fur trader, a profession that had attracted a wide variety of scoundrels as well as a few good men. His previous career as a scout for the English had earned him the respect of red and white alike, and his fairness in trade had done nothing to tarnish that respect.

He had first come to Tonowaugh more than twenty years before with a packhorse and a sack full of traps. The Seneca, understandably, were less than keen on seeing another white trapper sharing in their beaver catch. Already the Iroquois had to range deep into hostile territory, the fur-bearing population of their country having been depleted.

There had been something different about this tall, strong man. He could communicate with them, and although he was only about twenty years old at the time, he had a quiet dignity that they could not help but admire. He did not yet speak their language, but could sign as well as they could. He was more like a Frenchman than an Englishman in that he did not look down on the Indians like most of the English did.

And he was the deadliest shot they had ever seen. When the game was hard to find, he was the one who brought down a deer or a brace of birds, and when he did, he gave with an open hand, as if he were a great chief. He did not horde his goods greedily, like most white men they knew.

In fact, he was like nobody they knew. At first he did not know the woods as well as they did. Once, he left the village for an overnight hunt and was gone for five days. When he returned hungry, gameless, tired, and scratched—as if he'd lost a wrestling match with a catamount—they asked him where he had been. Had he been dodging Shawnee in the hills? Had he been stalking a giant buck clear to Niagara?

"No," he said guilelessly. "I got lost."

They stared at him as if he had suddenly sprouted the features of a False Face, the grotesque carved, ceremonial masks common to all the Iroquois. Then they began to laugh, cruelly, derisively, at the tall, slender young white man. But instead of reddening with anger, he tilted his head to one side for a moment, considered the situation, and joined them in their laughter.

By that time he had made a friend of one of the Seneca, a lazy good-natured man named Sad Eye who spent his days on the Genesee River with a fishnet instead of tramping through the forest chasing deer. But Sad Eye probably contributed more food to his family that way than most of the keen-eyed deer killers. He spoke slowly to Sam in the simplest Seneca he could conceive.

"They are laughing at you in front of everybody," he murmured. "They are making a fool of you."

"*They* can't do that," Sam responded. "*I* did that." With that he turned to the circle of Seneca men having such a good time around the fire at his expense. "Do you know," he said to them in the Seneca tongue he had been learning so slowly and painfully, "that for two days I walked in a very wide circle around the village following my own trail?" He made a huge sweeping motion with his arm to show just how wide a circle he had made. They looked at each other, stunned into silence as they imagined him following his own footsteps for days within shouting distance of his home village. But before they could explode into renewed laughter, he held up a hand for a few more moments of silence.

"And, hear me now. Each time I came around, the path became clearer and clearer, until I thought I was on the main trail from the Mohawk Valley to the land of the Erie." Now they did explode, only this time the laughter was full of the admiration Indians feel for a man who can appreciate a good joke at his own expense.

"How did you get back, Big Oak?" a warrior asked, using a name that was beginning to settle comfortably on his broad shoulders, like the epaulets of a British uniform.

"How? Well, that trail I'd been following for two days, I guess I must have . . . lost it"—more laughter—"and for three miles I plowed through thornbushes. I hit the village down at the other end, and until I saw old Lucy there"—he pointed to a particularly fat, particularly odd-shaped old woman—"I thought I'd stumbled upon a different village. Why, I hid out for a while, trying to decide if it was a friendly village." This last statement was untrue and everybody knew it, but they loved it nevertheless, and laughed about it for many years.

Sam loved the village, a simple town at peace for so long that the palisades that guarded it for many years had rotted away long ago. There were several bark-covered longhouses about twenty feet wide by fifty to a hundred feet long, plus a number of small cabins occupied by families who had broken away from the traditional Iroquois dwelling. The houses lined up along straight dirt streets shaded by beautiful old oak and elm trees. In the center of the village was a large open space where the men would hold council in the summer. The village was surrounded on three sides by broad fields of corn and beans, lovingly tended by the women, with some help by a couple of very individualistic men.

On the fourth side was the Genesee River, the Seneca highway north to Lake Ontario. The people of this tiny village were gregarious, and spent much of each summer paddling up and down the river, visiting family and friends in other villages. Maybe their fields weren't as well-attended as they should have been. Maybe their berry gathering was always a little short. Maybe they spent less time in the summer preparing for the long Seneca winter, and maybe they fell sometimes a little short of stockpiling what they needed to carry them through the winter, but they did love their visiting and their friends and relatives who lived a day or two's journey away.

The Senecas put up with Big Oak out of natural Indian hospitality for a couple of months, until they took in the full impact of his deadly marksmanship, added to their discovery that he could not only shoot a rifle, he could fix one too. They realized he could be a tremendous asset to the village. Life among the Indians, after all, was a constant quest for greater military security, and this man might be the key to many more years of peace along the Genesee.

Maybe wise old Kendee had that in mind when he brought Big Oak home for dinner one night. Kendee was a respected man in the village who sought no leadership positions but was always reliable when it came to meeting the needs of the community. He had outlived three wives, and of his seven children, only one shared his portion of the longhouse.

Her name was, simply, Willow. She was sixteen years old, and Kendee was determined to make a match with the tall white trapper. The reason was more than just respect for the young man. The Seneca village of Tonowaugh may have known peace for many years, but that did not mean its young men stayed home when there were adventures to be had, ambushes to be laid, laurels to be won, scalps to be collected. And when these young men went out into the wilderness, pursuing their dreams of glory, it was inevitable that some of them would not come back. Consequently, there were always more eligible women around than men, and few of the men were successful enough to support more than one wife at a time. Kendee was a good man, and he was determined to find not just a man for his daughter, but a good man.

So he brought Big Oak home to meet Willow.

The first moment Big Oak saw the face of Willow flickering in the light of her home fire, he knew that part of his life was no longer his.

She was stirring the big cast-iron kettle that was bubbling over the fire. Her eyes were cast down at the kettle's contents, obscured by lowered eyelids and lashes so long that they might have been those of a young doe. Kendee announced his guest and introduced him to her. She looked up, and Big Oak stood fixed in the gaze of a pair of eyes so big and dark that he thought he was about to get lost in them, and he did not want to get lost again.

She rose from her knees, and he saw that she was very tall for an Indian woman, above five and a half feet, and thin, but not painfully so. Her face was round and dark, her lips full, and her hair in braids, and to his surprise, she was wearing a simple blue cotton dress.

She smiled. "I have heard about you. They say you cannot find your way in the woods." It was a playful tease, and he knew it.

"There was a time when a shot from my rifle could not have hit the side of a longhouse," he replied, omitting that that time would have been when he was seven years of age. "Yet today I can kill a deer at a distance at which no one else can even see it." It was a simple statement, not a boast. "I can take apart the pieces of my rifle and put them back together in the heart of the night. I will learn the woods as well."

The courtship was swift and intense. Each knew they wanted the other, and neither made a secret of it. In a short time he had moved into his wife's home, as men of the Iroquois do. Almost immediately she was with child, a strong man child who grew so tall and rawboned so early that to the village he was Little Oak just as surely as his father was Big Oak.

As the years went by, the men of Big Oak's village and all

the other Seneca villages he visited learned to trust him as a man of exceptional honesty and decency. Nearly all of the white men they traded with were villainous knaves, or at least men who couldn't resist the temptation to hoodwink people strange to the ways of European commerce. When crooked words failed, there was always rum, and rum almost never failed. When a trader came to a Seneca village, as much as the Seneca looked forward to the goods they were about to receive, many dreaded the thought that some way or other, the trader, who any of them could crush with half an effort, would somehow find a way to cheat them.

The idea of having one of their own supplying their needs made the Seneca plead with Big Oak to abandon his traps for pack trains. For Sam, it was an opportunity to raise his family in comfort, so he seized it.

But before he was able to build his business, war broke out between the French and the English. War was always breaking out between the French and the English in Europe, and when it did, their colonists generally fought it out in North America. This little tiff was known as King George's War, and the British won some major conquests in the new world, which they were persuaded to give back by treaty at the end of the war. Sam had learned to find his way around the forests of New York as well as any white man west of the Hudson River, so he spent the entire war scouting for the British.

In the meantime, Thad was growing up into a young copy of his father, except that he was an Indian copy.

When Sam finally made it home from the war, he was told that Willow had sickened and died only a month before he arrived at the village with his cohorts. There had been no general outbreak, no smallpox or measles or flu that had carried off half the village. Perhaps she had eaten something bad. One day she was healthy, the next day she was sick, and the day after that she was dead. So said her broken-hearted father Kendee. "She didn't know she was dying. We didn't know she was dying. And suddenly, in the middle of the night, she was gone."

Big Oak cried then, great big tears of grief and emptiness that crushed Kendee's spirit even more. He walked to the door of the longhouse for a moment. Big Oak was a son to him, and he could not stand to see his son cry.

"Don't worry," he said. "You'll find another woman. Fine women in Tonowaugh," he insisted.

"Where is my son?" Big Oak asked, finally succeeding in bringing his emotions under control.

He discovered, then, that while he had been blazing trails in the name of commerce and war, Little Oak had grown into a fine Seneca boy.

Big Oak had learned in his travels that growing up Iroquois was not necessarily the best thing for a boy, considering the future of the Iroquois and the rest of the eastern tribes. So he decided to send his son off to get a white boy's education. Schools were scarce and expensive, but he had found a Presbyterian preacher at Oquaga, down on the Susquehanna River, who boarded a few boys and taught them to write and do sums.

He told Little Oak that when the leaves began to turn, he would be going off to learn books. The boy bucked like a deer that had been butt-shot. "I'm a Seneca," he spat in flawless Seneca dialect, for his English was spotty. "I will stay with the people of my mother." Little Oak, who had just turned eleven, now turned on his moccasins and started to walk away. Big Oak, instinctively wise to the ways of boys, then said the words that quelled his son's rebellion and changed the boy's future.

"We won't talk of this now, son. In two days you and I will be on the trail to Albany. You are ready to do your first trading."

The boy turned back toward his father, his eyes shining. Thoughts of school vanished like a summer shower. He thought of all the shining things traders carried with them, and imagined himself appearing in Tonowaugh one sunny afternoon with a string of canoes loaded with trade goods, while the villagers spilled down the banks of the Genesee eager to see what he had brought.

A sharp pang reminded him that his mother would not be there to show her pride in him. And he remembered that young men of the Iroquois Confederacy did not ferry kettles and cloth along the trails from the stinking cities. Their trails were warpaths to distant villages, to teach other tribes lessons of Iroquois might and bring back tales of their prowess. He and his friends, Skoiyasi and John Thompson, often pretended to be back from the warpath, boasting of the scalps they had taken, the fear they had inspired in their enemies, and the brave men who had resisted only to be conquered, for the Iroquois always conquered. Stripped down to loincloths, painted in savage stripes and circles, they had carried off their friend, little Kawia, many times, and adopted her into the tribe, where she was always happy to tell them how much greater were they, the people of the Western Door, than the Huron, or Chippewa, or Shawnee with whom she had lived before they had stormed her village and made her an Iroquois.

They all adored Kawia and took turns teasing or spoiling her in the manner in which boys everywhere show their love, and she showed hers by taking it and coming back for more. Little Oak couldn't wait to tell Kawia that he was to spend the summer on the trail to Albany with his father. The Seneca all respected Big Oak, and therefore the things that Big Oak did were worthy of respect. With a confusing mixture of sadness and anticipation, the boy Little Oak had walked back into the longhouse, picked up the heavy rifle that his father had been saving for him, and begun to clean it as his father had taught him the year before, during one of his frequent self-styled furloughs.

In the years that had followed, the Presbyterian Reverend Heflin, his father, and the woods had given Thad an education both deep and wide, until Sam regarded his boy as much a partner as a son.

Both Sam and Thad were tall, a shade more than six-foot-two apiece. They wore animal skins from head to foot, though the younger wore beneath his shirt a bright blue silk scarf which Kawia had given him before they had left To-nowaugh.

They each carried a small pack filled with parched corn and pressed venison and berries, a water pouch, and a large, heavy pack of skins that they had traded for on the French side of Lake Ontario—a dangerous bit of business, because in the Canadas, the King of France was the law, and the king did not value the lives of English colonists. There were five more similar packs cached beneath the floor of a secluded cave close to the Te-non-an-at-che River, the River Flowing Through Mountains, known to the whites as the Mohawk.

They had hoped to transport their furs via canoe down the river to Fort Albany. But war was again in the air, and canoes on the river were like ducks on the pond to the indigenous Onondagas and Mohawks, marauding Mingoes and Caughnawagas, and the various cutthroats and murderers, red and white alike, that war and rumors of war tended to stir up.

So they took enough furs on their broad backs to tide them over till times got better, and struck out through the sweet-smelling green canopy that covered most of the length and breadth of New York in 1755.

Filled with the kind of distrust that fosters survival in such times, father and son traveled on remote trails and traces along the tough, rocky ridge lines, and consequently they saw no one during the first three days of their journey. In a wide-striding lope, they covered mile after mile, single file, father in the lead, son watching the back trail, speaking rarely until they hit camp.

And then, one afternoon, as they were descending one of the endless succession of hills in the country southwest of

Canajoharie Castle, Sam froze like a hound on the point. There was a voice or two missing from the forest choir. He motioned silently for Thad to drop his fur pack. His son knew what that meant. They stood, still as tree trunks, waiting until it finally came, the thin snap of a small twig beneath a moccasined foot. Suddenly, like flushed rabbits, the two bounded forward in a long-legged run down the trail, a swift gait yet short of a sprint, knowing this would be a lengthy footrace and that their lives might depend upon the outcome.

Five strides forward they heard voices, then the shrill toot of an eagle-bone whistle, and the forest was alive with rapid footsteps behind and to the left of them. Instinctively, Big Oak veered off the trail to his right, away from the flankers, his son three steps behind and matching him stride for stride. Beneath the dense, shaded canopy, they had to concentrate on the ground in front of them. One misstep and a life would be lost.

Down the hillside they sped, fleet and sure-footed as the whitetail deer, willing themselves calm. Panic may be good for the short run, but for the long chase it is the thief of energy and endurance.

Now from behind they could hear more rapid footsteps as one of their faster pursuers began to sprint, attempting to force father and son into a dash that would quickly wear them down. Big Oak picked up the pace a bit, aware that the lone sprinter had more than a hundred yards to make up and daring him to do it.

Soon they could hear his footsteps receding to the pack immediately behind them. There were no whoops or shrieks coming from the pursuers. All energy was devoted to the chase, which by now had exceeded a mile in length and showed no signs of a finish. Sam veered right a little more, farther away from the flankers on the left. Their pursuers took note and sent a few flankers to the right. From here on in it would be a straight chase, or at least as straight as a chase could be down a wooded hillside.

Swiftly they ran down a slope paved with grass, smooth dirt, and small pebbles, around a large outcropping of granite, then worked their way along a steep, rugged incline, bounding from boulder to boulder, ducking low-hanging boughs and hurdling over fallen branches. Several braves, both behind them and on their flank, let out shrieking whoops to inspire themselves, but the flankers, who had to plow through heavy woodland, were hard put to keep up.

Sam and Thad jumped a stream and cleared a few small boulders, then plunged through some dried-up undergrowth. Dappled sunlight winked at them through the overhanging branches of birch and elm. The growth was beginning to thin out and the downslope leveled off.

Their breathing was deeper now, and labored, but still strong. Thad could see sunlight ahead, signs of meadow or cleared land. They went into a full sprint, and suddenly they exploded into a full clearing, a meadow of at least twenty acres, grazed to the stubble.

"If we can make it to the center of this field, we can hold off half the Mohawk nation," Sam said.

Their sudden sprint had so surprised their pursuers that Sam and Thad were a good hundred yards out from the woods by the time the first Indians made it to the edge of the clearing. A shot rang out and echoed off the hills but Sam took no notice. Ten, twenty, forty strides more and then Sam abruptly turned, fell to one knee and cocked his rifle. It was then that Thad got his first look at his pursuers.

Surprised at Sam's stand, they had all stopped and dropped into the sparse long grass. Even at a distance of an eighth of a mile, Thad could see their chests heaving, as was his, and he wondered if their hearts were pumping with the same excitement.

He had never before seen Mohawks over a rifle sight, scalp locks standing stiff like porcupine quills, stripped bare to the waist in deerskin leggings, painted in reds, yellows, and blacks, ready to kill. Ready to kill them.

There were seven of them, all armed with rifles or muskets. Two of them fired, but their bullets kicked up dust well in front of where the two woodsmen lay. Thad laughed.

"Can any of 'em shoot?" he asked.

"Maybe. Never seen one who could," Sam answered. "They're kinda poor, most of them, 'cause they never learned to save or get greedy." Sam was good at seeing both sides of a question. Were they wasteful or just not greedy enough to get rich? He never judged. He lived his life, and that was enough.

"They can't buy good rifles and they can't afford enough powder and shot to get a lot of practice. Aw, they're all right for about twenty-five yards in an ambush, but from where they are, they can pepper us all day without drawin' blood unless they get real lucky. But be careful. Sometimes they *do* get lucky." Another puff of smoke, followed by a soft boom, and an echo. "Now that feller there, he thinks he can save powder by chargin' her light, that or someone sold him some bad powder. He'd have to point her halfway to heaven for his ball to reach us, and then you could prob'ly catch it in your hat if you were of a mind to. Poor devils."

Little Oak shook his head. Here was a party of angry Mohawks trying as hard as they could to collect a couple of scalps, and Sam just sitting there kind of interested, probably trying to figure out how to help his enemy become better shooters.

The Mohawks were fanning out around them, creeping in closer, considering a rush. Sam shook his head. "Can't let 'em do that, now, can we?" he said, assuming a prone position and sighting down his long barrel. "I'll just skin one a little. If they keep coming, nail one dead center and reload. We'd get three or four of them before they could get close enough to hurt us. They wouldn't like that."

He squeezed off a shot and caught a little more Indian than he wanted, spun him around and put him on his back.

"Reckon I broke his arm. I don't think they'll come. 'Least not for now."

Sam was right. Two men were tending to their wounded

comrade, and three others fired ineffectually at them. A fourth pulled the trigger and sent a message that thudded into the earth five yards in front of Thad.

"That one's got an idea," Sam observed. "We'd better hunker down. Sam had found them a natural bowl about three yards across and just deep enough to offer them some cover from distant shooting on all sides. The Indians retreated into the woods.

"Waitin' till dark," Sam said.

"Grandfather said they didn't attack in the dark."

"If it feels right to them, they'll attack in the dark."

"That works two ways, Pa. If we can't see them comin', they can't see us goin'. We can be gone five hours before they know."

"They can see. Believe me, they can see better from the woods at night than we can see to the end of our nose. You had best close your eyes and get some sleep because you're gonna need to be awake tonight."

But Thad couldn't sleep. The thought of being surrounded by a deadly enemy with night approaching kept his eyelids wide apart.

"Can't we make a run for it, Pa?" he asked desperately.

"Put us right back in the woods with those devils," he said softly. "Don't worry, son. I've been in tighter spots. We'll get out of this." But Thad could see the worried furrows in his father's forehead, and he felt his stomach tighten.

They watched and waited, chewing on small amounts of venison and parched corn, and washing it down with a few swallows of water. The cool July evening swept in on a beautiful pink sunset, but all Thad could see was the darkening tree line, and the Mohawks who would soon be blending in with the darkness, silently creeping up on them, knives at the ready, ready to stab, slash, and scalp.

They lay side by side in opposite directions, rifles, knives, and hatches in hand or close by, each watching half the surrounding field. The sky was fading from blue to black, with no moon and little starlight.

"Pa," Thad whispered. "When will they come?"

"Just before dawn, when they figger we're worn out from watchin' all night. Half of them are sleepin' about now."

Thad swallowed dry, thought for a moment, and whispered again. "Pa?"

"Yes," the older man answered patiently.

"If we're a part of the Seneca nation, and the Mohawks are the Senecas' brothers, then why are they trying to kill us?"

"Well, they don't know we're Seneca, they think we're just reg'lar white men."

"Then why don't we just tell 'em?"

"Wouldn't make no difference to them. Guess you never heard. Senecas and Mohawks don't like each other much."

"But they're brothers in the Iroquois League."

"You read your Bible down in Oquaga. Brothers sometimes hate each other's guts. Now you take this here Iroquois Confederacy. There's six different nations in this confederacy, but they ain't all equal. The Seneca, Onondaga, and the Mohawks are like the big brothers, and the Oneida and the Cayuga are the little brothers. The Tuscarora are new members and they don't hardly count at all. Now, amongst the big brothers, Seneca and Mohawk each think they're leaders of the league. So they squabble from time to time and do little spite things to each other, and sooner or later the whole dang confederacy is gonna fall apart because maybe sometimes the Seneca and the Mohawk hate each other more than they hate the white man."

Sam patted Thad on the back of his calf, then listened to the wind for a moment. He patted Thad again, an all-clear sign.

"Pa?"

"Yes, son."

"Am I red or white?"

"Well, I'd say you can be what you want. The Seneca claim you for their own, but you've got the tongue and the writing and the religion of the white man.

"After your ma died I got to thinkin' a lot about what you

oughta be, and that's why I packed you off to Reverend
Heflin for seven years to get educated. For once I did right
by you, he taught you good, so I reckon you can be a white
man if you want, and I think that's what you should be."

"Are white men better people?"

"What do you think?"

Thad didn't know what to think. The two seemed a lot
alike to him. Both drank too much, though some Seneca
acted worse when they got drunk, and when they drank
they *always* got drunk.

Otherwise the Seneca were kinder and more generous,
and knew more about the woods, but the whites seemed to
know more about the world. Seneca were better fighters, yet
the whites were more powerful. Thad was confused. He
liked Tonowaugh better than he liked the white towns he
and his father had visited during their many travels together.
Of course, all towns, red and white, stank, so what he liked
most was the forest.

"Wanna know why you should be white? 'Cause the
whites are gonna win, that's why. The Indians can't stick
together like the whites. They were squabblin' with each
other before we came, and they're still squabblin' with each
other even while we're nibblin' at them. Sometimes I think
an Iroquois brave would rather bring home a Huron scalp
than a white scalp. And the Iroquois and the Huron are
cousins.

"No, Thad, you don't want to be a Seneca or any other
red man, because their day is done."

He looked out across the blackness of the field before
him. "Now these here Mohawk we got out there, I don't
think a one of them will live to see forty." That seemed to
Thad like a strange thing to say right then because the way
things were going, he'd be lucky to make it to nineteen.

In the dark the earth spoke to Big Oak, the white man
who could see the future, who would, if he could, save the
men who were coming to kill him. And they *were* coming, he
could feel them in the wind. Slow minutes went by. They

watched and saw nothing but the barest trace of tree line against the sky.

"If rum don't get 'em, the measles or the smallpox will. If the pox don't get 'em, the white men will," Sam mused sadly. "If the white men don't get 'em—well, the Mingoes might. Or some other wanderin' savage out of the west. There's Mohawk now who can't even find their way around the woodland anymore. If they can't survive in the woods, and the white man takes all the other land, where will they live?"

And then, to Sam's front, maybe fifty yards away, there was motion, then faint shapes, six of them, ten yards apart but all crawling from one direction in a frontal assault. Why? Sam thought. Why all from one direction? They stopped. He laid his sights on one blurry shape, troubled, his mind astir, trying to understand. They began to move forward again, and it was then, as he pulled the trigger, that he knew.

"To your front, Thad!" he cried, and when Thad looked he saw what appeared to him was an army. Overnight the seven who had pursued them had become three times that many, hanging back on the flanks until Big Oak had fired his weapon. Then they were up in a quick rush from all four sides.

Thad fired his rifle at a human being for the first time in his life, but missed. They reversed their weapons and swung them by their muzzles in wide arcs, connecting occasionally and keeping some of their enemy at bay. Thad did not feel fear, only the adrenaline rush of primal struggle as he felt his weapon connect with something human.

Everywhere he looked there were shrieking, screaming Mohawks flourishing tomahawks. A muzzle flashed so close that he could feel the powder burns on his cheek, but somehow the bullet failed to find its mark. A tomahawk whizzed by his ear, leaving a light sting but doing no damage. The enemy was making horrifying noises, but there were so many of them and so few of their adversaries, and the night was so dark, that they had to be careful lest they injure one of their own.

In the midst of the fight, Thad caught a glimpse of his father, tirelessly flailing away with his knife in one hand and his tomahawk in another.

So fearsome was his activity that he was holding seven of the attackers at bay. Again and again, grunting with the effort, he swung his tomahawk wide while protecting his midsection with his knife. His enemy knew a formidable foe when they saw one, and mostly kept out of range of his chopping and slashing, but in the end there were far too many of them.

While Big Oak's attention was on the small multitude to his front, two braves grabbed him from the rear. He shook off one as a bear might shake off water, but the second managed to pull him down. There was a Mohawk on Thad's back too, dragging him to the ground. His strength was slipping away from him. As he fell, the last thing he remembered seeing was the dark shape of an arm with a knife in the air then plunging downward, and the last thing he remembered hearing was a groan from his father as the blade found its home, followed by the soft hiss of his breath leaving his body.

# ❧2❧

**H**E WAS OUT FOR ONLY A MOMENT. THE
weight of at least three Mohawks was on his back. One had
his knee on Thad's neck. He had grabbed hold of Thad's
hair and was jerking his head back. Thad knew that the
scalping knife was next, followed by the exquisite pain that
comes from having the top of your head torn from your
skull.

The whooping and screeching were terrible, and under it
all, like the sad mourning sound of a cello, came a long, low
moan from Big Oak. Their lives, Thad thought helplessly,
were about to end together.

Above the din came a new voice, shouting something
Thad could not understand. Then he remembered that the
two greatest tribes in the Iroquois confederacy could not
perfectly understand each other's words.

The voice was excited, insistent, authoritative. The
screeching stopped. The fist let go of Thad's hair. Two of
the Mohawks grabbed his arms in viselike grips and lifted
him to his feet. Then the entire group commenced to run. In
the distance Thad could hear rifle shots, and the thick cloud
of warriors that had surrounded him and his father had
thinned out considerably.

"*Pa! Pa!*" Thad shouted, trying to shake himself free, digging in his heels, his eyes filling with tears. Never before

had he seen his father betray the slightest sign of pain and weakness, yet behind him, as his captors dragged him, he could still hear Big Oak's low, mournful moan. He heard the sound of two solid objects meeting. The groan abruptly ceased.

A third, very strong Indian clubbed Thad on the side of the head, sending a flashing pain from head to foot. He grabbed Thad from the back and, along with the other two who held him, forced him into a run. Dazed with pain, Thad yielded.

The remaining hours of darkness were the worst in Thad's life. Mile after mile the Mohawks ran. Thad ran with them, knowing that if he weakened and slowed down, they would quickly kill him. Whenever the pain and despair got to be too much and his energy flagged, one of his captors stuck him cruelly in the backside with a knife and laughed. Thad was willing to run through Hell itself to avoid another jab from that knife and the humiliating laughter that went with it. Once he stumbled and fell, only to be jerked to his feet by one of his conquerors. Another time, as they ran across the side of a hill, he pretended to fall, intending to roll down the side of the hill and try to make his escape, but his captor had too strong a grip on his buckskin shirt for him to break free. Instead he received a sharp rap with the side of a tomahawk that raised a bump on the side of his head and gave him a pounding headache that he would not feel until later.

And still he ran, blindly, mechanically, through the dark, with his Mohawk captors. Paralyzed by terror and anger, the only thinking part of his brain that still functioned was the one that asked questions. Where was his father? Was he alive? Would these "brothers" of his let them live? Why was this suddenly happening to him? For just a moment his mind floated off and he and Big Oak were again walking the hills of the Mohawk Valley, happy as any two human beings on the face of the earth. Then he returned to the ghastly pres-

ent and he could not imagine how the before and after
could possibly be connected in this life.

His breath came in explosive gasps. His legs had lost all
response. Let them kill him where he stood, he didn't care.
At that moment they finally came to a halt and let him go.
He fell to the ground, gasping desperately for breath. His
captors were also breathing hard, jabbering to each other in
their odd tongue, laughing about their conquest and their
narrow escape; from whom, he could not figure out. They
began to make camp. He lay still, catching his breath, hoping they might believe him unconscious. If they forgot
about him long enough, he'd lead them a chase all the way
back to the Genesee. In Seneca country they would soon
find out how loosely their scalps were attached to their
heads.

Without warning, the toe of a Mohawk moccasin found
his rib cage and what little breath he had went out of him.
He looked up and found the youngest of the Mohawks in
the party glaring at him. He grabbed Little Oak's wrists and
bound them together tightly with a leather thong, then did
the same to his ankles.

Slowly his breath returned to him. His head ached and
every inch of his body felt sore and abused, but nothing felt
broken. He looked around for his father, but Big Oak was
nowhere to be seen. He counted only eight Mohawks. The
group must have split up when they fled.

They were fearful-looking creatures, he thought. So fero-
ciously painted, so much uglier than his Seneca relatives.
And their horrible, guttural speech! Mohawks were not
completely unknown to him. He had seen one or two occasionally in his village or on the trail, and they had seemed
like people to him, but here, now, together in a war party,
they resembled the stories his Seneca grandfather Kendee
would tell him by the campfire.

"Fearsome allies, fearsome enemies," the old man had said.
Mohawk was an Algonquin word that some said meant

"Maneaters." They had that reputation, although they denied it.

They did not call themselves Mohawks. To themselves they were simply Ganiengehaka: People of the Flint Country. Others insisted that when the blood fever seized them, the Mohawks devoured the interior parts of their conquered enemies.

Thad had little doubt that they had terrible things in store for him, and his split culture sent his thoughts careening in two directions. The part of him which was white was ready to do anything to survive, including begging, if need be; while the part of him that was red surrendered to fate and tried to steel him for the trials to come, the devilish tortures and death that were a part of Iroquois ritual. The white side won, because he was determined to be there for his father if his father still lived.

Gently, he kicked the ankle of the Mohawk who stood nearest him, a stocky fellow whose war paint failed to hide the good-humored lines around his eyes. But as the red man turned to stare at his captive, his face darkened like a storm cloud and he pulled back his foot to give Thad a severe kick in the ribs.

"Where is my father?" Thad asked in the Seneca tongue, and was rewarded by a look of frank astonishment on the Indian's face. Perhaps, like a man who has just heard a dog speak, he couldn't quite believe his ears, for he continued to stand over Thad, staring.

"Where is my father?" he repeated in a louder voice, his annoyance betrayed by inflections known only to Indians. The Mohawk walked quickly over to the warrior who was obviously the leader of this party, a short man of about thirty years who was already turning gray and who had two silver loops in each ear and a third in his nose. His face held the expression of one who had vinegar flowing through his veins instead of blood. He looked strong and cruel enough to break even Thad in two.

He walked quickly over to Thad and muttered something

in the Seneca tongue that Thad couldn't quite catch. Thad inclined his head and the leader repeated his question:

"You speak the language of the Western Door?"

"I speak the language of your brother people. I bear the blood of your brother people. Do Mohawk always attack their brothers?"

"You are white!"

"I am Seneca. My father is Big Oak. Have you killed him?"

Now it was the turn of the leader to be astonished. "The man who felt my keen blade is the mighty Big Oak?" The man seemed pleased with himself.

"He is Big Oak, blood brother to the Seneca. We were coming in peace to your villages. You spilled the blood of your brother!" Young as he was, Little Oak was too angry to be afraid. If his father was dead, his eyes rested on his father's murderer.

"Paughhh!" The man spat on the ground. "Brothers do not send the French devils to do their dirty deeds."

Thad knew that some of the Seneca were rumored to be under the influence of the French and their Catholic missions, but he did not believe the stories. "We are Seneca of the Iroquois League. The English are your allies and so they are our allies. If a man would kill his brother, he would surely lie about why he did it."

The other members of the war party, hearing the debate, stopped their activity and paid attention. Their leader, proud of having felled a great man, explained the gist of the conversation, and his listeners made sounds of approval and admiration. Red Hawk, for that was his name, was gaining great stature on this night. He turned back to Thad and assumed a look of utter contempt.

"Then you deny that your chiefs led the French to our towns?"

"*My* chiefs talk of peace, especially with their brothers. And since I am too young to attend war councils, I could not say how our war chiefs feel about the Mohawks. But *my* people keep our promises. They are tied to the Keepers of the Eastern Door as long as the council fire burns in Onondaga, but if you cut my bonds, they will soon know of your treachery. Tell me now, where is Big Oak?"

"I have chopped the Big Oak down," boasted Red Hawk, "and I will pull a few feathers from his little rooster too." As he spoke, he signed to his followers. Several laughed, and one, the youth who had bound Thad so tightly that his fingers were beginning to lose their feeling, pulled a knife and felt the keenness of his blade, staring at Thad through narrowed, threatening eyes.

"How did you learn to talk like us?" Thad asked.

"I spent several winters with the Seneca trapping beaver in Canada," Red Hawk responded sourly, as if the thought brought back unpleasant memories.

"And now like a cruel dog you attack and kill the Seneca?"

"You wear clothes like a white man. We could not tell."

"We are Seneca. You must let us go."

"The Seneca do not tell the Ganiengehaka what to do. In two days we will be back in our village, and there we will decide among ourselves what to do with you and Big Oak, if my knife did not send him to the white spirit land."

"If you have killed Big Oak, you will answer to the Confederacy."

"I will answer you by stuffing your mouth with your liver, it certainly is big enough for it." More laughter, and the way the young warrior was smiling at the blade of his knife, Thad knew who had been sticking his hind end during the run through the woods. I owe you, he thought, looking first at the boy, then at Red Hawk. I owe both of you. And if you do not kill me first, I will pay you back and dance over you.

The camp now ignored Thad and began to eat. In spite of the young man's grief, his stomach demanded attention. He was surprised to find the good-humored Mohawk standing over him and handing him a bowl filled with corn.

"Thank you," he said.

The good-natured Mohawk smiled and retreated, cuffing

the younger boy on the side of the head as he passed by him.

Enough pain and fatigue can make the strongest man quake with fear. Perhaps Thad was fearful that night, but the following morning found his youthful body much improved, and so was his spirit. The hostile youngster with the sharp knife kicked him awake, cut his ankle thongs and attempted to kick Thad again, but Thad rolled free, bounded to his feet and faced his antagonist.

"You are a brave boy waving your little knife at a man with his arms tied behind his back!" he sneered. The boy did not understand the meaning of the words, but Thad's contempt was clear. Perhaps the boy would have ignored them had the insulting sounds come from a Seneca brave with a scalp lock and a breechcloth, but to him Thad was white, and he was not about to swallow insults—even those he did not understand—from a white captive little older than himself. Knife flashing in the morning sun, he lunged at Thad's unprotected abdomen.

Thad's life depended on one kick, and his feet did not fail him. His right foot struck the wrist of the young Mohawk. The knife flew high in the air and stuck into a dead branch ten feet off the ground. The three braves nearest the pair took one look at the suddenly suspended knife and laughed in a derisive chorus.

"You'd better not try to get it unless you can fly, Corn Boy," said one.

"Corn Boy," said another, "shall I bind his legs again so the fight between you and him can be even?"

The young Mohawk had disliked Thad on sight, but now that Thad had humiliated him in front of the older warriors, the dislike exploded into a seething, writhing hatred in his tortured belly.

"I will kill you one day!" the boy hissed at Thad. Then, realizing that Thad might not understand, he signed the words, in stiff, angry hand movements. Thad had to stand

and take it; with his hands bound behind his back, he could not respond.

Red Hawk had appointed himself Thad's guard for this day's march. As they walked eastward, he trailed close behind, softly pouring Seneca words into Thad's ear, in his atrocious Mohawk accent.

"Runner and his group will be bringing your father with them, if he survives the journey."

Thad listened but said nothing.

"I don't know, though. I buried my knife deep in his chest. You heard the mighty Oak moan when I did it?"

So this was the lay of the land, Thad thought, determined to show no sign that the words disturbed him, regardless of the pain they caused.

"I silenced him with a blow from the butt of my rifle. You heard the moans stop? I did that."

Thad had heard about Mohawk cruelty, but years of following his father on the trading trails had taught him that the Mohawks were not the only cruel people in the world. Seneca could be cruel, just as the Twightwee could be cruel, just as the French could be cruel, or the English or the Dutch or the Germans. His father and his Seneca grandfather had both told him that the way to fight cruelty was to store it away, in silence, then, when the right day comes, to take it out and use it. His grandfather told him that revenge, at the right moment, is, after first love, the sweetest, most satisfying feeling in this life.

Thad's father was a Christian, and Christians were not supposed to feel that way, but Big Oak admitted that one of his best days was a day on the Chenango River when he tracked down the German trader who had married his sister-in-law and later murdered her. He had tracked the German for days across the New York–Pennsylvania border country. Three times the German had laid in ambush for Big Oak, and three times Big Oak's finely honed senses had allowed him to survive. Once a fall had left him unconscious for hours, but he had shaken off his aches and pains and contin-

ued the chase. He took to traveling day and night to overtake the German, and the German took to traveling day and
night to escape Big Oak's wrath.

And then, one dark moment just before dawn, Big Oak
found the German asleep beneath an old hemlock tree, his
rifle beneath the pack on which his head lay. Gently Big
Oak had eased the rifle out from under the pack, but the
murderer did not stir. The long chase had finally exhausted
him beyond caring. Big Oak knelt by the sleeping man and
studied his face, imagining what he had looked like the day
he had plunged his knife into the heart of Willow's sister.
The story was that he had wanted her to get up and cook
his supper, but she was too weak from sickness to leave her
bed. He had lost his temper, said the people from the cabin
next door.

Big Oak did not lose his temper. Coolly, with exquisite
pleasure, he had reached down and strangled the German
with his bare hands. The German had awakened mid-stran-
gle, kicked his feet and reached feebly with his hands for Big
Oak, but Big Oak had the German's throat locked in an
unbreakable grip. The struggle subsided to gurgled protest,
then surrender, and finally the stillness of death. There had
been no regrets, only satisfaction at doing a job that the law
would not have done for him.

"The great warrior Big Oak," Red Hawk crooned, "laid
low by this hand." Thad did not turn around, but he could
picture Red Hawk gazing at his hand with amazement.

"You do not answer, but I am not surprised. You fear the
strong arm of the brave that killed your mighty father."

*There* was a challenge that begged for a response. Thad
stopped in his tracks, and the brave was so caught up in
contemplating his warlike deed that he nearly walked into
Thad's back. Thad turned on him with a snarl.

"There were seven of you and two of us. Man-to-man he
would have made you happy to beg for mercy."

"And his son, who walks with us like an obedient dog?"

"His son will have you walking with your ancestors if you have the courage to untie him."

"We defeated you. You are ours. Do you set free a pony whose manhood you have taken?"

Thad blew a contemptuous blast of air through his lips, turned and continued walking. *When the time comes, you will be mine,* he thought, but he felt down and disheartened. Red Hawk continued his running narrative: how easily Big Oak's chest had yielded to the knife, how gently the mighty warrior had slid to the ground before the erect body of Red Hawk.

Tears came to Thad's eyes, and again his salvation came from the inner confidence that when the time came, he would avenge his father's death at the hand of this filthy, boasting, unworthy murderer.

## ❈3❈

**T**WO DAYS LATER THAD AND HIS CAPTORS AR-
rived at the village, a substantial one surrounded by a stockade fifteen feet high. Inside were several longhouses of
sturdy wood frames sheathed in elm bark and topped by
pitched roofs with several smoke holes lined up down the
center. Each of these longhouses was eighty to one hundred
feet long and held a number of families belonging to the
same clan. Numerous smaller lodges also fronted on the
neat, straight streets that crisscrossed the village. Outside
the stockade were a few more lodges in various stages of
disrepair, from a time when the population of the village
had outstripped the ability of the stockade to contain it.
That time was long gone.

Although Thad had shaken all the physical effects of the
Mohawk attack, his anxieties about his father had continued
to grow as the days on the trail passed. In the evenings on
the trail, Thad had sat by the fire with the warriors, listening
to them speak about the encounter. They said it was a
shame that Red Hawk should defeat the mighty Big Oak
only to have Runner take his scalp while the trader lay unconscious. To an Iroquois, the taking of a scalp was a high
honor.

But only Corn Boy claimed to have seen the body of Big
Oak bereft of its scalp, and the other braves gave Corn Boy's

word no credibility. Like a hungry man clinging to his last morsel, Thad clung to the hope that his father might yet live.

The town was located on top of a hill that long ago had been stripped of trees. It looked down upon the vast woodland and a small stream that wound in and out of the woods, its tumbling water winking brightly in the sunlight. At the foot of the hill, in the floodplain of the creek, grew well-kept fields of corn, beans, and squash, the "three sisters" that sustained the Iroquois throughout their magnificent history.

Red Hawk and his band were met at the gate to the palisade by most of the village, anxious that so many of their young men were out at one time. The first to speak to Red Hawk was an old, stern warrior with many scars on his face and body. He was pleased to see that the entire party had returned, and he wondered why they had returned so soon.

They had intended to go west toward Lake Erie, and there strike the Mingoes, groups of Iroquois who had migrated west and were showing inclinations toward the French and away from the council fire in Onondaga. This was just a group of braves looking for a way to win some honor for themselves. The old men didn't like it, but there was nothing they could do about it. Boys will be boys, and in the Longhouse, boys looked for enemy to kill and capture. The old ones understood. They too had been boys not so long ago, looking for ways to win renown, and not too particular who would furnish the opposition.

The old man turned his attention to Thad. Red Hawk swelled with pride as he boasted about his conquest of the great white hunter. The old man was not interested. He wanted to know why they had curtailed their journey to the land of the Mingoes to attack a couple of white fur traders. Indeed by now the whole village was gathered around them, asking about their adventures and whether they had seen the other, larger party that had gone out after them.

Thad was surprised to see that the Mohawks in the village wore more white man's clothing than did the Senecas. In fact, there was evidence of white trade goods all over the place, from the blankets to the higher quality weapons, cooking pots, and the spinning wheel that stood in the doorway of one of the longhouses. It was obvious that the Mohawks lived their lives much closer to the English than did the Seneca.

The old man took Thad to his lodge, which was inhabited only by his wife's extended family, a group big enough to occupy an entire longhouse.

"I am Gingego," he told Thad in English. "I know who you are. I know your father. You will be my guest. You will not leave my longhouse."

Thad nodded and understood. Because of his father and his Seneca lineage, he was to be treated as a guest, without being bound, but he was not free to leave the village. Deep in the dim, smoky recesses of the longhouse, he was introduced to various members of the family, given a bark cup of a hot sassafras tea to drink, and provided a seat of honor in front of the fire. Weary from his ordeal, Thad was pleased to take a blanket and nod off by the fire. After the long days on the trail, filled with tension and abuse, the fatigue and the warmth of the fire acted like a beautiful drug, wooing him into a shallow but untroubled sleep.

He was awakened by a tap on his shoulder from a young girl with a dish of stewed venison. He picked out a choice piece for himself and took a bite. The girl smiled and sat down across the fire from him. She had a beautiful smile, he thought, and for a moment he imagined what it would be like to walk this beautiful country with a sweet, laughing, pretty girl who would smile at him the way this girl did.

She made him think of Kawia, his Seneca playmate since their early childhood. As early in his life as he could remember, Kawia had followed him around like a puppy dog.

More than once he had taken a licking from a bigger boy to protect her from the nasty things that bigger boys sometimes do to little girls. In autumn when he departed the village to spend the cold months learning his letters and numbers with the Reverend Heflin, she cried bitterly each time the hour of his leaving drew near.

As he grew toward manhood, the nasty boys ceased tormenting Kawia, knowing that the price for making her unhappy was having to deal with Little Oak. They had become close in an older way, and spent a lot of time together over the past spring, walking in the woods or sitting by the Genesee, fishing but not really fishing. Her pretty little face fit so perfectly into his life that he had even imagined that someday she would become his wife.

Quietly, the young Mohawk girl left him and he let his eyes drift toward the fire. From his early childhood he had loved to stare into a bright open fire and allow himself to be hypnotized by the dancing flames. When his grandfather told him stories, Thad could peer into the flickering yellows, oranges, and blues and see his forebears who founded the mighty Iroquois League.

"So many years ago," his grandfather had told him, "the five great peoples made war on each other, until the green valleys of the Mohawk, the Delaware, and the Susquehanna were covered with the blood of dying braves.

"Then came Deganawida and Hayenwatha, with words instead of tomahawks. With words the five tribes made peace with each other, and today are the mightiest of nations. They rule the Huron, they rule the Abnaki. They dressed the Delaware in petticoats and made them women who must get permission from the Ganonsyoni even to break wind—Ganonsyoni being the name the Iroquois called themselves. Even in the land of the Twightwee, beyond the mountains, when the league sends word, the others do as they are told. Far to the south, to the land of the Cherokee, it is the same. The Iroquois are the rulers of all the people," he said, meaning all the *Indians*.

But his grandfather's stories served only to confuse Thad. Big Oak had a different point of view. "That may be the way it *was*," he said, "but today England and France play the music, and that's the tune the Ganonsyoni must dance to."

Thad could not understand. To him the Indians seemed to be mighty warriors, while the white men scratched in the dirt like Iroquois women.

Big Oak had to remind his son that the whites could do things of which the Indians could only dream. The whites could make new rifles and fix broken ones. The whites could make and shoot big cannon that would send the bravest of the braves fleeing like rabbits. The whites could make mirrors. Mirrors were now a must for Indian warriors when they applied their war paint. The Indians could not make the metal knives, hatchets, bullets, and gunpowder necessary for their survival.

Even the clothes on their back more and more were made by whites, from the cotton weaves about which they knew little or nothing. So too their blankets. And their rum.

"And there you have it," his father had told him. "The Indian will lose his country because he needs the white man more than the white man needs the Indian. The white man needs the Indian for only one thing: to help him on the war path, to find and kill other Indians. Without Indians to guide them through the forests," he said, "the white armies lose their way and fall easy prey to tribes who know how to fight in the woods, or they find only empty villages, for the Indians will have long received word of the white man's coming and fled.

"But once the Indians become so weak the whites no longer need to kill them, why, they will no longer need the Indian at all. Then what will happen to your powerful Iroquois confederacy?" Big Oak did not laugh as he said these words. He looked very sad.

"Why do we live with the Seneca, then?" Thad asked him.

"Because I trap with them. And I trade with them for their furs. And I like them better than I like the whites," Sam replied. "But God must like the whites better, because God has delivered the red man into the hands of the white for destruction." Little Oak had been surprised to hear his father talk like a preacher, because he had often told his son that his Christianity had a lot to do with Jesus and very little to do with preachers.

Now, Thad chewed his venison slowly and stared through the jumping, dancing flames at the glowing coals beneath. If Big Oak was right, then where had the mighty white men been when the Mohawk surrounded them and cut down his father as if he were an old dead tree that for only a brief moment stood in their path? And now where was Big Oak? Did he lay in the field, food for the wolves and the crows, his skull a sea of gore?

Where was the other Mohawk raiding party? If one of the warriors returned with his father's scalp in his belt, Thad knew he would pretend not to notice, yet he would somehow find his way to a knife, bide his time, and cut the heart out of the coward who did it.

But then he would never have the chance to do the same to Red Hawk, who, after all, was the true murderer.

The draft of the fire failed for a moment, filling his eyes with smoke and tears. Then the smoke cleared and the fire again cast its spell. No longer hungry, but still weary from the journey and the loss, Thad let his chin sink to his chest and his eyes close.

In his dream they were paddling their canoe downstream on the upper Genesee, letting the current carry them along, stroking just enough to keep them midstream. Dappled sunlight filtered through the overhanging sycamores and oaks. The canoe was loaded with furs and trade goods, and yet it rode high and easy in the water.

He was in the bow, his sharp eyes peeled for rocks, stumps, and sunken logs. Behind him he could feel his father's strong, certain touch steering the craft through the deep channel of the river. He felt the joy of a healthy appetite, gauged the angle of the sun, and knew that the time was near to make camp. There would be clear water to slake his thirst, a plump deer haunch to roast over the open fire, and the voice of his father, praising him for work well done, and speaking of the deeds of his adopted tribe.

They paddled the canoe close to shore, jumped out, and began to extract bundles of furs from the floor of the canoe. Then they pulled the canoe from the water. Instead of a clumsy Iroquois elm bark canoe, it was a graceful light birch-bark canoe like those known to the Chippewa and the tribes of the Canadas. Quietly they made camp, gathering wood, kindling a small fire, and starting their roast. Thad started to speak to his father, but Big Oak put his finger to his mouth, then cupped his ear—listen.

Thad listened, and to the east he heard the sound of drums, faint but certain. As he listened, as he tended to the campfire, the drums got louder and louder. Abruptly the drumming disintegrated into a cacophony, as if each drummer had decided to play to his own rhythm without regard to what any of the others was doing. Thad clapped his hands over his ears and looked up at his father, but Big Oak had disappeared. Thad was alone, except for the quarreling drums.

He woke to the sound of angry voices, and he was certain that the voices spoke about him. Quietly he listened, not daring to breathe lest he miss something that would give him a clue concerning his fate. The voices rose to a crescendo, then subsided, and a moment later Gingego walked in and beckoned Thad to his feet. Thad took a deep breath and composed himself, although his heart was trying to find the shortest trail to his throat. He was a Seneca; he would betray no emotion in front of the great Mohawk warriors.

Thad followed Gingego to the council fire in the middle of the village. The entire village was present, from the wise elders and proud warriors near the fire to the old women in the shadows. As he neared the fire, a few soft exclamations of approval arose from the shadows. He had lost his cap on the trail, and what they saw was a tall, handsome young Indian man with jet-black hair tied in a single queue. He hid his flagging spirit and stood straight and proud before the village.

Gingego faced him. "Who are you?" he asked in a formal manner.

"I am Thad Watley," he signed as he spoke. "I come from the People of the Great Hill, from the village of Tonowaugh on the Genesee River. My mother was Willow, daughter of Kendee, who long ago was known among his people as a great warrior.

"I am also the son of Sam Watley, who everybody knows as Big Oak of the Seneca, Guardians of the Western Door," he said, and at the mention of his father, several "ahs" arose from the sages by the council fire who had known that good man for many years.

Nobody responded immediately, so Thad continued. "I see that many of you are pleased at the mention of my father's name. It isn't every boy who is fortunate enough to have a father so well-regarded. It would be a fine day to die if I knew that my father could say the same of his son. And yet I do not know if my father will ever see his son's face again, because only three suns ago your people attacked my father and me. That man"—he pointed dramatically at Red Hawk—"opened my father's body with his knife." There were a few surprised gasps as a translator relayed Thad's words, but Red Hawk, far from being offended, stood straight and proud, arms folded, as if Thad were praising him.

"Somewhere out there lies my father, maybe dead, killed by his Mohawk brothers. When a brother kills a brother for no good reason, should he not be punished?"

Red Hawk could not let that pass. Arms unfolded, he walked toward Thad—but not too close, for Thad was a solid seven inches taller—and fastened his glowing, angry eyes on the young man.

"Who is this boy, that he can come before our people and decree punishment for a warrior of the Turtle Clan? The son of a white man, a man whose famed rifle has sped many red men to the spirit world. I have been to the dung heap on the Genesee that he calls his village. I met many of those who lived there, and they were not like the great Seneca braves who fought beside us in the great wars. Of course, I did not meet this boy or his 'great white warrior father' and his 'great red warrior grandfather.'" His sarcasm was thick as a freshly cut side of deer meat.

"I have heard the wise men speak of the olden times when the Ganonsyoni filled the valleys from the eastern river to the Ontario. When the beaver ran free and man fought man close, with arrows of stone, not bullets that even the keenest eye cannot see. It took a brave man to fight battles then, hand-to-hand with an enemy so close he could feel his breath on his cheek.

"I feel good when I look across the fire and see so many of my own, the mighty Ganiengehaka, looking upon my face. But many of you are here because your own villages are no more. The white men have taken your land. They have given your people their sickness, or made them crazy with strong drink.

"They take our women too, and you let them, and from such things come this!" He stretched his hand toward Thad. "He is the most dangerous, because he can deceive you that he is one of us. He speaks the tongue of our western brothers, the Seneca. His skin is dark. His hair is dark and straight, his eyes are dark, like those of the Flint People. Strip his shirt from his back and cut his trousers into leggings, and he would look like one of us.

"And yet he is *not* one of us! He speaks the white man's speech. He makes the white man's marks, marks like those they use to take away our land. He knows how to live like a white man. His father is a white man, from the stinking white cities in the land that once belonged to the Abnaki and the Pequot.

"He lives like the Ganonsyoni. He does now. But hard times are coming for us. Every year our people are fewer, and theirs more. When the day finally comes that we must fight the English for our lives, where will he be? And when our mighty nation is scattered to the winds, where will he be? Will he be in the hills striving and struggling with his mother's people, our brothers, the Seneca? He will not. He will be planting corn with a metal plow and an ox, like a white man. He will be in the towns, like a white man. Counting his wampum and trying to think of more ways to cheat his 'brothers' out of what little they have left. He is a white man with red skin. He is a betrayer.

"I say that if he is one of us, he should prove it now, by dying like an Indian." Having said that, Red Hawk mounted the log platform behind him, where, Little Oak understood, they would erect the stake that bound captives who were to submit to the tortures.

In spite of his resolution to keep his courage, Thad's belly turned cold. Red Hawk's arrow had hit home. Many of those seated before him had indeed come from other villages whose population had been decimated in one way or the other, and almost everyone there felt the fear of too many white people, many of them too aggressive, and all of them too close.

Thad looked around to see if anyone there was willing to speak for him, but all remained silent, even Gingego, even Ganaoga the good-natured brave who had been kind to him on the trail. All turned to him to see how he would save himself. The only resources he had were his father's thoughts, his father's words, his father's wisdom.

He stood before them and closed his eyes until the words came. He did not hurry, and the people gathered around the fire waited with patience. And when the words came, the cold fear left his belly. He knew the words were right, and once you've done your best, the rest is in the hands of the Lord.

"How do I answer the mighty Red Hawk, this man who struck down my father, the best man I have ever known?" There were a few murmurs of agreement from the older men of the village.

"I am young yet and have never known the war path. I have never killed a man. The day I know that my father is dead, I will vow to kill Red Hawk, for what he did to my father was unjust. My father has never harmed Red Hawk. Somewhere in time, my father may have aided Red Hawk, for he has aided many of the Ganiengehaka. Red Hawk and his braves attacked us only because he believed us to be white men. In doing so, he attacked his own kinsman, for my mother was of the Turtle Clan, therefore I am of the Turtle Clan.

Now there was real excitement among the assembled Mohawks. The Turtle Clan was one of several clans common to all the nations of the Iroquois confederacy, and it was these clan relationships as much as anything that kept the league together. Thad pressed his advantage.

"Or does Red Hawk believe that he is chosen to judge who may and who may not be of the Turtle Clan? Or how much Iroquois blood it takes to make a man a part of the Turtle Clan? Is he a law unto himself?"

For the first time anger could be heard. Although warfare among members of the same clan was not unheard of, when such events actually arose, it ran contrary to the Iroquois sense of what was right and lawful. Even Red Hawk was shaken.

"I did not know," he said, calmly but with some feeling. "How could I have known?"

The angry murmurs continued, until Gingego raised a knotted, arthritic hand. Then the crowd grew silent.

"He did not know," Thad agreed. "And had it not been my father, I could forgive him." He paused and let his gaze wander from face to face, as if to draw each one into his heart, that they could feel as he felt.

"I am a selfish young man. I wanted my father to live long, for he is a great man, with so much to teach me. I wanted to learn *all* he had to teach me." The old men nodded, most of them wishing that their sons were like the youth who stood before them. Like all old men, they felt they had wisdom to pass on, and like so many old men, they had sons who thought their fathers to be fools.

"My father's wisdom was mine to acquire. Every moment with him in camp or on the trail was an education for me." He turned toward Red Hawk and pointed at him, but his voice did not rise in anger. "You stole that from me, Red Hawk. It is beyond my power to take it back. It is beyond your power to ever give it back. How *can* I forgive you?"

Cleverly, Thad had changed the terms of debate from whether he should burn at the stake to whether he should forgive Red Hawk. But mere survival was not the gist of the wisdom his father had taught him. He raised his hands toward the attentive crowd, who were divided between those who had been so proud of their victory, and the rest of the village, most of whom were appalled by their deed.

"Now that I know you understand what is in my heart, I must tell you that much of what Red Hawk has said is true. My father has told me the same and I must not hide it from you.

"Most white men do not care to live side by side with the red man. They do not understand the red man, and mean only to take what you have and send you beyond this river, then beyond that mountain, until you live on land they do not need for themselves.

"And my father says they can do it. There are so many of them and so few of us. He said that over the water where the king lives, there is a city with more people than all the Iroquois, all the Huron, all the Delaware and all the Twightwee put together. Just one city. And there are other cities almost as big. And many of the people who live there are poor and unhappy, so they come here. More and more of them to dig up the soil and kill the game and take your land away from you.

"The chiefs of the Onondaga fire, he says, are very wise. They see that the French and the English fight each other. Sometimes they help the one, sometimes they help the other, so neither one becomes too powerful.

"We think the English are our friends, because they sell us goods more cheaply than do the French. But he has said that we should not let cheap trade goods make us too close to the English, for they are the ones who have the most power, and when they no longer need us, they will throw us away."

Here Red Hawk could no longer keep silence. Although Thad had used his father's words to credit the speech of the Mohawk brave, in Thad he could see only a white man.

"You are very good at using the word *us*," he said, sneering. "But I still see that you are my enemy."

"I am also your kinsman," he reminded Red Hawk. "But if you crave my blood, I am not afraid. Let it be knives or tomahawks. But do not expect me to be easy, like my father was when he had three others to fight off when you slid your cowardly knife between his ribs. Come to me, you brother-killing dog, and I will tap your throat like a tavern keeper taps a keg of ale. Am I an Indian? Your scalp on my belt will answer that question!"

The sun was setting blood red in a field of blood red clouds as the two men eyed each other. Aside from those few who stood with Red Hawk, there was no blood lust in the village. Too many people had lost too much in recent years for the people to stand for more bloodletting between brother Iroquois nations.

But the young warriors longed to see this combat. They were confident that their leader was on his way to becoming a mighty war chief, and they were certain that a man-to-man contest would mean death to the son of Big Oak and greater prestige for their leader. They were about to stir up the community when a guard from atop the parapet of the stockade wall shouted that the other raiding party was returning.

The meeting immediately broke up, as most of the community made for the open gate. Among the first to arrive at the gate was Thad, followed closely by Corn Boy, who was still determined to wreak revenge on Thad for the humiliation he had dealt him while they were on the trail.

"Don't think you can escape now," he told Thad. "I am right here, ready to kill you if you run."

"If I decided to run, I will take you to the woods with me, pull out your liver and eat it," Thad responded. "I will call the crows and the vultures and tell them that I have scattered little bits of you here and there and that they are welcome to you if they can find any pieces big enough to be worth eating." The youngster eyed Thad's large hands and massive shoulders and decided Thad was capable of doing what he said he'd do.

"Just don't try to escape," the boy sulked.

"Escape, you say? What do you see? A litter, with a man on it? That man is my father, and I will never leave his side until the day he grows strong enough to avenge your cowardly attack. I was raised to believe that the Ganiengehaka were all strong and brave, but I suppose that every village, even on the Te-non-an-at-che has a few cowardly dogs like you and your master, Red Hawk."

Thad now noticed that there were three litters, not one, and that five of those walking bore visible marks of a terrible struggle.

"They must have had a big fight with somebody," Thad observed.

The boy sneered at Thad, but behind him Ganoaga laughed. "Somebody yes," he said. "You and your father."

"Mmm," Thad responded, aching to run out to his father's litter, to see his face and do whatever was necessary to return him to health.

"Well, just don't you try to run away," mumbled Corn Boy, whose tone of voice indicated a respect he hadn't shown when Thad was bruised, lacerated, and defeated, his arms bound behind his back and his spirit nearly crushed.

But as he and Corn Boy rushed out the gate and toward the litter, Thad felt a rush of hot tears coursing down his dust-covered cheeks. The clothes of the man on the first litter were those of his father, all right, but the face was that of a stranger, misshapen and bloated, eyes clouded and unfocused, cheeks and jaw terribly discolored and mouth hanging open, revealing several teeth missing from within and the lolling tongue of a human being who had completely lost his mind.

## ❖4❖

SOME LONGHOUSES ARE LONGER THAN OTH-
ers. One of the buildings, in the southeast corner of the
Mohawk stockade, was a very short longhouse. Originally
built for an obscure purpose long forgotten, it stood droop-
ing in sad disuse, its curved bark roof barely clinging to the
rest of the structure.

Although Sam and Thad had inflicted damage on nearly a
dozen of the braves who had attacked them, Sam was by far
the worst injured. Gingego was honored to take him into his
house, but the big man, insensible and in great pain, moaned
terribly. Nobody in Gingego's longhouse was going to get
any sleep on this night, so when Thad asked if there were
any empty buildings he could take his father to, Gingego
sent two of his younger daughters along with his eldest
granddaughter to clean out the small lodge and equip it for
Sam's comfort.

When the lodge had been made ready, a fire was laid
beneath the chimney hole and Sam was carried carefully
inside. By now the evening was well along. Thad requested
that everybody leave but Gingego and his wife, who knew
as much about caring for the injured as anybody west of Fort
Albany.

In the wavering light of the fire, Gingego and Thad sat on
either side of the badly injured man. Even close up he

looked like a stranger. The flush on his face from the fever was quite different from the windburn that usually colored his pale features. His head and face were one-fourth larger than normal owing to the blows they had received during the skirmish. His eyes opened and blinked, but they did not focus. His nose was broken and swollen.

His hideous moans broke Thad's heart. Everybody who knew Big Oak knew that he bore pain and suffering in silence. One time, Thad's grandfather told him, a wandering war party of Chippewas had ambushed Big Oak and several Senecas from Tonowaugh while they were out together trapping near Lake Erie. In the first moments of the ambush, he had caught a bullet in his right shoulder. He had stuffed a rag under his shirt to "plug the leak," as he said later, and had continued to fire his rifle with deadly effect during the entire long morning without a murmur. Only later did they discover that the bullet had broken his shoulder.

The good news was that the knife wound had not pierced a vital place, nor did the wound seem to be infected. Somebody in the raiding party had been skilled with herbs and poultice. His breathing was regular. His lungs were clear.

"His life is not right now in danger," declared Gingego's wife. "I will leave you for a while to tend my family, but if you need me, just call for me and I will come quickly.

"Thank you," Thad said sincerely. "I'd like to be alone with him for a while."

Gingego nodded and he and his wife walked out past the fire, into the night, leaving Thad alone with the insensible Big Oak. Thad sat cross-legged, holding his father's hand, staring at his face.

But Gingego's wife was wrong. Shortly after she and Gingego left, Big Oak began to experience difficulty breathing. Then his breathing became regular but shallow. Fearing that if he left the lodge to go for help, his father might die alone, Thad moved closer and watched in anguish. Then came another breathing spasm, followed by a vain struggle to take a breath. His chest twitched, then convulsed, but no breath came. The feverish red cast on his face turned pale, then blue. Frantically, Thad grabbed Big Oak by the shoulders and shook him, without effect. He slapped his face once, twice, but the injured man still could not take a breath. Finally, desperately panicked, he reached into Big Oak's open mouth and pulled out his swollen tongue, which had been blocking his windpipe. Slowly, slowly, Big Oak's breathing returned to normal.

Thad sat for hours, watching the face of the stranger who was his father as he breathed slowly, deeply, rhythmically. As long as he still breathes, as long as his heart still beats, there is hope, Thad thought, and not for a moment did he ever wish for his father's death to ease the man's suffering. Thad knew that above all else, his father loved life, and would suffer untold pain in order to reassert his hold on it.

If my father can live through his suffering, then I can live through his suffering, he told himself. Throwing aside his own anguish, Thad waited for Big Oak to show his first sign of real consciousness.

Early in the morning, Gingego's wife brought broth, which Thad fed to his father, holding his head up and pouring small spoonfuls into his mouth. He changed his father's dressings and cleaned him, poured plenty of water down his throat and watched the fever recede. Otherwise the first day brought no sign of improvement, nor did the second, or the third.

As he sat with his father over the first three days, watching him, he thought back to that first summer after his mother had died, his first long trading trip with his father. They had paddled south down the Susquehanna River into northern Pennsylvania, where they hoped to trade in a village of the Lenni Lenape. When the Iroquois had lashed out in savage warfare with their neighbors, they had forced a humiliating peace on the remnants of all the tribes that spoke a language similar to their own. The Algonquian tribes had refused to yield, except for the once powerful

Delaware, whom the Iroquois referred to as their "children," or "women."

Although the Iroquois behaved toward the Delaware with extreme arrogance, at least Big Oak could trade with them, and so their canoe set out from the village of Oquaga laden with porcelain beads, cloths, blankets, kettles, hatchet pipes, musket flints, vermilion, and other Indian necessities. Compared to other traders, Big Oak ran a small operation, but his overhead was small, he needed to depend on no drunken boatmen, and he was shrewd in his ability to accumulate and preserve capital. Someday, maybe, when his desire to prosper outgrew his love of the simple journey, he thought, he would expand his operation, but in the meantime, alone or with his strong young son, and with the land at peace, life was pleasant, and simple.

Summer on the Susquehanna was special even to someone who had spent most of his life living along the Genesee. In many places the oaks and sycamores grew right up to the banks, casting their green shade over the quiet waters. If the river had once been thick with Indian villages, wars and disease had taken care of that. Mile after mile they paddled, sometimes idly, with relaxed sweeps of their paddles; sometimes they just drifted, with an occasional dip to keep the canoe in its proper channel. Life was sweet and sad and sentimental, with both father and son thinking much about Willow, yet pleasantly drugged by the warm breezes that rippled the waters of the Susquehanna.

For days they saw no villages along the river. Sometimes, while Thad paddled, Big Oak would toss a baited line into the river, and often was rewarded with a succulent bass or perch for the evening's meal. In the evening, when the sun's mirrored yellow would seem to disappear around a western bend, the man and the boy would haul their goods ashore, pull the canoe onto the bank, and prepare camp.

To Little Oak, that summer was the dividing line of his life, when he began to know his father as a friend, rather than as a man who was mostly gone from the village and occasionally stayed home during the winter long enough to experience a sample of his son's rambunctious behavior. During the long winter snowstorms, when families were cooped up and tempers ran short, Big Oak would often warn the boy angrily that he had better treat his mother with more respect. Thad had never understood why his father would berate him so. In Tonowaugh, Seneca fathers, and mothers for that matter, generally allowed their boy children to do pretty much as they wished. How could he know that where his father came from, parents were stern disciplinarians and children who disobeyed were often punished far worse than the inconvenience of an angry fatherly lecture?

On the Susquehanna the lectures were forgotten. Away from the village his father seemed so much more relaxed and self-confident than he did during the long winter months by the fire in Willow's longhouse.

Once in camp, the man and the boy would prepare a fire big enough to warm their tired muscles. Even in summer, nights along the Susquehanna could be cool enough make a body shiver. With blankets wrapped around them, Indian style, they would cook a delicious fish and corn stew. Thad would teach his father songs the children learned in the village, and Big Oak would teach his son songs from his childhood in New England, mostly hymns. By their third night on the Susquehanna, they were singing each other's songs, and singing them together.

Finally they arrived at the village of the Lenni Lenape. Although Little Oak's grandfather Kendee had often told Little Oak that men of the Lenni Lenape were scarcely men at all, Big Oak insisted that they had once been a great tribe and that they would somehow survive their tribulations long after many of the other tribes had disappeared from the face of the earth.

The village chief had a Delaware name that sounded unpronounceable to Little Oak, but he announced proudly that the white men called him Captain Thomas. He and one or two other Delaware greeted Big Oak and Thad as they scrambled ashore, but there was no general welcome from the village, as Little Oak would later come to expect in his travels with his father.

The reason became apparent when they entered the village and found that they had been beaten there by a contingent of traders who had come up the Susquehanna from Baltimore and had traded with Indian villages all the way. Villagers were inspecting the wares of the Baltimore traders. Their stocks were severely depleted, Big Oak noticed, and the traders did not sign very well. Big Oak explained to Captain Thomas that although they did not have a huge stock of goods, he was certain that the chief would find that his goods were much better than those of the traders from the south.

The chief walked back down to the shore and watched while Big Oak opened two of the twelve bundles of items they carried. Captain Thomas hefted one of the kettles and nodded, and inspected a handful of flints with a satisfied smile.

"The flints you hold in your hands are yours," Big Oak said.

"I will talk to the others," Captain Thomas told them. "But meanwhile, you must stay here."

When Captain Thomas had disappeared, Big Oak expressed his concern to his son. "Help me close these bundles and get them back in the canoe. I'm not sure I like the way this feels." Little Oak did as he was told and then seated himself in the stern of the canoe. Big Oak put his foot against the bow and pushed it out into the current.

"Paddle the canoe around yonder bend and don't come back until I whistle for you." The boy nodded. A half-dozen strong strokes and he was out of sight.

Big Oak waited by the river for Captain Thomas. Above the breezy hiss of summer leaves he could hear the buzz of commerce in the village, nothing to heighten concern in his careful, suspicious nature. He turned to look toward the river and was pleased that Little Oak was keeping the canoe out of sight. Up until now the trip had been successful in that the hellion he had sired had turned out to be a good companion to have on a trading trip—quiet, alert, attuned to the forest.

After three or four minutes Captain Thomas returned to the river with an older warrior, who commenced to speak in understandable Seneca dialect.

His name, he said, was Beaver's Heart, and he was honored to meet the famous white scout called Big Oak. The chief, he said, wanted very badly to trade with the Big Oak, whose name was known to all tribes from Lake Erie to the big river. But he had given his word to the traders from Chesapeake Bay that his people would buy from them.

"Did he say he would buy *only* from them?" Big Oak asked. Beaver's Heart put the question to the Delaware chief in his own language. The chief looked back with a stone face that may have been covering up something, but he said nothing.

"My goods are better, he can see that. And he knows that I will deal fairly with him," Big Oak said, looking first at Beaver's Heart and then at the chief, who looked away.

A look of unspeakable sadness came over Captain Thomas. He began to speak. The translator listened, but said nothing until the chief had finished.

"My brother Big Oak," said Beaver's Heart, now speaking for himself as well as the chief, with great feeling. "We have seen your goods and they are better than those of the other traders. But they are selling rum and we must have it."

Big Oak looked deep into the dark eyes of the Delaware chief. "I would not sell you rum. I was raised to believe that it would be wrong," he said. And the translator translated.

"I am glad you feel this way," Captain Thomas replied. "But next time you come this way, you must bring us rum, for we must have it."

"It is killing the men of the Lenni Lenape."

"You speak the truth, my brother Big Oak," said Captain

Thomas through Beaver's Heart. "But we love it so. Next time, bring us rum."

When the chief and Beaver's Heart went back to the village, Big Oak whistled for his son and then told him the story.

"To tell you the truth, son," he finished, "I was counting on tradin' along the Susquehanna. If these traders have been selling all the way up from the Chesapeake, then I don't know who'll have any furs left to buy our goods."

Thad nodded but said nothing. He knew his father was just thinking out loud, not asking for advice.

"Here's what I think we'll do, since we don't really have much choice. We'll go back downriver maybe a half a mile, and we'll wait till tomorrow. If the trading in the village today is not satisfactory, maybe we'll be able to do business." Big Oak stared out at the wind-rippled water, and Thad knew his father really wished they could be on their way.

"Truth is, you know, that once they break out the rum, any deal that includes the rum'll look good to them."

They shoved off and headed upriver, and spent the day fishing, then later, eating what they caught. Early in the evening they relaxed in the camp, listening to the sounds of the forest and thinking their own thoughts. Little Oak had found that his father enjoyed those moments of contemplation in what he called "the warm cool of the evening." Little Oak also loved that time, when everything to be done had been done.

It started as the sound of chatter, as if the commander of Fort Oswego were holding a big party and all the officers were lining up at the punch bowl. Then the chatter grew in excitement. All this went on for two hours or so. Through the talk came some good singing, then some bad singing, then shouting, and at last an angry cry followed by screams. There was a shot, followed by more shouting, very angry this time, then a whoop, and finally all hell broke loose in the Delaware village.

Big Oak and Thad picked up their bedding and moved

from the clearing into the brush, rifles primed, loaded and ready, just in case. Pandemonium was loose in the village. Several more shots were fired and the voices of women and children briefly joined the deeper sounds of the men. Then the high-pitched voices subsided, but the sounds of male discord continued.

Big Oak raised himself on one elbow and picked a new sound out of the chorus of forest night noises. Soon the sound grew clearer, quick footsteps in panic along the forest floor. A misstep and a body sprawled in old dry leaves. "Ooh," came the voice of a child, followed by a woman's sharp command, and then the footsteps started again.

Big Oak stood up, stepped out into the clearing and waved his arms at the frightened woman and three terrified children as they ran out from a thick grouping of birch. The woman came to a sudden halt, started to reverse her direction, then stood before Big Oak, rattling off the rapid-fire Algonquian tongue of the Delaware.

Big Oak hadn't a clue to what she was saying, but he didn't have to. He knew what was happening in the village. Follow me, he signed to the woman in the light of a half-moon as he led the woman and her children to the canoe. Soon Little Oak and her oldest boy were paddling the canoe farther up the Susquehanna, and Big Oak was watching her anxious hands tell the story of terror in the village.

"Tomorrow morning," Big Oak told his son, "We will bring this family back to the village. I'm afraid they had a bad night."

They paddled north for half an hour and pulled the canoe ashore. Big Oak broke into his stock of blankets and passed them out, and they all laid down to try for a short night's sleep. Blessedly, the distance and the intervening trees and terrain hid the awful sounds of a village at war with itself. It took a while, but at last exhaustion found them and they all drifted off.

They awakened early, but Big Oak refused to let the family go back to the village just yet. "Let the fools wake up themselves and give their heads time to shrink back to normal size before we pay them a visit." The woman, who was called Lost Moon, did not object. She seated herself and told her three boys to do the same, while Big Oak presented them with the leftovers of the previous night's banquet. They waited more than an hour before they returned to the canoe and slowly made their way downstream to the village.

It could have been worse. "At least they didn't burn the place down," Big Oak grumped as they surveyed the damage. Indians were lying everywhere, all of them men, the women and children having vanished into the woods for protection. At first Thad thought that they might have killed each other, but then he realized they were still sleeping off the previous night's drunken rampage. There were a number of empty kegs scattered about, but, Big Oak noticed, the stock of trade goods that still lay where the traders had left them was pathetically small.

A few of the Delaware were already up, and they were suffering from terrible hangovers. One was suffering more than the others. His face was caked with dried blood and his left eye was completely shut. Big Oak looked more closely and realized that the left eye was permanently shut, for there was no eyeball left in its socket.

Other men were beginning to stir, and it seemed that at least one in five had some form of injury or other. This one was missing a chunk of ear, that one's face was striped with red as if it had been clawed by a lioness. One soundlessly nursed a painful gunshot wound in his thigh, and one had lost so much blood from a tomahawk gash in his shoulder that he lay babbling insensibly. He was the husband of Lost Moon, who gave a small scream of distress and ran to the woods for a piece of bark to stop up the wound.

At the doorway of one of the lodges stood an old gray-haired woman past forty, wailing piteously. Next to her stood a young man half her age, and tears glistened in his eyes, although the expression on his face remained impassive.

Suddenly Beaver's Heart was standing next to Big Oak. The trader had not seen him approach, so engrossed was he in the misery he saw around him. A few women, with their children, were beginning to approach the village warily, but it seemed clear that many of them would stay in the woods until they were certain the danger was past.

"Tell me how bad it was, my brother," Big Oak said to Beaver's Heart.

The interpreter grimaced at the sound of Big Oak's voice and held the sides of his head as if to balance it on top of his shoulders. With the other hand he pointed to where the old woman and the young man stood together lost in grief.

"This is from the white man's rum," he said. "Last night the woman had two big strong sons. This morning she has one. And the young man standing beside her is the murderer of his brother.

"When we start drinking the rum, at first everything is wonderful. We hug our brothers and laugh and sing and feel the warm good within our bellies. But we always want more. And when we have more, some of us get mean and angry, and remember a friend or a brother who once displeased us with something he said or did. And we . . . we do bad things then."

He pointed to the man who lay on the ground, with Lost Moon ministering to his shoulder. "I have seen such wounds before. Yesterday that man could hurl a tomahawk from here into the trunk of that beech tree." He pointed to a tree thirty yards distant. "Every throw," he added. "But he will never again lift his arm above his shoulder—if he lives long enough for the wound to heal."

"Where is the chief?" Big Oak asked.

"Ah, that is worst of all," replied Beaver's Heart. "Come."

Big Oak and Thad followed Beaver's Heart into a lodge under a group of tall pine trees. There, on a platform covered with deerskins, tended by two young girls who might have been his daughters or his wives, lay Captain Thomas.

His eyes moved in the direction of his visitors and he blinked twice, but he did not turn his head.

"He does not move," Beaver's Heart said softly. "Spirits have seized his body and tied it too tightly to the earth. He sees us. He knows who we are, but he cannot speak to us."

The two men and the boy stood silently and stared down at the stricken village chief. "Most of the men in the village do not even know. They are either still sleeping or they feel too sick to care what is going on around them." He looked into the eyes of Big Oak. The look was not friendly. "Let us leave the lodge," he said.

When they were outside, he spoke again. "It would be better that you leave our village now. When the men are feeling better, they will be very angry at the white men."

Big Oak bristled. "My brother, I did not bring rum to the village. If I could have stopped it, I would have stopped it. My eyes have seen much since I came into the village. Your braves were so greedy for the drink that they did not even put away the trade goods before they began to drink. These traders, they gave you much rum and little goods of any use for the skins you sold them. How will you get through the winter without new blankets? Did they sell you any powder?"

Beaver's Heart shook his head. "We have very little ammunition left for hunting."

"I did not bring much, but we have some," replied Big Oak. "If you want, we will remain in the village for one moon. If your men will go out and trap furs, I will let you have what I have brought, even though I could get more furs for my goods elsewhere."

"Go to your canoe for now and do not speak of it," said Beaver's Heart. "Tomorrow I will talk to the older men, and then I will visit your camp and give you their answer."

Big Oak and Thad stayed no longer in the village that day.

"What will we do?" Thad asked when they had returned

to the screen of overhanging branches where they had hidden their canoe.

"We will wait," his father replied. "But we will also watch."

Big Oak left his son in the concealed canoe and returned to the outskirts of the village, where he hid himself and listened. He was not surprised to see Beaver's Heart walking around the village, rousting men from their hung-over lethargy with animated rhetoric and gesticulations. Big Oak had learned that in some ways, Indian nature was no different from white nature. A terrible thing had happened in the village, and the men were not about to blame themselves for it. Since the white men had sold them the rum they craved, and left few of the goods the Indians would need for survival over the winter, the Delaware were determined to avenge themselves on any whites handy. Big Oak had heard of numerous times when the whites had done the same to the Indians.

When he saw men appearing with their weapons, then moving off toward the river, he waited no longer, crawling for about a hundred yards, then scrambling to his feet and racing toward the canoe, where it was parked upstream from the village. He would have to get a big head start on these Indians. There was no way he and his eleven-year-old son would be able to outrun three or four strong paddlers in a swift canoe.

"We've got to get moving now," he hissed as he neared the place where the canoe was hidden. Little Oak, hearing his approaching footsteps, had paddled the canoe out from behind the branches and gotten it moving upstream by the time Big Oak appeared. A carefully timed running jump landed him by the stern, where his paddle was waiting.

With strong, deft strokes of the paddle he propelled the canoe into the middle channel. Big Oak and Thad then made the river fairly boil past the bow of the canoe, and Big Oak could hardly fail to notice how powerful and coordinated were the strokes of his young son. They moved the canoe toward the opposite bank, where the current was slow, and really put their shoulders and backs into their work. Big Oak knew that it would take a few minutes for the Delaware to launch their canoes and sort themselves out, and he was counting on the poisons still tormenting their bodies to slow them down.

His first thought was to put as much distance as they could between them and their pursuers, but about three miles up the river they entered a long, fairly straight stretch and an idea hit him. Just beyond the bend following the straight path of the river, he stopped the canoe and reached for his rifle. While his son held the canoe steady, Big Oak lay across the bow, pointing the long barrel of his rifle downstream. About ten minutes later the first Delaware canoe hove into view less than two hundred yards away. Big Oak took careful aim, waited for the canoe to come a little closer, then fired and splintered the blade of the lead paddle. The stern paddler immediately stopped, and they waited for the other pursuing canoes to catch up, while Big Oak quickly reloaded his rifle.

There were three of them, and when they had all stopped, Big Oak rose to his knees.

"Beaver's Heart," he hollered in the Seneca tongue. "Why are you doing this?"

The translator answered, but between the distance and his accent, Big Oak could not understand.

"You, and only you," he shouted, "I will talk to. I pledge my word not to shoot." The men in the four canoes conferred for a minute, then two men left the canoe of Beaver's Heart and he alone paddled forward. When he was within ten yards of Big Oak's canoe, he stopped.

"Watch the other canoes, son," Big Oak said. "I will talk with this deceiving devil."

Big Oak raised his voice: "I made you a good offer, Beaver's Heart, and yet you tried to attack us. Why?"

The Indian knew better than to try to lie his way out of his predicament. "We would have our vengeance. We need the goods you carry, and we will not work half the summer for you to earn the goods that the traders from the Chesapeake should have given us."

"And yet, my deceiving brother, you chose rum over the things your families needed to get them through the winter. How could you do that?"

"How? I have heard that far to the west there are lands where you can travel for days without finding water. If you had to go for days without water, would you not sell your soul for a taste of it? That is how we crave your rum."

"Not *my* rum, my brother."

"Big Oak," the Delaware said, "When the white man came to these shores, the Lenni Lenape were there to help them. They gave us rum and we loved it. We never dreamed that anything so good could be so bad, else why would our white brothers give it to us?

"For the taste of rum we gave them our hearts, our land, and finally our manhood. They who we had once helped allied with the Iroquois and gave them guns to conquer us with. We who were once the most powerful and the most noble now must do what the Iroquois tell us to do. They call us their women. And it is the English who did this to us. Without the English to arm the Iroquois, we would still be our own masters.

"It is the twilight of our people. Where we were many, we are now so few. But our forebears look down upon us and call for us to make a fight of it.

"And yet we cannot fight. Not when we crave our rum more than we crave our guns and ammunition."

Big Oak kept his silence for a few moments to let Beaver's Heart know that his words had been heard.

"Most of what you say is true. But you made a mistake when you chose to treat us as white enemies. We are of the Seneca, and if we chose to return to the Longhouse and tell our brothers what you tried to do to us, they would send their warriors down this river, wipe out your village, eat your men, and make slaves of your women and children. If they were angry enough, they would see that the great name of the Lenni Lenape was never heard again in the land."

Beaver's Heart could not help but show fear when he heard these words.

"I will not do this, for the sake of the memory of the noble Lenni Lenape. All people have their good times and their bad times. Take heart, my brother, for the day may again come when the Lenni Lenape will be a great people.

"Where I was raised, we were taught to return good for evil. I wanted to deal with your village because I knew that the Chesapeake traders had probably dealt with villages all the way down the Susquehanna as they had dealt with you. I needed to sell my goods for furs because that is how I make my living. Because you have refused our offer and tried to attack us, we must take our goods back to Oquaga, and it will go hard with me.

"And yet I know you must have powder and bullets to hunt this winter or your village will starve. Here, my brother." And he reached down among his goods and lifted a small keg of powder and several bars of lead, as well as a handful of flints, which he passed over to the Beaver's Heart.

"My heart is heavy for the Lenni Lenape, for I know that there was a time when you were mighty, and yet you did not wipe out your neighbors, like my brothers the Ganonsyoni have done.

"I wish you health, my brother. Now go from me and do not follow us or we will bring the Iroquois down upon you and wipe you from the face of the earth. Farewell."

Big Oak ordered Thad back to his position in the bow, and waited until Beaver's Heart had paddled back to where his fellow villagers were waiting. Then with three swift pulls on his paddle, his canoe rounded the bend and vanished from the lives of the Susquehanna Lenni Lenape.

# ❈5❈

SEVEN YEARS HAD PASSED SINCE LITTLE OAK'S first trading trip with his father. The mighty man who had once laid down the law to the Delaware, alone in their own country, still clung to life by a brittle thread.

The fourth day after the near death of Big Oak, he opened his eyes, searched out the opening to the lodge, and his voice croaked something unintelligible. The fifth day, he began to move his limbs, and on the seventh day he fastened his eyes on Thad and said, "Son."

"Pa," Thad responded excitedly. "Pa," he repeated, again and again. Now Sam pointed toward the light streaming through the doorway opening. "Sun!" he cried with feeling.

"Yes, Pa, yes!"

An hour later he looked at Gingego and said "son," or "sun." He grabbed the bowl from Gingego's fingers, took a couple of sips of broth, pointed to it and said "son," or "sun." Or was it "it's done," or something else?

Thad had to be thrilled. He had been raised to be an optimist, and if his father was croaking gibberish, at least he was saying something. He stared at his father, at his pathetically swollen head and his unfocused eyes, and let his mind again wander back to a time before a gaggle of young Mohawk glory seekers had robbed Big Oak of his reason.

He remembered a bright summer morning when his father loaded him, his mother, and a sack of tools and spare rifle parts in a canoe and paddled down the Genesee River to visit Old Belt's village. They were spotted from the woods by a band of children, and by the time they had arrived at the village, nearly everybody was down by the river to greet them.

Some of them attempted to carry Big Oak's baggage for him, but Big Oak rejected their help. He knew that his ability to repair broken weapons seemed almost mystical to these villagers, and he chose to add to the mystery by treating his bag of tools and spare parts as if they were a medicine bundle. As they entered the village, Old Belt came out to greet him, conducting him to his longhouse, where the two, along with other important men of the village, and a pair of visitors from another Seneca village, dined on the best that the chief had to offer, which was considerably good. In the meantime Little Oak and his mother joined some of her friends and their children for a less formal meal.

In the afternoon they set a large blanket out under a huge oak tree, and there Dr. Big Oak set up his office, while the men of the village brought him their ailing weapons. Most of the problems were simple, stemming from mediocre gunpowder and inadequate cleaning. The Indians marveled at the dexterity with which Big Oak disassembled their weapons. They admired the gleaming shine he put on the mechanisms, and the smoothness of their operation after he had finished his work. In some cases where there was actual breakage, he was able to tailor parts to make do, and when he did, there were always exclamations from his audience. Although the Senecas had had muskets and rifles for many years, they could never seem to master the mechanics of these weapons.

In truth, Big Oak was no gunsmith. He was limited in what he was able to do to repair firearms, but what he could do was sufficient to take care of most ailing muskets and rifles. Tolerant as Big Oak was of other people's limitations, he couldn't help but shake his head at the limitations of his adopted brothers. They just would not understand that a bit of knowledge and timely care could save their lives someday in battle.

Big Oak was careful not to lose caste. When one brave brought him an old musket with a broken stock and arrogantly demanded, "give me new wood," Big Oak eyed him with contempt and told him that gunsmiths do not work wood and that he should go out and carve his own stock. The warrior erupted in fury, but when his hand reached for his knife, Big Oak rapped him on the knuckles with the barrel of the broken gun and promised to wrap it around his neck if he didn't take the useless thing and get it out of sight.

"Bury it," Big Oak advised. "Bury it shallow, then maybe some wandering Huron might find it, try to shoot it, and then die when it blows up. That's the only way you're ever gonna kill an enemy with it," he told the brave in fluent Seneca dialect. With that, the brave took his rusty old weapon and slunk out of sight, to the sound of raucous laughter from some of his fellow warriors.

When he was repairing Old Belt's weapon, he took considerable care, first cleaning the piece with extra thoroughness, and then, after working the mechanism, replacing the fair French flint with an excellent black flint from the fine craftsmen of Suffolk, in England. Old Belt, who was sitting next to him, made a sheepish confession:

"Certain Death," he said softly, uttering his pet name for the fabled sharpshooter. "I must tell you that this year I have been shooting my gun very bad. I could never shoot like you, but this year I cannot seem to kill anything. And yet my eyesight is as keen as ever."

One of his braves overheard the confession and made a rude noise. "He would be more likely to bring down a deer by throwing his gun at it than by shooting it." Again there was laughter from the men who surrounded Big Oak. The white man sighted down the barrel, first from the flintlock side and then from the muzzle. "Uh-huh," he grunted, and smiled at the chief.

"There is nothing wrong with your shooting, Old Belt," he insisted. Taking a pliars-like device from among the tools that he had laid out on the blanket, he made a minute adjustment of the sight.

"This is not a rifle, it's a musket," Big Oak reminded the chief. "Good for maybe—from here to that tree." He pointed to the tree in question. "And your sight was off enough to make the difference. And here . . ."

He reached into his sack and took out a small pouch. "In this pouch," he said, "is the finest gunpowder in North America. With it you cannot miss." Although he was telling the truth about the quality of the powder, it was not likely to improve the chief's shooting very much, but Big Oak knew that confidence was important for a shooter.

"Tell you what," he said. "Let's test it out." He gestured with the barrel of the musket for the audience to clear a path so he could take a shot at the tree he had pointed out earlier. He pointed to a branch and told them he would clip it off. Although the distance was only forty yards, the branch was a scant two inches thick. He loaded the piece carefully, brought it up slowly, took a deep breath and let it out just a bit, then squeezed the trigger.

The musket cracked and the branch disappeared, to the oohs and ahs of his audience.

"Now you do it, Old Belt," he said. The chief shook his head to more laughter.

Old Belt poured powder into his musket followed by wad and ball, then pointed to a limb on a closer tree, this one perhaps half again as thick as the one Big Oak had splintered. He brought the weapon to his shoulder and sighed his target. He leaned forward slightly, filled his lungs half full of air, and fired.

\*   \*   \*

A week after Big Oak had spoken his first syllables, everything was "son" or "gun" or "drum." By now it was certain that he didn't have the faintest idea what he was saying.

His knife wound was sufficiently healed that he could take walks, leaning on a patient Thad, who had no trouble supporting him, for he had lost a lot of weight in a very short time. His body was emaciated, yet his head was still swollen and lopsided. His once incredible vision was so impaired that when he reached for his bowl, his hand sometimes grasped three inches short of its goal.

Late at night Thad would lie beside his father, feeling frustrated and discouraged. Progress was so slow that sometimes he doubted he would ever again exchange words with Big Oak, much less walk the forest trails with him. But in the morning he would feed him his broth, then lift him to his feet and walk him around the camp.

By the fourth week the walks were up to fifteen minutes. Big Oak's appetite was considerably better, and his vocabulary had increased. But what he was saying still made no sense, and he walked like an old man. Every day Thad held long conversations with his father that often went something like this:

"Beautiful day for hunting, Pa."

"Got legs on that bird no more Oswego umgot."

"That's what you always taught me, Pa."

"Your ma putta tree under her wigwam."

"What did Ma do?"

"White man fool—red man fooler. So it . . ."

Here Big Oak would lapse into some Indian dialect, but not one that Thad could remember having heard. Nor had Gingego ever heard it before. He'd shake his head, take Big Oak's hand and squeeze his shoulder. Big Oak never seemed to notice.

"Little Oak," Gingego said one day. "Your father not yet come out of the shadow. But you cannot hide in the shadow with him. I will stay with him for a while, but you must come out, see the sun and feel the earth."

The sounds and smells filled Thad's senses as he walked from the house, stretched, and looked across the valley. He recalled his favorite trip with his father one autumn, up beyond Lake George for otter skins, and just a few thoughts that his father had shared with him on that trip.

"Autumn is a funny time," Big Oak had told him. "It makes some men think of livin' and some men think of dyin', but it changes everybody."

"My favorite time is the spring," Thad told his father. "What's yours?"

"What's mine? I like the seasons. All of them. I love to mark the changes year after year. They make life worth livin'. When the leaves have all died, they get a clean blanket of snow to cover 'em, and then comes the sun to fill the streams with sweet new water from the mountaintops."

Would his father ever mark another season? Thad took a walk into the hills, and in spite of his flagging spirits, could not help but feel the joy of stretching out his long legs and making his lungs expand with the exertion of climbing up, up, until he found a ridge line that looked northeast toward the Adirondack Mountains, across the valley to the next line of hills that stretched mile after mile of green, undulating in the mild summer breeze.

He stood still for nearly a half hour, watching the green parade marching toward the blue horizon, and his heart ached that a man could not walk this beautiful land forever. He looked to the east and saw, just this side of the horizon, what he thought was smoke filtering up through the bright-colored canopy. White man? His father had once told him that some day white men would fill the Mohawk Valley, and that a man wouldn't be able to walk a trail for thirty minutes at a time without coming in sight of one lodge or another.

His heart ached as he imagined the forests chopped into clearings for the iron plow. Sam had once told him that it might even happen within his lifetime.

Hungry, Thad walked back down the hill toward the village and headed for his father's lodge. But as he entered the

village through the front gate, he found Corn Boy waiting
for him.

"I thought you had run away, like a bad child," signed the
young Mohawk.

"My father is still not well," Little Oak signed back.
"Maybe you would run out on your father when he needs
you. I would not."

"I have seen your father. He has turned into a fool."

"Maybe so. But better to have lost your reason in battle
than to have been born a fool like Corn Boy."

Corn Boy's temper was the first to crack. "You think me a
fool? This fool will split your skull with one blow of his
tomahawk, you half-person." Indians of many tribes went
around thinking of their tribe as "the people," or "the only
real men." Allied tribes may be "people," but white men
certainly were not.

"You talk big but you are much smaller than the plant you
are named for."

The Mohawk sneered. "I am nearly as tall as you."

"Your smallness is in your heart, not in your height. It is
time I chopped you down to size," Little Oak suggested.

Suddenly words were not sufficient. With a deadly gleam
in his eye, Corn Boy slid his tomahawk from his belt.

"You see that I am not armed," Little Oak said, leaning
forward on his toes, hands in front of him, ready.

"You are as big a fool as your father. Come to me, white
boy, and I will split you in two." Little Oak did not move.
Corn Boy circled in on him. He was agile, Little Oak knew,
and strong enough, he was certain, to do what he wanted to
do. Even quickness would not be enough to save Little Oak.
He needed to break his enemy's concentration.

Corn Boy moved closer, feinted to his left and laughed
when Little Oak reacted to the feint.

"Ha! Your scalp hangs loose on your head. I could almost
pluck it off with my bare hands," he snarled in Mohawk
tongue. Little Oak puzzled over the meaning of the words,
some of which he could almost but not quite understand,

and nearly forgot to dodge when Corn Boy charged him and swung his tomahawk. He heard it whistle past his ear. It drew no blood but it did inspire an idea.

Little Oak circled around a few times, stepped back and began to shout nasty insults at Corn Boy in the Seneca tongue, but every so often he'd slip in one of the few Mohawk words he knew. It all sounded like a furious diatribe, and he turned it up another notch when Corn Boy closed in on him again. He saw the boy hesitate for just a moment at the sound of the Mohawk word for "skunk." It was the lapse Little Oak had hoped for. Quick as the shadow of a nighthawk, he reached out with his left hand and snatched at the handle of Corn Boy's tomahawk. He grabbed it with a grip of iron and then brought his right hand to the young Mohawk's face, where his fingers began to gouge at Corn Boy's eyes.

Now the two moved in slow, dusty circles, each with both hands on the tomahawk. Both tugged hard at the handle, trying to throw the other off balance. Then Little Oak pulled so hard that the Mohawk left his feet for a moment and flew through the air a third of the way around Little Oak. He landed on his knees, and Little Oak began to twist the tomahawk out of Corn Boy's grip.

The young Mohawk regained his feet, kicked out hard at Little Oak's groin and came close enough to draw a grunt from deep in Little Oak's chest. Little Oak gave the tomahawk one last desperate twist before he surrendered to the pain and fell to his knees, his breath coming in rasping gasps. The tomahawk fell into the grass about ten feet away.

Corn Boy tried to dash past the kneeling form of Little Oak to retrieve the tomahawk, but Little Oak grabbed his foot and sent him sprawling. Little Oak ran to Corn Boy before the Mohawk could stand up, pulled him to his feet by his shoulders and flung him again, as hard as he could, away from where the tomahawk lay in the dust. The Mohawk crashed against the wall of the stockade and crumpled to the ground. Little Oak ran to the tomahawk, picked it up, and leaped back to where Corn Boy was still struggling to rise. He clubbed him down with a blow from the flat of the tomahawk. The Mohawk sank back into the dust, his eyes glassy. Little Oak thought about Corn Boy making fun of his father and started to raise his tomahawk above his head.

He heard a single gasp, looked around him, and for the first time noticed that half the village had come out to witness the fight. He also knew that as outsiders, he and Big Oak would be in deep trouble with the village if he killed Corn Boy right here on his own soil. He had yet to kill a man, and did not have the heart to start now. Suddenly he stood up, cocked his arm, and threw the tomahawk high over the stockade wall. This one had nice balance, and his arm was very strong. The tomahawk disappeared over the wall and flew down the side of the hill like a diving hawk.

Seated astride the stunned Mohawk, Little Oak surveyed the sea of hostile faces around him and decided they would not even be willing to tolerate a thrashing. Little Oak waited fifteen seconds, until Corn Boy's eyes cleared. Then he poked his index finger into the boy's chest and said, "I want you to stay away from me, or I will surely cut you into pieces. And I promise you that those pieces will not know where to find each other. Do you understand?" Corn Boy did not understand, of course. He just glared back at Little Oak with a look of pure bile. How he hates me, the young Seneca thought. Little Oak told him again, this time in sign. Breathing hard, Corn Boy merely growled in response. Little Oak stood up and dusted himself off, eyeing his audience defiantly.

Corn Boy sat in the dust and waited until Little Oak headed for his father's lodge before he moved. He had finally received the message. Little Oak was too tough to bully. Corn Boy would have to wait for the next new boy in town.

Weary from his forest stroll and the fight, Little Oak walked past the silent witnesses, into Gingego's longhouse. He found some boiled corn in the pot of Gingego's lodge fire, and brought it home to share with his father. Gingego had been feeding him and his father for weeks now. Tomorrow morning he would go out and kill a deer for Gingego and his family.

The next morning, very early, Thad checked his rifle carefully, replaced the priming in the pan, and headed out to find a deer. He disappeared into the edge of the woods along the creek bank and followed the creek for a mile or two without seeing any fresh deer sign.

Eventually the woods receded from the north bank of the creek, while on the south bank stood a thin screen of trees and, beyond, a hillside of long yellow grass, perhaps an old field still cleared from the days when more people lived in the village and the women grew more food on more land. Maybe they still grazed livestock there at times, he thought.

He crossed over to the other side. Some of the long grass had a trampled look to it. Good news and bad news. There might be deer in the field, but in the long grass he'd be lucky to spot one. A doe could crouch in the thick growth fifty yards away and he'd never see her.

He shrugged his shoulders. His father was a philosophical hunter. If the weather went against them, or the terrain went against them, or the deer decided to be somewhere else on the day they were out, he'd just shoulder his rifle without complaint and tramp on home. He'd find himself a deer another day.

So Thad was a philosophical hunter. On this warm day, a walk in the woods was privilege enough for him. Slowly he made his way along the creek, eyes on the bank and on the field, his world in sharp focus.

His mind wandered back to Kawia. The summer before, he had taken her with him on a deer hunt that had brought them not a sign of the animal the entire morning. The day got hotter and hotter, and the river looked more and more inviting, until she begged him to go for a swim with her.

He decided that he didn't really need a deer that badly

that day. They peeled off their clothes and plunged into the cool water of the Genesee. It was then that he had caught sight of the deer. Kawia had been watching him, pleased by the effect she knew she was having on him, thrilled to watch his expression as he approached her, and surprised to see his glance turn toward the shore, and then to see that his legs were following his glance.

Quietly he pulled himself onto the bank. Buck naked, he crept to where his rifle stood against an oak sapling. He reached for the rifle and drew it to his shoulder. Kawia watched him, totally absorbed in the deer and the rifle, and her brief moment of anticipation turned to anger.

"He-*yah!*" she shouted, and the deer bounded into a thicket. Thad jumped into the thicket after it and fired a wild, ineffectual shot, then tore himself away from the thicket and walked back toward the river, so disgusted that at first he didn't notice the scratches all over his body. The thicket had clawed him like an irate panther from his shoulders to his knees.

"Oh," she said. "Oh." She made him lie down while she scooped up cool mud from the river bottom and rubbed it tenderly on his back, his stomach, his arms, his legs, everywhere. Little Oak didn't know if the mud did his wounds any good, but he found the experience to be the finest thing to have ever happened to him in his young life—that is, until a moment later, when she kissed him.

The tall grass in front of him exploded and so did his reverie. A deer leaped from where she lay, and Thad's heart almost leaped through his chest as he pulled the rifle to his shoulder. Her next leap was right where he knew it would be. He pulled the trigger and down she went, dead and still by the time he got to her ten seconds later.

He brought most of it in on his back, then gave the lion's share of it to Gingego's wife. He saved one beautiful hunk for himself and his father, carried it back to their lodge, put it on a stick, and slowly, slowly roasted it over his hearth fire. He and his father would dine better than King George tonight.

The next morning, just after breakfast, Thad's father turned to him and said, "What year is this, son?"

Thad smiled. "Seventeen fifty-five, Pa."

Big Oak nodded. "You know, there's gonna be war soon, don't you?"

Thad never thought he would greet the news of war with such joy. Those were the first sensible words that Big Oak had uttered since he had been brought in from the forest.

Then he fell silent, and Thad did not attempt to force more words from him. The following day, Big Oak was back to speaking gibberish, but Thad was now convinced that soon he would have his father back.

Three days later, suddenly, late in the afternoon, Big Oak turned to Thad and said, "Son, where are we at?"

"In the Mohawk village of Gingego," Thad replied.

"Ah, Gingego, my old friend. How I'd love to see him again. We might journey there to visit him someday soon."

"Pa, I can bring him to you before the shadow of the sun moves."

"Good, good," Big Oak said. Thad sighed, and Big Oak again lapsed into passive silence.

But the next day Big Oak awakened, rose to his feet and stretched. His face was by now close to normal, but Thad noticed him working his jaw, as if he were aware for the first time that something about him was not quite right.

"Take me to Gingego," Sam growled. "I need to see that old frog killer."

He still walked slowly, but on his own, erect. His eyes retained the bug-eyed look they'd had since they brought him in on a litter.

"How long have we been here?"

"Nearly two moons."

"It must have been bad, then."

"Pa, you were holding on to this world by some real greasy fingers."

"They were Mohawks who ambushed us, weren't they?" Thad nodded. "From this village. They—"

"Shhh, listen." Big Oak had stopped in his tracks near a lodge set right by the north wall. Thad halted too, and held his breath that he might hear what his father heard.

What they heard, faintly but clearly within the lodge, was French being spoken by Indians. They moved a step or two closer to the lodge and stood facing in another direction, as if searching for their destination.

There were three voices. In spite of the strangeness of the language, Thad recognized one of them.

"Red Hawk," he whispered. "The one who nearly killed you." Big Oak nodded, and they began to walk again.

"The Mohawk are great allies of the English," Big Oak said. "But among them are some who have been bewitched by the priests of the French. Most live in mission villages, but some carry on their treachery among the 'English' Mohawks. Red Hawk is probably one of those. The other two are not Iroquois. Their speech gives them away."

Gingego stood at the door of his lodge. Even before Big Oak could open his mouth, the venerable warrior sensed the change. "My old friend." He smiled, brushing a strand of gray hair from his cheek. "It's so good to see you again." He threw a stringy arm around Big Oak and thumped him on his broad back with the other. "This day I am very happy."

For once, Big Oak had no words with which to respond. He simply nodded, and with great effort swallowed the lump in his throat.

Thad started taking Big Oak for long walks in the woods. His sense of balance was terrible, and he fell off the trail once and slid fifty feet down a hill, into a creek. He laughed at himself, called himself the world's clumsiest frontiersman, and spent the next ten minutes climbing the slope back to the trail.

But gradually his balance improved, and his strength returned quickly once he was back in his element. There were gaps in his memory, and his fingers still had minds of their own. When he loaded primer, he spilled half the powder on the ground. Once it took him six tries to get the rammer to go down the barrel instead of down one side or the other. He might as well have been trying to thread a needle.

But for Thad these were good days. His patience was long and his hopes high, for he had seen how far his father had come since the first day he had grunted "son," or whatever it was he had grunted.

During this time, Big Oak let his son lead him. He recognized that until his thoughts were working in a steady stream instead of in coughs and hiccoughs, his son's judgment was superior to his own.

Finally the time had come for Big Oak to challenge his shooting eye. At first the stock felt strange against his cheek and the barrel heavy over his arm. The target weaved back and forth in his sights, the kick jarred his shoulder, and the noise nearly burst his eardrums, but he was determined to regain the skill that had saved his life so many times in the forest.

The shooter's touch is a delicate thing, but a man who has it never loses it as long as his hands are steady and his vision is clear. It took time, but gradually the great healing powers of his body made him nearly the man that he had been.

In one way though, he was different. Never again would he feel bulletproof. Never again would he feel invincible. As cautious as he had been by instinct, now he was cautious by conscious habit.

"We must make the most of our time, son," he said a week later. "You have seen me shoot."

"Still the best shot this side of the ocean, Pa."

"I raised my son to tell the truth. I will be better, but I will never be what I was before. I do not believe that my hand will ever be as steady, or my eye so clear. I am glad that you have inherited the shooter's touch."

"Pa, I don't—"

"Now, you must understand what is happening. Gingego is my friend, and he remains a powerful man among the Mohawks. Mohawk braves travel far and wide across New York and Pennsylvania, and along the Ohio, and even down into Virginia. And when they return, they stop here and tell their stories to Gingego because he is a good listener. Last year the Mohawk chief Hendrick was at Fort Albany. He told the English that the French were preparing for war, like men. The English, he told, 'You are like women, bare and open, without any fortifications.' He has always been a good friend to the English, and he was trying to warn them that the French would soon be comin' down on the English settlements.

"Gingego says that there's a rumor goin' 'round about an English army that got itself ambushed near Fort Duquesne down in Pennsylvania and just about wiped out by the French, and the Ottawas, and Chippewa, and even a few of Chief White Eyes's Delaware."

"What? Did the Delaware dare to make war on the allies of the Iroquois?"

Big Oak nodded. "With the French there to give them courage. The French and the English have fought many times over this land. Wherever there are French and English, they fight, because they do not like each other. They get in each other's way. In this land it is the furs that they fight over. In other lands they find other things to fight over. We won the last war, but then over the water they made a peace that gave the French back everything we had won from them. But I believe that this war will finally decide who will stay and who will go."

"And will we fight?"

Big Oak put a hand on his son's shoulder. "While I lay babbling on the floor of the longhouse and you sat with me, you passed your nineteenth birthday. It is right that you ask me for advice, son, but I no longer decide your future for you."

Little Oak stared at his moccasins for a moment, embarrassed. When he raised his eyes, he looked into the eyes not of his father, but of his friend.

"Do you feel ready to travel?" he asked.

His father nodded.

"We should spend some time gathering provisions and readying our weapons. Where is it best that we go?"

"Fort Albany." Big Oak smiled. "According to the runners, they are raising an army there, and they'll be wantin' scouts.

"Gingego got our furs back for us," he added. The party that brought me in also had our packs. Gingego nearly whipped one of them when he found out they intended to keep them. You wouldn't believe that these young braves still fear the might of his arm. He was a great warrior in his time. And a great man even today.

"I believe we need to stay here another week, get out in the woods and give me a chance to toughen up a little more. My body has stopped complaining to me, but my breath is still short. Then we will head for Albany. Before we report to Colonel Johnson, we will sell our furs. It is always good to take care of business first."

## ❖ 6 ❖

**T**HAD'S EYES WERE WIDE WITH EXCITEMENT ON the day the little party arrived at Albany. All the traveling he had done on the heels of his father—the Seneca and Cayuga villages, the lands of the Delaware, an occasional colonial hamlet, and the vast woodsy cathedrals, had left him unprepared for this city of three thousand souls, now doubled by the colonial militia forces squatting in the woods just north of the city's palisades.

Although the community boasted some impressive buildings, notably the towering, steep sloping roof of the Dutch Reformed Church, Thad's first impression was that of dust, from the town streets inside and the company streets outside —dust that coated the plain, practical one- and two-story brick houses, and settled on the clothes of those who walked its streets.

The stench of horse manure rotting in the late spring heat clung to the nostrils of one who was accustomed to the sweet smells of the woods. Above the dust, like a halo from Hell, floated a persistent pall of smoke; the militia, by way of settling in, were still cutting and burning the woods around Albany to clear space for their huts and tents.

When Big Oak announced his intention to march to Albany to fight the French, the Mohawk village had erupted with conflicting emotions. As much as they hated the

French, at this time they were no great admirers of the English either. The English were fond of proclaiming their brotherhood with the Iroquois when they wanted to use Iroquois claims in the west against the French, but when they sent their Iroquois allies into battle against the French in the east, they weren't above selling the French arms to fire back at the Iroquois.

"We don't trust the French. We don't trust the English. Why should we?" Red Hawk had spat one night at a late night discussion among the warriors.

Big Oak had retaliated by reciting the familiar roll of massacres and murders perpetrated by the French and their Indian allies against the Mohawks over the past seventy-five years. "You were once an even mightier nation," he reminded Red Hawk. "The French did this to you."

"So you tell us. But I say it is not all the French. We die just by being near the white man. You turn the very air that we breathe against us. I do not understand how it happens. It is not just battle. It is not just rum. It is not just the sickness. It is the presence of the white man. When he passes through an Indian nation, he is like the wind and we are like the leaves. When you are done passing through, our pieces are scattered to the ends of the earth, and then we are no more."

"You must trust your white friends, Red Hawk. Men like William Johnson are your true brothers. Without men like him, you are surely lost."

Anger rose in Red Hawk, so hot that only with great effort could he cool it. The big white man was speaking to him as Iroquois spoke to Delaware. How he hated this white man. How he wanted his life.

"We are still the fiercest of warriors," Red Hawk had growled back. "Look how easy we took you, great one." Whenever Red Hawk was in the presence of Big Oak or Thad, he wore a sour expression, as if either one or both exuded an unpleasant odor.

"Great warriors," Big Oak had agreed. "But see how few of you remain."

"Ah, and yet you wish to see us throw away our lives against French cannon. If there are so few of us left, we will not die cheaply, like white men do in the big battle. Maybe we will come later, when we see what happens."

"When you see who is on the winning side!" Big Oak snapped.

"We cannot afford to be on the losing side!" Red Hawk shot back.

"No, you cannot afford it, but if the English lose, the French will still call you enemy, for you are the enemy of their friends, the Hurons."

"We will come later," Red Hawk insisted, and Big Oak was surprised how many braves agreed with him. Among the Iroquois, and most other Indian nations, men did not rule, they led by persuasion, and on this night Red Hawk was persuasive.

And so when they arrived at Albany, there were only Big Oak, Little Oak, Gingego, and Ganaoga, the stocky young brave who had befriended Little Oak in captivity.

Although Thad wanted to spend more time on the streets of Albany, Sam insisted that first they must report to whomever was in charge of the military organization forming in the camp north of the town. Tents and rough log cabins tumbled all over each other in the clearings still being hacked out of the woods. Here and there some enterprising captain had set up the semblance of an organized community, with a company street flanked by neat rows of tents, but most of the companies had turned their living areas into filthy barnyards, and camp sanitation was not even a rumor.

"You notice," Big Oak told his son as they explored their environment, "that there are almost no Indians here yet. In this war there is no way to win a battle without having Indians fighting on your side. I don't know that these two sides could even find each other in the woods without Indians. I'll bet William Johnson is gettin' ready to pitch a fit. He expects his Indians to *be* here when he needs them."

"They will be here," Gingego insisted.

"And what about Red Hawk?" Big Oak asked the old Mohawk.

"When the battle begins, Red Hawk will be there," Gingego said cryptically.

Big Oak laughed. "On whose side?" he asked. Gingego did not answer.

Sam spotted four loitering soldiers. At least he assumed they were soldiers, because they carried muskets, though their mode of dress was more that of townspeople. They wore work clothes, with their breeches tucked into gaiters that buttoned halfway up their thighs. Two of them were leaning against a lone tree that had been left standing to shade someone's tent, and the other two were facing them. They were having a conversation, but it must not have been very important because they were not annoyed when Big Oak interrupted them. In fact, they seemed fascinated by the two woodsmen and their Indian comrades.

"Where do we sign up?" he asked the one who seemed least unmilitary.

"Depends on who yer signin' up with," the man responded.

"The English, of course. Do I look like a Frencher?"

The soldiers laughed. Their leader poked the nearest one to him hard as he could. "Listen to him, why doncha? Tell you what there, Mr. Trapper. There's Governor Shirley what's raisin' an army to go west to Niagara. And then there's Colonel William Johnson, who's raisin' an army to go north and fight the Frenchers up there somewhere. 'N then, Lieutenant Governor De Lancey, he—"

"Johnson," Gingego interrupted.

Sam nodded in agreement, but he wanted to know more. "This Shirley, what's he governor of?"

"Why, Massachusetts," explained the soldier, as if he were talking to a child. "And he thinks he's a general too. 'Course, from what I hear now, Johnson don't have much experience leadin' an army."

"Johnson," Gingego repeated, smiling.

"He means Johnson has always been fair to the Mohawk. I'm sure they can use some men who know their way around the woods," Sam added dubiously, looking the soldiers up and down.

"He can sure use some Indians, I know that," the soldier replied. "I don't think fifty have come in yet. He's hopin' for a thousand, though why,"—he looked at the stooped figure of Gingego—"I don't exactly know."

"You'll find out soon enough," Sam said cheerfully. "If you'll just point us in the right direction, we'll join up. By the way, you didn't mention who you were with."

"And a good reason I didn't too. Our captain, you see, hasn't yet decided. Those two fellows, Shirley and Johnson, they don't like each other very much, see, and we don't rightly know which is the man to follow."

"Johnson," Gingego said one more time, indicating that he understood a lot more English than he let on.

The soldiers argued a bit with each other over the best directions to Johnson's tent, finally achieved a consensus and pointed out the way. Sam, Thad, Gingego, and Ganaoga made their way past a number of tents and shacks, drawing more than a few curious stares before they found themselves in front of the finest tent they ever saw. The front flaps were wide open, revealing a table around which sat five men dining on cold meats and lemon punch.

The seated men all looked very much like gentlemen, which immediately irritated Thad. Four of them ignored the visitors completely, but the fifth scanned their faces, and as soon as his eyes rested on Gingego, he leaped to his feet, walked around the table and clapped his hands on the old Indian's shoulders.

"Gingego!" he fairly shouted in the old man's ear. In fluent Mohawk he told the Indian how glad he was to see him, how much better he would feel going into battle knowing that his old and honored friend would be fighting by his side, and asked how many braves Gingego thought would join up from his village. He inquired about his village and his family and asked several questions about his associates before turning to Sam and Thad and apologizing for his rudeness.

"It's just that Gingego and I are such dear old friends," he exclaimed. "But I had no idea he was traveling with the famed Big Oak." Johnson was a big man, nearly six feet tall, with broad shoulders and a confiding smile, and clean-shaven like most of the English and Irish Big Oak had met. Although his face had more a sensitive than a hard look, his manner exuded power and authority.

"I'm sorry it has taken so long for us to meet," Johnson continued. "I am honored." Heartily, he shook hands with Sam, and seemed genuinely pleased to meet him. "I have heard so much good about you from the warriors of the Ganonsyoni. You are the only white man they trust when they are running the long trail. I knew that someday our paths would cross."

Then Johnson turned toward the table. "Gentlemen," he said, smiling, "this is my good friend, Gingego."

They made grunting noises of greeting but did not rise. Nor did they rise when he introduced the noted western scout and trapper Sam Watley. Sam presented Thad and Ganaoga to Johnson, who was cordial, and to his luncheon guests, who were not. After another minute or two of conversation, Johnson's associates excused themselves and left Johnson with Sam and his party.

Neither Sam nor Gingego took much notice of the rudeness. To them it was the everyday pretension of ordinary white men who called themselves "gentlemen" and therefore felt themselves entitled to feelings of superiority. Did Johnson notice? Perhaps, but he had other things on his mind.

"Gingego," he said. "I have sent wampum to all the villages of the Ganiengehaka. They have always come before, but I must tell you, they are not coming now. I have fewer than fifty braves. Where are they? Have they forgotten the man who has been their constant friend?"

Gingego looked sadly at the most powerful white trader in the land of the Iroquois. "They will be here, Warraghiyagey," he said, addressing him by the name the Mohawks had given him, a jawbreaking jumble that translated into, among others, Man Who Undertakes Great Things. "Not as many as you would wish, but many nevertheless. But I must warn you that some will be with the French. My heart hurts that this is so."

Johnson smiled and clapped Gingego on the back. "It has always been so," he said. "The French are clever. They know how to persuade. But we are your brothers. And we will win. Those who fight for the French must know that when they are beaten, King George will cast them from his longhouse."

"Do not think about them," Gingego replied. "Think of those who will come to fight beside Warraghiyagey. They are your mightiest warriors."

"I would trust them with my life."

"And we would trust you with ours."

Thad and Sam followed the dialogue with interest. Sam knew that the loyalty of the Mohawks had enriched Johnson in the nearly two decades since he had arrived in America from Ireland. But his instincts told him that Johnson was sincere, and that whatever his military experience, or lack of it, he was a natural leader of men. Nor did Sam fault Johnson for using the Mohawks to make him rich. After all, he reasoned, wasn't Johnson doing, on a large scale with the Mohawks, what he, Sam Watley, was doing on a smaller scale with his adopted people, the Seneca?

"A good scout is worth a battalion of foot troops," Johnson said to both Sam and Gingego. "Will you scout for me?"

The deal was struck then and there, before Governor Shirley even knew that Big Oak and Gingego were in Albany.

* * *

At first there wasn't a lot for them to do in camp. Building a small shack for the four of them was a matter of two days' work, chopping, fitting, splitting, laying, and chinking. They spent a few days watching would-be soldiers marching and performing manual of arms, and Sam and Thad were bored with the inactivity, being used to constant involvement in the serious business of trade and survival.

Gingego, who had heeded the arthritic messages of his bones, had given up the warrior's life for that of the aging sage and occasional hunter, but he was pleased to find his body rested, mended, and, once he had gotten used to the long trail, ready for useful service. Soon both Oaks were out in the field teaching marksmanship, while Gingego and Ganaoga had the job of teaching tradesmen and farmers the art of bashing and slashing with tomahawk and knife.

The militiamen were equipped with a variety of muskets, few of which came with bayonets. Sam and Thad thought of muskets as a degrading weapon. Although their large, smooth bore permitted fast loading, it was difficult to hit anything with a musket. "Dang noisemakers to scare officers' horses," was Sam's comment, but he and Thad did their best to teach the men that a steady grip and sure aim might someday save their lives.

Gingego and Ganaoga had a much more difficult task. It was tough enough to get these men within smelling distance of a scalp-locked brave swathed in the odor of rancid bear grease, much less engage them in hand-to-hand combat. One large, stolid Dutchman named Brom Van Damm from halfway down the Hudson River was particularly disenchanted with Gingego. So naturally the old Indian selected him out of a group of onlookers as a demonstration volunteer.

The farmer must have been twice the size of Gingego. The tomahawk the Indian gave him almost disappeared in the man's huge right hand. The sight of Gingego standing thirty feet away, painted and armed, must have raised an ancestral memory or two. The man went berserk and charged Gingego like an angry bull, waving his tomahawk murderously. The onlookers held their breaths and waited for disaster to overtake the little old Indian.

With long heavy steps the Dutchman closed the space between them. Gingego stood his ground until Brom was almost upon him, then gave a loud whoop that nearly halted Brom in his tracks. The Dutchman's tomahawk came down, then stopped in midair as his wrist found the iron grip of Gingego. The Indian put a well-placed knee in Van Damm's groin, threw him to the ground, and gave him the tiniest tap on the noggin with the blunt tomahawk. The Dutchman rolled over gently and lay staring at the sky with a peaceful look on his face that seemed a lot like a smile, but might have been a grimace.

The men watching the demonstration stared openmouthed, unable to believe that this mighty bully had been bested so easily by the small Indian with the drawn, ugly face, the overhanging belly, and the stringy muscles.

He had made instant believers of them all, but try as they might to get the hang of what he had to show them, only a very few showed any signs of being able to master the challenge of hand-to-hand combat. Gingego looked at his pupils and blanched at the thought of going into combat with them on his side. He'd much rather be their enemy, he told an equally concerned Ganaoga, and Ganaoga agreed that these militiamen would make a wonderful enemy.

One afternoon, following a shooting session with a particularly inept company that had journeyed all the way up the Hudson from New York City, Thad found his way into the stockade that was Fort Albany. There had been a heavy rain the night before, and the streets had instantly turned into a deep mudhole that daunted horses and pedestrians alike. The quagmire nearly sucked the moccasins off his feet, and mosquitoes bit him on his neck and behind the ears as he squished from street to street, looking for a place that would serve a better table than the army's monotonous diet of salt pork and hard biscuits. Some of the townspeople he passed were walking through the mud in their bare feet, carrying their shoes in their hands. He considered doing the same thing, but his moccasins, which he had tailored himself, stubbornly clung to his feet no matter how deeply they sank into the muck.

He turned a corner, walked down an alley past a neat row of solid brick houses, and spotted a girl prettier than anything he had ever imagined.

She wore a dress so short that her white-stockinged ankles showed, and her sleeves ballooned above the elbows. Her skin was pale and lightly freckled. Her hair was long and bright yellow and tied in the back with a purple ribbon. She had a little nose and large eyes the color of robin's eggs. Though she wasn't looking at anybody, her mouth had a pretty little smile, as if she went about every day thinking private, happy little thoughts. It was the private little smile that made him catch his breath.

She had a large basket with a cloth neatly covering the contents. It hung from her forearm and swung gently as she crossed the street, walking in his direction, heading for home, Thad was certain. She walked so lightly, he thought, that her shoes did not sink very far into the mud. A stranger to polite society, Thad could not look away and feign indifference. His gaze was so open and intense that her lips parted for a moment and *she* had to catch *her* breath as she passed by him.

He was speechless, crushed, blushed, and nearly paralyzed. He turned to catch a glimpse of her back at about the same time she turned to look at him. They both turned back quickly, and this time they both caught their breath, both embarrassed, both happy and excited that messages had been sent and received. Suddenly he was angry for allowing himself to be frightened about meeting a girl. He turned around again, boldly, and watched her walk up the street. The street sloped slightly upward, so he was able to stand, watching, for a full three minutes as she walked two blocks, then crossed the street and turned left.

She did not look back again. Maybe she wasn't as interested as he was, Thad thought, or maybe he had more nerve than she did, or maybe she was just determined to be a lady. Her gait was more a bounce than a walk. One could never have guessed by the way she strolled along the streets of Albany that of all the cities of any size in the colonies, Albany was the one closest to the war. In the taverns and inns, men gathering for lunch talked nervously about the coming battles, and every night the women double-checked the locks on their shutters and doors, frightened that drunken French Indians would soon be climbing the walls, burning the houses and murdering the citizens.

But there was no way that this young girl with the blond hair and the basket could have been thinking of bloodthirsty Indians on this day. Nor could she have been thinking about the mud in the streets, which was doing a dirtier job on her shoes than Little Oak noticed.

It wasn't until she was well out of sight that he realized he had no idea whatever where she lived. No matter. She couldn't have been too far from home. He remembered the place and resolved to come back whenever he had the time to do so. For the moment, every female he had ever known was wiped from his mind like so much chalk off a schoolmaster's slate. He spent the rest of the day imagining what her voice sounded like, what her first words to him might be, what she might be thinking about him. He was sure that whatever she thought of him, he was certain to be different from the pale-complected town boys and the foul-mouthed soldiers that made up whatever social life she might have had.

Shy as he was in the presence of a colonial girl, for he had never before *been* in the presence of one, he had confidence in what he was. He was a man, and what's more, he was a gentleman with manners and some education. Little Oak knew that someday he would meet this girl, because he wanted to meet her, and that when they did meet, she would be pleased with what she found.

When he got back to camp, he did not mention his encounter to his father. After all, what had happened? He had passed a girl on the street and felt attracted to her. It occurred to him that his first battle was almost at hand, and that anything might happen in battle. But he did not tell himself that he must meet this girl before the battle, lest he die without having met her. He was, like his father, a philosophical man. If he were to die in battle, why, it wouldn't matter very much that he hadn't had a chance to meet her.

On the other hand, should he live, should the English be victorious, should he come back to Albany a hero, then it would be important for him to have met her before he went off to battle. Then when he came back, she'd run up to him and ask, "How was the battle?" And then he would tell her. It just wouldn't do for him to come back to Albany after the battle and stop her on the street, a total stranger, to say something like, "You'll never guess what a wonderful battle I just fought."

No, he would have to find a way to meet her. He welcomed the challenge. It would give him something to do with his time when he and his father weren't busy teaching clumsy militiamen not to hurt themselves with the weapons they were being taught to carry around.

Thoughts such as these occupied his mind for the rest of the day and into the night, when he took her smile to bed with him and slept the sleep of the contented.

# ❖7❖

FORTY MILES WEST OF ALBANY LAY MOUNT Johnson, part of the vast country estate of William Johnson. There was no home among the Six Nations to rival Johnson's either for comfort, taste or hospitality. Johnson was determined to live a life of grace and elegance in the savage woodlands of North America. His idea of grace and elegance had a style that would have been thought of as unique anywhere in the world.

Surrounded by acres and acres of pasture, farmland, and wooded hillside, an aqueduct and a mill, a bake house and quarters for tradesmen, servants, and slaves, the house had two stories capped by a high, lead-sheathed gambrel roof and beautifully appointed rooms to pleasure his company. Johnson loved company. He loved the soft, flirting company of females, red or white. He loved the roistering, boisterous company of men, red or white. At this time, in the middle of June, he had all the male company he could have wished for, and more.

Eleven hundred Indians assembled, tore up Johnson's meadows, ate his food, drank his rum, and all in all had a glorious time. He was glad to give it to them. That was about all he was glad about, for this ten-day council was primarily a recruiting party, and too many of his Iroquois were not interested in fighting the French.

He daubed his face with red paint, put on his Indian garb

and danced with the Iroquois. He held formal meetings with the entire rambunctious assemblage, at which there were many opportunities for dramatic speechmaking, both by Johnson and by his red associates. He gave great outdoor feasts and filled his guests with fine food and drink as they sat at long tables spread across his front lawn, which looked down upon the Mohawk River.

He went from group to group, exhorting them until he was hoarse from the shouting, but only his faithful Mohawks seemed ready to follow him against the French, and there were simply not enough of them, even if they all came, to satisfy Johnson. Camping among the Indians like a white speck among the bronze was Big Oak, saying little but missing nothing.

"Will he still fight if they don't follow him?" Thad asked.

Sam laughed. "He'll get enough of them, you'll see," he shouted in his son's ear above the roar of a thousand contentious Iroquois. "When he is not making big speeches to the entire crowd, he has grabbed one sachem or another war chief by the scalp lock and sat him down behind closed doors. I saw him this afternoon. With a pair of Caughnawa-gas—*Caughnawagas, if you can believe it!*" he shouted above the tumult into Thad's astonished face. "He was telling them what great warriors they were. He was promising to help keep the peace between the Caughnawaga and their Mohawk brothers.

"Oh, he was wonderful. He told them he loved them better than the French could ever love them, and then he gave them each a heap of presents, so that when they carried them from the house you couldn't see their faces above the heaps."

"Surely he couldn't make the Caughnawaga forsake the French."

Big Oak laughed. "I doubt it, but he sure will try, and if anybody can do it—"

He turned abruptly in the direction of a voice that rose above the tumult; Johnson again, always Johnson, nose to nose with yet another chief, reminding the Indian of his, Johnson's, loyalty, and French perfidy, begging, demanding, browbeating, promising.

The chief remained unmoved, but Johnson persisted until, finally exhausted by the effort, with a promise that they would talk again, Johnson moved to the next group, to begin anew his harangue.

"Did you ever see such a man?" Sam asked, laughing. "He never gives up. I can't wait to see him in battle. He will be a roaring catamount."

A large hand gripped Sam's shoulder from behind.

"Big Oak, my friend," said a voice in the familiar tones of the Seneca tongue. Thad turned around and smiled. After weeks and weeks of strangers, his eyes at last fell on the face of a friend.

Sam smiled too as he turned to face his longtime ally, Seneca chief Grota Younga, but the smile faded before the dark shadow that lay across the face of the chief. He gripped the chief's hand with both of his and stared into the man's eyes. "What is wrong, my brother?" he asked before even inquiring about the health of his village.

The chief pointed to a man who sat several rows away from them, talking with animated hand gestures to a small group of Oneida. The man had one eye, and that one had a malevolent cast to it.

"Ah, Lydius," Sam barked contemptuously. "Might have known he'd turn up here. Who's he trying to swindle today?"

Grota Younga shook his head. "This day he is recruiting warriors for Shirley."

Sam chuckled. "Stealing men from under Johnson's nose, eh? Johnson won't like that."

"I'll roast that devil," the Seneca chief muttered. He stood up, raised both hands and waited, still and patient. As the others took notice of this respected chief, the noise died, until even the preoccupied Johnson paid attention.

"Brother Warraghiyagey," Grota Younga began. "Why have you allowed that snake to come into this council?" He extended a steady arm toward Lydius. "That man gets us alone, makes us drunk, and steals our lands." Many pairs of dark eyes turned toward the object of Grota Younga's disgust. Lydius stopped talking for a moment, sat quietly among the Oneida and took a bite from a hard-boiled egg, seemingly unperturbed.

Johnson turned crimson. He detested John Lydius, who had once been his deputy but later set himself up as Johnson's rival among the Indians. Years before, when the Mohawks had rioted against the Dutch, Lydius had spread the rumor that Johnson had instigated the riot.

"I didn't invite the egg-sucking snake," Johnson responded, referring to the eggs the detestable Lydius was always eating. "And I want him off my lands!"

His mighty voice reached to the edges of the assembly, but Lydius ignored the insult. He had the ear of the Oneidas and was determined to do business. But when Warraghiyagey spoke, his words went straight to his Iroquois brothers. A rising wave of angry noise convinced the audacious Lydius that he had better make his exit. Sweeping several eggs into a capacious coat pocket, he arose with all the dignity he could muster and managed to sweep out of the assembly as if he were a visiting potentate, oblivious to shaking fists and Indian imprecations, which he knew only too well.

"Who is he?" Thad asked Grota Younga and his father. The Indian disdained to reply, but Sam laughed.

"He is your brother, adopted into the Turtle Clan many years ago. And half the men here would gladly slit his throat if they could catch him alone on a dark night."

Now, desperately, Johnson stood up before his audience and made one more urgent plea. The French, he said, would march. If they were not stopped at Lac St. Sacrement, they would burn the longhouses of the Canajoharie Castle and every Iroquois village that had fought on the side of the English.

"But will the English stand with us today?" an Onondaga

sachem cried. "Or will they let us down again? Our lodges have grown few. We cannot afford to sacrifice our warriors, or our nation will be no more. Warraghiyagey, how can we count on people who fight, then do not fight?"

"Count on me," replied Johnson. "I will bring you arms and three thousand soldiers to fight the main battle. But I need your eyes, and your strong arms, to find the enemy and help finish him off."

Gingego stood up. "I have seen your soldiers, Warraghiyagey. And they are no soldiers. They are not even women. Women can at least bear the pain of childbirth. These men are good for nothing. They cannot march. They cannot fight. They are not brave enough to stand still and fight, and they do not have enough strength to run away. They do what they want when they want to, and they are very dirty."

"They will be soldiers when I am through with them, Gingego," Johnson responded. "And when they are soldiers, I will march them to Lac St. Sacrement, and we will spill so much French blood that they will never again approach a Mohawk longhouse. Then we can live in peace—the English and the Ganonsyoni—at last."

"Can we?" cried the Onondaga sachem. "Every year there are more English and fewer Ganonsyoni. We sell you our land, and then you want more. Sometimes I think we should have smoked our pipe with the French. Most of them stick to the woods. They are not so hungry for land. And there are not so many of them."

"No, there are not so many of them, and that is why the English will win," Johnson insisted, "and that is why you must stay with us. I have always been on your side. You are my brothers and I love you. The blood of the Ganiengehaka runs through the hearts of my children. I will not let you down. But this day I need you to defeat the French. For if I lose tomorrow, the next day they will come down from Canada and burn your children in your longhouses. We are men. We must not let them come down here and murder our women and children. We will find them in the northern woods, where they skulk like the sneaking thieves they are. My brothers, my war kettle is on the fire, my canoe is ready to put in the water, my gun is loaded, my sword by my side, and my ax sharpened! I desire and expect you will now take up the hatchet and join us. Come with me and let us once and for all run the French and their priests back across the water."

The front lawn of Mount Johnson erupted with the roar of a thousand Indian voices, inspired by Johnson's rhetoric. Johnson's Indians respected him because they believed he was the one white man who could and would protect them from the bad whites, the ones who were stealing their lives from them in ways they could not comprehend.

While the Iroquois and Johnson played politics with zeal, Little Oak had time to do some exploring. He was impressed by Johnson's home. Although it was by no means the splendid palace he would have years later when he built Johnson Hall, it was far superior to anything Little Oak had lived in during his life. Over the years, he had heard English officers talk of their huge ancestral manor houses back in England, with their cultivated rose gardens, breathtaking paintings and tapestries, and awe-inspiring dining halls with many-candled chandeliers, crystal, china and silver serving sets. It was easy for him to look at the large dimensions of Mount Johnson, with its internal clutter of furniture, paintings, wall-mounted swords, and domestic appointments and associate it with those lordly castles. The house was also cluttered with Indians who, it seemed, had the free run of it. In fact, he had to step over a sleeping warrior just to enter the front hallway.

But as he explored the home, he became aware of a part, somewhat isolated from the whole, where Indians did not go. His acute hearing picked up an unaccustomed sound coming from a room down the hall. The sound was laughter, a young girl's laughter. Before he could move closer, the door to the room opened and two slender girl-children, led by an older woman, left the room and exited through a side door into one of the gardens.

He could see them through a hall window; there were several benches shaded by cherry trees, and there the girls took up their stations. One of them, an adolescent close to womanhood, was reading a book. The other, several years younger, occupied herself with some form of needlework. The older woman stood aside, as if to watch for intruders. He had heard that Johnson, in addition to his multitude of half-Indian children, had two white daughters. It was hard to imagine these children living in sweet isolation, behind the walls of a back-country fort under the thumb of an old biddy reading romances and doing needlework, while in the meadows only a few hundred yards away a huge assemblage of warriors was debating if, when, and how they intended to go to war in their tender Indian fashion. The girls wore beautiful dresses of expensive fabric, and their innocent expressions were blessedly free from the horror Thad remembered seeing on the faces of the Delaware children the night their fathers uncorked the rum kegs.

All things considered, Thad judged that being a rich white man had it all over being a poor Indian.

By the time Johnson had made his way back to Albany, his Mohawks had begun to trickle in, together with a scattering of fighting men from the other five members of the Iroquois Longhouse. First there were a dozen more, then fifty, then close to a hundred; not nearly the number Johnson felt he needed, but enough to let him know that more would come.

And they did come. Johnson had a powerful ally who roamed the Mohawk Valley for him. He was the aging Mohawk chief Hendrick, Tiyanoga to his people, daring warriors to come out of their hidey-holes and fight the big fight at Lac St. Sacrement.

Soon the persuasion and intimidation of Tiyanoga had brought three hundred fierce-looking, fully blooded Mohawks into Johnson's camp, painted and ready to kill. They ran shrieking through the dreams of the many militia men who had never been this close to the "man-eaters" before.

Johnson now had time to digest the news that would have intimidated a lesser man. Major General Edward Braddock, the man England had shipped to the colonies to put the French in place, had been ambushed down south on the Monongahela River. Two-thirds of his fourteen hundred men had either been killed or wounded, and Braddock himself had died of his wounds shortly after the battle had ended. His last words were reported to have been, "We shall better know how to deal with them another time." They had buried him in the middle of the road back to Virginia.

The news of the massacre with its scalpings and tortures was bad enough, but once the creative rumor carriers added their embellishments, half of Albany was ready to flee for their lives, for they knew that war on the frontier had begun, and Albany *was* the frontier.

The reports of Braddock's disaster seemed to dwell on Braddock's determination to have his troops stand in ranks and fire their organized volleys as if they were fighting a set-piece battle on a European plain. They'd gotten wiped out by Indians firing from hills and trees into the massed troops caught in a valley, while the unfortunate English found themselves firing at red ghosts who hid behind trees like the ungentlemanly curs they were.

Warraghiyagey was determined that such would not be his fortune. He hailed the three hundred new warriors like the long-lost brothers they were, and set up a huge feast, serving the barbecued beef himself to his new warriors, and handing his sword to Hendrick to cut the first slice. In the dances that followed, Thad was astonished to see the bulky white colonel, stripped to the loincloth, painted all over the upper half of his body, feathered and bejeweled, leaping and dancing and screeching, stirring his Mohawks to a fever as he buried his tomahawk in the painted war post. The Mohawks feasted on the beef as if they had not eaten in a month. One of the "gentlemen" who so often shared Johnson's table with him wrote home wryly that he hoped the Mohawks would fight with as much enthusiasm as they ate Johnson's meat and drank his wine. As for Thad, he was glad to have the beef. He and his father had spent a long hungry day teaching militia how to load a musket in the middle of a battle without overloading it and killing themselves.

Thad was also surprised at the appearance of the great war chief Tiyanoga. He was past seventy, an ancient age for an Indian male to reach. He could not see well, he could not hear well, he carried his belly before him and lost his breath over very little exertion, but he and his warriors taught the militiamen lessons that would save their lives in the future.

Johnson sent them out to fight mock battles that turned fierce when Indian and Irish tempers clashed and each bellowed their war cries at the other. It didn't take even the dullest of Dutchmen long to realize that when massed ranks try to stand their ground in the forest against seasoned tree fighters, the masses disappear in a hurry man by man, and seldom get in a lick themselves.

They watched the Indians running from cover to cover, swift and crouched over, from shadow to sunshine and back to shadow again, and they learned. Time and again the Indians would appear, firing blank charges into their vulnerable flanks, then disappear before the militia could react as a unit. Johnson would gallop one of his blooded horses into the melee and curse this or that young officer for his stupidity, then exhort him to do heroic deeds, and finally leave him transfixed before his men, ready to plumb the darkest depths of hell, should Johnson only ask it of him.

And slowly, slowly, the left-footed farmers and tradesmen of Johnson's ragtag mob turned itself into an army determined to fight, prevail, and if necessary die on the field of battle.

"**D**O YOU LOVE THIS COUNTRY?" RED HAWK asked, stirring the campfire with a long stick.

The question was posed to a dark, muscular Indian of average size named Helps Enemy. At least, that's the name the whites knew him by, a bad translation of a Mohawk phrase that really meant Helps to Defeat the Enemy. Helps Enemy was a born follower, a man at least ten years older than Red Hawk, who had loped down many trails with Gingego when Gingego was still a warrior of renown. He was a man with no political interests, whose loyalty was absolute, so long as his leader was strong for the war path.

And so when Red Hawk showed himself to be the man in the village most willing to lead daring men, Helps Enemy attached himself to the younger man like a tick to a deer. When Red Hawk, Helps Enemy, and Corn Boy first left the village, two days after Big Oak's party departed for Albany, Helps Enemy neither asked nor cared exactly where they were going. At the end of the first day's journey, when Red Hawk told him they were on their way to Caughnawaga, near Montreal, Helps Enemy assumed they were out hunting for Caughnawaga scalps. Then Red Hawk explained to Helps Enemy that they were going to join these Catholic Canadian Mohawks in making war on the English. The old veteran just shrugged his shoulders and began to work up in his mind why, instead of being angry with the Caughnawaga, he should be furious with the English.

It wasn't hard to come up with reasons. When he went into the English settlements, they treated him like he was a wild dog. What he really wanted was to go back to Schenectady and pluck a few hairy souvenirs in the course of a quick midnight visit. But Red Hawk was bound for Caughnawaga, and Helps Enemy was bound to follow Red Hawk. Helps Enemy was not a stupid man; in fact, in battle he could be crafty and creative. He lived a simple life. His interests were, first, war, and second, rum, except when he was drinking. Then his interests were, first, rum, and second, rum.

"It's all right, I suppose," answered Helps Enemy, whose only reservation about Red Hawk was that he talked too much, even when he wasn't making speeches in front of a crowd. When Red Hawk talked to him, he had to listen, and then answer, or Red Hawk would get angry. As strong and tough as Helps Enemy was, he feared the aggressive might of Red Hawk, which was fine with him; he liked following someone he feared, it gave him a feeling of security.

"I like it up here much better than down on the Te-non-an-at-che. You know why?" Red Hawk asked him.

"Because you are closer to your French brothers?"

"Pah!" Red Hawk spat into the fire. The spittle sizzled on the hot coals. "I have no white brothers."

Corn Boy had been pacing restlessly around the perimeter of their campsite, which was in a small clearing a half mile inland from the St. Lawrence River. Now he joined the two older men at the campfire.

"I like it up here because the English do not live here yet. I like it anywhere the English have not yet come to."

Red Hawk wanted Helps Enemy or Corn Boy to ask him why he hated the English so much. He wanted them to say something nice about the English so he could argue with them, but they must have agreed with him, since they maintained their silence.

"We can burn our campfire to the sky if we wish. There are no English here, only our brother Caughnawagas. They are happier among the French. They say the French are like *real* brothers, though I believe they are deceived. They wear the cross with the man being tortured at the stake, like the French. Maybe the French *are* more like the Ganonsyoni than the English."

Red Hawk looked deep into the eyes of Helps Enemy, and he felt alone. Helps Enemy was a fine man to have at your shoulder in battle, but he did not like to think about things. Nevertheless, he was the only man to talk to, and Red Hawk was determined to unload his thoughts.

"I must tell you about a village I lived in as a child. My mother had grown up in that village, and her mother, and her mother before. We were so close to the falls of the Te-non-an-at-che that at night that we could lie abed in our longhouse and let the sound of the rushing water carry us to sleep.

"The women of the village were great farmers. They planted big fields of corn, squash, and beans, and no matter how long and hard the winter, we never went hungry. There was plenty of game too, most of the time, and our men had learned to shoot their guns well. Our kettles were always full, our people happy. Nobody dared to menace the Ganiengehaka—not the Abnaki, not the Huron, not the French, not the English. And so it could have gone on forever. But it was not to be so.

"One day an Englishman came to the village with some soldiers and some words scratched on skins. He told us that a chief who was no chief to us had sold the land on which stood our village. Our village chief said that the land was not that other chief's land to sell. The white man with the skins acted as if he did not hear our chief's words. He told us we had to go away before harvest time. Our chief was smart. He said, 'Ah, you want us out now so *you* can harvest the crop *we* planted.' So it is with the English. They love to take the fruit of the land we have worked.

"Then our chief said, 'You did not buy land from us. We do not sell our land.'

"The white man said, 'We are not going to deal with every fool of a village chief. The land is ours and this skin is the proof. You will leave by the middle of the hot season or we will force you to leave.' I could not believe a man would speak so rudely to our village chief. The chief should have roasted them right then, but instead he just smiled and said, 'We will not leave.' "

Red Hawk was now into the rhythm of his story. He had the attention of his two followers, and he enjoyed it.

"So we stayed where we were and they did not attack us, but in the thick of summer they came at night and burned our fields. Then this same man came back, and pretended not to know who did it. He said, 'Because you are breaking the law, the traders will not be allowed to come to your village. That is what we have decided.'

" 'But we need ammunition to hunt,' our chief told him.

" 'You will have your ammunition when you give up your village,' he said.

" 'We will not give up our village,' our chief shouted in his face.

" 'You will give up and move,' was how the white man answered him, so sure of himself. Then he turned his back on our village chief and walked out.

"The winter was very cold and snow covered the ground in smooth, deep, flat layers of white. Without our corn, we were hungry, and the men had no powder and bullets to hunt with. Some of the older ones tried to make bows, but our skill with flints had gone away, so there were no good arrowheads. Some warriors tried to put the points of their old knives on the ends of arrows, and others tied their knives to sticks to make long spears. But the white men had been so long in our forests that much of the game was gone and the rest was too frightened to let a man get close enough to make a kill.

"The village was nearly wiped from the earth that winter.

We had no corn, we had no powder to hunt deer, and when our men went out with the bow, they couldn't come close enough to a deer to kill it. You should have seen the arrowheads we tried to make. One man struck a deer with an arrow. It bounced off.

"Our people starved for half the winter. Mothers could not make milk for their babies. The bones showed through the skins of our children as if they were already long dead. Some of the women told their husbands that they were no good because they could not put food in the lodges of their families. One woman threatened to go to the whites and find one who was man enough to feed her children if she would share her bed with him. Her husband told her that her tongue was too sharp, and then he tried to cut it out. The other women stopped him.

"Our chief could no longer stand the suffering in his village. He went to the white men and begged for food. They didn't have any for us, they said. He begged for a little powder and lead, enough to kill food for our people. 'Certainly,' they said. 'Just sign a paper promising us that you will move before planting time.'

" 'Where will we move?' he asked them.

"They showed him a white man drawing with lines and told him that all the land this side of that snake"—Red Hawk wiggled his finger to depict a squiggly line on a map —"all that land belongs to you. 'You can settle anywhere you want—on that side of the snake.'

" 'And how long will it be before you want more land, and we must move again?'

" 'Our king has told us that we must stay on this side of the snake and let you live on that side,' the white men answered.

"The chief finally put his mark on their paper. He did not believe them because they were such liars, but he could not go home with empty hands to hungry children, and starving babies, and lodges where the men and women quarreled because they had nothing to eat. He and the braves he had brought along with him went home with several sledges piled high with goods—blankets, powder and lead, bags of corn and flour that the white man had told him they didn't have.

"When he and his braves returned to the village, the people cheered him for saving them. But then some of the men began to wonder and they asked him, 'What did you have to give the white men to get all these good things?'

"He looked them in the eyes and told them, 'I gave them our land.'

"And they said, 'Our land is our mother! You gave them our mother! Better that we should all starve to death than give the white man our mother.'

"The chief was ashamed. He went to his lodge and told his family to go visit their uncles and stay until he called them back. And he told the people of the village to stay away from his lodge until he called them in. And then he went inside.

"The people expected him to call them in, but he never did, and he never called his family to come home. He was a sachem, not a war chief. No war chief would take up the tomahawk. The white men were too powerful.

"For days the people in the village waited for their chief to appear, but he did not. Finally, his wife could stand it no more, and she walked into the lodge and found him there, dead, very cold.

"How did he die? I'll tell you what my mother said. She said that my father died because the white men shamed him. What powerful devils they must be who can shame a man to death."

Neither Helps Enemy nor Corn Boy were great thinkers, but both were moved to silence, staring at the orange tongues of fire and the sparks that rose toward the black sky.

"Tomorrow," Red Hawk said, "we will cross over the St. Lawrence."

* * *

The rain was pelting down on the roof of the lodge of Chief Iptowee. Here and there small leaks were letting drops of water in, but the dirt floor quickly absorbed the moisture. The lodge was good, the fire was good, the food was good, and the tobacco was good on a cool summer night north of the St. Lawrence River.

"Red Hawk, my brother," said Iptowee courteously, although until this evening he had never before met the man. "It is good that you are with us. But I must know, will there be more Mohawks come north to join us against the English?"

"The Mohawk do not love the English," Red Hawk replied. "But they love Warraghiyagey. I believe that some will stay home, and some will join him, but none will fight against him."

Iptowee shook his head in wonder. "What is wrong with you Mohawks? Can you not see the future when it stands before your eyes? On this side of the river are the French, a few trappers and farmers. They live with us, they become part of our tribes. They send good priests to teach us about God and his son, who gives us eternal life. They trade much with us and steal little from us.

"On your side of the river are the English. They are like a swarm of insects that devour everything in their path. Their ministers preach to you about souls, but they kill you as if you had none. And yet you stay with the English. Why? Just because in ancient times one Frenchmen and his men fired their guns at the Iroquois? That is so long ago. Since then you have fought wars and made treaties with many tribes. Since then you have been cheated so many times by the English.

"Come with us. Help us wipe the English from our land. The French are brave allies. They do not let us down. See us here in Caughnawaga, so close to Montreal? There are no villainous councils meeting in Montreal to talk about wiping out Caughnawaga or about how to cheat the Caughnawaga out of their land."

Red Hawk felt as if someone had wrapped a warm blanket around him on a cold night. "My brother Iptowee. Your words are sweet in my ears. For so long now I have labored in my village to make the people understand. They see, but they do not see. What they see is that the English are mighty, that they have greater power than the French, and that no matter how many battles they lose, they will win their wars. I have tried to tell my people that if the English defeat the French, they will next turn on us, for they have no true friends but their own. My people say, 'No, remember, there is Warraghiyagey. He is a true friend.'

"I say, even if this is so, which it may not be, since Warraghiyagey is with the English, and so he cares only for himself—even if he is the good man you think he is, he is only one man, and when he is gone, there will not be another like him. But they do not care what I say. 'The English gave us this,' they say. 'The English gave us that.' I say, whatever the English gave you they took away so much more in furs and land, always our very best land.

"I will be by your side when you go down to fight the English. And so will Helps Enemy and Corn Boy. But the other Mohawks are fools. They will not listen, and I am sick of talking to them."

"Hear me, my brother Red Hawk," Iptowee said gently. "We know how bad the English are for us, but what is worse is when we fight each other. That is when we are doing the white man's work for him. We *are* the Mohawks. The Mohawks are us. We have the same grandmothers and we must not shed each other's blood."

Iptowee's friend Atahro, sitting beside them watching occasional drops of rain fall through the smoke hole and sizzle on the fire, now spoke for the first time.

"Iptowee, you are not used to hearing my voice in council. It is my strong arm and my keen eyes that make me big in the eyes of my brothers. But I must tell you. We have for

many years now been on the opposite side of the river from
the Mohawk. Our blood might be the same, but our feelings
are not. We have fought each other before and we will
again. When we go into battle against our enemy, we must
fight our enemy or it will be as if we were going into battle
with our guns unloaded and our knives unsharpened. I know
their guns will be loaded and their blades keen and bright.
They love their Warraghiyagey and they love the sting of
battle. Once the battle starts we will be no different to them
than the French. So if we are to fight the English, we must
be ready to kill Mohawks."

"I have heard you, Atahro," Iptowee responded. "It pleases
me to hear your thoughts. You are my strong right arm and I
trust my life to you."

They sat silently, smoking, listening to the rain fall upon
the bark roof, each with his own thoughts. Although the
Caughnawaga had been apart from the Mohawks for many
years, the legends of the Iroquois remained strong in the
heart of Iptowee. He was a brave man, a man of purpose
who longed for battle against the English but longed for
peace with the Mohawks. His mind could conceive of no
way to have both of his wishes.

At last Red Hawk broke the silence. "My brother Iptowee,
I have told you that I am half Mohawk. I am ashamed of that
half. The Mohawk in my village remind me of the foolish
men who shamed my father long ago. They complain about
the English but they are afraid to cast them away because
they need the English. And so, year after year, they get
weaker and weaker. Do not be afraid to kill Mohawks. At
least they will die bravely, in battle, instead of dying in their
lodges of English disease or English rum. As you love the
friends of your friends, you must hate the friends of your
enemy. How can I hate the Mohawks any less than I hate
the English? It is the Mohawks who make it possible for the
English to be the English. They have wiped out so many of
the tribes who would have fought the English. In the woods

and hills of the west, they do the dirty work of the English. I hate the Mohawk so for being such fools. When they are dead, it will be by their *own* hand, not yours or mine. I just want to speed them on their way.

## ❖9❖

A WEEK AFTER THEIR FIRST ENCOUNTER, Thad saw the yellow-haired girl again on the street. They were passing each other, going in opposite directions. The closer they came, the more Thad pretended to take an extraordinary interest in the third story of a house behind her. But there was no way he could miss the look of concern that flashed across her face when she saw the array of bruises, swellings, and contusions that made his face look like a map of Hell. In the course of Johnson's sham warfare, he and a militia private had taken a personal dislike to each other while they battled at close quarters and emerged looking like a pair of beaten-up prizefighters.

She quickly recovered her poise and passed him by, her eyes modestly cast toward the ground, her face warm and colored.

Then she was gone, leaving a yearning ache in his heart that felt strange to him. She seemed, from a distance, so totally unlike any girl he had ever known, that he longed to discover more about her, maybe even to talk to her.

Thad walked around town some more, and as he walked, he thought about the girl. She liked him, of that he was certain, even though the two had never met. But he was in a war, and his father had told him often that in time of war a man will survive only if he pays attention. Thoughts of women, he said, make a man absentminded, and absent-minded warriors are unlucky warriors. That was why many Indian nations abstained from sex before going into battle, why Iroquois warriors did not generally take a wife as young men, why rape of female captives by the Iroquois was unusual.

More and more he was beginning to find that he liked the smells of Albany. There was a Dutch bakery that made his mouth water, close to where the girl always seemed to appear, and a bootmaker's shop with the strong odor of shoe leather. The smells of home-cooked delights that he had never tasted wafted out the windows of a hundred homes. And down by the mighty Hudson River, where fishing boats and transport craft lay moored side by side, the memorable odors of fresh fish, naval stores, and sawdust made him dream of places far beyond the woodlands of New York.

The sights and the sounds of this white man's town were different from those of Tonowaugh. Only one thing seemed pretty much the same, and that was the children. He watched them as they played in the streets, the boys at war and the girls with dolls, and he was surprised. He had never considered that white children were interested in the same things as Indian children. Again he thought of the girl with the yellow hair, and for a moment his spirit sagged. Realistically, how much of a chance did he have with her? Her father was probably a local burgher with a purse full of gold where his heart should be. He would take a dim view of her giving her heart to a half-breed, half-wild woodsman.

Half-breed was just a word to Thad with no horrible stigma because he had spent so little time in the white communities where Indians were hated and distrusted. Most of the whites he had known knew him only as the son of the legendary Sam Watley, and therefore someone to be accounted for. But he knew that as the time neared for standing up on his own, he would have to deal with some small minds. His father had warned him.

He wondered how he looked in the eyes of the blond

girl. Back in the Seneca village, he knew, the girls thought him handsome, especially Kawia, whose blue silk scarf he still wore beneath his hunting shirt. He thought about her and wondered how she and the rest of the village fared in this summer of approaching war.

His grandfather had once told him that in their valley, when you heard thunder echoing in the east, you could expect rain from the west. Sam said it meant that when war came to the Mohawk in the east, you could expect the French to be stirring up the western tribes and the Mingoes to attack the Seneca. War at one wall of the Longhouse, he said, meant war all around the Longhouse, and if the Six Nations did not stand together, they would surely fall.

Thad left the town by the front gate of the palisade and headed for the camp. He knew that today he would find out when they would start the march north to meet the French. They had not far to go to find war, since Albany was near the edge of the northern frontier.

As he walked down a bustling company street, the conversation of a gaggle of New Englanders reminded him how difficult it was for Johnson to create a unified army that would follow him, untested as he was, into the wilderness:

". . . and then the minister said to the old heathen, 'How do you expect to go into battle with the Lord on your side when you bed down every night with harlots of every color?' And you know what Johnson says?"

A chorus of murmurs showed that they didn't know, but that they certainly wanted to.

"He says, 'If you are referring to the women you have noticed visiting my camp, sir, you are talking about ladies. And I'll thank you not to slander them.'"

A refrain of no's and "you don't says" erupted.

" 'Besides, Reverend,' says Colonel Johnson, 'if you want one, why don't you just ask, instead of actin' like a little boy with his nose pressed up against the window of a bakery?' And then the preacher got so red in the face, I thought he was gonna fall down and have a spittin' fit!"

The speaker was about to regale them with more details when a corporal stepped into their midst.

"If you can hold off on the gossip for a moment, you'll want to know about this," the corporal said, and since he was the principal gossip in the company, he immediately caught their attention. "In one week's time, men, we march."

William Johnson had more immediate worries than his lady friends and a discontented dominie. He called his chiefs together and probed them for any knowledge they may have had of the Braddock massacre. When he learned that the news had not yet reached many of them, he told them the news himself, made a great speech about how they all would have to pull together to save their homes and families from the thieving, murdering French, and extracted from them undying pledges of loyalty.

If the citizens of Fort Albany still suffered from collective insomnia, Johnson, with faith in his Indians and loving affection from his women, slept well. His sleep might have been less tranquil had he known that the French had captured the papers of the late General Braddock, and that among those papers were war plans which included a march on Crown Point, on Lake Champlain, to be led by one Colonel William Johnson.

And so, in early August he sent two thousand men north up the Hudson River; on the fourteenth of August, in 1755, he joined the rest of the army as they marched north to their destiny.

They weren't as ready as they should have been.

The transport boats for the artillery leaked. Some of Johnson's New England troops had failed to arrive. New Yorkers did not like New Englanders and vice versa, and many of each were still nervous about going into battle alongside the exotic Mohawks, with their painted faces and bejeweled noses and their eternal, rancid bear grease, which repelled the militiamen at least as much as it repelled bugs and mosquitoes.

Worst of all, Johnson had sent some of his Indians to visit

their Caughnawaga brethren up in Canada. They had begged these "praying Indians" to stay out of the fight. Instead, Iptowee had advised the emissaries to steer clear because the French and their red allies would field eight thousand fighters ready to crush the tiny British forces in the coming battle.

He added that they had no desire to harm their Mohawk brothers, but Atahro and some of his more ardent warrior friends insisted that if the Mohawks continued to hang on to "their useless English alliance," then they too would perish.

"We do not fear the Mohawks anymore. All the tribes of Canada," Iptowee added, "have taken up the French tomahawk and are ready to march with the French against the English and the Iroquois." Baron Ludwig August Dieskau, the new leader of the French forces, was, they advised, ready to ambush the English in the carrying place near Lake Champlain. In other words, it would be another Braddock massacre, only worse.

When the returning Mohawks told him of what they had learned from their Canadian brothers, the only effect this doleful news had on the irrepressible Johnson was to make him order his axmen to alter the route of the road they were cutting through the barely penetrable north woods.

The New Hampshire troops, who had been blundering half lost through the forest for weeks because they refused to travel on the ocean to New York, had finally arrived at Albany. By now the entire army of militia was under way, heading north, dragging heavy cannon and themselves toward their doom, a little over three thousand whites with little battle experience, a handful of Indians—Tiyanoga's Mohawks had gone home, leaving only a promise that they would return for the fight—and a leader who had yet to spend a day, an hour, a *minute* in battle.

Yet to the citizens of Albany, they made a fine sight, that long line of strong, musket-bearing Americans who marched bravely up the trail north, and they came out to see the soldiers off. Old men who had survived even more uncertain times on the New York frontier stood with grave looks on their faces; while young women in ribbons waved, and barefoot children ran alongside the soldiers.

Although Sam was in the advance and would be scouting ahead for the whole march, Thad lingered long enough to catch a glimpse of the girl he adored from afar. With a battle before him, the idea of speaking to this girl was not nearly so intimidating. What, after all, did he have to lose? She was standing with a few of her giggling friends by the side of the trail, but her expression was serious—for his sake, perhaps? Before he passed her, he dropped out of line for only a moment, and barely remembered to take off his cap before he spoke.

"Will you tell me your name?" he asked, leaning stiffly on the barrel of his long rifle.

"Katherine," she replied.

"I'm Thad," he said, taking in every detail about her in the brief moment they locked glances. Her face was a mass of conflict. Her brow frowned, and so did her mouth, but her eyes twinkled to the roll of the drums as she looked directly into his.

"Do you remember seeing me in Albany?" he asked, because he hadn't any idea what else to say.

"Of course," she answered. And she smiled her full smile, not just the secret little smile he saw her smile on the streets of Albany. "I'm glad we got to meet before you had to go away."

"Me too," he agreed.

Her smile faded.

He replaced his cap, cradled his rifle in the crook of his arm and marched up the trail, not looking back, but showing her a crimson strip of neck between the collar of his hunting shirt and the bottom of his cap.

Once he was out of sight of the stockade and its citizens, he jumped out of line and began jogging through the woods to catch up with his father, Gingego, and Ganaoga. Catching up was easy, because the troops were moving at the pace of the heavier wagons of equipment, ammunition, and supplies.

The prime substance of the journey was sweat: the sweat of the militiamen carrying their heavy weapons and packs. The sweat of the draft horses in their traces, straining at the six three-ton cannon that would support the English attack. The sweat of the sixty or so Indians as they flitted like shadowy phantoms through the forest, covering the main body of troops. The gnats loved the sweat, and so did the mosquitoes. Proud militiamen longed for Indian bear grease and slapped irritably at the insects that tormented their bodies.

And ahead, the forest rang with the sound of axmen chopping trees, clearing the way and filling the forest with the fragrance of fresh sap to go along with the more mundane odor of unbathed marchers.

Ahead of the axmen, among the Indians, ranged Thad and Sam, running the forest trails Thad had once doubted they would ever run together again. Like hunting dogs on the point, their nostrils twitched and their eyes roamed, always alert, always seeking out the deadly.

Although it was only fifty miles to where the previous units had assembled, the going was slow. To make things worse, rumors were rife in the ranks that in the west the Indians were running wild and feeding the blood of their enemies into the ash-blackened earth. It wasn't often that Shawnee, Delaware, Potawatomie, and Huron had the chance to spill blood as they did on the Monongahela. Who were the English, that they thought they were so invincible? Their towns could burn too. And so could their people!

And they did, again and again, in Virginia and Pennsylvania and New York. And the stories somehow filtered back to the soldiers on the march, in all their bloody horror, further magnified by imaginative retelling.

Sometimes at night, or during a break from their routine, father and son talked about it.

"This is the battle we have to win or we'll have to start

learning to speak French," Sam said. "No, that's not right. They'll cut our tongues out and other pieces as well, and we won't have to worry about anything but meeting our maker. We have to win this battle, and our leader ain't ever commanded troops in battle before." Sam shook his head.

"Can we win?" Thad asked calmly.

"Well, you know, war's a funny thing. Luck has a lot to do with who wins. Bit of good fortune for us at the right time, the Frenchers lose their hair. Bit of luck for them, and we lose ours."

Thad wondered if this bit of philosophy was supposed to make him feel better. He wondered if he'd stand and fight if things got hot, and he wondered if it was right to run when things got too hot.

"Little Oak," Sam said. When speaking of very important things, he often used the name the Seneca had given Thad. Reading the boy's silence, he read his mind. "When the battle begins, I want you to stay close to me." He had more to say, but he didn't say it.

# ❖10❖

**I**N CAUGHNAWAGA, RED HAWK READIED HIM-
self for traitorous action against the Mohawks. He and his
two disciples were pleased to draw brand new rifles from the
French, along with other first-rate war supplies.

September found them with the French army of Baron
Ludwig August Dieskau at Lac St. Sacrement, newly named
Lake George by Major General William Johnson, proving
that under a monarchy, even great men will occasionally
indulge in a bit of butt kissing. The French, of course, were
not aware of Johnson's map revisionism, and neither were
their Indian allies, the Caughnawaga and the Abnaki. Red
Hawk felt very much at home with the Caughnawaga except
for the Catholic religion that had been presented to them
by the patriotic French priests who had carefully weaned
them from the Longhouse.

The English had a general idea of where the French army
was, but the French knew the exact location of the English
army, and were ready for it. Johnson had camped on Lake
George just a few miles from the newly constructed English
Fort Lyman. He had created a three-sided rampart out of
felled tree trunks, bateaux, and wagon bodies to defend the
camp in case of enemy attack. Believing that the French
would attack Fort Lyman, Johnson decided to send a thousand men down the road to reinforce the fort.

His friend, the great Mohawk chief Tiyanoga, spoke to posterity when he said, "If those thousand are to be killed, they are too many. And if they are to fight, too few." Johnson was a trader, not a real general. He sent the thousand forward anyway, even though he knew the French forces far outnumbered them.

And that was why Red Hawk and his Caughnawaga friends were fairly drooling with anticipation as they heard the English force tramping noisily down the road.

The French Indians and Canadians disappeared in silence into the forest on either side of the road, where they waited behind trees and rocks for their enemy to come, ready to strike them with deadly force and to give no quarter. Well to the rear, in their ridiculous, very visible white uniforms, stood the French regulars, waiting for the trap to be sprung. Then they would come forward with their massed firepower and bayonets, to complete the slaughter. Quietly they waited, hearts thumping, sweating in the still forest, for the killing to begin.

Suddenly a single horse appeared, ridden by the old, fat, valiant great chief of the Mohawks, Tiyanoga, who had once been to London to see the queen. Behind him, stretching far down the trail in single file, walked two hundred Mohawks, who had, as promised, rejoined Warraghiyagey in time for the battle. With them were two white scouts from the Seneca nation, followed by hundreds of colonial militiamen.

Like Big Oak, Tiyanoga knew the songs of the forest choir. He could no longer hear very well, but he could hear well enough, and his dimmed vision helped him concentrate on the sounds to tell him what his eyes could no longer see. What he heard made him stop his pony and tilt his head to one side in order to make better sense of what his senses were telling him.

From the brush came a loud voice: "Old man, who are you?"

"Who skulks in the brush like a fox?" Tiyanoga said to the bushes. Three warriors stepped out from cover. They were

Chief Iptowee, Atahro, and one other. Watching the drama from his place on the road, Big Oak tapped Little Oak and pointed out a clump of trees ten feet off the road. With all eyes on the conversants, no one noticed the two men in deerskins slip off into the clump.

"Tiyanoga is a dead man, and he knows it," Sam said. "In a few moments death will fill the forest with his friends. From here we can fight."

The three Caughnawaga were stripped to breechcloths and painted, like Tiyanoga's Mohawks. Tiyanoga said his force represented the six confederated Indian nations that ruled all the Indians in the land. The tallest of the three warriors said he was chief of the Caughnawaga, of the seven confederated nations of Canada.

Now came the debate. "Out of the way so we may fight our enemies, the English," said the Caughnawaga chief. "We do not wish to hurt you. It is the English we come to kill, and we will have them."

"You who used to be real Mohawks," answered Tiyanoga, "before the French sprinkled water on your heads and gave you dolls to pray to, come back to the Longhouse, where you would still be welcome." In the stillness of the forest by Lake George, mouths went dry. Fingers tightened on triggers. Men counted their remaining life span in seconds.

"You must go back," said Iptowee, his voice filled with quiet desperation. As badly as he wanted to kill English, that is how badly he did not want to do battle with people of his own blood.

The Caughnawaga chief started to speak again, but his silent lips were interrupted by a single shot from a young Mohawk warrior, which knocked him to the ground.

For a brief moment those hiding in the brush and those standing on the road froze and watched the smoke drift like a signal from Hell. The sudden death of a single Caughnawaga chief sent a wave of shock through every Indian who stood in the road or hid in the forest alongside it. Most of the Mohawks and Caughnawagas had truly hoped they would not have to fight each other. But blood had been spilled. Then the Caughnawagas struck.

In the first thunderous salvo, dozens of precious, irreplaceable Mohawks fell, including one from the muzzle of the traitorous Red Hawk. Englishmen likewise tumbled into grotesque postures of death as the dense fire struck home. The woods echoed with the battle cries of the Indians, voices of life so unlike the shrill shrieks of the dying and wounded. Blue-gray smoke clouded the forest but failed to provide merciful concealment for those caught in the horrible meat grinder.

Red and white men alike dove for cover off the road and returned a deadly fire, but nothing to compare with the fire directed at them. The French regulars firing in ranks sent scythes of lead down the road, harvesting militiamen by the score.

Indians and bush lopers darted from tree to tree in search of targets, and when they found one, they often killed it. Here and there a Mohawk from one side or the other of the St. Lawrence River traded his rifle for a scalping knife long enough to reap a bloody, hairy trophy. Loading, firing, and screeching creatures leaped from one cover to another, swift shadows searching for brothers to kill.

They ignored the sting of powder smoke in their eyes; ignored, if they could, the pain of bullet wounds. Their lives depended on avoiding the rifle sights of others even as they pulled the trigger on those who had somehow stumbled into theirs.

Well-covered in their clump of trees, father and son searched out hostile targets while presenting as little of themselves as possible to the enemy. Big Oak loaded and fired rhythmically, almost mechanically, but Little Oak was having trouble finding something to shoot at.

"Keep your eyes open. You'll get the hang of it," his father said. A close shot sent a splinter of wood into the youngster's cheekbone. "There. Watch where he pops up."

And sure enough, the head popped up where Big Oak

thought it would. Both father and son fired at once. Thad's shot missed, but Sam's bullet tore the upper half off the head of a careless French Canadian. *His* body would yield no scalp.

Thirty yards away Thad saw a familiar figure pausing by a tree to fire a shot into the poor, massed militiamen being decimated down the road. One of Red Hawk's braves, he remembered from his terrifying capture by the Mohawk raiding party. This was too simple. The man was protected from the militiamen but exposed to Thad, who hesitated a moment, then fired a ball into Helps Enemy's chest, which launched him on one last leap into eternity. It was Thad's first kill.

The smoke continued to thicken, held from the heavens by the forest canopy. The smell of powder was so powerful, it stung throats and nostrils. Officers were shouting curses and striving desperately to hold their ranks together and keep them firing, but it was obvious that position and numbers gave the French and their allies the upper hand.

The sounds of rifle and musket fire, war cries, curses, and hurled insults, were continuous and deafening; so were the screams of pain and the shrieks of fury from reds and whites alike. In a few places the fighting was so close that Indian engaged Indian with tomahawk, knife, and war whoop. Thad felt fear but no panic. Nor did he feel pain from the wood splinter, even though drops of blood were rolling down his cheek like crimson tears.

The lessons of his father, and pure luck, saved him through minute after endless minute of the fierce firefight. Only briefly did he offer an eyeball as a target from behind a tree, and then only behind the sight of his formidable Pennsylvania long rifle. Often as not, he was firing into bushes where the enemy had last been seen, and only once had his guesswork been rewarded, by the fatal thrashing fall of a stricken Abnaki.

"Load, prime, and fire. Load, prime, and fire," Big Oak muttered, ramming a ball home as he lay flat against the earth. Little Oak did not have to be told to do the same. His chest was tight with fear that rose toward his throat. He respected that fear, and heeded it even as he struggled to swallow it back down. Once again he exposed an eyeball and pulled the trigger. Spark from the flint, no fire.

"Primer, son!"

"Damn!" Thad said, charging the priming pan with too much powder. He leveled his weapon, pulled the trigger, and almost lost his eyebrows from the flash, but a French curse from the bush he aimed for meant he had at least come close. Then came smoke from the bush and the buzz of a bullet past his ear.

"Get your fool head down!" his father growled. Thad poured powder down the barrel, pushed in a patch, spat a ball in after it, laid down and rammed the whole mess home, and nearly lost his hearing as his father fired across him, past his head, to bring down a Caughnawaga who had just about flanked their position.

Their tree trunk was fast accumulating a load of lead from the muzzles of a dozen sworn enemy. The firing from the English side was beginning to slacken. Big Oak noted the difference immediately. So he was ready when he heard an English officer shouting orders. He couldn't hear the words above the deafening crackle of gunfire, but his battle sense told him that the officer was ordering a retreat.

"Run like hell!" he yelled. "And keep low!"

Little Oak didn't need to be told twice. He followed his father as they ran doubled over. Panicked, he had to force himself to do what his father did the way his father did it. He wanted to straighten up and run as fast as he could. He wanted to lie down and pull the earth over him. Never had he been so thoroughly terrified.

There were no troops behind him. They had withdrawn toward the fortified camp on Lake George, and Big Oak could feel the enemy following right behind them, threatening to close the trap. He hollered an alarm in the Mohawk tongue and off they ran, toward Lake George, with a hundred and fifty screaming allies ahead of them, and two thousand howling hostiles behind them.

Bullets ripped through the branches around them and plucked at their clothes as they flew through the woods toward the camp. Big Oak, who could load a rifle in flight, watched the enemy running for the road to cut them off. He aimed his deadly rifle at those closing the trap. His great reputation kept them distant, until one came too close and Sam blasted him into the hereafter.

Thad yelped as a bullet carved a groove across the fleshy part of his shoulder.

Another shouted command brought the last handful of troops to a halt. From behind their tree trunks they fired a volley that stopped their pursuing enemy in their tracks. This stalwart rear guard loaded rapidly and fired again. More French and Canadians were down. The momentum of the attack had been blunted for a moment. Gratefully, Thad, Sam, and most of the remaining Mohawks ran past the line of covering militiamen, and in that moment the rear guard resumed their dash to safety.

"Keep running," Sam commanded.

Again Thad did not need to be told. Ahead of him ran Tiyanoga's Mohawks, considerably fewer than at the beginning of the fight. Abnakis were breaking off their pursuit in order to mutilate the dead and dying Mohawks left behind. First one then another and another whoop of triumph rang through the forest as the warriors tore scalps off their victims' skulls and flourished them, bloody and reeking, high above their heads.

From the rear came the sounds of quarreling among Indians who could not understand each other. The Caughnawaga were not about to allow the Abnaki to mutilate the bodies of their Mohawk brothers. Angrily they grabbed hold of their allies and demanded that they continue to pursue the Englishmen, their real enemies. The Abnakis had a different point of view. They and the Mohawks had been killing each other for years, but it was the Mohawks who had reaped most of the honors, and the scalps. For the Abnakis, this was payback time.

The Abnaki trophy hunt allowed the remaining English fighters just enough time to get a head start down the road toward the fortified camp. Gradually the shooting subsided, save for an occasional pistol shot from a French officer dispatching a badly wounded Englishman.

Red Hawk did not share the Caughnawaga aversion to mutilating Mohawks. On the contrary, he searched the forest until he found the still-living remains of a Mohawk from his home village. He took some water from his pouch and splashed it on the Mohawk until he regained consciousness. The wounded man smiled when he discovered the familiar face of Red Hawk, until he saw him using the priming pan of his rifle to kindle a fire in a little pile of dried grass. Red Hawk heaped a few twigs on the grass, then a few sticks on the twigs, until he had a nice little fire going and the feeble, badly injured Mohawk knew what was in store for him.

"No, my brother," he whispered as Red Hawk dragged him close to the fire. Red Hawk pulled his knife and deftly separated the man from his scalp, then pulled the helpless Mohawk to the fire and threw him facedown upon the flames.

In spite of his injuries, the man rolled out of the fire with a horrified shriek, and lay still but conscious, breathing hard, his face already red from the flames that had kissed it. Red Hawk took him by the arm, turned him facedown again, and dragged him so that only his face would touch the fire. He then leaped upon the Mohawk's back and reveled in the warrior's feeble thrashings as the flames consumed the flesh of his face and finally the life of the brave.

There was still a war on. Red Hawk had no more time to enjoy his triumph. Satisfied, he tucked the scalp into his belt, smearing his own abdomen with blood as he did so. He did not bother to wipe the blood off his knife before sliding it into his belt. Then he stood up, careful not to slip in the

gore around the body, and joined in the pursuit of the fleeing English and their frightened, beaten Mohawks.

The English militia were in a desperate situation, but they
refused to scatter in disorganized panic. They had learned
their lessons well at the camp north of Albany. Thanks to
their training and a few good officers, most of them retreated rapidly but in the right direction and in good order.
The French troops chasing them down the road fired volley
after volley into their rear, while the Canadians, Caughnawagas, and Abnakis harassed them on the flanks as if they
were running a deadly gauntlet.

By the time they were close to the makeshift walls, they
had been joined by many of the Mohawks, whose light
dress and superior physical condition had allowed them to
catch up to the main body of militia.

Together they continued their headlong retreat in a painful, breathless run until they gained their second wind, then
saved themselves with another sprint across the naked plain
and through the opening of the flimsy barricade that served
to fortify the camp.

After the first wave came the orderly troops who had
slowed down the pursuit with their well-aimed volleys,
interlaced with the remainder of the surviving Mohawks,
falling back, reloading, firing, and falling back again,
preventing the blood lust of the pursuers from turning the
retreat into a rout. Finally came the few who had failed to
get the message until it was nearly too late, struggling to
catch up with the main body, one cut down by the stray
bullets of his own forces, a few pulled down by the pursuing
Caughnawagas and their lives quickly ended with a blow
from a tomahawk. Among them were many wounded, limp-
ing painfully or being helped by their comrades.

In the camp, General Johnson had his troops' weapons
loaded and pointing toward the woods from which they
knew the enemy must come, waiting for their own to finish
their last desperate dash through the gate and flop down,
exhausted. As soon as the pursuers appeared at the edge of

the forest, the defenders let loose a deadly volley that put a sudden halt to any thoughts of a quick victory for the French.

Now came a brief, chaotic respite. The inexperienced militiamen behind the barricades struggled to swallow their panic while Johnson and other officers walked among them, soothing them with gentle words, like riders calming their horses before a thunderstorm. In the meantime the French were trying to reorganize their Indian allies, who wanted either to enjoy a few prisoner burnings or pick up their scalps and go home. The Caughnawagas had no desire to allow the Abnakis to torture or mutilate any more of their Mohawk brothers, and were ready to go to war with them to prevent it.

The French commander Dieskau thundered at his charges and demanded they get ready to attack, but the Caughnawagas and Abnakis claimed a victory and felt no need to fight another battle, this time against cannon that might rip them to pieces. He nagged at them and he called them cowards, and at last Dieskau achieved order and got his men pointed in the right direction.

Near the edge of the woods, Canadians and Indians peered from behind the trees at the fort. They were out of effective rifle range but they could see the makeshift ramparts and, more forbidding, the cannon, which seemed to be pointing their large gaping mouths at each of them. More than death, the Indians desperately feared dismemberment.

Red Hawk stared at the makeshift fort from behind a massive elm tree. He knew that this attack was not for him. He had killed three or more of the enemy, and the two Mohawks were at least as satisfying as the young militiaman he had cut down with a mighty chop from his tomahawk that had sunk halfway through his neck. As stealthily as he had lain in wait for Tiyanoga and his Mohawks, Red Hawk now slunk into the woods, invisible to the French officers who would attempt to prod him with their swords into a foolish, suicidal attack. White men, Red Hawk reasoned, were of no account in the silence of the woods, but they were deadly firing the long rifle across a clear field from behind the walls of a fortress.

Red Hawk would have no part of this action.

There was a short silence. Behind the barricade, recovering from their mad dash to safety, their deadly long rifles pointed down the road, Thad and Sam felt the quiet before the tumult, broken only by the calming encouragement of officers and noncoms.

"Steady now."

"They'll be coming soon. Aim low."

"Don't worry, boys, if you hit what you aim at, we'll have 'em."

"If I see a one of you leave your post, I'll run a blade through your cowardly gut!"

Steady old hands already recovered from their panicked retreat took positions next to breathless recruits in a horseshoe shape, backs to the water, fronts to the road.

The early course of the war stood balanced on the nerve and skill of these men, white and red, many of whom would rather have been almost anywhere but where they were at that moment.

Mostly frightened militiamen, scarcely trained and held together by the will and courage of a handful of leaders, they struggled to control their wild, terrified breathing while they awaited the approach of the enemy that had just routed them and effortlessly slain their closest comrades in arms.

Wordlessly they looked across the empty stretch of ground at the woods that held how many hundreds of cruel, pitiless *sauvages* and *couriers de bois*—and how many thousands of cold, machinelike cogs of the vaunted French killing machine?

Their backs were up against Lake George. There was nowhere to run.

ACROSS THE OPEN SPACE, OUT OF THE woods on the road, marched the ranks of French regulars, their white uniforms presenting gorgeous targets. While the hearts of the inexperienced militiamen leaped and their mouths went dry, the veterans were thrilled to find enemy that did not flit from tree to tree in the shifting shadows of the forest.

Here was some meat for a lion to sink his teeth into and chew on, but before the lion could pounce, hundreds of Canadians and Indians exploded from the forest, howling and screeching like a primal nightmare.

As if the plain before the barricades were a parade ground, the French troops formed themselves into three ranks and began firing volleys into the barricade of the improvised English fort. A young lieutenant licked his chops while his crews trained the two front-facing cannon, mighty thirty-two-pounders, point-blank on the French ranks.

A volley from the French wounded three members of the crews serving the artillery pieces.

"Fire!" the lieutenant cried. The guns boomed and recoiled on their wheels, and several gaps appeared in the French ranks, as if a giant dentist had suddenly pulled a few teeth. It took a few seconds for the officer in charge to restore order among them, during which time the cannon barrels were swabbed and the guns were charged again with powder and grape.

The French fired another volley, but it was ragged and wild. Like the professionals they were, they swallowed their fear and stood their ground, and it cost them their lives.

The gunners aimed their pieces again, more accurately this time, and stood back. *"Fire!"* the lieutenant shouted. Matches fed fire to the touch holes, and once again the guns bucked against their axles. This time the guns were right on target. A hailstorm of grapeshot buzzed through the French, carrying off half a score of brave soldiers.

Another volley. Now many of the white uniforms bore the spread of red across their facings. Men were writhing in the dust, silent or screaming. Key officers and sergeants were down, and the ranks could not maintain their discipline in the face of the deadly muzzles of the guns.

The third artillery volley did less damage than the previous two, for now even these courageous French veterans had stood up to the mouths of the murderous cannons as long as was humanly possible. Yet still they did not flee. Instead they broke ranks and scattered around the field, disorganized but still deadly, willing to continue the fight against rifles and muskets as long as they did not have to face the certain death of well aimed grapeshot. The Caughnawagas and Abnakis were so dismayed by the bursts of grape that they melted back into the trees and became spectators, and so did their Canadian allies.

Red Hawk flitted through the woods silent as a shadow. The battle no longer held his interest. Let the white men kill each other. He had two scalps in his belt and would have more. In the light of the high sun that filtered through the green forest canopy, scattered like windblown chaff, were bodies—militia, Caughnawaga, Canadian, Abnaki, French regular, Mohawk, Oneida. They lay on their backs or doubled up on their sides, leaned against tree trunks or draped over boulders, or were sprawled spread-eagled on their stomachs. Dead bodies were all the same, he thought, no matter what they had been when they were alive.

Except for the ones who were scalped, burned, sliced, or dismembered. They were different.

Red Hawk at last found what he was looking for, a body that was not yet dead. He knelt down beside it and studied it. He was a Mohawk or a Caughnawaga. He could not tell. He took his water bag, spilled a few drops of water on the man's tongue and rubbed his face and hands. The man had a chest wound and had blood all over him and around him. His breath was rapid and shallow. Red Hawk continued to work on him, and yet he remained unconscious. Then Red Hawk noticed a thong around the Indian's neck. He tugged on it, and from beneath the surface of a pool of blood on his chest he pulled a crucifix.

Caughnawaga! Red Hawk thought, and even as he thought the word, the Indian sounded his death rattle.

Red Hawk then found the body of the Mohawk whose face he had roasted after the ambush, lying facedown by the still warm coals of the fire he had kindled. He knew the Abnakis would soon appear, and he had no desire to let them mutilate this body further. There was a scummy pond close by. Red Hawk picked up the body of the Mohawk, carried it to the pond and threw it in. Let them swim for it, if they want it so bad, he thought.

Closer to the site of the ambush he heard a soft moan. Quickly, running in a crouch out of habit, Red Hawk made his way toward the sound, which came from a colonial boy who could not have been more than sixteen years old. He lay propped up against a tree, feeding his blood to the earth, but his heavy-lidded eyes were open, and his lips barely far enough apart to emit the faint moaning sounds that had brought Red Hawk to him.

The boy was so far gone that the sight of Red Hawk brought no fear to his eyes.

"Awta," he said, and Red Hawk recognized the universal cry of the wounded for water. Even Red Hawk, fresh from

the heat of remorseless combat, could feel a moment of
sorrow for a child who would never grow to be an adult.
Like bodies, children have no race. Take this boy home to
an Indian village, and in five years he would mold into a
good Mohawk. Pah! he thought. Pity for the enemy makes a
people die.

The boy had blond hair that fell nearly to his shoulders.
Red Hawk gathered it and lifted it, pulled his knife and
carved the circle. There was still a lot of blood left in the
boy, and it flowed down over his face as the knife made its
way above his brow and over his ears. The boy did not seem
to notice. Big Oak put his left hand on the boy's shoulder
and with his right tugged hard at the boy's scalp. The boy
closed his eyes to the pain. Then the scalp came free. The
features of the boy's face sagged. The eyes remained closed.
The moans ceased.

By now Red Hawk was not the only Indian prowling the
scene of the ambush. A faint noise behind him drove him
behind a tree, from where he watched a handful of Abnakis
creeping through the woods, looking for scalps. They were
followed by a number of mistrustful Caughnawagas.

Red Hawk had had enough mayhem for the day. Tucking
the bloody blond scalp in his breechclout, he was about to
join the Caughnawagas when his eyes lit on Iptowee, the
Caughnawaga chief who had hoped to avoid bloodshed
with his brothers the Mohawks. He had been gunned down
by an inconsequential young Mohawk warrior whose name
Red Hawk didn't even know. Red Hawk walked to where
the Caughnawaga chief lay. A quick look told him the chief
was indeed dead. Red Hawk felt no pity for him. Had
Iptowee been less occupied with peace and more occupied
with victory, he thought, they probably could have wiped
out most of the red and white enemy before they'd had the
chance to make it back to the ramparts on Lake George, and
he would in all likelihood still be alive.

Red Hawk also found the bodies of Helps Enemy and
Corn Boy. He had no idea how Corn Boy had met his end,

but he had seen Little Oak dispatch Helps Enemy with a single sure shot from his rifle. Anger surged through his veins. For a veteran warrior like Helps Enemy to meet his end from the bullet of a boy like Little Oak stuck in his throat like dried corn. There was no justice. In the old days of stone arrows, a man like Helps Enemy, wearing a wooden breastplate, his powerful arms driving arrows straight and swift, would have been invincible to the likes of children like Little Oak. The rifle was as great an evil as rum, and if the Indians would ever drive the white men back across the ocean, the powder and lead would soon run out, and the value of the great arrow maker would return. The great stalker and hunter would once again be a hero to his village. Warfare would return to the hands of great warriors and be taken out of the hands of children with good shooting eyes, cowards who kill from afar with only enough strength to pull a trigger.

He fingered his own rifle, stood up and began to walk north. Other warriors were also pointing their footsteps toward Canada. In the distance the sound of battle gave Red Hawk the glad news that French and English were killing each other. Let them fight, he thought. A dead white man, no matter what tongue he spoke when alive, brought joy to the eye of Red Hawk.

Thad's adrenaline acted like morphia on the deep laceration in his shoulder carved by a Caughnawaga bullet. He could only wonder at the deadly effect his long rifle was having on the milling targets who were struggling to close in on the English defenders. By this time in his life he had fired at enough targets and animals to know that his eye was as deadly as that of his famous father, but firing at a deer was one thing, pulling trigger on an armed human enemy was another.

He'd squeeze off a shot, and one or two hundred yards off a body would leap and crumple, then lie still or wriggle in agony. He would then duck below the barricade to load under cover, rise up to eye level, take a look, bring his weapon to bear, squeeze the trigger, and another body would leap or crumple. It was too easy. Too deadly. If it was easy for him, it must be easy for them, and then he would hunker even lower to load, and remove his hat to expose still less of himself over the barricade.

A young militia boy firing beside him was either careless or unlucky. A buzzing bullet bit him in the neck, pinwheeling blood all over Thad as the boy fell. Thad glanced over and saw quick death in the boy's eyes, then dropped below the barricade to load and prime still one more time. Suddenly it was no longer so easy. The next time he aimed his weapon, it was with less care and greater haste. The Canadian in his sights seemed to weave back and forth, and the shot he fired went high and wide.

French regular officers in the field, true to their training, kept trying to return their troops to the formations that could bring rapid, deadly, concentrated fire on the English defenders, but every time they reformed, they were scattered by the murderous fire from the barricade. Nor could the Canadians rush across the open space without being cut down. Again and again the gallant French officers exposed themselves to the deadly fire to inspire their men. Each time they were stopped in their tracks by the accurate fire of the colonial defenders.

The equation was simple. The English had the cover and the artillery. The French had only their courage. Good artillery smashes courage every time. A pair of cannon had shaken the faith of the veteran French troops and chilled their stout hearts.

Battles like this one were no stranger to Big Oak. He knew what he had to do, and he did it mechanically and unerringly. There were ways of drawing a bead on the enemy without giving them a clear shot at you. Big Oak knew them all. His position was betrayed only by a blue-gray puff of smoke each time he fired, and by then he was gone. And he could not miss. The range was too close and the enemy too exposed. It took him half a second to spot his target. Unless he could identify an officer, he simply chose the easiest one, the one who was closest or was standing still. He could hit a moving target as well as anyone, but a still target was a certain kill, and the lives of the English depended on certain kills.

Big Oak's heart soared with pride as he watched the young militia around him taking heart and directing a strong, withering fire on the poor French and Indians who remained in the field. Warraghiyagey may not have been an experienced general, but he was certainly a lucky one. Big Oak had no way of knowing that Johnson had been wounded and that the English were being led by Colonel Phineas Lyman, but he did know that the French were turning certain victory into a costly defeat by being too brave at the wrong time. Europeans were very wasteful of the lives of their brave soldiers, he thought, ramming home another bullet and rising to reap another life.

Thad pulled his trigger and his rifle did not fire. Down he ducked behind the rampart. First he cleared the burnt powder from the touch hole, then he unclamped the flint and replaced it with a fresh one. He checked the priming, found it intact, rose above the barricade and fired. By now he had learned not to linger long enough to find out whether his shot had found its target. As he knelt down to load one more time, it occurred to him that the French fire was thinning out. Above the roar of the gunfire around him he could hear the screams of English wounded. His own wound was beginning to throb now. It occurred to him that he had not seen Gingego or Ganaoga since the beginning of the fight.

He sneaked a brief look over the barricade and saw an older, probably high-ranking officer with an aide behind him, rallying his Canadians and waving his sword to beckon the white-shirted regulars forward. Quickly he slid his rifle forward, drew a bead on the brave officer, took a breath, let a little out and, along with half the front defenders, squeezed the trigger.

The officer fell backward and his uniform began to bloom red in several places.

Now the English officers shouted new orders, and without hesitation their men scrambled over the barricade, catching the attackers indecisive and astonished. Buoyed by victory and the scent of blood—other people's blood—militiamen became fearsome warriors, howling war cries as if they'd been born devils.

Suddenly, French bayonets were no match for English hatchets. Suddenly, the soft clerks and awkward plowmen of New York and New England were bloody avengers, showing no mercy as they drove their tomahawks into brains and their knives into underbellies.

Thad vaulted over the barricade in the first wave and almost immediately found a Canadian in front of him struggling to raise himself up from the dust and fire off a shot. Without a second thought, he clubbed the *courier* on top of his head with the butt of his rifle, then continued on without a second look.

The French regulars fled down the road, and the Canadians dashed for the woods. It was the regulars who felt most of the colonial wrath, dying in ones and twos and fours and fives, screaming and gurgling in their own blood.

Swift, lightly loaded colonials overtook the tired and demoralized French troops, and with their hatchets, cut them down from behind. One pair of youngsters worked as a team, the first one tackling a straggling soldier and the second driving his knife deep into the soldier's back.

The Mohawks, who had taken little part in the fight from the barricades, were also busy taking scalps, and soon some of the rawest of the militiamen were following suit. One hot-blooded colonial cut a deep gash in his own hand trying to slice into the top of a French corporal's head. That colonial was Thad.

His angry father pushed him away from the fallen Frenchman. "Come on, the battle ain't over!" he snarled in disgust. "If I had raised you to the scalping knife, I would have left you in Tonowaugh," he growled, and they continued the chase.

But it *was* over. Two battles had been fought by age-old enemies on the shores of Lake George, two bloody slaughters. The winner of the second and deciding battle was a wounded Major General·William Johnson, who soon would become both a legendary provincial hero and an English baronet. The losers were his great allies, the now less mighty Mohawks, who had claimed victory on the battle-field but who lost many brave men that they could not afford to lose.

Big Oak and Little Oak walked from body to body. "If you find a Frencher breathing, son, please take him prisoner, don't knock him on the head and cut off his ears," the older man said sarcastically.

For Thad, the mighty drug of battle had faded and left him depressed. His father had never before spoken to him this way. He was ashamed, and he wasn't sure why. His father had often fought with the Iroquois and witnessed the tortures and mutilations without judging them. Why was he, Little Oak, different?

"I am half Seneca," Thad replied, not in rebellion, but in confusion.

"You are a Christian," Big Oak said.

"But the militia—"

"No. There is no excuse for them, and no excuse for you. White men do not scalp."

"But the French—"

"They are savages. And because they are savages, we will run them off the continent."

"Are the Seneca savages too?" Thad felt anger toward his father, whom he had always admired because he did not make harsh judgments of others.

"The Indians are Indians. I love them and I like them, but I do not always understand them. Today you saw why the Indian will be driven from the land. The Caughnawaga and Mohawk had the same grandfathers, and yet they killed each other fighting a white man's war. And they enjoyed it. My God, did you see how they enjoyed it?"

"But Pa, did you not see the Caughnawaga try to keep from slaughtering their Mohawk brothers?"

"I will always honor the Caughnawaga chief for what he tried to do. But they fight the English because French priests sprinkled water on their heads. Where is the sense? Both tribes are more loyal to the white kings they'll never know than to their own blood."

Little Oak was indescribably weary, and ravenously hungry. It was very late afternoon. A high sun cast its bizarre glare upon red-stained bodies heaped on one another. Groans grew to screams and faded again as the wounded from both armies were brought into the camp, where medical care would be just as likely to kill them as to save them. With the silence of the guns, the birds had returned to the nearby woods, and their evening songs were a dirge for the dead and the dying.

"I'm sorry, Pa," Thad said. "There is enough killing of live people without killing the dead."

"You have never killed before, son. You killed many today. How do you feel?"

"Don't make me tell you how I feel, please."

His father nodded. "Do not get to liking it too much, son."

Five miles away a lone Mohawk made his way west from the shores of Lake George, bitter and vengeful. Dead were his two followers, including one who had been slain by the boy he could have killed on the trail many moons back. All the bloodshed had left him dissatisfied and vaguely depressed, as it had the young man he so despised, Little Oak. He knew that the hundreds of colonial Englishmen who had died that day would be replaced so easily, but there would be few to replace the Mohawks he had so willingly helped to slay.

Also dead, he knew, were his old friend Ganaoga, killed

and scalped by a fat Abnaki early in the fight, and Gingego, who should have stayed home warming his old bones in the light of a lodge fire. And a warrior even older than Gingego, the great chief Tiyanoga, lay in a clump of brush not too far from the ambush, killed and crudely scalped by a handful of Caughnawaga children.

Try as he might to save his fire for the hated English, Red Hawk had slain two Mohawks in the fight. How could the red man triumph if even he killed his own? And then he remembered what he had done to the one he had scalped— roasted him alive in a fire and enjoyed the power of watching his struggles weaken as he surrendered to the pain and death provided by the mighty Red Hawk. He wanted to sing about his battle prowess to his children, but he had no children, and anyway, how could he sing about killing and torturing a brother of the Ganiengehaka?

Amid the oranges, yellows, and light greens of the early New York autumn, a small body of Mohawks wound their way home along the back trails of the high country, then down into the valleys that led to the Te-non-an-at-che, the mother of their existence.

The slanting sunshine, the faint chill and soft pale haze, spread over the endless woodland. The easy living of summer was nearly over, the annual struggle of winter was soon to begin, and it pressed heavily on the hearts of the men as, single file, pigeon-toed, each to his own private silence, they ate up the distance between the battleground and their home.

Their hearts were also heavy with the loss of six of their number. The last had died of wounds only the day before they had left for home. The survivors were unwounded, or at least fit to travel full speed, so their journey would be a quick one.

And yet, strong in the hearts of this unhappy group was a feeling of satisfaction, for nothing could obliterate completely the joy of a great victory and of knowing they had been mighty in battle. The scalps they carried proved that. The memories they dwelled upon as they walked were those of well-placed shots that sent the hated French spinning to the ground, of solid tomahawk chops that broke the heads of their adversaries like so many eggshells, of deftly cut and ripped scalps to keep as mementos of their victory.

Like men of any culture, using the skills they had been taught, using them well, made them feel like a part of the whole, eased their doubts about their worthiness, assured them of their place on earth and in heaven.

Big Oak and Little Oak, who journeyed with them, understood.

Little Oak had entered the firestorm a child and emerged a man, at least in his own mind. Facing death and standing his ground had stilled his deepest fear, and made him a man. Killing men who would kill him, both from a distance and hand-to-hand, had made him a man.

His wounds had been light. He wondered, of all of the thousands of rounds fired, how many had come close to ending his life? What did it mean that they hadn't? Did he want to do this again? No, he didn't. But if he had to, he would.

Big Oak's thoughts were simpler. He had been through more intimate battles, where the enemy had become almost a dance partner, but those had been skirmishes, nothing like this all-day slaughter pen where men were blown down like cornstalks in the cold winds of November. His manhood passages were so long passed that they meant nothing anymore. Like any other active frontiersman, the call to battle stirred his blood, and death around him made him feel more alive, but he was disappointed that the last war had only led to this war.

He so loved his life that he hated the thought of losing it to a chance messenger. And yet he, who fled from death with such determination, was too valiant to flee from battle.

There were nine Mohawks in the party. Two of them, George and Louis, were the sons of Gingego. Strong and stalwart, they walked the trail tight-lipped, their vengeance unslaked in spite of the scalps they carried. For when they had walked the battlefield in search of their father, they had found his body where he had died, stripped, mutilated . . . and headless. They had spent an entire day searching the area for their father's head, and finally, in the twilight, they found it, they thought.

Scalpless, eyeless, earless. Skull crushed. Filth shoved into his mouth. Who would have so dishonored this good and venerable Mohawk man? Even his enemy loved Gingego. White man style, his sons had buried his parts all together and hoped the Great Spirit would take him as he was, but their faith was shaken in spite of the day's triumph.

That their father had died bravely, as he would have wished, was no consolation; that was a given with a great man like him. In this time of terrible change, all that was real was life. The rest was in doubt, for where was the Great Spirit hiding that weak and greedy men like these white men could come upon the mighty Mohawk and cheat them with written words even while they called them their friends and allies? Gingego's sons had no more illusions about the white men than did Red Hawk. And yet they, like their father, were willing to give their hearts and their trust to exceptions like William Johnson. It gave them hope. If there was one good white man, there must be more.

Big Oak was a good man. Their father had told them so.

There was little talk among the Indians and between the two white men. Both the victory and the costly losses had left them all feeling empty. By day they reveled in the open valleys and forest trails they conquered so swiftly with their feet. By night they made camp, roasted meat, and ate it, but made little fireside conversation. Their security was not what it should have been in time of war, but fortune smiled on them, for their red enemies were heading off in another direction, to Canada. They saw no other human beings on the long trail home. And three days after they had left the scene of the battle, they were in familiar territory. Their spirits picked up as they spied the recognized landmarks, only to come crashing down when they found themselves drawing near to their village.

Not six but eight lives had been lost, including the two who had run off with Red Hawk and died fighting for the French. Gingego would be missed terribly for his wisdom and his kindness, but six of the men had been prime hunters, acquirers of food for their families. Winter was over the next hill, and with it privation for those who did not have what to eat and wear.

Solemnly they entered the village through the front gate, scalps dangling from their belts, heads held high and proud. It was midday, under a deep, cloudless blue autumn sky, when eight Mohawk families heard the news that sent their world crashing down. Those who first whooped to honor the deeds of the living went silent or joined the keening cries of those so suddenly bereft.

What happened next almost unhinged Thad. Women screamed and began to give vent to the most heartrending cries of grief. Friends and relatives ran to them and tried to console them, only to be swept themselves into the pain and hopeless horror of sudden loss.

Of the bereaved women, only Gingego's widow refused to allow herself to lose herself in hysterical lamentation. While her sons grabbed hold of her on either side and supported her, she swallowed the choking cries that arose within her and said, "No, no. I'm all right. My husband died as he wished, and my sons are home to carry on his seed. My life is more full than I deserve."

For a few moments she stood by the gate of the village and took deep breaths. "Go to your families," she told her sons. "They need you right now more than I." Then she began to make her rounds to the weeping wives and mothers. "Shhh," she said soothingly to each. "You are Ganiengehaka. You are strong. You must bear this grief for the sake of our people. Hard times are ahead. Be strong and spring will come again for us all."

These words, from Gingego's wife, who had lost the no-blest Mohawk man of their time, did not stem the tears, but they helped to give the women back their dignity. "Do not fear," she told them. "The village will get your family through the winter."

When she had done all that the wife of a great chief should do, and more, she walked out the gate to her favorite hilltop west of the village, a peak that looked out across a valley toward the Oneida country, toward where she had first met Gingego while their families were both visiting an Oneida village. He was a man who treasured a wise woman, and it was that wisdom in her young eyes, rather than the lithe attractiveness of young Indian girls, that had turned Gingego her way.

Often, when Gingego was away and due to return, she would take some woman's work with her into the hills and find a spot from where she could watch for him while keeping up with her chores, perhaps cutting long strips from a deerskin with a sharp knife to make thongs, or mending a torn legging. Her keen eyes could pick his short, slight fig-ure out of a long Indian file, or out of the greenery if he was traveling alone. Her heart would flutter with pleasure as she thought of his gentle touches and his thoughtful words, which always reached the heart of the matter and made her feel secure.

Now she found herself a comfortable spot in the sun, stared off toward the tree lines he would never again walk, and allowed the hot bitter tears to flush down her cheeks. For more than an hour the tears flowed, noiselessly. She let the memories flow in an endless stream, recalling his young face, so full of purpose and discipline, but already bright with the lines of tolerance and good humor.

So long ago, she thought, in a day when all tribes feared the Ganonsyoni, and even the English dared not make a move in the valley of the Te-non-an-at-che without first securing the agreement of every village chief who called himself Ganiengehaka . . .

As the years passed, and the world closed in around the Mohawks so gradually that most could not feel the change, Gingego would tell her, "There will come a time when we will have to make so much room here for the white man that there will be no room left for us. When that time comes, *we* must be strong so the tribes of the Ohio River valley will make room for us. They will not do so willingly. We will have to fight for our place.

"We have done so before," he reminded her. "We did not always live here. There was a time we lived to the north, and a time long ago when we lived to the south. Do not fear. Wherever we go, the Ganiengehaka will be a great people."

As he aged, his body gave in to the years, but never his heart or his will. She remembered the last time he had returned from the great council fire in Onondaga. It was not so long ago, and he had found her on this hill, waiting, as he knew he would.

"As the years pass and the strange changes come," he told her that night, "sometimes it is hard to go on. At the council fire I heard dark words. It is harder and harder for the confederacy to hold together. Together is all makes us the great people we are. If our union fails, we shall fly apart and scatter to the winds. The other night, I heard words at the council fire and I was afraid. Then I thought of you, waiting on the hill, and my heart stopped its wild beating and found peace. You are my strength."

"You were wrong about that, Gingego," she said softly to the warm breeze of the late summer afternoon.

Then she said, aloud: "Your strength let me be a child for longer than I had the right to. It is time for me to be a woman. Forgive me, my love. I must put you aside for a while. You have grandchildren."

She stood and let the wind dry her tears, then she locked her sadness away inside of her, deep enough that others could not see, but nowhere near deep enough that she could not feel. And she made her way back to the village, to the longhouse where her daughters-in-law would be welcoming back their husbands.

## ❊12❊

THERE WAS MORE TO HER GRIEF THAN SIMPLY the loss of her companion. Winter was a few short weeks away, and meat was short in those homes that had been missing their hunter and would now be missing him forever.

White Bird—for that was her name, walked slowly back to the village. Forty-five years could be old for an Indian woman who had borne eight children and buried three, tilled the soil and felt every day of the harsh, damp, cold seasons in her bones. But until this day she had carried her years with the kind of grace that kindled the admiration of all the other women.

Now, suddenly, as she walked back to the village, she felt old and graceless. And poor. Great Mohawk chiefs like Gingego often *were* poor. They stayed that way by giving their wealth away to those who needed it more.

A practical woman, White Bird thought of the difference between white chiefs and red chiefs. White chiefs, she noticed, kept their wealth, and the people around them admired the wealth they kept. Red chiefs, on the other hand, gave away their wealth, and their people admired them for what they gave away. Because Gingego was a good man, his widow was a poor woman. Oh yes, she had four sons, but two of them lived in other villages, and all had families to take care of. One more mouth to feed in a harsh winter was too many mouths to feed.

As she walked up the last slope to the stockade, the sky was red with the last rays of daylight. The shrieks and keening had subsided, but inside the walls she could hear the quiet sobbing of a young girl who had become a wife only a year before. Sadly, White Bird chided herself for her selfishness. Dark Moon was only fifteen, with a new baby at her breast and no husband. Gingego's widow had been loved by a good man for a long time, and she had lived a good life. Like other women of stature in the Mohawk nation, she was a political force in choosing the leaders of the village. Even in her time of grief, White Bird wondered where the future leaders of the village would come from if the war continued to extract such a terrible toll on the warrior population. Without their best men, the village would drift, leaderless, and in wartime such a drift could be fatal.

Louis, her oldest son, named for the King of France when Gingego wanted to send the English a message, was waiting at the gateway to the stockade.

"Where is Big Oak?" she asked.

"Why do you need him?" was his searching reply. She gave him a look that told him who was the boss of the family. "In the small lodge," he said as she walked past him.

White Bird had known Big Oak for many years, almost as many as her husband. She considered him a friend. There was something about him that could buff the jagged edges off her fears. His powerful gentleness reminded her that not all the goodness of the world was wrapped up in the soul of Gingego. Softly she walked past the longhouses, past the quiet conversation within, past the smells of meat and vegetables cooking in pots. For the sake of the lost warriors and their families, and in their own grief, the surviving warriors had put away their trophies and related their war stories only to a friend or a spouse in the flickering shadows within the longhouses.

Finally White Bird arrived at the small lodge and knocked

softly at the door. Big Oak answered, took her hand and led her inside.

The chill of late summer brought Big Oak, his son, and White Bird close to the fire, which flickered warmly in the dark interior of the lodge. She pulled her blanket around her and stared at them both across the fire. Big Oak plunged his knife into the pot that rested on the fire, drew out a piece of meat, put it in a bark bowl and offered it to her. She shook her head.

"I climbed the hill outside the village," she said. "The day was fair and warm, like so many in my fortunate life.

"But as I walked back to the village, at my back I could feel the cold wind of approaching winter. We have lost so many of our people. In the Longhouse, from the Eastern Door of the Mohawk to the Western Door of your Seneca, there are fewer lodges in every village, and fewer people in every lodge. This I know, for I have heard of the empty lodges elsewhere. There are empty lodges in this village. The people on the outside talk about moving back within the walls of the stockade, but you cannot wall out the things that are making us a smaller people. It is clear to me, as it must be clear to you, that as the white people come from the sunrise, the flint people go to the sunset.

"I do not understand why our Master of Life is so weak before your god. Why so much disease, and why do we sicken and die, while white men leave their beds and live again? Why are there so many of you and so few of us, that you can lose a thousand and still grow and prosper, while those we lose cannot be replaced? I do not understand why you have been given things like guns, that are so much more powerful than what we have, and why even when we have those things, we still need a man like you to make them shoot. You can make the blankets, so light and warm. And you have the stone you can see through, that lets the light in but keeps the wind out.

"You can make the shining blades that cut so easily, and we cannot. And the silver stone that is like holding a pool of water—you look into it and it looks back at you. All these things you have mastered. We now have those things too, but we are like children, we use them without knowing how to make more of them, so we must give to you what is ours in order to get more of those things we need.

"You can always make more guns, but we cannot make more beaver. So we must roam farther and farther to get the beaver, and when we do, we must fight the Ottawa and the Chippewa for them.

"You can always make more blankets, and more mirrors, and more glass beads for our wampum, which we pay so dearly for—oh yes, I know how easy it is for your people to make those beads, a minister once told my father about that —you can go on making them forever out of the sand that never runs out, but where will we get more land to pay for it? And of course there is the rum that makes fools of our warriors. Even Gingego was a fool about rum."

Big Oak and his son stared attentively, motionlessly, across the fire. They did not interject, nor did they even nod their heads.

"You have seen many seasons pass, Big Oak. And yet your belly is flat and your eye still keen. Your bones do not ache on a cold morning in the forest. Not like so many of the Ganiengehaka who have your years. You are a white man and your years will be long."

She gestured toward Little Oak. "And your son, who comes from the people of the Western Door. Strong, honest, loyal. Two good men in a village that needs men. There are women here, beautiful young women who know how to satisfy a man, not like the spoiled white women in Fort Albany. Warraghiyagey knows the joy of our women.

"And our men. The mightiest of warriors. Why? Because they can be men—hunters and warriors—all the time, and never have to worry about their children or the crops or the village. That is what good women can do for a man.

"You are a great trader. Our men cover the land, even in the Canadas, to find the furs that will make you rich. Even though they are scarce here, our men find them elsewhere. That is why we have so many good things in our village.

"My time here is short. There was only one man to comfort me, and he is gone. But there are young women here, brand new in womanhood, filled with the kind of desire that makes men feel like men. If you stay you have your pick and no one will say no. You, Big Oak, know what the women of the Seneca are like. But have you ever been with one of ours? If you spend a week with a young woman of the Ganiengehaka, you will want to stay forever."

He had to admit to himself that the prospects were enticing. He was a man, he could not help but notice the beautiful young women of this Mohawk village, some of them young and inexperienced, longing for a man to bring into their lodge. It was not always easy for a young girl to find a man, because of the shortage of men during wartime, and because young braves often avoided attachments, believing that loving a woman deprived their bodies of strength in battle.

And there were young women who had been widowed in recent times, the price of being part of a warrior nation in the midst of a war. They too longed to have a man. And Big Oak, modest though he was, knew that a man of his means and reputation would be welcome in many a longhouse.

Big Oak continued to stare at Gingego's wife as he pondered the possibilities. He remained certain that the English would win this war, and that the Mohawk Valley had a great future for great men like Johnson. The Mohawk people were a great people. For centuries they had ruled the river valleys of eastern New York, and fought peacefully with the Seneca for leadership of the Longhouse.

But their time was disappearing. The day the devilish priests first set foot in a Mohawk village, that was when the day of the Mohawk was done, he thought. Big Oak had his own home down on the Genesee River, and though the pain of its emptiness still struck him when he crossed its threshold, those were his people, not the Mohawk. They needed him more than the people of this village. Down there he could be of some use. This village, he was certain, could not survive a long war, with him or without him.

"My home," he said, "is at the Western Door. My heart is still at the Lac St. Sacrement, with my friend Gingego. No one can replace that kind of man. I do not grieve for you, for you would not have me do that. But I grieve for me. Even the many years I have spent on the Genesee, the world was better because I knew that Gingego was alive on the Te-non-an-at-che. But war kills the best. I cannot replace him. I must go back to my people."

In the gloomy, flickering light of the hearth fire, White Bird looked deep into his eyes. There was more, he knew, to her request beyond the mere replenishment of population.

"The English are our friends," she said. "Sometimes you fear your friend more than you fear your enemy because you know how to fight your enemy. But sometimes we hear things. In the forests. In the wind."

"Rumors," Big Oak prompted.

Gingego's widow nodded. "That the English will attack in the night from Fort Albany and kill our men and make slaves of the women."

"Has that happened yet?" Big Oak asked.

"Have I died yet?" White Bird replied. "And yet I know that when my time comes, I will die. The white men are strange. We do not understand them. We cannot guess what they will do. But I know that when something stands in their way, they remove it. I am afraid for the village. If you were with us, then you would know their thoughts. And our children would be safe."

Big Oak felt sad, for he had in the past heard wild talk among the people of Albany about wiping out the nearby Indian villages. It would make Fort Albany safe from the savages, they had said; what they really meant was that it would open up a lot of land for speculation and development. But he knew it would do no good for him to confirm her fears.

"The king," he answered carefully, "knows that the Ganiengehaka are his loyal subjects, and he would never allow such a thing to happen."

"The king is very far away," White Bird responded, and he knew how right she was.

"I will always be your friend, and if I were to hear of such a thing in Albany, I would prevent it if I had to kill with my bare hands. But I cannot stay," he said with a catch in his voice.

She bowed her head, then nodded and rose to her feet.

"I am glad you were his friend. Please come by to visit me before you leave. I have something for you."

Head high, she walked out into the night.

The following morning found them in the hills early, their deadly rifles at the ready. While they were still close to the stockade, they knew they would find no game, so they talked about the war.

"I'm not sure this war has all that much to do with us, or the Indians, or the beavers, or anything else on this side of the ocean," Big Oak explained. "France and England are like the Mohawks and the Abnaki. They don't like each other. Never have. And whenever they have a chance to get at each other, why, they get at it. Now, I don't know if they're fighting anyplace else on earth this day, but if I were a gambling man, I'd wager that they will be, and soon."

"Why are you so sure the English are gonna win this thing, Pa? Just because they've got more folks to fight for them?"

"That's just what soldiers like you and me might think." Big Oak chuckled. "Fact is, the English are gonna win because they have got the best ships. The English like being at war with France because then their ships can come out and capture the French cargo ships on the seas. Then the prices of goods get higher and the Indians believe the French are trying to cheat them. Understand?"

Little Oak nodded. "So what it comes down to is, it's their

friends the English that put the Iroquois in a corner wherever they look. Right?"

"Yeah, well . . ." Big Oak said slowly, "our brothers the Iroquois are not God's angel band either. Iroquois is what the Algonkin call them. It means 'real adders.' And guess what the Ottawa call them."

Little Oak shrugged his shoulders.

" 'Bad snakes.' Our brothers of the Longhouse are not the princes of peace. But then I guess we shouldn't be too hard on them either. This is not what you'd call a peaceful land." And he laughed.

They had walked so many trails together, and they knew the woods and each other so well, that they both understood without a word from the other that the time had come for stealth. They walked and they walked until they found a place on the creek that bore all the signs of a watering place for deer. Then they waited, for hours, and were rewarded by the appearance of five adult deer, including a big, beautiful doe. They killed it, field-dressed it, and brought it back to the village.

The following day they roamed the harvested fields and shot pheasants and doves, dozens of them, and brought them back to the village.

Yet a third day they hunted, and this time, far from the village, they killed a bear so large they had to rig a sledge to drag it back to the stockade. All the food was for Gingego's wife. She would prepare it and hoard it, they knew, and save little of it for herself, but when the snows were deep and the supplies low, and the children of the village hungry, she could reach into her personal supply and feed them. It was the kind of woman she was, and the kind of man Gingego had been. It was the least Big Oak and Thad could do to help. It was the only thing they could do to help.

The last night, they went from longhouse to longhouse saying good-bye and wishing the village good fortune. With Red Hawk gone, the famous white hunter and his half-Seneca son had become favorites among most of the villagers.

As Big Oak looked in each face, big and little, he wondered how many would be there next year if they visited the village with their furs on the way to Fort Albany. Little Oak reflected on how different the village seemed to him now, compared to the day he had first been dragged in by Red Hawk. It had seemed an evil place then, populated by demons, a prison for him, and the place where he might well bury his father. Now he thought he might miss the village. He was certain that he would miss Gingego, and White Bird.

Early in the morning, just after first light, they stopped by the home of White Bird. She was already up, feeding the youngest of her grandchildren, who lived one fire over in their longhouse. She had told her daughter-in-law to stay awhile longer with her husband, who had been away so long. She told them both that their moments together were precious.

She spoke softly to the children as she fed them boiled corn. The children were young, three and four, and they adored their grandmother over all other living things. She put some maple sugar in the corn and stirred it around. Then she reached into her pouch and dropped another big hunk of the sugar into the corn. The children each took a spoonful and smiled and smacked their lips. They had never before tasted anything so sweet.

White Bird heard Big Oak call out, and she beckoned them to her hearth fire. "Would you like something to eat?" she asked.

"No," Big Oak replied. "We've already eaten, but today is the day we're leaving. We wanted to say good-bye."

She nodded. "Come with me," she said, walking them over to a dark corner, where she stored many of her possessions. "With all my heart, thank you for the meat you brought us yesterday. We worked long into the night preparing it for the winter months. It was a kind thing for you to do. We will remember."

She bent down and reached into a corner of the room, beneath a sleeping platform. "I told you I had something for you," she whispered. "Something that belonged to your friend, Gingego."

She had a large leather pouch that served as a closet for family possessions. From it she took a smaller leather pouch and brought it back to the fire. "I wanted you to have something that belonged to him, and I thought hard about it. I understand that what it is wouldn't matter to you as long as it belonged to him. His medicine is for his children. His weapons are for his children. He has no wealth, for although he acquired much in his life, he gave most of it away with an open hand that the Ganiengehaka will remember as long as we are still a people.

"But here is this white man thing that was made for him by an English lieutenant who was his friend in the last war. The pouch is something I made for Gingego, and I want you to have it to remember me. But the skin inside is something he wanted you to have. Many times he would take it out and look at the markings and say, 'I must show this to Big Oak the next time I see him.' He wouldn't trust any other white man to see it.

"But he was not thinking about it when they brought you to our village almost dead five moons ago."

"I would have died without you," Big Oak said earnestly. White Bird ignored Big Oak's words of thanks and pulled up the flap on the leather pouch.

"Gingego said this was what the white man called a map. He said that you would know what it said." She removed it from the finely worked leather case and unfolded it. It was a sheet of parchment about eighteen by twenty-four inches. The markings were in brown ink, which in some places was smeared from the effects of water, but on the whole, the map was quite readable.

Big Oak studied it for a while, then motioned for his son to view it with him. "Can you understand what area this map refers to?" he asked Little Oak.

Pleased to be consulted by his father, Little Oak studied it carefully but could hazard only a·few guesses.

"There is a shoreline here, that I can tell," Little Oak said. "But there is not much to go by. It could be Lake St. Sacrement, Canandaigua Lake, Skaneateles, any of many."

"Or it could be someplace out of New York," Big Oak added. "This map is one of those strange pieces of information that asks more questions than it answers. For what purpose was it made? Where is it? What are these markings? This writing may be in French. It sure doesn't make English sense."

He turned to White Bird. "What did Gingego know about this map?"

"I cannot say," she said. "When he brought it home, he told me the lieutenant had made the map when he was one of those men who go out to mark the land."

"A surveyor?" Big Oak asked, curious.

"I do not know the word," she said. "After that war was over, he did not think about it, except when he thought about you."

"Strange for an officer to be carrying such a map. It is not a battle map. There are no troop locations, no prominent military landmarks. Not even any route marks like roads or paths to guide a traveler. A very curious thing. He must have been an officer of the militia, but the map probably dates back before that."

He looked up from the map, into the eyes of Gingego's wife. "Were he and the lieutenant good friends?"

She thought for a moment. "Gingego said the lieutenant told him that someday this map could be important to Gingego. But Gingego must not have thought much about it, then. Because he never did anything with it but say that someday he must talk to you about it. Maybe he did not think it was so important."

Big Oak stood up and folded the map, placing it carefully inside the leather pouch. White Bird likewise rose. "I know that you must get an early start," she said. "Friend of my husband, return to us soon."

"Will you be all right?"

Her back stiffened as she looked up at the tall white man. "Women of the Ganiengehaka are strong. We love our men, but we also love life, and will fight hard to hold on to it."

"I know that what you say is true," Big Oak replied. His words were strained with the effort of containing his emotion. "I will think of you and Gingego on our journey back to the Genesee. We have all passed so many winters so quickly. It seems unbelievable that even a long life can be so short."

"It has always been so, Big Oak. Go now, I feel your need to be gone." White Bird choked on those last words, and Big Oak had to turn his head toward the doorway and pretend he had not heard. Outside, near the front gate, many villagers were assembled in spite of the early hour. Most of them, he noticed, were the women, the very old, and the very young. Some of the people wore the look, not of Mohawk, not even of Iroquois, but of Huron, or even Delaware, adopted into the Six Nations to replace the losses that occurred during years of warfare with surrounding tribes.

One last time they walked among the people, shaking hands, squeezing shoulders, letting them know about the feelings they had in their hearts. There was sadness on the faces of many men. There were tears in the eyes of many of the women. A few were weeping openly. Big Oak was touched. He had not realized they had been so attached to him and Thad. There were some things about Indians that he would never understand if he lived with them for the next fifty years.

Big Oak placed his hands on the shoulders of White Bird for a moment and stared into her eyes. No words came out. There was no need. Nor did the Indians at the gate have anything to say. That they were there told the father and son all they needed to know.

They shouldered their packs, rested their long rifles on

their forearms, and trudged off toward the distant hills in the west. They walked down the hill, across a valley, and through an orchard to the top of the next hill. Little Oak turned around for a last look at the stockade. Through the morning mist, not yet burned off by the morning sun, the villagers stood like ghostly apparitions, likewise longing for a last look of the legendary white friend of their beloved chief.

"Come on, son. You can't let yourself feel these feelings," Big Oak said. Yet he too paused in his journey for a minute, to get a last look at a village he would never forget, where there had lived a great man who was his friend.

# ❧13❧

ONCE THEY WERE OUT OF SIGHT OF THE VIL-
lage, Big Oak led his son south away from the river, to some
of the higher, more difficult trails that only the very few
knew.

The countryside was now ablaze in full-scale warfare between the French and the English, and when the French and
the English fought, the Indians fought even harder because
the survival of their entire nation was at stake.

"If we keep to the rough trails, and travel softly and carefully, I believe we will be safe," he told his son. "I was careless on the way east. I'm glad you were not the one who had
to suffer for my mistakes."

The winds blew on the high trails, muffling the sounds of
their footsteps as the dried fallen leaves crunched beneath
their feet. They could look down through the dazzling reds
and yellows at the low country, and search the clearings
below for hostile travelers. On the other hand, the going
was rougher and slower, overgrown and rocky, not natural
pathway at all. It was better, Big Oak reminded his son, that
they sacrifice ease for security, and Little Oak agreed. He
had had enough fighting to last him forever.

As they climbed higher into the hills, away from the Mohawk village, Little Oak's spirits rose. The forests held no
terrors for him, not in the day, not in the night. They were

his home, and every step along the way was a pleasure. The weather had turned just cool enough to chill his ears a bit, but the effort of traveling along the trail with a heavy rifle and pack kept him warm. He also felt the joy of following the broad shoulders of his father. Never again would he take that man for granted.

He found himself thinking about his friend Skoiyasi, boisterous, loud, full of the devil. It was Skoiyasi who had always wanted to know what Little Oak had learned during the winters he spent with the preacher's family. At first Skoiyasi had even tried to get Little Oak to teach him how to write the English words, but he grew impatient and then resentful at his own inability to concentrate. When the weather grew warm and the fish grew plentiful, a spear seemed so much more real to Skoiyasi than ink marks on paper.

"A Seneca brave can no more make words with a pen than he can make arrows from succotash," he grumped.

As quickly as it came, his interest vanished, and when it did, distance grew between the two friends. "We are of different places," he had told Little Oak. "I am a man of the woods, while you, my brother, linger awhile longer by the warm campfire." Little Oak had thought that a strange thing to say. Like most young braves, Skoiyasi had no qualms about settling in by a longhouse fire through much of the winter.

"Seneca braves dream of making a name for themselves on the warpath," Skoiyasi had said. "I think mostly you dream of Kawia." His friend was probably right about that. He didn't think he had opened his heart so wide that even Skoiyasi would notice.

Three hours on the trail had taken Little Oak and his father fifteen miles from the Mohawk village and given both men a tremendous appetite. They were crossing over a large gray rock formation into a clearing at the crest of the hill they'd been traversing.

"I would rather see than hide," he told his son. "Many

places to hide are death traps if they find you. From here, we will see them first."

"See who first?" Little Oak asked.

"For some time now, I have had a feeling that we were being followed. I don't know why, but I am certain that our footprints are being covered."

Little Oak had not yet acquired that sense, but he knew that when his father had a strong instinct, it was always true.

"Many following, or few?" he asked.

"That I do not know."

"Should we double back and let them pass?"

"I have been thinking that we should do that, but not yet."

They took a quick glance at their back trail, saw and heard nothing, and waited no longer, but walked on, gnawing on a bit of cold meat. "Don't eat any corn. If you drop a few grains along the trail, they might guess that we do not stop to eat because we know we are being followed."

They picked up the pace just a bit, running the downslope to the next hill. On the next hill the high trail did not meander along the top ridge, but stuck steadily along a ledge on the side of the hill. They trudged another mile along the trail, until they found an area of exposed rock that extended up the hill for forty or fifty feet. There would be no footprints on a rock shelf. There they left the trail and moved about a hundred feet upslope, then doubled back for about half a mile until they found some thick undergrowth that would conceal them while permitting them to watch the trail.

Meanwhile the wind had died down, allowing them to use their ears, and their noses. With the patience possessed only by deer hunters, they lay in the brush, breathing softly, each with his senses on high alert, mostly keeping a sharp eye on the trail below, but intermittently checking their backs and their flanks.

Fifteen minutes later Big Oak poked his son and pointed toward his ear. Although Little Oak listened, he could hear only the birds, the wind, and the leaves on the trees. But he had never known Big Oak's hearing to fail him, so he listened harder. Two minutes later he thought he heard a twig crack or a leaf crunch. Then, through the successive layers of branches and leaves, he thought he saw movement.

A face, and then a body, appeared over a rise on the trail below them. He moved swiftly, yet so silently that only occasionally could Little Oak hear any kind of noise over the usual soft forest cacophony. The stranger's body was lean and muscular. His look was certainly Iroquois, probably that of a Mohawk. But his face was that of an enemy, stern and implacable, determined to kill. As the Mohawk moved closer, Little Oak was surprised to see that it was Louis, Gingego's oldest son. Ten feet behind Louis ran another Mohawk, whose face Little Oak remembered from the village but whose name he did not know, followed by seven more, five of them Mohawks, two of them Oneidas.

It occurred to him that except for Louis, all of the faces he could remember had either been part of Red Hawk's band or the group who had carried his wounded father back to the village and had attempted to maintain possession of the furs he and Big Oak had brought with them, until Gingego had forced the raiders to return them.

Silently, the nine Indians passed on the trail below, then moved out of sight where the trail rounded a bend. Big Oak signaled his son to hold his position awhile longer, which was a good thing, for, sure enough, a tenth Indian popped over the rise and ran silently by, eyes moving from side to side, alert to anything out of the ordinary.

Soon he was gone too. Big Oak allowed another few moments to pass, then he began to descend the reverse slope, away from their pursuers.

Why was a painted party of Mohawks, led by the son of his great friend, on their trail? Big Oak wondered. He had thought the hateful influence of Red Hawk had disappeared from the Mohawk village the day he had left to join the enemy. Big Oak reminded himself that in these precarious days, no white man was completely safe in an Iroquois village, no matter how much he felt a part of the Longhouse.

A half mile down the side of the hill, they found a creek, just a little bit of a thing, but enough for them to step into the icy water and walk for a mile or two. Another larger, wider creek joined this one, making a fairly powerful watercourse. Big Oak cocked an ear and smiled. Although the water was now knee deep, they continued to wade until Little Oak could hear the faint roar of falling water. They stopped for just an instant to listen, then climbed up the bank and walked beside the creek. The sound of the falling water grew louder and louder with each step, until they suddenly approached the edge of a precipice and saw the creek take a sheer drop of sixty feet onto the rocks below.

For a moment they watched the smooth band of water ten feet wide pour off the side of the mountain in a shiny ribbon, only to splatter like an endless crash of crystal onto the rocky valley floor. Then Big Oak pointed up the hill and began to climb, with Little Oak close behind.

"That's two hills between us and Louis," Big Oak said, once they had made it over to the other side and found an easier way toward the valley floor. "If I remember right, there's a trail you can hardly tell is a trail, which we can pick up right about there." He pointed toward a ridge of pine trees straight ahead of them.

Although there were several hours of daylight left, Big Oak decided to move just behind the ridge they were on and make camp where they were. When Little Oak asked why, his father took him back to the ridge and pointed through the trees at a distant hilltop with a bald summit.

"The trail they are taking," he said, "goes through that clearing, and the view from there commands the entire valley. We have to *cross* that valley to make it to the next trail. By now they probably have some youngster up there with eagle eyes, just waitin' for us to cross the valley, and when they see us crossin', they'll be on us like bad on Lucifer. So we're gonna cross in the dark."

They settled down in an area sheltered from the wind by trees and rocks. Little Oak was desperately hungry for hot food, but there would be no fire on this night, not even a small one.

"A Mohawk can smell smoke from halfway around the world," Big Oak insisted. "Give him a few minutes to walk around, and he'll figure out the direction."

"All right, no fire." Little Oak pulled a chunk of venison out of his pack and ripped a huge bite out of it. "But why are they after us now that they know who we are?"

"I'm not sure," Big Oak answered. "Maybe he blames us for the death of his father. Maybe he's angry because we came back and Gingego did not. Or maybe he's just lookin' for something to kill that will bring him some honor. I'm not sure that he cares about the confederacy. Maybe a lot of the younger ones don't. I believe that little pieces are beginnin' to fall off the Longhouse, like shakes off a roof, if you catch my drift."

Little Oak shook his head.

"You can still get a Mohawk to go into battle against the French so long as they don't have to face up to cannon. But it's just the battle they want. Then they go home and they get to thinkin' and they remember they can't much stand the English either, and that makes 'em mad. Now there's no Gingego left in the village to stand up for you and me. Tell you what I think, my boy. If they catch us, they'll roast us. And they'll do it real slow. And they might even make a meal out of us. And something else. If they get ahold of any rum they will cut off our heads and present them to White Bird, and they won't mind a bit if she screams a time or two."

They followed up their venison with a couple of handfuls of parched corn, washing them down with cool creek water. Then they rolled themselves up in the blankets they carried, rested their heads on their packs and waited for their body heat to gather inside their blankets and warm them up. Almost immediately both were asleep, their breathing inaudible, their bodies still.

* * *

About two dozen Caughnawaga plus Red Hawk made their way north along the shimmering glitter of Lake Champlain. The Caughnawaga knew all the trails along this route, for many of them made their living in the smuggling trade.

Red Hawk was not completely thrilled with his company. For one thing, three of the Caughnawagas were not Caughnawagas at all, but Abnakis, and he did not like Abnakis. For another, the Caughnawagas were Catholics who prated on incessantly about how, when they made it back to Caughnawaga, he should get himself baptized in thanks for having won so many great honors without so much as a scratch in the battle on Lac St. Sacrement. Red Hawk needed many things in his life. He needed a new firearm, since he had already abused the one he had received from the French, so that it failed to fire about one in five times, and when it did shoot it wouldn't hit anything farther than the length of a longhouse. He needed a new scalping knife; he had lost his good one in the battle, and his bad one would not hold an edge. He needed to make a new pair of moccasins as soon as he got around to killing and skinning a deer. But he did not need a new god. For him the old Iroquois gods were good enough, and he certainly didn't need a white one that spoke French.

In fact, he thought the Caughnawagas odd. They were Mohawks but they were not Mohawks. As much as he hated the English, he knew the English and their language was familiar to him, not like the nasal bleats of the *coureurs de bois* and those Indians who had learned to speak like them. But these were the men he had chosen the day he turned his back on his home village, and so he resolved to make the best of this bad situation. Perhaps in time he would get used to them.

For their part, once the Caughnawagas had seen Red Hawk in battle, they had immediately accepted him. He was a holy terror with a tomahawk in his hand, fearless and merciless, the very embodiment of the warrior ideal. And he had made one friend on the journey north from the battle-field. His name was Owaiskah, son of a Caughnawaga mother and a Seneca father. He had first caught Red Hawk's attention during the ambush when he had picked out the young Mohawk brave who had started the fight by killing Iptowee. Red Hawk had paused a few moments in the battle to watch Owaiskah stalk the young Mohawk under the cover of underbrush until he was within attacking distance. Then he had sprinted the final five steps, leaped upon the Mohawk's shoulders, brought him down and finished him by cleaving his skull with one mighty blow of a tomahawk. The whole attack could not have taken more than a few seconds, quicker than a cougar killing a deer.

The admiration had turned out to be mutual. Owaiskah later saw Red Hawk bring down a fleeing militiaman from behind, cut his throat with a knife, and regain his feet to continue the pursuit of the fleeing English army without bothering to pause and admire his handiwork. Not only were both men formidable warriors, both were great talkers, and both of them thought the English were the devil's dregs.

Like young whites bragging about their love conquests, the two warriors loitered at the end of the long line of Indians as they wove their loping way along the forest trail to the big Caughnawaga village, discussing their many mighty achievements in battle. These achievements had increased in stature every year until, yellowed and mellowed by time and space, they were now positively Homeric.

"One time," recalled Owaiskah, as they trotted easily along a moss-covered downslope, "we were bringing in about seven canoe loads of powder and lead from Albany, when we were attacked by Mohican—much shooting on both sides of the river. Two other men in my canoe, both killed at the beginning of the fight. I fell out of the canoe, pretending to be dead, and stayed underwater by the canoe. I gave it a little push so it would drift toward the shore. From under the water I could see two Mohican waiting for the canoe. Then they could not wait anymore. They went down the bank into the water to get the canoe.

"By the time the canoe was close to them, the water was shallow, up to their waist. I crawled under the water, around them, stood up, quiet as the big cat, and when one of them put one of his hands in the canoe, I swung my tomahawk like this"—here he swung his tomahawk within a foot of Red Hawk's head in a mighty downward motion—"and sunk it so deep into his head, I couldn't get it out. It went 'Sclack!'" He imitated the sound of a tomahawk splitting a skull: "And when the other Mohican heard the sound, he turned around with his eyes big and round." He made big circles around his eyes with his fingers, to show how big the Mohican's eyes looked. "I took his rifle away from him as if he were a child, and I smashed his face with it.

"By that time some of the Mohicans on the other shore had seen what happened and they were shooting at me. I scalped both Mohicans underwater. What else was there to do? I could not shoot back." He shrugged his shoulders like a Frenchman. "My rifle was in the canoe, and the rifles of the Mohicans I had killed were wet."

Red Hawk normally was not that interested in the war stories of other warriors, but this one was different.

"I do not understand one thing. You said that you traded for your goods in Albany. You traded with the English? The French let you do this thing?"

"The French see things as they are. When they found out that we traded with the English, they became very angry. But we told them that we could get what we needed only from the English and they understood. 'We cannot allow you to do this,' they said, 'but we will not stop you. We will turn our backs when you come back from Albany until the day comes when we have made them disappear. Then we will supply you with all you need, and we will not charge the thieves' prices that they do.'"

The English, always the English, thought Red Hawk. Mean, cruel, selfish, ruining everybody else's lives. And

when he thought about the English, he thought about Big
Oak and Thad, the Senecas who were English.

Red Hawk slowed his pace and Owaiskah did the same,
knowing that his new friend wanted to tell him something
for his ears alone. "There was a day," Red Hawk said in a
voice that Owaiskah could barely hear above the noises of
the forest, when this arm"—he extended his right arm and
stopped to admire it—"slew five Abnakis so quickly that the
sun did not even move."

They looked down the hill at the Abnakis among the long
file of Indians that continued their long easy jog along the
trail of Lake Champlain, north to Caughnawaga.

Real woodsmen have a clock inside their brain that runs
only when they sleep and wakes them up at a preset moment. Big Oak's clock rang three hours before dawn. The
still air settled a shivering chill on Little Oak as he unrolled
himself from his blanket. He would have gladly crept back
under the warm wool had he not been so aware that his life
was in jeopardy.

Slowly in the moonlit night they crept down the side of
the hill into the valley, where the coldest of the night air
had settled. Big Oak led, his sensitive toes feeling through
the thin soles of his moccasins, and Little Oak followed so
closely that his nose occasionally brushed his father's pack.
Soon they were on the east bank of the stream, about two
hundred yards below the waterfall. The stream was about
twenty feet wide and swift at that point, but there were a
number of large light-colored rocks that meandered from
one bank to the other, perhaps placed in the stream years
ago by enterprising Indians who preferred to bridge their
way across dry in the wintertime.

In the sky brushed-silver clouds scudded across the face
of the moon, which lit up the night so that they might as
well have been crossing at noon. But behind these lacy
clouds were thick, puffy ones, and a moment later they had
blotted out the moon and darkened the land.

As dark as the night was, these two keen-eyed hunters could make out the dim shapes of the rocks and the white of the water as it rushed past them. The roar of the falls upstream and the water before them made it necessary for Big Oak to put his face close to his son to communicate.

"It doesn't look hard, but the rocks may be slippery. The water's cold. The air is cold. If you fall in and get wet, you're in trouble."

Little Oak looked back at his father, smiled at him and nodded. Still and forever, he is my father, he thought.

North of the falls, Little Oak could see the dark shape of the hill where the Mohawks were, sleeping, he hoped, along the trail. The trail was on the other side of the hill, and even if they had been perched in a tree at the top of the hill, looking out toward the falls, the night was far too dark to see two tiny shapes crossing the broad valley. But Little Oak had an almost mythical perception of Indians' ability to track an enemy, and there was no doubt in his mind that these Mohawks considered him and his father to be their enemies. He just didn't understand why.

Carefully they stepped from rock to rock, feeling first with their moccasined toes before they put their weight down. A cold, cutting wind was blowing down the valley. Little Oak felt it on his skin, and he felt it push against his balance. In the middle of the creek it made him sway a little. He put one foot quickly onto the next rock to keep from falling. The rock had a bit of moss that made his toe slip forward. He almost did a split, and his knee felt the biting cold of the stream for a moment, but he did not lose his precious foothold on the rocks. Three quick steps later he was safely on the other side with Big Oak.

They paused only long enough to fill their canteens, then quickly climbed the bank, crossed the remaining open area of the valley, and vanished into the life-giving cover of the woods. Ten minutes later they stopped and pulled out some venison and corn. Neither man dared to speak until they finished eating, and then Big Oak whispered softly in his son's ear.

"We'll stop here until first light. That's a tough trail to find in the dark, and I'm afraid we might miss it."

Red Hawk had to admit that Caughnawaga was a very pleasant-looking town, with streets laid out in an organized manner and a large open common area.

In the common area Caughnawaga braves were riding horses up and down, and performing various maneuvers. He could not believe what he was seeing. Young Iroquois braves had little use for horses on the narrow trails that wound up, down, and around the wooded hills of the Te-non-an-at-che and the lake country. Horses were for old warriors grown too fat and blind to run from place to place anymore, like that old fool Tiyanoga who had been killed at Lac St. Sacrement.

And the Catholic priests scared him. He had attended a mass and did not feel at all good about being there. He watched his Caughnawaga kinsmen and wondered how they could have allowed the French to do this to them, to forsake the age-old faith of their fathers to worship a white man nailed to a stake. He wanted to be back on the other side of the big river of the north.

So he talked to his friend Owaiskah, and told him of an idea he had, one that would strike a blow against the English, who they both despised, and against the Longhouse people who continued to do the dirty work of the English, even though they should have known that when the dirty work was done, the English would destroy them.

Owaiskah loved the idea. He was like Red Hawk's old comrade Helps Enemy in that he craved the sting of battle, but unlike Helps Enemy, he had some solid notions of who were his friends and his enemies. He loved to strike a blow, and when Red Hawk presented his plan of action and his reasoning for it, it never occurred to Owaiskah to question whether the enemy deserved the disaster that Red Hawk had in mind.

Owaiskah brought Red Hawk to meet a trio of *coureurs de bois* who were very active partisans in the cause of the French. They were so pleased with Red Hawk's plan that they decided to join them on their excursion, and not only arranged for supplies for the entire war party, but managed to secure a brand new rifle and a pouch full of flints for Red Hawk. Red Hawk ran his fingers up and down the smooth gun metal and finished wood of the weapon. Never had the English been so generous. When he asked for a new scalping knife, he got one.

*This* was certainly the side to be on, he told himself as he fingered the keen blade of his new knife and slipped it into the waist of his breechclout.

Little Oak blinked his eyes and opened them. A faint bluish light filtered through the fall canopy. Big Oak was up already, checking the priming in his rifle and the edge on his knife, as he did every morning when he awakened in the woods. They took care of their morning needs and quickly packed their blankets. Each drank some water and cut a slice of meat. Each shouldered his pack and hoisted his rifle into carrying position. Well before the sun had made its appearance, they were climbing a steep hill in search of the trail that was barely a trail.

Little Oak hoped desperately that Louis's little band would not have the skill or the luck necessary to locate him and his father in the vast inland sea that was the great forest of the Mohawk Valley. But both he and Big Oak knew in their hearts that they and Louis would meet again, and that the time would not be long.

# ❦14❧

THE COLD WINDS OFF LAKE ONTARIO WERE blowing the leaves from the oaks and elms before their time. Maybe it was the dry summer that had just passed. Maybe it was the early chill. Away from the lakes, the trees were still in full yellow and red leaf, but within range of the Ontario winds, an eagle could have spotted the snaking file of loping Caughnawaga and allies, led by three Frenchmen just as bejeweled and painted as the Indians.

Red Hawk had disliked the Frenchmen on sight, and hated them more when he heard what their accent did to the Mohawk language, but when he heard what they had to say, he found himself thinking good thoughts about them.

"We are your true allies," one of them had told the war party their first night away from the village. His name was LeJeune, a small, wiry man of about thirty, with a scarred, red, ugly face; ugly not because of the scars, but ugly from the perpetual snarl that curled his mouth into the shape of a tadpole.

"We will go with you where you wish to go, but on the way we will stop everywhere we see an English face, an English farm, an English home. We will burn their farms, burn their homes, kill their women and children, torture their men, and once in a while set one free, burned and bloody, to take back to the English settlements word that being English in the land of the Iroquois is a bad thing."

He was saying these words to all the men in the raiding party, but most of the time his eyes rested on Red Hawk.

"You, Red Hawk," he continued, finally addressing him personally, "must get the word back to the Ganiengehaka that it is the French who are their real friends. I have never understood why the Mohawk—why the Longhouse—has been so stubborn and clung to the English. Has King Louis taken one foot of land from the Iroquois to hand over to his rich friends? Have the French come like locusts to crowd you out of the land that is yours by the blood your fathers shed to win it? What do the French do? Why, we live with your Canadian kinsmen, and take wives among them and trade with them. We send blacksmiths to them to mend their weapons, and priests to them to mend their souls. We do not treat them like *sauvages*, the way the English treat you."

"But when you make war upon the English, you also make war upon us," Red Hawk replied, surprised to find himself arguing for the people against whom he had so recently turned traitor.

"Only because you are the allies of the English."

"But you are the allies of our enemies—the Huron, the Chippewa—the Abnaki." The two Abnakis in the party turned to glare at him, but LeJeune showed his snarling smile.

"The Iroquois must learn that they can no longer afford to make war on their neighbors when the real snake lies coiled to strike them all, eh?" Red Hawk did not reply. He did not need a Frenchman to tell him how to teach a lesson to his people. He was curious to see how these white men would behave when the killing started.

The file of Caughnawagas, Abnakis, and Canadians made their way south along the easy trails, past the west end of Lake Oneida and down into the fertile lands among the

Finger Lakes. They saw no whites along the way and did not go out of their way to look for any.

And then, one unseasonably warm afternoon as they loped through a level stretch of woodland, they saw to their right the golden glow of sunlight that indicated a clearing where a clearing should not have been. Maybe if the man who had made that clearing had been a little less ambitious the winter before in the number of trees he had cut down and the number of stumps he had burned, then they would not have seen that sun glow for what it was. Maybe if they had passed through that part of the trail earlier in the day, the sun would not have been balanced above the western horizon, casting its rays through the open farmland. And then, a family consisting of one English colonial farmer, his wife, and his eight children, would not have perished on that day.

Maybe it was just meant to be. LeJeune, and not the sharp-eyed Caughnawagas, was the first to notice. He poked Moreau, his easygoing partner in marauding, and smiled. Moreau was tall and paunchy, bearded and handsome, a man who enjoyed life, especially the killing part of it. He nodded, grabbed Owaiskah by the shoulder and pointed. Soon all two dozen raiders were kneeling behind trees at the edge of the clearing, staring at a small, neat log house at least a hundred yards away.

They took in the whole tableau in an instant. The farmer was at the edge of the woods on the north side of the house, felling a tree for the winter firewood supply and to continue enlarging his planting area. Half the land still had stumps on it, with late season greens and pumpkins growing between the stumps.

A pair of boys between the ages of ten and twelve were playing in front of the cabin, but anybody else on the farm would have had to be inside. The French leader sized up the situation quickly and logically.

LeJeune dispatched a pair of warriors to that part of the forest closest to the farmer, and the rest of them spread themselves around the woodland's edge. He couldn't believe that the farmer was foolish enough to have gone into the woods without his gun.

From where they stood, most of the raiders could see the farmer with his ax, flailing away at the large white ash tree. He was strong and he made the chips fly as the blade bit deep into the wood with a loud *thunk*. A man like that, tall, strong, and tireless, could build a large, prosperous homestead for a large family in a few years time, on Mohawk land, thought Red Hawk, waiting with grand anticipation to see how his two Caughnawaga brothers would handle the situation. While he and the others waited, the farmer continued to rain mighty blows upon the tree from two sides, until it was nearly ready to fall. He lowered his ax and started to put his weight against the tree, to give it the *coup de gras*. It was then that the two Caughnawagas struck.

Red Hawk saw the man's mouth open as the first Caughnawaga jumped out of the forest and grabbed him from behind with an arm around his head, but before he could cry out, the Indian had plunged a knife into his neck above the collarbone. Blood flew into the air as the farmer's arms fluttered weakly in pointless resistance, then he collapsed. Desperately he climbed to one knee, but before he could stand, the second Caughnawaga sunk his tomahawk into the man's brain just above his right ear. As Indian killings went, this one was quick and merciful. The farmer would not live to see the unspeakable horrors about to be visited on his family.

Even before the farmer's scalp had been lifted, the rest of the raiders came boiling out of the woods from all sides, stripped to their loincloths and screeching their war cries. The boys playing in front of the house were just a shade too far from the front door to make it through before five warriors caught up with them, pulled them down, and dragged them by the legs, shrieking, away from the cabin.

The door flew open and a large, muscular woman came running out with a rifle in her hands, screaming at the Indians to let her boys loose. Three Caughnawagas who had approached the house from the rear attacked her from either side. She raised the rifle to her shoulder, turned to her left and fired a charge of buckshot that nearly cut one of the braves in half. Of the remaining two, one grabbed her by the hair and the other pulled the rifle away and smashed her across the face with it, knocking her senseless for the moment.

The front door slammed shut, and from the inside the Indians could hear the terrified cries of children. The woman quickly regained her senses enough to identify the Canadians as being white. On her knees she begged them in the name of the Almighty to spare her children. Her tears might have softened the heart of the Master of Life himself, but they did not move the Canadians. An Abnaki approached the woman from behind and, by putting his hands on her shoulders and leaning on her, he held her in a kneeling position while the Caughnawagas brought her two boys before her.

LeJeune spoke excellent English, and he chose to employ that gift. "You have killed one of our warriors," he said, "and for that, we must kill your sons."

Now she screamed and offered herself to anything they wished of her if only they would let her sons go. She might as well have spoken to the big ash at the edge of the woods behind the house, which still stood over the now bloodless body of her husband.

So frightened they could not stand by themselves, the weeping boys were brought to within five feet of the mother. First one was killed by a single blow to the brain by a tomahawk, while the other was allowed to live long enough to understand what was in store for him.

He did not plead for his life. Fear had deprived him of reason. He struggled like a madman in the grip of one of the warriors; then, suddenly, the struggles ceased and the boy crumpled beneath a mighty blow to the back of his head from a heavy Caughnawaga war club. A moment later the mother found herself gazing through terror-widened eyes at the severed scalps of the sons she adored.

One of the Caughnawaga approached her to deliver a fatal blow, but LeJeune grabbed his wrist. "No," he said. "She is the one who will live to tell of this."

But now there remained the business of the children in the cabin. The raiders could still hear them inside, huddled together, whimpering with fear and dread. Owaiskah and Red Hawk had no problem coming up with the solution. The house had stout shutters on the front, but the children inside were too young and paralyzed with fright to understand what to do with them. The two newfound friends had put together several bundles of dried sticks and kindled them into firebrands. Now they simply dropped them through the open windows and watched the curtains spread the fire to the walls, and then the ceiling. Held pressed so tightly to the ground that her mightiest struggles were of no avail, the woman was forced to listen to the screams of her children as the fire raced through the house. Mercifully, the smoke stilled their voices and their hearts before the flames consumed them.

Now what to do about the woman? A mere hour before she had had a home, a husband, and eight children to raise up, and now she had nothing. In her grief and despair she had no fear, and she was very strong. When the Indian who had been holding her down let go of her while he was watching the cabin burn, she climbed to her feet and wrapped her hands around LeJeune's neck. Her strength was overwhelming, her grip tight as a vise. He pummeled her midsection, but he might as well have been pummeling a water barrel. When he tried to gouge her eyes, one of his fingers slipped into her mouth and she bit clean through to the bone.

"Help me," he gurgled, and he would have died in front of his raiding party if one of the Abnakis hadn't knocked her unconscious with a blow from the stock of his rifle.

His neck bleeding from fingernail scratches, and purple

where her fingers had closed off his windpipe, his left little finger a pulpy mess, his face red with fury, he walked over to where the woman lay, pulled her head up by her hair, and slapped her back to consciousness. Then, while two Indians held her down, he took his hatchet from his belt and with one blow chopped the fingers off her right hand.

He stood up and watched, in pain and satisfaction, as the roof of the house caved into the inferno. He took from his backpack a bottle of brandy, poured some on his neck, some on his finger, some down his throat, and swore horrible oaths as the burning pain swept over him.

"Let's get back on the trail," he said. "We've stayed too long." A moment later, in single file, the warriors were covering the trails in their familiar, distance-eating stride, leaving behind a murdered farmer, two boys brained and scalped, a burning cabin full of dead children, and a woman who by God's mercy had lost her mind.

Big Oak and his son found the going slow but safe. They were not following a trail, but remnants of several old trails, from a time in history before the Iroquois confederacy.

"There was a time," Big Oak told his son, "when many tribes fought for this land, before the five nations came together and claimed this land as their own. In those days it was better not to be seen. You never knew who it was might see you."

"Looks like those days have come again," Little Oak commented.

His father nodded. "Times like these, trust comes hard." Walking the ridge lines, they kept their eyes always toward the distant Mohawk River valley, where they were certain, Gingego's son, Louis, and his men pursued them. They were now in the country of the Oneida, where they had cached their furs, and Big Oak felt the need to check on them before they proceeded on through the lake region.

When the trails they followed took them through the valleys, their travel kept them in the deep woods, or trudging through the thick underbrush that had overgrown the ancient trails, sometimes climbing over fallen oaks or hemlocks, or following the winding course of clear, cold, swift-running streams. Then, back up on the ridge lines, they sometimes crossed a clearing that gave them a startling view across the marching caravan of wooded hills and valleys that blanketed central New York. When the wind blew, it sent thick showers of brown and yellow leaves down on them from the exposed tops of the old forest giants. As they labored along the ridge lines, its chill stung their exposed faces, even while the sun drew sweat from them beneath their deerskin hunting shirts. The icy claws of north country winter would soon seize the land.

As the days passed without any further signs of their pursuers, they relaxed some of their anxious vigilance. One morning, craving fresh food, they descended to a deep creek, speared a few fish with their knives, tied to sticks. They encased the fish in thick, dried cakes of mud and baked them in a small open fire of sticks so dry that the thin wisps of smoke that filtered through the forest canopy were safe from even the acute senses of the distant Mohawk party.

By now Big Oak was certain the Mohawks, traveling the easier trails, were well ahead as well as to the north of them. Fresh fish, he said, was much better than old, tough deer meat when the trail was long and hard. Following breakfast, they turned north and came down from the hills, crossed a valley, then followed a small watercourse upstream for a mile, until they came in sight of a large rock formation above the valley floor.

They began to climb up the formation, rock by rock, not a vertical climb, but steep enough to require a strong effort from them with the weight they carried on their backs and in their arms. Fifty feet above the floor of the valley, Big Oak slid into a narrow crevasse between two rocks and walked into an open area about ten feet wide, covered with dirt and leaves and a few spindly birches and hemlocks.

When Little Oak caught up to him, his father put a finger to his mouth and froze, listening intently to the silence. Gradually, as the creatures in the immediate area grew used to their presence, the forest resumed its normal chorus. There was another rock formation beyond this clearing, one with an opening behind it hidden by a thick stand of wild berry bushes. Careful not to disturb the bushes, Big Oak made his way behind them and into a narrow passageway about three feet high.

Inside was a chamber not quite tall enough to stand up in but big enough to hold four or five small adults and nothing more. They entered and waited for their eyes to get used to the dim light.

Big Oak looked around in the dust and the spiderwebs for signs that anyone else had been inside the chamber since he had last visited it. Finding no such signs, he got down to the business at hand.

To the left of the entrance was a rock overhang that left the dirt beneath it in constant darkness. There were a few large, loose rocks strewn about underneath the overhang. These Big Oak removed, and scooped up a handful of the dirt they had stood on. He began to dig with his knife, six inches down, just deep enough for him to touch the old bearskins and deer hides wrapped around the furs. Carefully, he removed the covering of dirt, and with Thad's help began to pull the bundles out of the cache, then out of the cave, in order to examine them.

The day was sunny and warm, considering the lateness of the year, a fine day to sit cross-legged in a forest clearing and examine one's wealth, such as it was.

Thad watched as his father removed the coverings and examined the pelts.

" 'Pear to be in good shape," he said after a while.

"Pa, I've been runnin' traps and trails with you for years, and we never have talked much about what really happens to these skins after we get through with them."

"Well, then, I guess you ought to know, seein' as this whole war is bein' fought over furs."

Little Oak looked at his father in surprise. "I kind of thought that it was about whites and Indians."

Big Oak shook his head. "Not this war. This war is between the French and the English. Our Ganonsyoni chiefs understand this, and mostly they're just tryin' to keep out of the way, but of course the English and the French would love to get their Indians to do as much of the fighting for them as possible." Thad sat across the pile of furs from his father, nodding that he understood.

"Now, the English do mostly farming, but some of them, like us, are fur traders. The French, on the other hand, almost all they do is trap and trade pelts, and this war is about who is gonna get the whole fur business in this part of the world. Kind of funny how men'll risk their own skins for the skins of beavers."

"Now tell me what happens to these furs on the other side of the ocean," Thad said.

"Here's the way a trader in Albany explained it to me once.

"You know those big hats you see the important men in Albany wearing?"

Thad nodded.

"That's beaver."

"Don't look like no beaver I ever saw swimming around in a creek."

"That's because they don't really use the skin. They use what they call the beaver wool, strip it off the skin and make it into something they call 'felt,' and that's what they make the hat out of. I can tell you, you've got to have a lot of money to buy a hat like that."

Having inspected his furs and satisfied himself that they were in good condition, Big Oak repacked and reburied them, this time a bit deeper. He scattered rocks of various sizes over the area and convinced himself that no one would ever guess that there were valuable goods beneath the floor of the little cave.

As far as Big Oak knew, he and Little Oak were the only humans on the face of the earth who were aware of their cave. Now they would have to cover any outside signs of their having been there, and continue the journey. Outside, while they paid attention to minute detail and found nothing that would reveal human presence to any visitors, Big Oak felt the anxiety that came with the sense that someone was watching them. With the greatest of care he scanned every tree from roots to treetop, every rock, every square yard of dirt, of grass, for a sign that somebody else might be around.

They had begun to walk toward the passageway between the rocks when Big Oak abruptly stopped.

"Something is troubling me but I can't lay my finger on it. I don't wish to leave just yet. Let's make camp in back of the cave. We'll take alternate watches and see if we can catch a skulker."

# ❊15❊

**S**O INSTEAD OF LEAVING IMMEDIATELY, THEY stayed overnight, camping in a clearing under the crisp bright stars. They ate in silence as Big Oak tried to rid himself of the feeling that they were being watched. He had tried every trick he knew, including after-dark scouts around the area, but he found neither skulkers nor signs that anybody besides them had been in the area.

Finally they wrapped their blankets around them and ate. With a full stomach, his anxieties finally subsided. "Maybe it's just the war," he told Thad. "Maybe Louis and his lopers are just headin' west to do some mischief to the Shawnee. Maybe we should have just waited for them and joined up with them, then we'd be sharing a fire with a little army of Mohawks instead of shiverin' here in the dark. Maybe I'm not back to what I was before Red Hawk 'n them beat the bejeebers out of me."

Thad shrugged. He didn't like it when his father talked about that night. He changed the subject.

"How'd you find this place anyway?" he asked.

"It was Gingego who found it, maybe fourteen year back. I know it's hard to imagine, you saw him as an old man who loved his campfire more than he loved the tomahawk, but fourteen year ago he was still the mightiest warrior in the village. He didn't miss a chance for mischief in those days, and that's why we were out here, for mischief.

"We were on our way south to Wyoming Valley when we heard that a couple of Frenchmen were sneakin' around this area. An old Delaware named Bear Returns told us about them. Nowadays we would have just said, 'So what, let someone else clean 'em out of the valley,' but we were full of the devil then and maybe a little bored of looking for beaver where the beaver were about gone, so we decided to look for them. It wasn't just scalps. We figured they might have some good weapons, or some money, or some trade goods."

"You wanted to rob 'em," Thad interrupted him.

"And kill 'em," Sam continued with good humor. "Fortunes of war, you know. Well, we found them, all right—found them firin' down on us from up here, and if they'd been any kind of marksmen, you'd be an orphan today.

"So there we are, hot-footin' it down to the valley floor, half running, half rollin' end over end 'cause you could see this afternoon what a clear field of fire they'da had on us, no trees on the side of the hill and all. We get down the bottom of the hill, finally find us some cover, and there's Gingego all scratched and bruised and guffawin' like he had the hiccoughs. 'What's so funny?' I asked him, and he was so thrilled with the humor of it all that he can hardly catch his breath to answer. Finally he gets to breathin' right again and tells me that the old Delaware set us up for an ambush, and gets to laughin' that awful laugh of his again.

" 'That's the best joke I've heard since the Mississaugis almost roasted me five year back on the Ohio River,' I told him. He starts to laughin' again.

" 'Tell you what let's do,' he says in his own way. 'Let's go up there and take care of them, then we can come on down to Oquaga with their scalps hangin' from our belts and see if that old Delaware devil recognizes the hair.'

"What we did was head on out of the valley by that ridge yonder that you could see from the clearing in front of the cave, where they couldn't help but see us. I pretended to be walking with a terrible limp, as if one of them had maybe nicked me pretty good and that's why we were gettin' out of there, because their shootin' just kind of awed the hell out of us. You ever notice how them boys that can't shoot well enough to hit the next mountain over are always the ones who think they're mighty powerful shooters?

"That night we come at them from another direction, which was risky 'cause it's easy to miss a couple of sleeping anything in the middle of the night. But you know what? Them French boys must of had a nose full of brandy, 'cause they were both dead to the world and snorin'. so loud we could hear 'em when we were still half a mile away. We hadn't an idea where they were until we heard them. And it was so loud we thought it was a trap. We waited up half the night, waiting for them to stop fakin' it, but they didn't, so we dropped in on them and cut their throats, and then cut their hair, and they didn't seem to mind a bit."

"Whoa now, Pa," Little Oak interrupted. Big Oak looked up from his rifle, which he had been cleaning by the light of the moon. There was something in Thad's tone of voice. Was it anger? Was it hurt? A feeling of betrayal?

"You remember up at Lake George you hollered at me for going after a Frencher's scalp—you recollect?"

Big Oak thought for a moment. "A lot was happening then. I don't recollect, but I believe you."

"You told me that white men don't scalp, and when I told you to remember that I was half Indian, you said that don't matter, no son of yours is gonna take scalps. Now you remember?"

"I guess so," his father said. "My memory isn't as good as it used to be."

"Didn't you tell me that you scalped this Frencher whose throat you cut in his sleep?"

His father thought about it for a moment. "That was different. I think there was a bounty at the time. We might of got a heap of money for them scalps."

"So you're telling me it's okay to take a scalp for money, is that it?"

Big Oak thought about it. "Well, it wasn't worth anything to the dead Frencher anymore, right?"

"And mine didn't need his anymore either, right?"

Neither the father nor the son minded a bit of silence in the middle of an argument. Sam went back to cleaning his rifle, and Thad, who had been leaning forward toward his father, leaned back against a tree. Just when Thad figured that Sam had closed the subject because he didn't want to deal with it any longer, the older man looked up from his rifle with a sad expression on his face.

"I don't think white people should take scalps," he said. "I don't think anybody should take scalps. But it's something Indians do. They burn people and cut them up and sometimes they eat 'em too, and they shouldn't do that either, but it's not my job to tell them, just like it's not my job to tell the English not to liquor the Indians out of their land. That kind of stuff is for politicians. I'm a trapper and a trader, and I still get excited when there's a war on. I can't help it. I only kill when there's a war on with a legal enemy, but if you're gonna survive in a war, I figure you better enjoy killing your enemy, cause they're sure as hell gonna enjoy killin' you."

He paused for a moment, unscrewed the flint from his rifle and tried to inspect it. It was a little too dark to do a proper job, so he clamped it back in, pulled back the hammer and pulled the trigger, setting off a shower of sparks in the night. He primed the pan, loaded the piece, and set it back on his lap.

"I shouldn't have scalped that man," he said. "And I suppose we should have buried them and I should have read some scripture over him too. I'm a little lazy about some things. But let me ask you a question. Does it bother you that you didn't take that man's scalp when you had the chance?"

Thad smiled. "Well, just once it would have been nice, just to see what it—" He stopped and reflected for a moment. "No, not really. Sometimes, you see, I think you're more Indian than I am."

"Me too," Big Oak said. Now he began to inspect his powder horn, more with his hands than his eyes.

"Pa, you were telling me how you come to find this cave."

"Oh, that. Well, where we laid last night, in the clearing in front of the opening? That's where we found those Frenchers and let their blood loose."

"So maybe we slept on some dead man's old dried blood?"

"Well, you might say that. It's long washed away, of course. The earth has a way of cleaning itself that's a lot better than the way we clean ourselves. After we killed them and scalped them and shook the cooties out of their scalps and tucked them away, I got turned around and went through the wrong underbrush, and suddenly I'm in this cave, bumping my head up against the roof. That's really all there is to it. I came right out again and didn't think much about it until I was coming through the valley a few years later and thought what a good place it was to cache a load of anything between Tonowaugh and Albany."

"Did you ever catch up with the old Delaware?"

"Down in Oquaga, where we thought we might find him. Both of the Frenchers had hair almost as dark as an Indian, but one of them had a white streak that ran along the side. That was Gingego's scalp, and he was real proud of it. When we got to Oquaga we found the old Delaware, and Gingego hauled out the scalp.

" 'We went trapping a few days back,' Gingego told the Delaware. 'And we found this real odd skin. Looks almost like a skunk. Smelled like one too. We wondered if you might tell us what it is.' And he waved it in the old man's face."

"What did he do?"

"Didn't do a thing. Just sat there with no look at all on his face. After a while he looks up at us and says, 'Never seen anything like it before.'

"I told him it was a French whoreson. He nodded as if I

had said something that made sense, and told us that he was pleased we had trapped an unusual animal. That's what he said, but the next day he was gone from Oquaga, and I haven't seen him since."

Early the next morning they stepped out smartly, heading away from the Mohawk Valley, generally southwest to skirt the northern shores of what we call today the Finger Lakes region.

Throughout their journey along the northern edges of the Finger Lakes, Big Oak kept on his son to watch their back trail carefully.

"I don't think the Mohawks are anywhere near close to us," he said at one point. "Either that or they could track us over the clouds. But there's something out there that's botherin' me. Do you feel it?"

"Yes I do, but it might just be you."

Big Oak nodded, lifted his cap and scratched his head for a full minute. The day was mild and the afternoon sun was brilliant over a forest-green Lake Canandaigua. In another day or two they would be home. Their spirits rose. They were in Seneca country now. They were no longer the intruders. Let others beware.

But still they stopped every so often and crawled into the underbrush beside the trail to check for pursuers. Still they ate cold food without a campfire every night and every morning. Still Big Oak fidgeted irritably, as if he had taken his rifle apart and then, when he had cleaned it and tried to reassemble it, found that a piece was missing.

There he was, looking everywhere for the missing piece. Had he dropped it on the ground? Was it hidden in a fold of his jacket or his breeches? Maybe it wasn't missing at all. Maybe if he took the weapon apart and reassembled it he'd find that all the pieces were there, after all, if he could just fit them together correctly.

Their last morning on the trail they awoke to skies so dark it scarcely felt like daylight. From their packs they took fitted pieces of leather to cover the firing mechanisms of their rifles. Almost immediately after breakfast it started raining. Then it started pouring. Their moccasins began to slide on the wet leaves. Then they began to sink into the mud. Their clothes got heavier as they absorbed the moisture.

It began to rain even harder. The clouds were so black it seemed as if the rain had quenched the sun itself. Thunder rumbled in the distance, an almost unheard of event along the Genesee this late in the year. They labored forward, heads down, rifle barrels pointed down, each with his own thoughts of a warm, dry lodge and warm food. Once on a downslope, Little Oak lost his footing and had to grab a sapling to keep from sliding off the trail and down the side of a hill. Big Oak helped him to his feet and gave him time to unruffle his feathers. As Little Oak replaced the leather piece over his rifle, Big Oak raised his head and sniffed the air.

"Campfire," he said. "Not too far ahead."

They had to be more careful now. Any Senecas would be staying close to the village on a day like this, so the campfire might belong to an enemy. They left the trail and moved along a route roughly parallel to it, expecting to come upon the camp fairly quickly. What kind of campfire could stay lit in a downpour as heavy as this? A mile went by, then two, and there was no camp. Little Oak could also smell the smell of damp ashes, but if it got any stronger, it did so only gradually.

It took another two miles of off-trail struggle before Big Oak's head snapped erect and a moan escaped his lips. "Great God!" he cried. "Back on the trail, son. And make some swift tracks." They covered the last three miles to the village in a run, through rain that came down in sheets, soaking them to the bone, with fear clutching at their stomachs and their eyes dreading what they would soon have to witness. From behind him Little Oak could hear his father muttering something—a prayer perhaps—so rapidly and indistinctly that he wasn't sure whether the language was English or Seneca.

And when the forest had thinned to a clearing, their worst fears were facts.

Stunned, they stood before a lifeless, black ruin of a village. For a moment they could not move. For a moment, surveying the scene through a wall of falling water, they thought that their senses were deceived. Every longhouse was a charred hovel. From the edge of the clearing they could see dark bundles strewn about, at least some of which had to be bodies. Amid the smell of damp wood ash, Big Oak was certain he could detect the stench of burned flesh.

Everywhere there was death.

Slowly, they entered the village, so stunned by the devastation of their home community that for the moment a lone skulking coward with a knife might have dispatched them both without either lifting a hand to stop him. Most of the dead lying in the clearings between buildings were women and old men. The old men had simply been killed and scalped, quickly, as if their feeble resistance had been meaningless. Many of the women had been stripped and mutilated before and after their deaths.

Here and there too lay an infant, head easily crushed, or a young boy, quickly hacked to death and thrown into the crackling inferno of a burning longhouse, his charred body later reemerging as the building burned to windblown ashes. One horror heaped itself upon another as Big Oak and his son forced themselves to look at the faces they had known for so long.

Sweet Berry, wife of the best hunter in the village, mother of three children, who was the cleverest craftsman of all the women in Tonowaugh. Sadakaniti, a mighty warrior in his early years, grown stiff and ill with age, but the best storyteller in the village, so patient with the children, who learned from him of the bow and arrow, for he was the last in the village to preserve the knowledge of stone arrowheads. Looking Glass, Little Oak's uncle, who had made toys for him out of cleverly carved pieces of driftwood. His clever right hand had been cut off.

They knew them all, and grieved for them all. And then, charred almost beyond recognition amid the ruins of his lodge, lay Little Oak's grandfather, Big Oak's father-in-law Kendee. His hands clutched the remains of an old Dutch musket. Much of him was badly burned, but Big Oak could see that he had been killed quickly by a bullet to the brain while he defended his burning home against the raiders.

Little Oak fell to his knees then, and wept as he had not wept since the death of his mother many years before. Men of the Ganonsyoni did not weep, but for the moment Little Oak was a weak, inconsolable child, aching with longing and pity for the old man who had filled the years of his childhood with love and reverence for his Seneca home and culture.

Big Oak took him by the shoulders. "Come, we must see if they left anybody alive. Then we must go to the stone house. They might come back. Come."

They found Little Oak's old friend Long Racer, unburned but missing his scalp, an ear, and several fingers. Near his body they found a bloodstained hatchet, gory evidence that he had not died without striking the enemy.

Long Racer was ten years older than Little Oak, but he had taken early notice of the boy, and when Big Oak was on the trail, had been like a big brother to Little Oak. He was as strong and fast as his name. Little Oak could not imagine Long Racer lying in the unnatural stillness a body assumes in death. If it was possible for his heart to grind into even greater pain, finding his friend Long Racer did the trick.

But the sight of his friend also reminded him that he *was* a Seneca. He let his heart grind, silently, inside himself, and they continued their search for the living.

Not far away from him was the body of a naked woman. She was headless.

The actual living area of the village covered a scant six acres, and the raiders didn't leave a single building un-

scathed. Even as the day's deluge continued to wash away
the horrible smell of this Seneca holocaust, they continued
to find more bodies. And the more they found, the more
they dreaded what they had yet to find. There was no
Kawia, no John Thompson, no Skoiyasi. In fact, with the
one exception, there were no warriors.

Big Oak's emotional paralysis quickly gave way to slow,
seething anger. On the north side of the village, barely visible through the wet gray mist of this autumn afternoon, he
could see a line of five tall stakes, with a dark figure hanging
from each of them. Instantly his mind constructed the sce-
nario and the devilish intellect that could have conceived
such a sadistic script.

Apparently, a large force had secretly surrounded the village and determined that most of its men were ranging far
away, hunting and trapping. They had attacked so swiftly
and bloodlessly that they must have convinced the meager
half-dozen braves present in the village that surrender
seemed a sensible decision.

When the raiders were satisfied that they had captured all
the braves in the village, they tied them to the stakes and
forced them to watch while they burned the village and
massacred the people, including the mothers, fathers, wives,
and children of the braves. As he and Little Oak slogged
through the rain, Big Oak did not know who he would find
dangling from the stakes, but he had no doubt *what* he
would find. After torturing their souls with the sight of
watching their loved ones killed and mutilated, the raiders
had tortured their bodies with the diabolical skill conceiv-
able only to imaginations of the warrior tribes of the Northeast.

The fires were kindled far enough from the stakes that
they would not burn the Seneca warriors to death too
quickly, but would roast them slowly, with indescribable
agony. As the outside skin cooked, the raiders used long
sticks to break the blistered skin and peel it. No matter how
brave these warriors, how reluctant to show their pain and

distress, these unfortunate men must have screamed enough to satisfy even the most fiendish of their tormentors.

Little Oak approached the stakes with unspeakable dread, and forced himself to look at men whose last day on earth must have been so ghastly that now heaven itself wept for them.

He knew them all, and liked them all, but he loved the last one in the row, young John Thompson, named for a Scotsman who had once saved the life of John's father. A year older than Little Oak, John and Little Oak had played together, hunted together, and were schooled together at the feet of the wise men of the village. John had learned English from Little Oak just by listening to him talk to his father, and had at one time talked of taking up the white man's way, but instead had become one of the promising young warriors of the village. And now he hung from a wooden stake, cooked almost beyond recognition, his hair so singed that no one had even bothered to take his scalp.

Next to John was an older warrior, Swerusse. Before he died, his torturers had presented him with a special treat, the severed head of his wife, which now lay at his feet but which, Big Oak was certain, they had waved triumphantly in his face as he suffered his death agonies.

The other three warriors must have also died in unimaginable pain and despair. How does one summon the courage to die bravely when you have just seen your loved ones murdered without mercy before your eyes? Even Big Oak, who had seen so much in his many years on the frontier, had never encountered such complete, uncompromising cruelty.

Tears rolled silently down Little Oak's cheeks as he stumbled away from the scene to the bank of the Genesee River, where he fell to his knees and wept in great sobs. His father called him back.

"We've got work to do here, son," he said gruffly, in a voice that did not sound like his. He had his knife out and was cutting the bonds that bound the bodies of the Seneca warriors to the stakes. "I need your help, son. I can't do this by myself."

Gently, they seized hold of each warrior and, with the greatest care, lowered them to the ground. They were cold, very cold, and their naked bodies seemed to have somehow absorbed huge quantities of water, making them heavy. Little Oak's will and his strength nearly failed him as they cut John Thompson down from his stake and brought him to earth. Little Oak closed his eyes and refused to view the details of what had been done to him. He had seen enough.

"It's the hardest work there is, but it's real man's work," Big Oak said. He looked into the boy's eyes.

Little Oak nodded. His father's eyes, too, held a deep film of tears. He had never before seen his father show this much emotion, and the sight made his body begin to shake once again. "Oh, Pa," he cried. "Who would do such a thing, and why?" Only with the greatest effort did he manage to bring himself under control. He looked away from his father and took one deep breath after another, determined to regain control of himself. But a great force behind his forehead continued to push tears out of the corners of his eyes. The pain was unbearable. He longed to set his emotions free.

But his father was right. In Tonowaugh that day, as the rain fell in drenching torrents, there was work to be done, real man's work.

Together, in the gray of a rainy, raw autumn afternoon, they began the long, difficult task of preparing a funeral for an entire Seneca village, their Seneca village.

# ❦16❧

THERE IS A PLACE ON THE GENESEE RIVER where the trees and bushes grow to within thirty feet of the bank. From the river, you could peer through that growth and see what looked like a pile of rock, but was in reality the home of Big Oak.

The home had no real front door, though there was a fake door facing away from the river. It was built into the stone facade of the house front. Entrance was through one of two tunnels that emerged from hillsides fifty feet on either side of the house.

The building was walled in solid stone, with windows on the top floor but only gun loops on the ground floor. Also on the second floor, all four sides had niches into which small swivel cannon might be mounted and fired from within. The stones were so cunningly fitted that the walls were too smooth to climb, and no trees grew within one hundred feet of the house except the thin layer of camouflage growth near the riverbank.

The growth was there primarily to hide the house from chance passing intruders when the occupants were not home, during which time the second-story windows were secured with shutters of thick, heavy old oak.

Riverstone, as the house had been called, had been built fifty years before by one Robert DeBerry, the youngest son of the Duke of Owneby. Young DeBerry was a spoiled, headstrong child of thirty-three who had achieved a reputation for picking quarrels with gentlemen who took exception to his bad manners. When the old duke died, Robert was sent to the new world by his brother, the new Duke of Owneby, because he was such an embarrassment to the family. The new duke had financed the expedition in the earnest hope that he would thereby rid himself forever of his obnoxious younger brother. His plan succeeded beyond his wildest expectations.

Robert came west with a half-dozen slaves, a secretary, an overseer, and five farming families, with the intention of founding a trading empire on the Genesee River. His family had somehow wangled a grant of several thousand acres, with the idea that the farming families and some of the slaves would make the little colony self-sufficient in food production, while the rest of the population would concern themselves with accumulating and shipping huge quantities of animal skins.

Heeding the warnings of veteran colonists back east, they had constructed a serviceable stockade, and Robert's overseer, an old army officer who had been cashiered from service for drunkenness even beyond the norm for army officers, had suggested the fortresslike home.

His besotted mind had conceived a brilliant, modest two-story country house that may well have resisted assault by the entire Iroquois confederacy. A superb engineer, the old lieutenant superintended the entire construction, and when it was completed, the local Senecas were so thoroughly awed that they relocated their village five miles down the river just to make sure they wouldn't have to deal with the strong house, as they called it.

But the house was not grand enough for Robert, so he built a pair of massive one-story wings, north and south, of unhewn logs. Inside those wings were massive halls for holding lavish balls, although dukes and duchesses to attend such galas were scarce on the Genesee River. The architectural effect was striking in a rustic way, but it nullified the military advantages of the original house. His overseer had been on a trip east in quest of trade goods when the wings were begun. When he returned and saw what was happening, he and Robert had such a row that the overseer quit on the spot and headed east. He never made it as far as Albany, and nobody ever found out what became of him.

In the meantime, Robert began to conduct trade negotiations with the local Indian trappers. Having no business sense at all, he gave the Indians more generous deals than did other traders, and was soon receiving trade delegations from among the Miami and Shawnee. Then he began to tighten his trading policies, which angered all the tribes, but still the Miami and Shawnee kept coming, because Robert was the only Englishman they knew with the courage, or the stupidity, to deal directly with them instead of going through the Iroquois, as everybody else did.

One morning he received a visit from Black Jaw, a chief from one of the Seneca villages up on Lake Ontario. Through a Cayuga interpreter, Black Jaw tried to explain that in the New York fur trade, the Iroquois were the middlemen between the whites and the "lesser" tribes that surrounded the Iroquois. It made things easier, explained Black Jaw. The Iroquois obtained furs that otherwise would have gone to the French, and they got them cheaply because their power over all these tribes allowed them to pay what Black Jaw called "fair prices" for the furs. Then the Iroquois could deal in volume with the English, strike a fair deal, and everybody would be happy, except, of course, the Hurons, Miamis, Shawnees, Delawares, and the rest.

The parley might have worked out well except, alas, the Cayuga interpreter had learned his English from the foulmouthed soldiers of the western garrisons. Consequently, the noble-blooded Robert found himself subjected to some astonishing rhetoric.

"Black Jaw say you one mighty big bassard, you Robberberry," which of course wasn't at all what Black Jaw meant to say. The Cayuga's creative translations from the English tongue back to the Seneca weren't very helpful either.

He didn't have to translate, however, when Robert turned red as a wild strawberry and told the chief that *he* was certainly not about to pay some naked Seneca savage three times as much as he would have to pay if he traded direct with the Miami, the Shawnee, or the Delaware.

Black Jaw laughed in Robert's face. "The Delaware are our children," he tried to explain. "You don't trade with the children, you trade with the fathers."

"Of all the blasted cheek," Robert said, which came through the Cayuga translator to Black Jaw as, "Your face is full of holes." This didn't sit well with Black Jaw, who had as a child survived a smallpox outbreak in his village, but had been ever after sensitive about his ravaged complexion.

Black Jaw suddenly became very quiet, and listened politely to the Cayuga's faithful translation of Robert's message that if the Seneca wanted to trade with him, they were welcome, but that in the future they would receive the same trade rates as the Delaware or Huron, and that they had better not make an effort to restrain his trade with those tribes or he and his men would sortie from the strong house and teach the Seneca a lesson that they would never forget.

Black Jaw smiled and had the Cayuga interpreter tell Robert that he understood the words, and that he would see to it that all his braves behaved as good Indians.

Two weeks later four canoes carrying twenty-five Seneca led by Black Jaw paddled down the Genesee in the dead of night. They carried their canoes up to the low-roofed, log-walled north wing of the strong house and leaned them up against the sides of the wings. Using the canoes as ladders, they scrambled silently up the rough, elm-bark sides, onto the roof. From there it was a simple matter to climb through the second-story windows into the main part of Riverstone and silently slit the throats of Robert, his half-breed concubine, their two children, and their three house servants.

They then burned the wooden wings and every outbuilding, and killed or captured most of Robert's wilderness community. Leaving the air thick with gray and black smoke from the flaming ruins of DeBerry Farms, they transported their captives up the river to their village. Some died in torment and some were adopted into the tribe, depending upon the will of the village, but none were ever heard from again.

The interior of Riverstone quickly fell into ruin, but the building itself remained strong and stalwart the day Big Oak first glimpsed it through the summer foliage. By that time the Seneca village had long been reestablished in the area, but although his father-in-law could tell him about the massacre of Robert DeBerry, none of them had ever wasted much of their time trying to figure out how to get into the house, much less lay claim to it. To them it was just an old ruin, not worth any effort on their part.

But Big Oak found the false front door fascinating, and it did not take him long to figure out that there must be carefully hidden, secret passages into the house. Once he found them, he laid claim to the house as his own, and none of his Seneca brothers cared to dispute the issue with him. So he fixed up the house and brought into it his baby son and his young wife Willow.

Living in a white man's house must not have agreed with Willow. Within the year she had sickened and died, leaving Big Oak to raise Thad alone, for nobody from the village cared to move in with them.

When the Watleys were home, the house could be comfortable, if not particularly roomy. Fireplaces heated each room of the four-room structure, and the thick stone held the heat within.

After months on the trail, exposed to the various whims of nature, the two would normally have appreciated their comfort and their hot meals during the three days they stayed, repairing their equipment, stockpiling food, and planning their next moves. But now, as they contemplated the ash-covered ruins of the village and the horrible deaths of the people closest to them on this earth, they found themselves in shock, heartbroken and depressed, and temporarily deprived of the will to act.

From the south-side windows of the house they could look out and in the distance make out the black remains of the lodges and the stumps of the stakes that Big Oak had chopped down after he had cut the final bonds of the martyred braves. They spent part of the following morning sitting on the windowsills, staring out at what was once Tonowaugh.

"I can't believe that I'll never see Kendee again," Thad said as they gazed at the ruined village. "When you weren't here, he was like my father."

"Then he was like your father most of the time. I was away more than I should have been." Big Oak smiled as his son's Seneca grandfather came alive in his memory. "You remember him as an old man. Even when I first knew him, soon after I came to the village, his days on the warpath were over. He had been wounded in a fight with the Huron, and he walked with a bad limp, but by then the stories about him were famous up and down the Genesee River."

This surprised Thad. His grandfather had told him many stories, but never about himself, and to the youngsters who prowled the riverbanks with Thad, he was just an old man who used to shoo them out of the longhouse when they disturbed his sleep.

"He taught me a whole lot but he was cranky too," he said to his father.

"He was cranky when that old wound hurt him worse than usual. I guess he never told you about his first warpath."

Thad shook his head.

"When he was young, Kendee stuck pretty close to home. He was smaller than most boys his age, and though he went on many hunts, his blood didn't get to boilin' like the other boys when some young man who would be a war chief ran around the village trying to raise a war party. So he got teased by most of the boys until he was almost your age, and then he suddenly got his growth, not just height, but muscles. Soon all of the boys near his age were proven warriors but him, and it didn't matter how many deer he came home with, to the rest of the boys he was just a woman.

"One night he announced to the whole village that he was going raiding. Half the young men in the village volunteered to go with him; they were all anxious to see how he would stand up on the warpath, and besides, it had been a boring spring.

"But he was gonna do it his way, he said. He was going on his own, and he was going to bring back a scalp from a strange tribe none of them had ever seen before.

"He left the village and headed south until he found the shores of the Monongahela. There he stumbled upon a Delaware canoe, stole it, and headed down the Ohio River then on down the Mississippi. Imagine, just Grampa alone on that big river, not knowin' where he was goin', just goin'. He said that every night he dreamed the same dream, and that dream had him paddlin' south on the river, and that when the dreams told him to drop the paddle and grab ahold of his rifle, that's when he'd know the time had come to find himself a brave to kill. It wasn't till he got to Chickasaw country that the dream changed. Now your grampa was no fool, and he had no wish to get the Chickasaws mad at him, but a deal was a deal, so he ditched the canoe and went out to hunt up a Chickasaw brave.

"But when he found one, he also found six more, and they all had their big ol' rifles pointed at his head. They got real excited when he signed to him that he came from the Ganonsyoni, because they had never burned a Ganonsyoni before and they'd heard they were pretty tough.

"While they were bringin' him back to their village they asked him what he was doing so far away from home, and he figured he might as well tell them the truth. So he told them that he was on his first warpath, but he added that his dreams told him his quest lay on the other side of the big river.

"Ah, that put everything in a different light. How could they not help this young brave on his first warpath? Obviously the Osage were just the folks to furnish the scalps for him to bring back north. Instead of entering the village as a sacrifice victim, he entered as a brother in arms.

"They had a feast that night, and in the morning seventeen of the mighty Chickasaw and your grampa crossed the Mississippi and headed west until they struck the Arkansas River, and then they followed the river until they ran into a war party of Osage huntin' scalps of their own.

"Now, there were a lot more Chickasaw than Osage, so the Osage pulled foot and some of them got away, but your grampa caught one and chopped him down like a tree, and five of the Chickasaws each got their man.

"Well, I don't know what that preacher taught you besides letters and numbers, but there's a whole lot of Osage in that country west of the Mississippi River, or at least that's what the Chickasaws told your grampa. So once their scalps were collected, they lit out for home, expecting at every turn to find themselves surrounded by the whole Osage nation. Kendee said that the Osage were known for cutting the heads off people, and nobody wanted any part of that so they didn't stop runnin' until they were back at the Mississippi.

"When they crossed the river, they had another big feast in their village, and then it turned out that though your grampa really did kill him an Osage, his new friends had to help him take the scalp because he was doing such a raggedy job himself.

"And now, back at the village, he decided to get up and make a speech. They'd all had a little whiskey, not much, just all there was left in the village, but there was enough to make him wanna get up and talk. So he talked to the whole village in Seneca they didn't understand, and sign that they did understand, and he told them how much he loved his

Chickasaw brothers and how good they'd been to him and how much he'd miss them and in the middle he started crying—the whiskey, you know—and then the braves who'd been with him started crying, and then most of the village was crying or at least snufflin'. The braves offered to give him the scalps they'd collected in the raid, and he tried to refuse, but they insisted and they got a little angry when he kept on refusin'. Then he remembered that he was supposed to have been roasted in the village, so he decided to accept, and the next day he pulled out his canoe and headed for home with a canoe load of gifts from the village plus the six scalps.

"You can only guess what his village thought when he came home from his first warpath loaded down with gifts from the Chickasaw plus six scalps of a kind they had never seen before in their lives. He tried to tell the truth, that only one of the scalps was his, but they'd heard that the Choctaw and Chickasaw never gave away the scalps they took. Now, Indians hate false modesty, so he came around to their way of thinkin' that, yes, he was a mighty warrior who left six Osage dead in the field with their bloody hair fluttering from his belt."

Little Oak found it hard to imagine his gentle Seneca grandfather making war on perfect strangers, but it was like him to turn his first warpath into a funny story. Years later, fighting the tribes in Canada, he showed his people the stuff he was really made of. But age takes the best out of all of us, he thought, and the ones who came and killed him along with the rest of the villagers had probably found him easy to defeat, even with a rifle in his hand. Only then, nursing the empty ache deep in his chest as he looked across a field at the ashes and the charred bark and timbers, did Little Oak remember how much he had been looking forward to telling his grandfather about *his* first warpath.

Big Oak, long conditioned to the hardships and tragedies of the frontier, did not allow this period of helpless mourning to last. "No more," he growled as the darkness began to

close in on the second day. "We have not the time to spend
on the dead or on our dead past." And they got to work,
while they waited for the survivors to return.

Their hearts were broken but their spirits were not. When
they were not doing their sit-down chores, they were out
hunting and scouting around the remains of the village.
There was no doubt that the raiding party consisted of more
than twenty individuals. Although they were unable to tell
who the raiders were, they were certain that not all of them
were Indians. The raiders had made no attempt to hide their
tracks, knowing that they had annihilated most of the village, and daring those who had escaped or been away during the massacre to follow and do battle with them.

The trail led straight north toward Lake Ontario. At first
Big Oak wondered why, if they were heading north, they
did not simply steal a few Seneca canoes and travel down
the Genesee River, but then he discovered that prior to the
attack the raiders had thoughtlessly destroyed all the canoes
in order to prevent fleeing Senecas from escaping on the
river.

One other fact aroused his curiosity. The head of the
wife, placed at the foot of the tortured warrior Swerusse,
suggested that at least one of the parties knew the Seneca
village, or perhaps one family in the village. Cold fury
gripped Big Oak. With great effort he pushed it away from
himself. Most Indian warriors are boasters. Sooner or later
they would find out who the culprits were, and it would be a
pleasure to snuff their lives out one at a time, with the
squeeze of a trigger, the twist of a knife, the slash of a
hatchet.

"You know," he suggested the second night, "we could
pick up their trail and follow them until they got careless,
then we could bloody them up some. Maybe free some prisoners if they have them. What do you think?"

It was as if a great rock had been lifted from Little Oak's
chest. "Just the two of us?"

"Whoever escaped won't be back for days, if ever. Every

hour we delay, the trail grows colder. We should leave in the morning.

"They've got a good head start, but if they have prisoners or wounded, they won't travel as fast as we can. We can gain a lot of time on them if we go by canoe the first day or two, then move east to strike their trail and follow them from there."

"Can we find them?" Little Oak asked.

"We have to take that chance. With all those men, and prisoners, and with them feeling mighty big about themselves, they should leave a pretty gaudy trail."

Very early the next morning they pulled out the elm-bark canoe they kept hidden in a cunning hollow they had dug half a mile downstream from the stone house. They performed some minor repairs on it, and by the time the sun had made its full red entrance above the eastern horizon, they had taken their first strokes down the Genesee toward Lake Ontario.

A full day of canoeing on a river is long, boring work. Big Oak and his son had long ago taken up an old chant to speed their boat swiftly over the water.

> Dip, dip, the paddles bright
> Flashing like silver

Straight as an arrow the canoe shot down the Genesee, the water churning past the sharp bow as the canoe sliced through it. They sang their chant again and again, sometimes together, sometimes in octave, but always so softly that it could not be heard above the wind as it hummed its way through the quivering bare branches of the trees.

And that wind was turning cold as the season wore on. Only the endless flexing of arms and shoulders kept the two woodsmen warm. As they chanted, their eyes were in constant motion, looking for life or suspicious movement along either shore, but hour after hour they saw only birds, squirrels, and a deer or two. The chant faded into silence now, as the wind died and the afternoon sun warmed their bodies, and both men thought about what might lie ahead for them.

Big Oak was wondering how far north he could go without overshooting the raiders. If they had rum or brandy, they might be making very slow time, but if they had Frenchmen with them, then their mission might take on a sense of purpose beyond the simple enjoyment of slaughter and torture.

Just as the sun was touching the western horizon, casting an orange glow across the winding, dappled waters of the Genesee, a lone canoer appeared around a distant bend. Hoping he had not been seen, the paddler ducked into a cove, pulled his canoe from the river and hid himself among the sycamores. But the eagle-eyed Little Oak urged his father to continue on. As they came abreast of the hidden canoe, a voice from the woods identified the stranger as their friend Skoiyasi. Quickly they pulled to shore and rushed out to meet him.

The Seneca brave spent little time on pleasantries.

"This morning," he said, "I almost fell into a nest of Caughnawaga and Abnaki. They were painted and they would have roasted me had they caught me, so I made myself disappear."

"Were there French with them?" Big Oak asked. "Did they have prisoners?"

"I am not crazy enough to stop and find out. I want to get back to Tonowaugh and round up a war party to teach them a lesson about where they skulk about."

Big Oak and his son gave Skoiyasi such strange looks that the eager warrior halted mid-sentence and asked, "What is it? You think I can't get a war party together? They'll follow me, and we'll give those loping dogs a beating too."

Big Oak shook his head. "You'll have to change your plans, Scoke. There is no Tonowaugh anymore."

The young brave's eyes widened. "What?"

Big Oak and Little Oak told the story as quickly as possible, without the most shocking details, for the dead included several of Skoiyasi's close relatives.

The warrior took in the story like a man watching death approach him on horseback, and made no sounds for a long time after Big Oak completed his narrative.

"I must continue home to take care of them," he cried, and began to tug at the prow of his canoe, to get it back in the water.

Big Oak put a big hand over the grip the Indian had on his canoe and shook his head. "What could be done for those poor people, Little Oak and I have done. There is nothing left to do but free the captives, if there are any, and send these devils back to the hell they came from as soon as we can."

They helped him pull his canoe ashore and hide it in the brush. Then they boarded Big Oak's canoe and continued their journey north until the last dim red-slanted light faded from the water. It was the young warrior's turn to mourn, and the way he mourned, deeply but silently, did honor to his training.

"Here," said Skoiyasi, after they had paddled for maybe three more miles. Wordlessly they hauled the canoe up the bank and into the deep brush that grew at the edge of the woods. When they were satisfied that it was invisible to river travelers, they found a clearing and made camp. They ate quickly and sparingly, pulled their blankets around them and slept immediately.

First light found Skoiyasi in a swift jog through the forest, followed by Little Oak, with Big Oak bringing up the rear. Little Oak watched his friend carefully, and when they faced each other, noted the lines of awful purpose that stretched across the other's forehead. All three of them knew that the raiding party was too big for them to attack by themselves, but they resolved to find out who they were, strike a blow, and vanish. This was classic Indian warfare, and they were determined to give the raiders a nasty taste of their own medicine.

They struck the trail of their quarry exactly where Skoiyasi had expected them to, and followed cautiously, although they suspected that the villains were by now several miles to the north. Little Oak was restless with anticipation. He could scarcely believe that they were already so near to the first people in his life that he had ever hated with all his heart and soul. How he thirsted for the taste of their blood. As yet they were faceless to him, and so as he walked he created faces and bodies and then destroyed them with his weapons.

Skoiyasi halted suddenly, peered intently down the trail, and then rushed forward, followed by Little Oak. Big Oak alone hung back, rifle at the ready, forever suspicious. In the middle of the trail was the body of a woman. Skoiyasi and Little Oak kneeled down beside her. She had been stripped, her breasts had been sliced, and her skull crushed. She had been left where they had killed her, surrounded by the dark of blood-soaked earth. Both immediately recognized her as Speaks Softly, the wife of a warrior who must have been out hunting at the time of the massacre.

She had two young children. She had probably been forced to watch while the raiders had killed both as swiftly and casually as they might crush a tick between their fingernails. She had been a good wife, a loving mother whose judgment and wisdom were respected by the villagers of Tonowaugh. She had lived a happy life until the day the fiends had sneaked into Tonowaugh and given her enough grief and pain to last her ten lifetimes.

What they saw of her convinced them that she had been captured, used, killed, and thrown away with the inhuman disregard that comes upon so many men in time of war. Quickly, angrily, they placed her in a dry creek bed, piled rocks on top of her, and proceeded on their way, more determined than ever to extract deadly vengeance.

They picked up the pace, and within three hours they could hear faint voices ahead of them. So arrogant and self-confident was this team of mighty slayers of women and old men that they did not seem the least bit concerned about who might hear them on their way back to Canada.

Now that they had made contact with the enemy, Big Oak took the lead and slowed the pace, even lengthened the gap between the two groups.

"The nighttime will be ours," he told his two cohorts confidently. They nodded with understanding.

The large raiding party made camp an hour before nightfall, began gathering wood, and by dark had several roaring campfires lighting up the forest. Big Oak, Little Oak and Skoiyasi lurked in the deep dark, well away from the camp. If the raiders suspected that they were being pursued, then all was lost. The three decided to scout the area and regroup in about an hour. Keen-eyed and stealthy, by the time they reassembled, they knew a good deal about their would-be prey.

There were twenty-three of them, they agreed, nineteen of them Indians and four of them *coureurs de bois*, French Canadians who lived like Indians, married Indians, and fought like Indians. In short, they were French versions of Big Oak and Little Oak, except, Big Oak reasoned, that they were the most vile, savage beasts in God's woodland.

The three agreed that the Indians were a mixture of Mingoes—Senecas and Cayugas who had split from the Longhouse—Caughnawagas, and Abnakis.

And there was one other piece of information, observed by a breathless Little Oak from his scout on the western flank of the camp. The raiders had taken not one prisoner, but two. One was the unfortunate Speaks Softly. The other, still very much alive, but frightened and badly bruised, was Thad's and Skoiyasi's friend from childhood, Kawia.

Skoiyasi reacted strongly to this news, clenching his jaw and squeezing the barrel of his rifle as if he would strangle it. His nostrils flared and his eyes narrowed to hostile slits. Unconsciously his hand reached for the hilt of his knife.

"Now listen," Big Oak said, staring hard at Skoiyasi. "If we pay attention to what we're doing, I believe that tonight we will free Kawia and cut us a bit of devil hair. Okay?"

The two younger men both grunted their assent. "One other thing." He looked at Little Oak. "Among these vile creatures creeps one who is of the Longhouse, not only a murderer, but a traitor. He is Red Hawk."

They lay in a depression a couple of hundred yards away from the camp and listened. There was brandy in the camp, enough to make the warriors sleepy, but not enough to make them wild. Gradually the voices grew less, and then they softened, and then, finally, there was complete silence, but for the occasional crackle of a damp twig in one of the dying fires.

The three men crept directly to where Kawia lay, bound hand and foot into the shape of a J. Little Oak moved in behind her and put a hand over her mouth, while Skoiyasi quickly cut her bonds, then motioned to her to lie still. She had three guards around her, and just a few yards away from this group lay Red Hawk, leaning against a tree but asleep nevertheless.

Their plan was to take the three bodyguards first, then proceed to dispatch the renegade Mohawk. Big Oak moved to the first one, a big, ugly Mingo with a crescent-shaped scar stretching from the left-hand corner of his mouth to his earlobe. He was sleeping on his back. Big Oak approached him from behind his head, pinned the shoulders beneath his knees and clapped his hand over the Mingo's face. The Mingo awoke just long enough for his eyes to widen with fear and twitch violently as he felt Big Oak's knife carve another crescent, this one across his neck. The blood spurted, and after a while the eyes closed.

Little Oak and Skoiyasi took no such chances. Their knives flashed and death followed quickly. While Big Oak crept toward Red Hawk, Little Oak and Skoiyasi helped Kawia to her feet and thought they had made it out of camp undetected, but just as they left the circle of light from the dwindling campfire, Red Hawk's keen sense of change awakened him.

Drowsily, he looked straight into the campfire, then looked away and listened while his night vision returned to him. Hearing nothing but the everlasting night winds of approaching winter, he started to wrap his blanket close around him when he noticed that the light of the campfire reflected off the eyes of one of the sleeping guards.

He was sleeping with his eyes wide open!

Red Hawk leaped to his feet and immediately saw that his prisoner was gone. He shouted an alarm that had the whole camp on its feet within seconds, scrambling for their arms. From the north the long rifle of Big Oak cracked, and a Caughnawaga staggered screaming into the central campfire.

Those who spotted the muzzle flash chased it, but they were chasing smoke. Skoiyasi, Little Oak, and Kawia were heading south while Big Oak, who in the woods at night could outrun any man, red or white, immediately put critical distance between himself and his sleepy, confused pursuers. They were shouting and colliding with each other in their confusion. A shot rang out and an Abnaki went down, holding his knee and moaning, fearing a wound fatal to his career, if not to his life.

Sensing rather than seeing the trees that barred his way, Big Oak zigzagged through the forest in a northerly direction, while his sleepy enemy, who never particularly cared for night fighting anyway, stumbled over roots and rocks in their vain effort to chase him down.

When Big Oak thought the distance between himself and his enemy might be sufficient, he ran in a wide arc that doubled back south in the direction of his cohorts and their freed prisoner.

As he had expected, her experiences of the past few days had slowed Kawia down considerably. Skoiyasi and Little Oak had to push and pull her along the trail. Her lungs were close to exploding and her breath came in weeping bursts.

Although the raiders were all heading north in pursuit of Big Oak, the two young men were taking no chances. But as the howls and screeches of the aroused enemy faded farther and farther into the distance, they slowed down to give Kawia a chance to catch her breath. They were still a considerable distance from the canoe when Big Oak caught up to them.

"They'll be on to us soon, I'm sure," said Big Oak. "Come on, Kawia, do your best!"

She nodded. The numbness from being bound tightly by rawhide thongs was gone now. Her legs were working better, and hope for escape among friends drew air into lungs where there had been none. They could hear pursuit now, but the canoe was close.

"Here!" Little Oak snapped, and the three men ran the canoe into the water.

The raiders nearest in the chase heard the splash and exclaimed warnings to their associates. Kawia lay in the bottom of the canoe, gasping desperately for a breath of air, while the three paddlers cleaved the water with powerful strokes. They knew that if they paddled to the middle of the river, they would present easy targets to the onshore marksmen, so they shot up the river around the bend and close to the shore, hoping they could outdistance their chasers.

They almost did.

One agile Mingo, quicker, cleverer, and bolder than his friends, had made it down to the shore more than a hundred yards ahead of the rest, and as he ran, he spotted the canoe just below the bank where he ran. A quick jump and a kick, and he knew he had a good chance of upsetting the canoe, rendering the occupants as good as dead. But he was not thinking, he was reacting, and so as he jumped he gave a mighty whoop.

Big Oak was watching the shore anyway. He saw the Mingo appear and then he saw the Mingo jump, and it was not a great feat for him to smash the Mingo's face with the blade of his paddle. The Mingo, stunned but still conscious, began to thrash and rock the canoe. A blow from the butt of Skoiyasi's paddle and the Mingo lay still at the bottom of their boat.

The three men now paddled for all they were worth, first along the shore, and then, when they felt they had opened a decent interval between themselves and their enemy, toward the middle of the river, where the going was safer. They knew that even paddling upstream they could outdistance men running through the underbrush in the dark of night. After a while they moved close to the opposite shore, where they could paddle at a steady pace, knowing they would be virtually invisible against the dark forest background.

"He still lives," Kawia said in a flat voice.

"Can you paddle?" Skoiyasi asked, handing her his paddle. She nodded and took it.

Skoiyasi and Little Oak moved to the unconscious Indian at the center of the canoe, while Kawia paddled in the bow and Big Oak kept up his powerful stroke from the stern.

Little Oak found the Mingo's knife and threw it overboard, then positioned himself on the Mingo's chest, his knees pinning the man's shoulders against the thin hull of the canoe. From behind the Mingo's head Skoiyasi reached into the river, then threw a handful of water on the Mingo's bloody face.

His eyes opened, took in his predicament, and then his body tensed as he steeled himself for the ordeal he knew was about to come.

"Can you hear me?" Skoiyasi asked.

"I hear you." He was a Seneca-speaking Mingo.

"Why did you come to our village?"

"Village? There is no village. Just a dung heap for pigs to root in," the Mingo spat.

Calmly, Skoiyasi stuck his knife behind the left ear of the Mingo, sliced it off, and flipped it into the night. It landed in the river with a soft splash. He did the same to the right ear and handed it to Kawia, who flung it away from her.

"Can you hear my words better now? Why would you kill the women and children of your brothers?"

"Filthy lovers of the English. We killed them with ease. They died screaming." In spite of his desire to be brave and arrogant, he then ceased his bold speech. In the dark the Mingo could see the deep hatred in Skoiyasi's eyes.

Skoiyasi stepped over Little Oak and made a slash in the Mingo's abdomen. He pulled out a length of intestine and let it trail in the river. The Mingo gritted his teeth. In spite of himself, breathy grunts of pain escaped from deep within his throat. And yet he did not cry out.

"Who are the French dogs who led this raid?"

"Was it your wife or your mother that I took? I will tell you that they enjoyed it, even as I killed them after I finished," he gasped.

Skoiyasi made his way back up to the Mingo's head, then carved a circle deep into his shaved scalp. Skoiyasi's strong hand grabbed the scalp lock in an iron grip and tore the scalp free. The Mingo gave a distressed "aahhh," but still he did not scream.

"You no longer have a scalp. You are of no further use to us," Skoiyasi observed. "How do you feel about that?"

"I am ready to die if you are ready to kill me," said the Mingo.

"Kill you? We don't have to kill you. Look at you. You are weak as a rabbit. You cannot hurt anybody anymore. Take a breath. Feel how sweet the air is as it fills your chest. There are very few breaths like that left for you. Each breath hurts, doesn't it? We are your enemy, we look down at you and laugh at you. Watch me breathe. I have many breaths left, sweet, easy breaths. You have few left, and they come hard, do they not? I can see the stars. They are beautiful on the river at night. Can you see them, my Mingo brother? You cannot.

"I have years of life left. I will fight. I will hunt the deer. I will love. You have but a few bitter moments left. You have no scalp. You are nothing."

Skoiyasi and Little Oak almost but not quite swamped the canoe as they threw the still living Mingo overboard and let him drift home to his creator. Then Skoiyasi reached into the river and let it wash the gore from their hands.

They decided to paddle in shifts. Kawia and Skoiyasi slept, while for three hours the powerful strokes of father and son put more distance between themselves and the raiders; unnecessary distance. Unknown to the paddlers, the French had given up the chase and returned to camp to finish their night's sleep—this time with more watchful guards—and resume their march north to the shores of Lake Ontario. When several of the Caughnawaga and Red Hawk insisted that they must avenge their losses by catching their unknown assailants and putting them to a long, slow, painful death, LeJeune reminded them that their attackers had only a dead village to return home to, and what could be more painful than that?

That seemed to mollify the Caughnawagas. Only the bitter Red Hawk remained adamant, but the French pointed out that there were battles to fight and English to kill. Red Hawk wrapped his blanket around him, sank to the ground and sulked. But he did not sleep long, for his dreams were haunted by Mingoes with wide-open, stone-dead eyes.

# ❧17❧

"**I** DO NOT BELIEVE THAT THERE WILL BE MUCH fighting before spring," Big Oak told his son and their friends.

The past two weeks had been terribly painful. Following the rescue of Kawia, they had made it back to Tonowaugh and found several braves returned from hunting trips only to discover that their families had been blotted from the earth by marauders.

Two days later a family that had been visiting relatives in a distant village had come home to the desolate scene. Every few days another family or trapper or group of hunters came home to find there was no longer a home or a village. Each return brought a fresh outbreak of grief among both the new returnees and those who had been back for a while. Big Oak and Little Oak had begun to dread each return, with the fresh scabs of each emotion to rub raw and bleed again.

Then came the few, the pitifully few, who for one reason or another had been able to flee the scene when the raiders first appeared. Perhaps they had not liked the look of them when they had entered the village. Or maybe they were far enough away from the center of the village that the raiders had missed them when they had rounded up the villagers and begun their killing. When they heard the commotion and saw the slaughter taking place, they had fled to the nearest villages, which in all cases were many miles away. When they returned, some came with armed friends and relatives in search of revenge. Some of them took as long as three weeks to venture back, and they did so still round-eyed with fear and dread.

As for Kawia, with the ordeal of escape and captivity behind her, she now had time to feel the crushing pain of loss. Suddenly she was an orphan, almost a woman, but with no one there to teach her how to be a woman. Both Little Oak and Skoiyasi were tender and solicitous, but their awkward male sympathy held little satisfaction for her.

As the dark, gloomy winter settled in on the banks of the Genesee, she talked very little. Mostly she sat in the kitchen of the stone house and stared at the huge fire that constantly roared in the kitchen fireplace. It was December now, and the snow was piling up outside the cozy home with the four small low-ceilinged rooms, two on each level. The population of the village, which had once totaled more than a hundred, now consisted of ten men, eight women, and eleven children. The men decided to move the location of the village nearer the stone house. There were some objections from those who had seen too much of the Frenchmen and did not want to be near anything that made them think of white men, but Skoiyasi insisted. The men immediately began constructing a longhouse to shelter the returnees.

They then split their work force in two, with some out hunting and fishing to stockpile food for the little village, and others building a small stockade that incorporated both the longhouse and the stone house into their walls. Over the years Big Oak had cleared much of the area around his house to create clear fields of fire in the event of attack. The villagers extended those fields, stockpiling trunks for the stockade and leaving the smaller wood to dry for their hearth fires. They dug a narrow ditch around the stone house and the longhouse and raised the stockade wall one log at a time, using hatchets to flatten the sides of the logs so they would fit together securely. When the walls were completed, they built a catwalk near the top so the men could defend it from within. It was a simple affair, without blockhouses, but all the men felt it was sufficient for the time being. In the event that an enemy penetrated the stockade, everybody would retreat to the stone house, which, with just a few determined defenders, could stand up to anything but heavy artillery.

Building the stockade with such a small number of men available to do the work would take time, but most of the men agreed that it would be worth the effort. Then, about a month after the massacre, when the ground was covered with snow, one of the hunters came running along the riverbank path, to announce the approach of a strange war party.

"Here we go again," Big Oak grouched to his son as he buried his ax deep into a nine-inch poplar tree. "Everybody in the stone house!" They all ran for the entrance farthest from the river, for only Big Oak and his son knew about the other entrance. The women, who had been engaged in smoking fish, deer, and other creatures hunted down by the men, streamed toward the stone house with their children in tow. Men took their positions by the loopholes on the first floor and the shuttered windows on the second. The women and older children gathered all the spare firearms and began loading them.

Before long they had completed all their essential chores and now had nothing to do but await the enemy.

"There were about ten of them," said the hunter. "They were not painted for war but they were all well-armed."

"Only ten!" Skoiyasi snorted. "Let us ambush them and wipe them out."

The idea won instant support among most of the men, but not the women. Big Oak raised a hand.

"We do not know whether they are friend or enemy. But even if they are enemy, we cannot afford to meet them in open battle. We cannot afford to lose five men, or three men or one. Let them attack us here. We are secure."

"We would be secure if the stockade were completed, but it is not," said one of the men.

"Their bullets cannot enter our stone walls, and their fire arrows cannot harm our slate roof," Big Oak insisted. "We have swivel cannon and plenty of powder and shot. We have food for two weeks. Let them come."

They were not long in coming. Less than one hour after the hunter sounded his alarm, Little Oak, from his lair on the second floor, could see a file of Indians strung out twenty feet apart, snowshoeing over the snow-covered ice of the Genesee.

"They're here," he said quietly to his father, and aimed a swivel gun filled with lead shot in the direction of the leader.

He watched closely as the leader approached the spot where the river ran by the stone house. Big Oak peered down intently as he drew closer, and almost immediately recognized him, even though he was wrapped in layers of skins and blankets.

"Son of Gingego," he called out.

The man froze in his tracks, turned his head toward the voice and found himself staring into the muzzle of a swivel gun little more than a hundred feet away. If it pleased the gunner, Louis, the son of Gingego, was a dead man.

"Who calls out from behind stone walls?" Louis demanded.

"Big Oak," came the answer, and Louis's shoulders relaxed just a touch.

"Is this your village?" Louis asked, remembering his father's tales about Big Oak's home down on the Genesee.

"It was, before the murderous Mingoes and Caughnawagas fell upon the defenseless ones and wiped out most of the people."

Louis nodded, as if he had already heard of the massacre. "We are going home. We mean no harm to your people. May I see you?"

"My people are concerned that you might be the enemy.

Lead your braves around to the front of the stone house.
There you will see a longhouse. Have your men, all of them,
wait in front of the stone house. You hand your weapons to
one of your men and enter the longhouse. Little Oak and I
will meet you there."

"Why should I trust you and your son, alone and unarmed
in the longhouse?"

"Because your father trusted us and we never let him
down, and this you know."

"But I am my father's son. Why do you not trust me?"

"Because we know that you and your father were not
close."

"Uhh." Louis nodded again. "If he were alive today," he
said with emotion, "we would be close. I have learned much
since his death."

"For most fathers and sons, it is always too late. Give up
your rifle but keep your other weapons. We will meet you in
the longhouse."

Big Oak and Little Oak hurried down the stairs and out
the passage that led away from the river. By the time Louis
and his band of Mohawks had climbed the bank and found
their way to the front of the house, Big Oak had stirred the
embers of a longhouse hearth into a fire.

At the end of the longhouse a deerhide flap was pulled
open and daylight revealed the silhouette of a man. Like his
father, Louis was small, with stringy muscles, but possessing
a wiry toughness that promised endurance if not swift action.

Cautiously, Louis walked toward the fire, which was still
too low to reveal the faces of the two seated occupants to a
man unused to the darkness in the longhouse. Big Oak
tossed a handful of dry twigs on the fire. They blazed up,
throwing some light on the faces of the trader and his son.

"Ah," Louis exclaimed, seating himself across the fire from
his hosts. He packed his pipe with kinnikinick and lit it with
the glowing end of a twig.

"I must talk to you, Big Oak."

"I am listening," Big Oak answered in a voice neither warm nor cold, merely mildly interested, as he loaded and lit his own pipe.

"My father told me you were wise. I did not believe him, just as I did not believe in many things he believed." He paused for a moment, uncertain how to go on. "We have been to see Obwondiyag—the Ottawa chief whites call Pontiac. We went to see him because we thought he was strong enough to unite the red people to defeat the white people."

Big Oak nodded. "I have heard the same."

"But it is not so. He fights for the French. The Ottawa, Shawnee, Delaware, Huron—many others, wish to tear down the Longhouse, and they will give their souls to the French to do it. Not only your village has been destroyed. The French have led these Indians to attack other English and Iroquois places. They have told them to kill the women and children of the Ganonsyoni and sow misery everywhere there are English or English allies.

"I have always hated the English. They are not like the French, who are few, and who live with the Indians and marry them. The English are many and eat up the land. No man can own the land. Only the Master of Life can own the land."

"And yet the Longhouse shares the Mohawk Valley with no other nation," Big Oak replied.

"It is *our* land. We paid for it with our blood. Only blood can pay for land, not trinkets, or rifles, or rum."

"You are right, Louis, and in the end only English blood will purchase the land for the English."

"But it is wrong, Big Oak."

"I too wish it were otherwise, son of my friend. Louis, Gingego did not fight for the English because he loved them. He fought for them because he knew the white men were powerful, and that of them all, only William Johnson treated them fairly. Like your great chief, Tiyanoga, your father fought for Johnson."

"If we fight for the English, will they not someday take all our land?"

"I believe they will. But if you do not fight for the English, they will annihilate your people."

"Suppose we fought with the French, as Obwondiyag would have us do?"

"You have made too many enemies among the other tribes. You nearly wiped out the Huron, you made war on the Attiwondaronk, and the Tionontat, and the Erie, all of your own blood, and then the Delaware, until the cry, 'The Iroquois are coming!' chilled the blood of their mightiest braves. Instead of making allies, the Iroquois made enemies of all their neighbors."

"We are great warriors."

"The Iroquois may remember great victories. What the Huron and the Delaware and the Shawnee and the Tobacco People remember are the great defeats: burned villages, kidnapped women, and tortured warriors."

"It was our right!"

"They don't think so."

"Delaware? Shawnee? Pah! We tell them where to live and what to eat."

"But when they all come together? When they have good weapons? The French have no heart. If they win, they will watch and let the other tribes have their way with you."

"We can defeat them all."

"Maybe you can, but if the Indians had a great war, the French, or the English, would stand by until there was almost nothing left, then they would pick up your pieces and send you north to where there is forever snow."

"You say that if the French win, then we will lose, and if the English win, then we will lose. Then suppose we all got together against the whites, could we win?"

Big Oak shrugged his shoulders. "You will never get together. You have been killing each other for too long. The hate runs so deep that you cannot even learn to hate the white man as much as you hate the Abnaki."

"You are of the Longhouse, Big Oak. What would you do to save your brothers?"

"I would fight for the English and hope for honest men like Johnson to triumph over the corrupt Englishmen who have been so bad to you over the years."

Louis's face twisted in frustration. "But we are the Ganiengehaka! All the other Indians run when we sneeze. And the whites in the settlements soil their clothes when they hear our battle cry. How can such soft people defeat us?"

"Because when they have to be hard, they can be very hard people. They have better weapons, and they know how to use them better. And there are one hundred of them for every one of you."

"With furs we can buy better weapons."

"Son of the wise and loved Gingego, let me speak in words you will understand. The weapons you buy are not the best, and even when they are good, they do not stay good because among you nobody knows how to take care of them. You once had great arrowmakers who all their lives worked at the craft of making fine arrowheads of flint, fastening them to straight shafts and fletching them with the finest of feathers. And yet today nobody steps forward to learn the craft of repairing broken rifles, replacing worn barrels, and knapping flints so they will spark every time."

"That is white man's work!" Louis spat, with grand contempt.

"White men are maybe not so proud as Indians. You may be great warriors, caring much for honor and glory, but we care more for victory. To you there is victory and there is glory. To the smart white men, the ones who are chiefs and rich men, victory, and the wealth it brings, are the only glory. You may spit on such ideas, but they make the white man victorious, again and again.

"My son here has fought only one battle in his life, but give you each a rifle and put two hundred yards between you, and he will take you as easily as he takes the doe.

"He is not better than you, or braver than you, or more of a man than you. But when a better rifle is made, he, not you, will have it. And he will know how to care for it and make it speak the truth for him. In a new world, the rifle speaks louder than the strong arm and the tomahawk."

"The tomahawk spoke well for Obwondiyag down on the Monongahela."

"The English general did not know how to fight in the woods. But the English will learn. They are good learners, and that makes them the most powerful nation in the world, even though they are not the best fighters in the world. And when they have learned, the French and their allies will pay." Now there was silence, both men having spoken their minds. Then Big Oak made one last speech.

"I am sorry we have never talked before. You are a worthy son of Gingego. The Ganiengehaka are old allies of the English, and ancient enemies of those who fight on the side of the French. We—you and I—cannot choose sides. Our sides have been chosen for us."

"And Red Hawk has chosen his side!" an angry Louis hissed.

"Ah, I thought you might speak his name. He is a traitor to his people, but he is not a Caughnawaga. He is a man without a people. He destroyed this village—so many of the Turtle Clan in this village, and he a member of the Turtle Clan. He will perish. You know he was with those who killed your father."

Louis's face betrayed frank astonishment. "I have heard that this was so, but I did not see it, so I did not believe it. Friend of my father, you would not lie to me about this."

"I would not lie to you about this or anything else," Big Oak said, tapping his heart with his fist. "I am sorry. The Iroquois are a great people. If the white man had stayed home, the Iroquois might be a great people forever. But the white man did not stay home, and the Indians will never unite against him. You know that, don't you?"

Louis agreed, but said nothing.

"Louis, there is a thing that I do not understand. Red Hawk is truly a devil, but what of those who were with him? In all my years of fighting with the Indians and against them, I have never seen anything as cruel as the thing that they did to the people of my village."

Louis looked at his father's friend and nodded.

"What is happening to the Iroquois?"

Louis took a deep breath and hesitated, choosing his words carefully:

"You know, my brother, that the Ganonsyoni have conquered many tribes, even down to the big mountains in the south. There the tribes are like animals. They love the screams of pain that come from their enemies. To them it is like the sweetest music of the flute.

"The Ganonsyoni have never loved torture in that way. When we tortured a captive, we respected him. We did not do it to entertain ourselves. Let me tell you a story that my father once told me."

Big Oak repacked his pipe and both he and Thad sat back to listen. Big Oak loved stories of the Iroquois tradition, and he loved the sound of Louis's voice, as he had once loved the sound of Gingego's voice.

"Many moons ago the Huron were a mighty people, with so many braves even the white man could not have counted them. But they were no match for the Ganonsyoni. One Iroquois warrior was worth ten Huron—or ten of any people, for that matter. And so we conquered them, in battle after battle, until they were but a small people, and a small people they are still.

"But our wars were bitter. We lost many brave men fighting them, and all the other people we conquered. One night a great warrior brought in a prisoner named Anaysa. Anaysa had fought bravely and would have died in battle but his right arm had been hacked by a tomahawk and made useless. The warrior gave his prisoner over to the village chief, Tsontat, who had lost his son in battle some time before.

"Tsontat looked at Anaysa and saw a young man strong

enough and brave enough to take the place of his son in his wife's longhouse. But then he looked at the young Huron's right arm and saw that it hung by his side, bloody and useless.

" 'I am sorry,' he told the Huron. 'I wish I could make you my son, but you will never use that arm again. Tomorrow night you must die. I hope you will honor us with your courage.'

"That night the women in Tsontat's family took the greatest care of his injured arm, easing the pain with soothing herbs and his hunger with fresh venison. In the morning they washed him, dressed his hair, and served him the finest foods. People from around the village came by to visit him and mourn for him. They told him how they wished he could be a part of them and that they hoped he would bear his sufferings well.

"When the sun reached the top of the sky, they tied him to the stake, and throughout the day, long into the dark hours, they burned him with fire. He was a strong man, with a great heart, and it took him a very long time to die. Sometimes, when his eyes closed and his head hung, they would take away the fire, soothe his face with cool water and give him water to drink to slake his thirst. Then, when he was feeling better he would talk to the village, and tell them of the Iroquois captives who had been adopted into his Huron village—this one brought home the biggest buck in the north woods, that one came home from a raid with two Mississaugi scalps. And the people were kind to him, spoke to him as their son and their brother, spoke to him with love.

"The next time they let him rest, he told them of a dream he had, of a place where great fish swam in a lake so clear you could see their shapes far out into the water. So tame were they that all you needed to do to catch them was walk out to them and take them with your hands.

"And then, when his great heart finally ceased to beat, there was a great sadness in the village, but they were proud of his courage, and they divided him up and ate him, because he was so brave."

Big Oak and Thad had sat, motionless, fascinated by the tale. Louis and Big Oak continued to smoke, while Thad sat still and cross-legged, watching both.

"But because of the white man, things began to change. In a white man's war, one must kill or die. There is not much honor left in war. I have not heard of such a slaughter before among the Iroquois like this one here. My father once said he thought we were becoming too much like the Cherokee." He stopped, suddenly, as if he had realized that he had said too much, and let the white man and his son in too close. "Maybe he was right. . . ." His voice trailed off. Big Oak nodded his head and for a while sat still and puffed silently on his pipe.

"Will your brother and his wife take good care of your mother?" he asked after a long silence.

"Hah! It will be the other way around. My mother takes care of the village. Iroquois women are strong and brave. That is why they raise strong and brave Iroquois men. Do not worry about my mother. She will be all right with my brother and his family."

"Then stay the winter with us. In the spring I will bring you north, and together we will kill the French and their 'praying Indians.'"

"We will see. We have been on the trail too long, and are weary. We will stay for a while. Then we must return to the Te-non-an-at-che. When there is war, it is bad to stay away from the castle for too long."

Now the work on the stockade accelerated, and half of Louis's Mohawk band had to join the other hunters in the field, for there were more mouths to feed. Game was not easy to come by, so numerous small birds, squirrels, and other less relished creatures joined the deer in the huge stew pot that always bubbled in the kitchen of the stone house.

Slowly, as winter continued to deepen, a sense of survival lifted spirits within the new stockade.

The sole exception was Kawia, who had begun to talk to Little Oak and Skoiyasi, but who otherwise kept aloof and had no desire to smile.

Gradually the story came out of her. While the Frenchmen had stayed in the woods, half of the Mingoes and Caughnawaga had walked into the village and partaken of the hospitality Iroquois villages usually extend to their brothers. To the villagers of Tonowaugh, these Indians were merely Senecas and Mohawks together for a winter hunt. While they ate in the village's most affluent longhouse, the visitors learned that all the warriors but six were out hunting.

In the spirit of friendship, the Mohawk Red Hawk expressed his desire to meet his Seneca warrior brothers, but when they were ushered into their presence, the raiders pulled weapons on them and told them their brother Warraghiyagey demanded their attendance at a coming battle. The Seneca warriors objected, but their weapons were not at hand so they submitted to being bound and led outside.

Seeing that Red Hawk had accomplished his goal, the French and the rest of the Indians had dashed into the village, rounded up all the villagers, and kept their weapons pointed at them while the five—for one of the warriors had hidden himself—were tied to the stake. The attack had been well planned. There was no arguing among the Indian raiders or between the Indians and the Frenchmen, until the short Frenchman, who was the one with the biggest mouth, gave an order in French to one of the warriors.

The warrior told the Frenchman that what he wanted was wrong, that he wasn't going to do it, but then Red Hawk fixed his vicious eye on the warrior and said something in great anger. The warrior took a step back and his proud features seemed to shrink before the eyes of the villagers.

As Kawia told her story, the dull gray went out of her eyes, replaced by a white-hot fury. It was only then, Big

Oak realized, that she had lost the depressing, lingering fear
that the raiders would return and finish the job they had
begun on her, and that she would have to see the rest of her
village tortured and killed before her eyes.

The raiders, she continued, then formed a circle around
the villagers and ran wild among them, clubbing and stab-
bing and shooting the old men first, then the women and
children as they ran in panic, attempting to break through
the circle. But those few who did were pursued by the
French bush lopers, who chased them back into the circle.
One after another the villagers were struck down, or shot
down. Very few had weapons handy with which to defend
themselves. Kawia was certain her time had come, but the
ugly little Frenchman took hold of her and carried her away
before the last of the villagers were killed.

The streets of Tonowaugh were as they were after a rainstorm, except that the puddles were the blood of the villagers, which flowed too freely to be absorbed even by the
earth itself.

Soon the only villagers left alive were the five horrified
men tied to their stakes and a few of the more attractive
women. Egged on by the French, and French brandy, the
raiders took their turns with the women, and let the French
have their turn, and then, as each woman had served her
purpose, she was clubbed to death and scalped, and then on
they went to the next.

Now the only Senecas left alive in the village besides the
five warriors about to be martyred were Kawia and Speaks
Softly. They had been taken by the raiders for use on the
trail, but first they were to be made to watch the torture and
burning of the five braves.

Kawia had seen her mother and younger sister die quick
deaths at the hands of the blood-maddened avengers. As she
watched the death of her lifelong friend and playmate, John
Thompson, she vowed to keep her mind alive long enough
to find her own vengeance. This valiant, gallant young man,
how they made him scream and beg for mercy, and how

they laughed at him and called him a woman because he could not bear their inhumanities in silence. Kawia said she could no longer see in her mind the terrible things they had done to him, but she could still hear his screams. She would always hear his screams. As she told her story, she closed her eyes and tears began to squeeze out of them in big drops.

"You knew John Thompson. In the village he was a gentle man, and when things went bad for him, he never complained. On the trail he was a brave man, you told me so many times, Skoiyasi. On the last day of his life, the other braves suffered their tortures without a sound. Even Swerusse—oh, oh, poor Swerusse. He looked into the face of his wife and told her she had been a good wife and he was glad she did not have to see him like this. What a brave man he was.

"But John Thompson—our friend John Thompson could not bear the pain, and when he begged for his death, it was that devil Mohawk who tore open his blisters with a burning oak branch." Now that she had opened the door to the memories she had held back, she began to weep uncontrollably, in great, convulsive sobs. "And that spawn of a thousand demons, that Red Hawk, he said, 'Did we kill your mother back there?' And John Thompson said yes. Then Red Hawk said, 'If you will tell us that it made your heart feel good to see your mother die, then we will stop your torment.'

"John said nothing. Red Hawk dragged his burning branch across John Thompson's blistered body. 'Say it!' he screamed above John Thompson's screams. 'Say it!'"

As Little Oak listened, he turned away so neither his father nor Skoiyasi could see his tears. He could not stand to think about the last two hours of his closest friend's life.

Skoiyasi, on the other hand, listened in impassive silence, betraying his emotions only by the fierce glint in his eyes. John Thompson had been his friend too, and Skoiyasi was like a banker, adding up the debits, totaling them, assessing penalties and arriving at a price to be collected.

A wild look of anguish took control of Kawia's face. "And finally," she cried, "he said it!

"And that evil demon Red Hawk dragged the burning stick across John Thompson's body and put his face up to his and shouted, above John Thompson's screams, 'Say it again, you miserable woman!'

"And John Thompson said it again, and again, and again, until Red Hawk finally silenced him with his tomahawk." And she collapsed into uncontrollable hysteria.

Little Oak took hold of her and held her while, gradually, her hysteria subsided into great choking sobs, then finally into an unnatural calm.

On the trail, Kawia went on, she had been raped five times, mostly by the *coureurs de bois*. She remembered each and every face that hovered over her as they released themselves. She also took note of the laughing, evil faces that seemed to get such pleasure out of witnessing the rapes.

When Speaks Softly finally went mad in the midst of one of these orgies, Red Hawk had killed her quickly and left her on the trail. Had he committed an act of mercy, or did he want to end her agonized screeching, just in case there were enemies in the woods? Neither Big Oak nor Little Oak cared.

"I want that one!" she hissed as she completed her narrative. "He was the worst of all of them. They were all animals, but that Red Hawk, he was the devil who made men trust, and then made them watch their people suffer and perish, before they were tortured."

Little Oak remembered Red Hawk on the trail to the Mohawk village, boasting in detail about what he had done to Big Oak. He had never met a man like him before—so bitter, so completely evil. Nor had Skoiyasi, and the two made each other swear that Red Hawk's death, when it came, would be slow and so painful that he would promise them anything, no matter how humiliating, just to release him from his agonies.

As February turned to March and the endless Genesee winter marched on, Kawia found the will to carry on. She allowed herself to take part in excursions with Skoiyasi and Little Oak, skating on the river, fighting three-way snowball wars, tobogganing in the nearby hills. Sometimes the three of them went together, other times she went with either Little Oak or Skoiyasi. Big Oak smiled to see her spending her days active again instead of staring into the fire for days on end, as she had done for weeks and weeks after the massacre.

But he was anxious too. It was obvious that both Skoiyasi and Little Oak cared for Kawia. One of them was bound to be disappointed.

## ❧18❧

THE PEOPLE ON THE NEW YORK FRONTIER IN 1756, red and white, for the most part lived lives that the philosopher Thomas Hobbes would have described as "poor, nasty, brutish, and short." War, disease, malnutrition, childbirth, and accidents took a fearsome toll, but those who survived were tough and resilient, willing to trade the sorrows of the past for the hope of the future.

And so, as their ghastly autumn and heartbreaking winter mellowed toward springtime, the residents of the new reduced village of Tonowaugh took heart and went on with their lives. Here and there they welcomed back old friends who had either been visiting another village at the time of the massacre or had somehow avoided capture. As the news of the massacre spread among the Seneca villages, people came to visit their surviving friends in Tonowaugh.

Some of those who had escaped had fled in such complete panic that they didn't stop fleeing until they either perished in the woods or found sanctuary miles away. None of them dared return until they had news that convinced them there was still a village to go home to. Others never returned at all.

The population of the village was now close to fifty. Young men were paying attention to young women, the children were dreaming of swimming again in the Genesee, and the visiting Mohawks were giving a lot of thought to hunting Caughnawaga scalps once the weather turned warm.

Big Oak and his son had spent a lot of time with Louis and his closest friend, Tall Bear, during the weeks the Mohawks had stayed at Tonowaugh. It turned out that their trip west had not been merely a jaunt to visit Pontiac and contemplate alliances. The sachems in Onondaga had decided that their children, the Delaware, had been behaving too independently of late, and had sent Louis and his associates south as chastisers, to persuade their charges to improve their conduct.

"These Delaware, these 'only real men,' as they like to call themselves, have been spending too much time with the Ottawa and the Shawnee. They suddenly think that they have grown up, and we had to take their sugar away from them," Louis told Big Oak as they sat in the stone house kitchen by the big warm hearth fire, the day before they were scheduled to begin their journey home to the valley of the River Flowing Through Mountains.

"What did you do?"

"We didn't do anything like this, if that's what you are thinking," Louis said, pointing out the windows that looked south toward the blackened wood ends that poked out through the snow, headstones for a murdered village. "We *did* like this." Tall Bear smiled, pointing in the same direction. "Except we let the Delaware leave their little village before we burned it. We told them to go to their Shawnee friends for the winter. If they are such good friends, then they will keep you until the snow leaves. Then you can build your new village far enough away from the Shawnee that they will not teach you to think bad things about your parents, the Iroquois.

"This was after we had counseled with Obwondiyag," Louis added. "So the message was for Obwondiyag as well as the Delaware. They must not think that the Ganonsyoni have grown so weak that they can no longer extend a heavy hand to punish. That we came in the winter, when most people stay close to the lodge fires, tells them that they must always look over their shoulder, lest the Ganonsyoni sneak up on them and steal their *orenda* while they are not looking."

Louis put an arm on Big Oak's shoulder. "Friend of my father," he said, "I am glad we spent this time. You will be my friend, as you were my father's. This spring we will be fighting the French. It is my dream that you will be at my side, as you were so many times with my father."

The next morning they donned their packs and blankets and headed east, toward their distant home village. Big Oak, Little Oak, and some of the Seneca men and women gave Louis and his departing Mohawks what meager presents they were able to contrive from their poor store of goods, and watched them vanish into the forest.

Little Oak was spending much of his time with Kawia, alone when possible. By this time it seemed to him that she was Kawia again, almost.

There came a day in April, warmer than most April days on the Genesee, when they took a walk downriver and sat on the bank throwing pebbles and watching the ripples. He watched her as she tossed a rock. Her sandy hair made a strange contrast to her clear olive skin. He had always adored her. And she had always followed him wherever he went, with a happy puppy smile on her face. Now that he finally felt right about making something deeper of their long friendship, he felt distance, and it made him anxious.

"You don't look at me like I was your little sister anymore, Little Oak," she said as he nearly conked a turtle on its shell with a well-thrown pebble.

"You don't look like you did when I used to look at you that way," he said.

"I wish we could be like we were then."

"Do you not see me as a man for you?" he asked.

"I do not see me as a woman."

"You are still very young," he agreed. "So am I. At least that is what my father says."

"You do look like a man to me. And that makes me afraid."

In fact she did not look afraid at all. Although she spoke of emotions, her voice was flat, as if she was not very interested in the conversation, but was just going through the motions because that was what she was supposed to do.

He looked into her dark eyes, eyes far too old to be those of a fifteen-year-old.

"I am still Little Oak, the brother you always trusted."

"Then do not be my lover or I will not trust you."

Her words shocked him and made him dizzy. "What does that mean?" he asked.

She smiled, not a happy smile, but a wooden smile, such as he had never before seen on her face. "You do *not* want to love me," she said firmly, as if talking to a child.

"I do not understand. We always told each other what was in our hearts. Why do you talk to me this way?" His voice rose and she flinched.

"Go away from me, you." Her words were angry, but her tone of voice held no feeling.

"Not until you tell me the truth," he responded.

"I will tell you nothing!"

He waited for her tears to come, as they always had in the days when she used to come to him to soothe her hurts. Then he would hold her in his arms until she had cried her way out of her mood. She would be grateful, and spend the rest of the day chattering about how someday she would take him into her lodge and give him children. And they would laugh because it was so absurd to talk about such things.

But this time there were no tears. She did not want to be consoled by him, and she did not feel any responsibility for his feelings. He was, suddenly, a stranger to her, and she to him. He tried to look into her eyes, to find a clue there and understand what was happening, but her eyes avoided his, sleepily staring out at the river without passion. Her fingers, he noted, flexed impatiently.

He reached for her hand to help her to her feet. "It's time to eat," he said. "Let's go back."

She pulled her hand away, as if he held a fire in his. "I will go back in a little while," she said, leaving no doubt that she meant "a little while after you."

As the population of the little community grew, and the people of Tonowaugh began to lose their fear of a new attack, some of the men spoke of their desire to move back to the old site, away from the stone house. "We are Seneca," they said. "We don't need a white man to be a father to us."

Big Oak understood, but suggested that they at least stay close enough for the stone house to cover them with the swivel guns.

"No," responded Skoiyasi, who in spite of his youth had gained considerable influence over the shrunken Seneca community. "We want no cannon to rain iron shot down upon us."

"At least think of the palisade around my house as your fort," Big Oak suggested, "so that if an enemy approaches, we can fight them together."

"No," said Olida, a woman who had been out gathering roots with her children at the time of the attack, had fled to her father's people, and had returned to become a leader in the village. "When the Indians live with white men, after a while there are always fewer Indians. I wish you would leave us, but if you will not, at least stay separate from us."

"We did not attack your village," Big Oak replied, taken aback by the woman's vehemence. "Iroquois traitors attacked your village."

"We were one before the white man drove us apart. Before the French sprinkled water on the Caughnawaga. Before our people and the Cayuga went west and became Mingoes. You make our people angry. You make our people afraid. You make our people drunk. You make our people everything except Iroquois. Why did you come? Why did you not stay across the water, where you belonged? Before you, we were happy."

Big Oak's face flushed with anger. "Everything you say about the white man is true," he replied. "But what you say about the red man is not.

"Before a single Englishman set foot on this land, Iroquois were killing Huron, Iroquois were killing Delaware, Iroquois were killing Abnaki—and when those people had the chance to strike back, they would strike back. Why is it that when the Iroquois wipe out the Huron, they are brave warriors, but when the white men kill the Ganonsyoni, they are murderers?"

"Because this is our land!" Skoiyasi snarled, his fist tightening around the handle of the tomahawk in his belt.

"Was it always your land? Your old men say that you came from down south, moved north of the St. Lawrence, then finally conquered this land."

"With blood and courage we conquered this land."

"Also with cleverness and unity?"

"We are clever, and we know how to act as one," Skoiyasi agreed.

"With blood and courage, and cleverness and unity, the English will conquer you if you do not find a way to stop them."

"The English do not have courage. Most of them are weak, and they are cowards."

"And yet they walk the land of the Pequot unchallenged, and the land of the Mohican, and the Abnaki and the Delaware too. And much of the land of your brothers the Ganiengehaka."

"You are a good man, Big Oak," Olida said. "You always speak the truth. And yet you are a white man too. You somehow grow rich trading furs, while we who command all the Indian fur traders just make it through from year to year. So you must be like the rest of them. Maybe somehow you deceive us, and do *not* always speak the truth. It would be better for us if you no longer went among us."

Big Oak did not wish to argue further with this woman. The sounds he heard from the braves who stood before him were sounds of assent.

"If you want to separate yourselves from me and my son, then you should do it," he said. "I am sorry that you feel that way about me. I have lived among you for many years, and until the attack, your village knew only peace and happiness."

"That is because the white man stayed away."

"But I was here. Little Oak was here."

"White man stayed away," she repeated, and he understood that she was telling him something complex beyond her ability to express it, that his whiteness meant grief for the Seneca even if he meant no harm.

"I will not betray my Seneca brothers," he told her. "And I will not try and make you stay. But if you need us, we are still here."

The next day the Indians began to build their new village. This time there were no longhouses. All the buildings were small lodges with rounded roofs. Big Oak and Little Oak stood forlornly in front of the stone house, watching the women as they moved their possessions from the buildings inside the palisade. Big Oak walked up to Olida to remind her that the men need not cut new trees for the palisades, that they could dig up the ones they had erected around his house and use them.

"I hear you," she said coldly, as if wondering what clever trick he had in mind involving the logs of the palisade. Big Oak reflected on the fact that although the survivors who were rebuilding the village wanted nothing to do with the white men, they were forsaking the Iroquoian longhouses for the white-man style single-family dwellings.

"I don't understand," Little Oak told his father. "It was the Mingoes and the praying Indians who attacked the village. Why do they blame that on us?"

"Because there was a time when no one dared attack an Iroquois village. To her the French and English are the same."

"How could she be so wrong?"

"To whites, Iroquois and Delaware are the same. I think the spring is a good time to get our furs to Albany. I'd say we should leave tomorrow, but I know you and Kawia have been spending time together."

Little Oak laughed a sad, humorless laugh. "Don't let that stop us," he said. And even as he said it, Kawia walked out of the longhouse carrying an iron cooking pot. Walking with her was Skoiyasi. He was talking. She was listening. And smiling. "I believe that Kawia is like Olida. She thinks I am too white. I think tomorrow might be a perfect time to leave," Little Oak said without much expression.

Big Oak saw what Little Oak saw. "Tomorrow, then. And on to Albany. I seem to remember this girl there you had your eye on."

"Maybe this time I'll get to know her a little better." Little Oak turned on his heel and headed for the not-so-secret front secret entrance. He had the sinking feeling in his stomach that a man only feels when his feelings have been betrayed by a woman. He did not look back for a last glimpse of Kawia with Skoiyasi. That she could love someone else hurt more than a little. That she could be so indifferent to him pierced his soul.

And yet, that night his thoughts were not of Kawia alone, but also of the village where he had been born. It was one thing to be rejected by a fickle girl, but quite another to be cast out by his home village. As tears ran down his cheeks, he realized with a terrible, aching feeling in his chest that this would be the last night he would ever spend in this house. He did not understand why the village pointed fingers at him and his father, and yet he felt guilt. People who should have loved him hated him. He must have done something to deserve their hate, for they were good people.

# ❧19❧

IN THE MIDDLE OF NEW YORK, BETWEEN THE lakes we call Owasco and Skaneateles, lived a family called Hayes. Like a number of New York farmers, their forebears had come west in search of better soil and relief from the vicious Indian wars that turned the soil of New England red with blood, mostly Indian blood.

George Hayes may not have known a man called Big Oak, but he was a longtime friend of a man named Sam Watley. He had scouted with Sam during the previous war between the French and the English in the 1740s, and had meant to go into the fur trade with Sam, but George's father had died, leaving only George to manage what was turning into a successful farming enterprise. So, Sam recalled, George and his wife Ida had settled down in their beautiful valley and raised their eight sons and three daughters to adulthood.

They were a strong and fortunate clan, the Hayeses. You had to be strong and fortunate in those days to see all eleven children survive to adulthood. The three girls had each married stalwart local farmers and begun raising their own tribes of sons.

They were religious too, believing Christians who would not have known whether God favored sprinkling infants or immersing children, but they knew their savior did not favor the rich over the poor or the white over the red. They preached to nobody but each other, drank strong liquor only for medicinal purposes, and went armed to their fields in times of war and peace, just in case. Their survival was not, after all, all luck.

Thad and Sam came down from the hills at dusk, when the apple trees in the orchard were budding but not blooming on the hillsides, the forest trees were bright green with their downy early foliage, and much of the valley was plowed but not yet planted.

Below him Thad could see men walking behind plows being pulled slowly by powerful oxen. He was thrilled by the panorama before him, for he had never seen such a large portion of land given over to agriculture by one family. The Seneca men he had lived with always preferred the hunt to the plow, and he had naturally assumed that all real men felt the same way.

As Thad and Sam made their way down toward the floor of the valley, the men behind the oxen paused to stare, and one of them stopped his plowing to approach them.

"Any way for me to help you folks?" the man asked, in tones neither friendly or hostile.

"We're lookin' for George Hayes," Sam responded, reading the face of the young man before him.

"I'm George Hayes," came the reply.

Sam looked at the young man, perplexed. Then he laughed. "Your pa, Jughead. I want to see your pa."

At the invocation of his childhood nickname, the young man's head snapped back in astonishment and he let loose a laugh that echoed off the rock face by the hill that Sam and Thad had just descended. "I know you. You're Long Sam, that's who you are."

"Long Sam?" a puzzled Thad asked.

"That's what I used to call my old rifle, son. The one that blew up and carved this half-moon above my eye." He turned his attention back to Jughead. "Where's your pa? Is he all right?"

"All right? He's better'n that. He's got himself a new wife, would you believe? Says he's aimin' to start himself a new family."

A shadow crossed Sam's brow. "New wife? What happened to your ma?"

"Lord took her five—no it was seven year back, I think."

"Oh, my lord, has it been so long since I've been by here? I'm sorry. She was a fine woman, your ma." The three men began walking toward a distant farmhouse. It was a long walk, pungent with the smell of fertile new-turned earth.

"Seen much in the way of redskins on your journey?" Jughead asked.

"Not since we left Tonowaugh." Big Oak laughed.

"That's right, now I remember, you live with them and you keep your hair. I have to tell you, they ain't been very popular this neck of the woods lately."

"Why, have they been raidin' much around here?"

" 'Bout forty mile north of here they wiped out a big family. Scalped the father and two boys, tortured the mother and burned the rest up in the house. Two days later the mother stumbled into a neighbor's yard babblin' so bad they couldn't make out what was ailin' her. They had to go back to her home to find out what really happened. I don't believe she's come back to her senses yet, poor woman."

"Heard anything else?" Sam asked.

"Not yet, but down in Pennsylvania it's got downright dangerous to live west of Philadelphia, and we believe that things'll be gettin' lively up here too." The three figures crossed the barnyard in silence and entered the house through the back door into the kitchen.

"Hey, *Pa!*" Jughead hollered, as if he were calling across a field. "You'll never guess who just come over your threshold."

"I saw you comin' in," came the voice, followed into the kitchen by the man himself, five feet, seven inches of solid muscle, except around the midriff, where years of prodigious food consumption had thickened him considerably. "And them other folks you drug in with you."

"Other folks? Pa, can't you recognize your old friend Long Sam here? And that there tall skinny boy is his son, don't you remember?"

George stared hard at Thad, but did not look at Sam. "I remember I *used* to have a friend I called Long Sam, good a man as there was too, until I heard he took up with them redskins out west on the Genesee."

Sam stared at his old friend, looking for a clue. George had a dry sense of humor that could string along an old friend for an hour at a time before finally a smile would break through the stone face. But Sam always knew how to spot the twinkle in George's eye. There was none there now. While acknowledging that Indians had souls, George had never been particularly fond of them. But judging by the look on his face as he stared at Thad, it was obvious that he was ready to roast the half of Thad that was Seneca, and maybe the other half just to make sure.

"Well now, George, don't you worry your head much about me and the Indians, just last week they kind of threw me out of the brotherhood, you might say."

"What now, kicked you out of the village? Ain't that like the ungrateful heathens, after all you done for them." Suddenly he was filled with outrage at the cruel injustice that had been meted out to his friend. "You never should of married that girl, Sam. Should of stuck to your own kind."

Sam gave his old friend a long hard look. "She was the truest woman who ever drew breath on this earth, George."

"That she was, Sam," George agreed, then was silent for a moment. "But the rest of them lopin', lurkin' thieves, I tell you Sam, I don't understand why you can't see what a bunch of lowlifes they are, every last one of them—except for your darling woman, of course. Even their women—egad, if I was to wake up next to one of them, I think I'd put a bullet through my own head. Ugly! Ugly! Ugly!"

"George, now calm yourself," Sam said placidly to the

red-faced farmer, who had worked his way into such a frenzy that he was having trouble catching his breath. "I don't remember you being such a hater."

"I don't remember me being a *lover* of Indians before, but you're right. Used to be a time I could *stand* bein' in the same valley with them. That was before they commenced to runnin' around in their altogether hackin' people up from Ontario down to the Monongahela."

"Well, I think this war has got them all kind of upset and worried, you know, and—"

"*Upset and worried*, you say! I'm upset and worried, but you don't see me runnin' around naked with paint all over me, hackin' and burnin' people! You know, when we were out scoutin' together and you and I were talkin' to them heathens, why, I thought that them bein' around us so much was having a civilizin' effect on them. But you heard the stories, haven't you?" George pulled the stopper on a barrel of cider and drew a cup for Sam, then pointed to Thad.

"Can he have one too?" he asked, and Sam nodded. He drew cider for himself and Jughead, and the four of them sat at the kitchen table, so warm beside the immense fireplace.

Sam leaned toward George, eyes narrowed with controlled anger. "George, I more than heard about it. I saw it. Women and children butchered, men tied to stakes and burned slowly to death. Headless people, handless people, people with their hearts cut out of their bodies. That was months ago, and I still see the bodies in my dreams, their eyes still frozen wide open."

"Then you know, there's no end to what those devils'll do to white men."

"Right, only those white men were Seneca Indians. They were the people Thad here grew up with!"

"Well I—" The loquacious George was suddenly stuck for words. "The devil, you say!" he said, and he lapsed into silence. His was not a pretty face. At this stage of his life, muscles and fat were fighting for control of his features, but both yielded to compassion for the moment as George contemplated his friend and Thad, and their tragedy.

They sat staring across the table at each other, wondering how much was left of the old friendship.

"You know there's a war on," Sam said.

"So we heard."

"If the French win, you'll lose your farm, and maybe everything else."

"The English whipped 'em pretty bad last time, and then that fool prime minister give back everything we won. Everything you and I fought to win. They'll whip the French again, only this time without us, old friend."

"Speak for yourself, George. I'll be there, and Thad'll be there, and some of your sons at least oughta be there."

George gave Sam a grim, hard look. "Forget it, Sam. My boys are staying home. Let's just say we're raisin' young'uns to fight the next war."

Sam shrugged his shoulders. "I understand."

"I wonder if you do. Sam, what's an army good for if it don't protect the people that do all the hard work? We are Englishmen who just happen to live on this side of the ocean. There are no Indians roamin' the valleys of Yorkshire or Wales burnin' children up in their houses. If they had a few thousand soldiers marchin' around this valley, we would feel safe enough to go out into the fields without bein' armed like a pirate. And tell me why they give back to the Frenchers what we won the last war. If we'da hung onto them forts and towns, the French would probably be gone from America and then there'd be no one stirrin' up the Indians."

George took a deep breath and let the apoplectic color drain from his face, then took a long pull from his cup of cider. "Now, I have this slave. He's gettin' on, and I don't like havin' a slave anyway. So I'm willin' to donate him to the cause. Why don't you take him, give him a gun, then if he don't get killed, you can make him a free man, which is what you would do anyway."

"Tell you what I need, George. I've got some goods I have to transport to Albany, and I could sure use a big ol' horse to help me. Do you have an extra one I can borrow?"

For the first time Thad saw George smile, not a happy smile, but a smile of relief. "I'll do better than that, Sam. I happen to have a genuine Virginia mule, and she'll carry better than a horse twice her size. If you promise to bring her back, I'll let you have her."

"Well now, there's a war on and I can't guarantee she'll make it back, any more than I can guarantee that I'll make it back. But I'll pay you rent for her and replace her if anything happens to her."

Now George positively beamed. "No rent for you, old friend. And I know you'll bring her back, if anyone can. Jughead, get Laban to bring ol' Sukey out back and introduce her to her new friends."

The old black slave George was talking about turned out to be a tall, thin man who didn't look much older than Sam or George. By the way he handled the mule, he looked capable of warfare or just about anything else he cared to tackle.

"Laban here is half Mohican, which is why you don't see no feelings on his face. You'd never knowed that a cow stomped on his foot yesterday." Sam's eyebrows rose. George thought Sam was appreciating his turn of phrase. In fact, Sam was thinking about how emotional Indians can be among their own, and how they hide their emotions from outsiders. He wondered what emotions Laban was feeling as he listened to his master describe his feelings.

"This here animal," George said, "will carry 'bout anything you can load on her. She ain't like a horse. She'll eat her fill, then she'll stop eating, while a horse'll keep eating till he founders. So you have to treat her like she's got some sense."

As they returned to the house, he delivered his set of instructions on how to care for "the finest beast of burden ever invented." He said, "Any animal this tough will be a bit peculiar. But if you can get to thinkin' like a mule, you can talk to her, and she'll just about answer you."

Big Oak mulled that over in his mind for a moment and decided that maybe men who hang around mules get just as peculiar as the mules they hang around with.

They sat down again around the kitchen table, George and Sam, alone. Jughead had returned to his oxen, his plow, and his furrow. Thad hung around the barn with Laban, getting the hang of the mule. For a while Sam and George drank in silence.

"Tell me about Ida, George." Sam's interest was not merely polite. He had always thought that George's wife was the glue of decency that held together George's undisciplined moral structure. Ida was the real Christian; George was the Bible quoter. Ida used the Bible as her guide, while George used it as a weapon. Sam wondered what path George would walk without Ida to lead him.

George's eyes grew bright and for a moment the muscles won the struggle with the flab for control of his face.

"Sam, you may not believe this, but she was with child one more time. She thought it was very funny, a grandmother pregnant, you know, and that Elisha—that was our first grandchild—would be older than his uncle, or his aunt, whatever it was gonna be.

"One day while she's still early in her term, she gets this craving for berries and she takes her bucket and goes into the woods to pick some. I figured she must be going after blackberries, you know, I never took much notice of that sort of thing. So out in the woods she goes and she comes back with a bucketful. I'm working in the field, you know, doing what I can't—yeah, I was down in the dust trying to figure out what it was, gettin' in the corn.

"She passes by me and kind of swings her bucket to show what a multitude of wild berries she has picked. I just laughed and told her not to be a pig, that I'd be in soon and that a little cool cream out of the springhouse on top of a mess of berries might be just the thing.

"But it took me all afternoon to get back to the house, what with all the chores I had to do that day, and when I got into the kitchen, she was on her knees crying that her insides was feelin' all twisted up and she can't move. I picked her up, carried her into our bedroom and laid her down as soft as I could and covered her up. I looked at her and asked her what I should do, because I knew that she'd know what to do if it was me lying there.

"She says just let her lay there because it was up to God almighty and nobody else. That scared me half to death, and I sent Laban to the Onondagas—" He had been telling his story to a clay mug, but now he looked up and told it to Sam's eyes. "I—figured they would know about things like that.

"I sat with her and held her hand. Her eyes were shut tight with the pain, and she laid on her side all curled up tight, her knees up against her body. She told me that it won't be too bad if only I don't try to touch her 'cause that would just make it worse. So I didn't touch her, except for her hand, and I sat with her until dark and still they didn't come. I lit a lamp in the room, but when I tried to light another, she told me not to because two lamps would hurt her eyes. And then for the first time she screamed, and I told the kids who were there to get out and don't come back in until I send for them.

"Now she didn't know who I was anymore, and then her breathing got fast, and then it got slow, and then . . . it stopped.

"It couldn't have been five minutes later, Laban came, with an old, old Onondaga on a mule, and so help me, he knew he was too late before he was in the room.

"I sat up in the chair, next to her, all night, wouldn't let any of the kids in the room. We buried her the next morning—about the same time she went out to pick berries the day before.

"I'll tell you something, my old friend. She birthed eleven children, and every single one of them is alive today. The youngest is twelve. The oldest twenty-six. *Nobody* births eleven children and they all live to grow up. I thought maybe there was something about this valley—I know I'm a fool, but I thought, maybe, this family was . . . The Indians never attacked here, the crops never failed here—and nobody ever died here except the animals we slaughtered and the deer we hunted. Was it possible that—well, hell, I knew it wasn't possible, but what's better than dreamin' that we could all stay together, always."

He looked sheepish, as if he'd just been caught playing a little boy's game. "The day after she died, I built a fence around her grave. And I built it big enough for me, for all the kids, for all the kids' wives, and for all the grandchildren. There was no graveyard until Ida died, and she's still alone there. I'll not send my children to fight for England. It's hard enough to bear, thinking about them fightin' for this valley.

"And Sam, I know that someday I'll have to." The afternoon was turning gray. A spring shower was in the offing. The back door opened and a lithe, graceful shape glided in. The shadow across George's face vanished, replaced by a young man's smile. He looked across the room lovingly, and when he turned to Sam, his eyes sparkled in the dim light.

"Sam, this is Rachel. I call her Rachel, and she answers to Rachel. Rachel is my wife."

Standing before them, dark and full-blooded, was a young woman of the Onondaga nation.

# ⊰20⊱

LITTLE OAK PUSHED. LITTLE OAK PULLED. LITtle Oak kicked at her withers and tried talking sweet reason to the creature. Little Oak tried a dozen creative ways of motivating her, but the mule stood like a statue of a mule.

Little Oak grinned, embarrassed. "I guess I've just never seen a thing like this before."

Jughead put his mouth to Sukey's ear and clicked his tongue twice. The mule took a few steps. "Like that," he told Little Oak, who dug into his pack and came up with a bit of maple sugar.

"She'll bite your hand, and you'll hate that," George warned. Little Oak ignored the warning, and only his quick reflexes saved him as the mule snapped his jaw shut where the hand had been.

The bribe must have done its work. Somehow the boy and the mule arranged a meeting of the minds, and soon the farm, and the beautiful valley, were two hills behind them.

Little Oak was spending quite a bit of his walking time thinking about the farm and Jughead and George Hayes; especially Mr. Hayes.

"He's not hard to figure out, my friend George, if you just put your mind to it," his father explained. "He's like most of us, wants to be a good man, and then turns out he's just a man. Now, I knew he wasn't gonna give me his sons, and I didn't want 'em anyway. But he knew he shouldn't be just sittin' around when New York is fighting for its life, so he wasn't feeling all that good until I asked for a critter, and that seemed dirt cheap to him compared to his sons, you see?"

"You're telling me that we went visiting your old friend so you could squeeze a pack animal out of him?"

"Well, there's friends, and then there's friends. Now George, he was my friend when we was scoutin' together, and my partner when we were gonna go into the fur business together. George had a brother who lived in New England. That brother knew his dad had a farm in the middle of New York, but he had no idea that the man owned a big fertile valley.

"When George's father died, George sent his brother a letter telling him about his dad's poor old rocky farm and how he was gonna give it a go but that his brother shouldn't waste his time comin' out and tryin' to plow rock. Now that's the kind of soil that New Englanders are used to plowing, and his brother naturally figured that if he can plow rock in New England, why should he go all the way to the middle of New York, just so he could plow more rock? George laid it on real thick, and he was so proud of himself; he showed me the letter before I carried it for him to Albany.

"Now that's the bad part of George. He cheated his brother, and, fact of the matter, he cheated me—argued me into payin' him about half again the price his share of the business was worth when we split up.

"The other part of George was that he was a good husband to a good woman and raised a mighty fine family. Honest folks too—like he knew what was right, and admired what was right, just couldn't do it himself when it come to business. But those boys of his, and the girlfolk too, they're everything George wishes he was. Of course, Ida had a lot to do with that, but then, it took a goodhearted man like George really is to appreciate a goodhearted female like Ida."

They fell back into silence, as was their habit in the woods, listening instead of talking. The birds were beginning to return, filling the forest with their sounds and making Little Oak think about Kawia.

In fact, his thoughts about Kawia weren't thoughts at all, just a jumble of emotions that made his face hurt as the tears pushed at his eyelids. His father saw his face, and as often happened, read his mind. He'd talk to the boy in camp tonight. Meantime he'd have to have eyes sharp enough for the both of them. The boy certainly wasn't paying much attention to what was going on around him.

What do you do with a mule in the middle of a forest in wartime when she won't shut up? If you tie her up close by, you give away the location of your camp to unfriendly lopers. If you tie her up a mile away, someone will surely steal her, and they'll know you're in the area anyway. If you turn her loose, it might take you half a day to find her and the rest of the day to catch her.

Big Oak decided to tether her less than a quarter of a mile away from camp; but though the mule brayed half the night, the two made no campfire and spoke softly to each other. The going had been nearly all uphill that day, and the mule had been balky. They had been traveling since dawn, and both were so tired that they were asleep before the sky had gone completely dark. The unmusical protests of the lonely mule were their lullaby.

Little Oak awoke first. It was still pitch-dark, and the mule was still complaining. Little Oak wanted to turn over and go back to sleep, but there was something not quite right about the sound. His father had heard him stirring and now opened his eyes.

"What?" he said. But before Little Oak could answer, his father held a hand up and cocked his head. Both slipped out from under their blankets and grabbed their rifles. Silently they stood up, each crouched motionless against a tree, and listened.

Whoever was out there was not much of a pioneer. Twigs cracked, leaves crunched, and sibilant whispers made their way between the trees into the ears of the vigilant woodsmen. As their night vision came, the forest lit up for them like day. Half the trees still had no foliage, and the others had only their tiny early growth, so the three-quarter moon and assorted stars and planets gave them a good idea of what was in store for them the rest of the night.

There were five of them, in red coats that were beginning to show the wear and tear of unaccustomed forest living. They were standing around the mule and softly, they thought, cursing it in the barbaric syllables of lower class London and Yorkshire. One of them was pulling on the reins and another was pushing on the rump, and they might as well have been trying to move one of the old oaks that towered over them. Big Oak signed "deserters" to his son, and commanded Thad to stay where he was. Meanwhile he slipped into the shadows of some thicker growth and took a position behind a large tree uphill from the soldiers. Then he pointed his rifle at the closest one and spoke.

"That's somebody else's mule," he said firmly, and they nearly jumped out of their dirty white breeches. "You know," Big Oak said, "a man who'll steal another man's mule might get himself shot in this part of the world."

The five soldiers stared down at their boots like whipped puppies.

"I could bring you back to your army, and they'd probably shoot you, and we'd get a reward." He thought he saw a flicker of fear in the eyes of the first one to look up.

"Get their weapons, son." Thad collected the muskets that the men had almost forgotten they were holding, then he pulled off them an assortment of ammunition, bayonets, and less official instruments of war.

"You goin' t' scalp us?" asked another.

"I might not even kill you if you do what I tell you."

"Haw, y' only have two rifles, and there's five of us. We can take you, you know."

"I know there's only two of us, and there's five of you. That makes two dead, and it'll be three pair of fists against two rifle butts. Care to take your chances?"

"Dick, shut up and do what the man tells you to do," said a third man, the only tall man among runts a good seven to eight inches shorter than Big Oak. "Mr. Woodsman, what would you have us do?"

"For a starter, sit down and take your boots off."

They obeyed, grunting with the effort of removing the tall, snug-fitting footwear, which was not very well designed for the infantrymen who wore them. They were the most demoralized group of soldiers Big Oak had ever seen. They looked as comfortable in the American wilderness as he imagined he would look in Buckingham Palace. He felt very sorry for them.

"Why did you desert?"

The tall one, who had the skinniest feet and therefore had his boots off first, looked up at Big Oak, tilted his head and squinted. "Well, now, I'm pleased you asked that question. We were up there at Fort Oswego with General Shirley, you see. I don't know if you've ever been there, but if you like to live, you really oughtn't go there. Reg'lar hellhole it is. Every morning they wheel a little wagon out with the boys what died the night before—disease, you know—and then they have parade, and every day there's fellows missin' from the ranks what was standin' next to you the mornin' before. I'm tellin' you, after a while it got a bit depressin'."

They had forgotten they were prisoners. Their capture had suddenly turned into a gripe session.

"God damn," said one of the runts, who up to that time had kept silent. "The officers has real food, with wine, always, of course, 'n' we don't even get our rum anymore, to keep us healthy, you know. I think they save all the rum for the goddamned Indians so they won't desert us."

"What are they all so sick from?"

"What? I'll tell you what. Every time we squat, blood shoots out of our arse is what. Makes us so weak there's mornings we can barely crawl out of our beds. Then the sergeant, he throws us out of bed, if you know what I mean. I have to tell you, we may be hungry out here, but we been feelin' a lot better in these 'ere woods than we did cooped up inside those walls."

"You can wager on that, gov'nor," said another. "Not a night goes by that we aren't scared out of our britches out here, but at least we don't feel like we're dyin' in there a little more every day."

"Hey!" said the tall one. "They send our Indians out to spy on the French, and when they come back they tell our Colonel Mercer there that the French has got more than a thousand of them bloody savages waitin' to attack us once we're too sick to hold them off. You know what that means?" He answered his own question, as Big Oak knew he would. "It means that after the French attack, there won't be a one of us with hair left on our heads. That's what it means."

"Why are you so sure the French will win?"

"Will y' listen to the man. You have never seen such a fort. Made of clay, is what that fort is made out of. They never have artillery practice there, know why?"

"Not enough ammunition?" Little Oak asked.

"Plenty of ammunition, I'll tell you. But when they fire the guns, all that bangin' and shakin' makes the walls crumble. You ever hear of such a thing? We have a fort, and we have cannon to protect the fort, only if they fire the cannon, the fort will bloody well fall to pieces. I'd like to meet the man who built that fort, I would. I'd shake his hand. Hell, I'd shake a couple other parts of his body until he sings like a little girl, I would."

So much for Fort Oswego, Big Oak thought. The trouble with being a woodsman was, you've got too much sense to want to serve under noble nincompoops, for they would surely get you killed if you gave them the chance. On the other hand, somebody had to serve under the nincompoops or the English wouldn't have a chance against the French, whose nincompoops were smarter than the English nincompoops. My lord, when they knighted someone at Buckingham Palace, Big Oak thought, was it part of the ceremony to remove the man's brains from his head?

Big Oak was a loyal Englishman, but he had no desire to throw his life away to satisfy the vanity of fools, and so he would continue to pick and choose his fights, not based on the odds, but based on who would be his leaders.

"Okay, lads, you can see, the dawn ain't come yet. Now, since we can't trust you very well, we are going to take your boots and weapons with us. If you can follow a trail, you'll find all this"—he pointed to the items Little Oak was busy lashing to the back of the mule—"piled up a few miles down the trail.

"Now, I wouldn't advise following us in the dark, because I will be cuttin' thorny branches along the way and dropping them like posies here and there. We grow some cruel thorns out here in the American woods. Your feet won't like them a bit. I'd wait until the sun was well up if I was you, before you set off after us."

The men did not like what they were hearing, not a bit.

"Now just a minute, sir. You would have us walkin' in these woods without boots, without our muskets and our knives. It's damned inhuman, is what it is," said the most outspoken of the runts.

"And if we gave you back your weapons and your boots, you'd follow us and wait till we were asleep and then you'd cut our throats. Sorry boys, when you spend your life in the woods, you learn to be real careful."

"How do we know you'll be leavin' our muskets 'n' packs down the trail there for us? You might just decide to take it all with you and sell it, 'n' where would that leave us?"

"Sorry boys, we don't have any time to talk about it. You'll just have to trust us because we've got the loaded rifles and you've got your tender bare feet."

They groaned and complained, and three of them looked

pathetic while the other two looked downright hostile, but Big Oak would not be moved.

He laughed. "Don't worry. I won't let you down. And I sure don't blame you for gettin' out of Oswego while you still had some flesh left on your bones and hair left on your heads. Now, just stay where you are until it gets light. That's a clear trail ahead of you, and you'll find your things right where I said you would."

With that, he and Little Oak hustled back to their camp, arranged their packs, and vanished down the trail, leaving the five soldiers as sulky and dispirited as they had been the moment they first saw the two frontiersman glaring at them down the muzzles of their long rifles.

Winters in the Mohawk Valley seem to go on forever. One reason is the ample amount of snow from the cold moisture blowing in off Lake Ontario and Lake Erie. Just when you think you've finally got winter licked, along comes a late April snowstorm to remind you that nature has another cold arrow left in her quiver.

But by May everybody begins to hope for better things, usually. This was not a usual year. Everybody knew that when the mild weather began, so would the raiding season. This spring, egged on by the French, the Canadian Indians and their bloodthirsty French Canadian friends, the *coureurs de bois*, would be knocking on their doors with sharp hatchets and ripping the tops off their heads.

Sam and Thad and a mule loaded down with furs were on their way to Albany. They had dug out their skins uneventfully, then decided to tarry with their friends at the Mohawk village, where they had discussed the war situation with Louis and his finest warriors. The Mohawks still did not know which way they wanted to jump.

Louis was still a young man but he had the force of personality of his father, and his days on the warpath had impressed many in the village. He was a natural leader. But he was anxious to have Big Oak's counsel, to help him decide in just what direction he should lead his warriors.

"We think the French will win," he told Big Oak the first night after Big Oak and Thad had arrived at the village. "They fight better than the English, and they have many Canadians who fight like Indians, and many Indians who will fight, even though they cannot fight like the Ganonsyoni. We would like to stay neutral, but we know that if the French win, the other tribes will demand that the French let them and the Huron make war on us.

"With the English gone, they will have the new French rifles, and it will go hard with us. So we do not want the French to win.

"On the other hand, if the English win, they will keep nibbling at our land until we have nothing left in the Mohawk Valley, so we do not want the English to win.

"You can think like a white man, Big Oak. What would you do?"

The tall, sincere woodsman, face burned red by the winds of the past winter, leaned across his long rifle and spoke to the anxious faces around the council fire.

"It makes me feel good that you ask for my opinion. We have talked about this before, son of Gingego. My own village, my Seneca village on the Genesee where I raised my son, threw us out. They blamed the white man for their massacre at the hands of the Caughnawaga and the Mingoes, and I'm not sure they're wrong.

"Your choices are very hard. I don't blame you for not trusting the English. Even the white man you trust most, Warraghiyagey, now has claim to thousands of acres of what were once Mohawk land. As much as he loves the Mohawk, I am not sure that he would love you as much if you were not so important to his purse.

"But you cannot let the French win this war. Their friends are your bitter enemies. If you stay neutral, the French will laugh at you behind your backs. Then, if they win, they will tell their brothers the Caughnawaga and the Huron to make their knives extra sharp when the war is over, that there will be Mohawk meat for their table."

There was a murmur of agreement around the council fire, especially from some of the older women who had known the English for so long. The men, for their part, were used to hating the Caughnawaga and the Huron, and liked the idea that some days life remained as it was in the good old days when it was open season on the tribes to the north.

"Like you, the forests are my home, and I would not give them up for the plow. If I were you, I'd fight for the English and learn all I can about the English law so I could keep my land."

"Haugh!" interrupted an older warrior. "The English law has cheated us out of so much land. My head would buzz like a honeycomb if I had to learn to lie like the law lies."

"I have heard people say that the law lies, but have you ever seen the law lie?" Big Oak asked.

"I did," shouted Tall Bear, suddenly angry, standing up and walking toward Big Oak. "It was at Teantontalogo. There was rum and lots of presents, and then an English war chief stands up with a big skin and tells us that this is a treaty of peace between the Ganiengehaka and the English. He's got a feather that he gives to the big men in the village—big drunk men of the village—and each one makes his mark on the skin.

"The next spring there are white men cutting down trees and building houses on our land. Instead of just killing them, like we should have done, we come to them and ask them what they are doing on our land, and they tell us it is their land, they bought it from us for some presents in Teantontalogo. And we found out that the 'treaty of peace' signed by the six drunk chiefs gave them land all up and down the south bank of the Te-non-an-at-che.

"The law says that the heart of the rich, beautiful land we won with our blood so long ago, we gave to a white man for a few barrels of rum and a wagon full of blankets. Could anybody really believe such a lie?"

"I have heard of this thing," Big Oak replied. "French law. English law. You must learn to protect yourselves from it or it will eat you up. It eats up many white men too, believe me. Still, you must fight for the English. If the French win, they will burn the Longhouse to the ground. If the English win, there is a chance for justice, because King George knows that the Ganiengehaka are his children."

"Sometimes, my brother," Tall Bear said looking deep into the eyes of Big Oak, "I think that King George is like your God. I cannot see him, and yet I must believe in him. If he is so powerful, and yet he is so just, then why has he allowed us to be cheated so much?"

Big Oak knew the right white man answer: because he is so far away, and his counselors do not always know the truth, or if they do, they do not tell him the truth. But the truth was that King George, like all the other men at court, and like the men who governed his colonies, was a politician. And if it was true that the Indians were close to King George's heart, which Big Oak personally doubted, it was also true that there were other things much closer to King George's heart, like the national treasury, for instance, and the contentment of the nation's most influential commoners and noblemen.

Under the rules of such a reality, what chance did the Ganonsyoni have of keeping their land, and their freedom?

"Friend of my father, now friend to me. Your heart is great and yet you cannot feel what we feel," Louis said. "You are a white man, better than most white men because you would have us save ourselves by becoming white men. Oh yes, we could become white men. If we did, our bodies would live but our spirits would die."

Big Oak let the silence follow the echo of Louis's words before he replied.

"You misjudge me, son of my dearest friend, because you do not know me. I am white and do not pretend to be anything else. I love the Ganonsyoni, and yet I do not understand the thoughts of the Ganonsyoni. Not really. I know how greedy white men are to possess Indian lands, and I want to say to you, 'This is how to stop them!' But I do not know how to stop them. And when the last forest is cut down to build houses, my tears will be as real as yours. Do I not love the forests as you do? You have never seen my hands on the plow, following an animal around a field.

"And yet that is the English way of life. They do not know any other. Your mother wishes for you to give up your tomahawk and go to Onondaga to trade words with the old men, a great honor, yet you will not because the warpath is your way of life.

"Little Oak and I go to Albany tomorrow, to sell our furs. After Albany, we will go to Fort Oswego. It is there that the next big battle will be fought. If the English lose there, I believe that they will still win the war, but it will be long and hard.

"It is my prayer that when the sun rises on Lake Ontario, you will be at Oswego with me to help the British win a great battle. I will speak no more about it." And he folded his arms and sat down upon the ground.

Later on, as he stood at the open gate of the stockade, looking out into the night, he felt a light tap on his shoulder.

"They will be there with you," said the voice of White Bird. "Much has passed since the night Red Hawk plunged his faithless knife into your body. Our men have seen your might in battle on what you call Lake George. Your rifle speaks, and a moment later a speck on the horizon falls to the ground. You not only tell them what the man was wearing, but where your bullet pierced him." White Bird had aged much in the few months since she had last seen her, but, lonely as she must have felt without the man she had loved through most of her life, her spirit was still strong as the heart of an oak.

"But would you like to know why they are so determined to be there for the great battle?"

Big Oak turned around and looked into the wise eyes of the old woman.

"It is because Red Hawk will be there. The Ganiengehaka can live with defeat, but we cannot stand to let a traitor live. As long as he lives, as long as he fights on the side of the Caughnawaga against his own people, then our men will know no rest until his scalp hangs drying in the longhouse of his broken father."

Big Oak looked down at his moccasins and scratched the back of his neck.

"You have known him for many years," he said. "Why did he betray his people?"

"Don't you know?"

Big Oak shrugged his shoulders. "Maybe. I'm not sure."

"Because he hates the white man more than he loves his own people. And because he hates anybody who does not hate the white man as much as he does. Do you know what he said to Gingego once? He said, you hate the white man, I know your heart. Your trouble is that you do not hate the white man enough. And that softness will someday get you killed."

Her eyes turned hard and terrible. "Friend of my husband, that is just one more way that the white man has divided my people against each other."

## ❖21❖

NEVER HAD BIG OAK FELT SO PROSPEROUS. A war was on and furs were hard to get. Prices were high and so was the quality of the furs he and Little Oak had brought in.

To Little Oak's surprise, his father, so generous to his friends, drove a hard bargain with the buyer, a Mr. Joachim van Zandt.

"Mr. Watley," Van Zandt complained. "You are asking so much more than I can afford to pay. There is no profit for me in such a transaction. I must ship my furs down the Hudson to New York. It is a very dangerous passage. The risks are great, my insurance rates are high, and the insurance company does not always pay off if the savages steal my furs."

Big Oak laughed. "His honor thinks deerskins on my body make me a fool. The savages, as you call them, do not need to steal your furs from ships going down to New York. They have furs of their own and are more likely to attack the ships coming upstream *from* New York with trade goods they need. And they probably *would* attack your ships if they ever learned to build giant canoes that carried cannon. Anyway, I know that much time has passed since the last time a ship was attacked on the Hudson by Indians. I know nothing about insurance, but if your insurers are telling you the things you're telling me about risks and such, then they are tellin' you tales and I would go to another insurer, if there is such a thing."

Van Zandt ignored the barb embedded in Big Oak's response. "And then we are at war with France, Mr. Watley. What if they sink our ships?"

"No one knows better than I, Mr. Van Zandt, that we are at war. The French can sink my canoe. They would murder me just for the pleasure it gives them if they caught me between Ontario and Albany. I have seen your warehouses and they are empty. It would seem that the French have caught many of the fur traders who deal with the English. My journey along the Mohawk must be more difficult than your journey down the Hudson, eh?"

"You are correct, sir," Van Zandt acknowledged. "These are dangerous times for the both of us. But there is a limit to what the fashionable in London will pay for their haberdashery. Your profit would leave no room for mine, I'm afraid. Come, Mr. Watley, let us be realistic."

And on and on like that. The furs are flawed. No, sir, the furs are perfect. These skins are smaller than the others. No sir, these skins are the same size (holds them up for comparison). You see? Mr. Watley, I don't see how I can do business with a man so obstinate. That's all right Mr. Van Zandt, I will be glad to take my business to Mr. Van Loon. That thief? You wouldn't!

"Come now, Mr. Van Zandt. We're not that far apart."

They struck a deal. Then they had to fight over whether the price meant New York pounds or English pounds. Van Zandt was so surprised that the trapper in the deerskins knew the difference—or maybe he was frightened by Big Oak's vehemence—that he gave in fairly easily, but not until he first threatened to call in the soldiers.

When he made that threat, Big Oak's face turned into a steely mask so frightening to the buyer that he truly sealed the deal, on the trapper's terms, at that moment. The merchant wrote out a short contract, which Big Oak read over very carefully and then returned to him.

"Make a copy, sign both, I'll sign both and I'll keep one," Big Oak said. "No, I'll tell you what. I'll save you the trouble by copying it myself. Then we can both sign both copies and we will have a deal. Is that fine for you, Mr. Van Zandt?"

"Certainly," came the reply. In short order father and son walked into the warm spring sunshine with enough money on their persons to tide them through for a long time in the simple manner of their lifestyle.

"Let's celebrate with a real tavern meal," Big Oak suggested. "And you know what else? We are goin' to sleep in a real inn tonight."

They found their meal in short order, at a run-down inn called the Bow and Musket. It was the first time in his young life that Little Oak had ever eaten a meal cooked and served in a public place for money, and he couldn't identify much of what he ate or drank. Little Oak took a look at the small mushrooms on his plate and said to his father, "I have seen bottles of wine before at the house of Warraghiyagey, but this is the first time anybody ever gave me the corks to eat." His father laughed and forked a mushroom into his mouth. "Eat it," he told his son. "You'll like it. After all, it's food, isn't it?" And he did eat and he did like it—in fact he liked the entire meal, which included some kind of meat, some kind of yam, and some kind of bean.

Around them the place was in an uproar, with seventeen monologues going on simultaneously at eleven tables, and each monologue getting louder and louder in order to compete with the other sixteen. This was strange to Little Oak. Iroquois listen, then they are silent, then they talk. This room was full of men who were all talk and no listen. The sound was brutal. Well, he thought, maybe it was the drink that gave them such bad manners. Drink seemed to give everybody bad manners, and like his father, Little Oak could not tolerate rudeness. The room stank of spilled ale and rum.

When they finished their meal and made inquiry to the innkeeper about a room, the innkeeper was so astonished he was barely able to keep his false teeth from popping out of his mouth.

"You gentlemen haven't been to Albany in a while, I suppose. We have more than a thousand soldiers being quartered in Albany right now, and thirty-six of them are sleeping in rooms right up there." He pointed to the ceiling. "I've only six rooms, and I couldn't stuff another soul in any of 'em, so I suppose you'll have to hie yourself back to the greenwood or wherever it is your sort sleeps."

Little Oak didn't like the tone of the man's voice, but his father simply laughed, and the two walked out.

"Pa, there are some things I do not understand. In the forest you are fearless against great odds. You kill mighty enemies with your rifle, your tomahawk, your knife, and your bare hands. How many have you killed in your life?"

"I don't remember." Big Oak was obviously not pleased by the question.

"And yet here in the city, with little people like the fur buyer and the man at the inn—men you could slice in half with a sharp look—you let insults pass."

"In the forests we are our own law. When you must fight to survive, you can let your weapons speak for you, but in the city the mightiest weapons are words. The men with these words are called counsels or somesuch. If I stuck a knife in the innkeeper, he would send a message to his counsel and the counsel would call a constable and the constable would come with several men and take me away and lock me up. Then I would have to give money to a counsel to get free.

"In the cities, the powerful men have, not strong arms or a clear eye, but strong words, and friends with strong words. I cannot fight those words. I'm sure another might have gotten much more money for his furs. The frontier is all afire. Trapping is very dangerous work this year. I would fear for our own scalps if we had to spend months in the forest at a time. So furs are scarce. The fur merchant's eyes were so hungry when he saw our furs that I was afraid he would eat them."

"I thought you struck a hard bargain."

"I did the best I could, but someone in ruffles and knee britches could have done much better. I won't worry about it, though. The innkeeper was right. We belong in the woods."

"Even with the Caughnawaga prowling like hungry wolves?"

"We'll stick close to Albany for now. There are too many soldiers here for the Indians or the French to strike this far south. Meantime, I believe we ought to get us some supplies."

They walked around the crowded shopping district. The normally patient Big Oak found himself annoyed by the constant crush of bodies splashing dirty water on each other as they made their way along the muddy streets, but Thad enjoyed the sight of so many oddly matched men and women in a hurry to travel from one place to another and tripping over each other to get there. There were the military people, of course, mostly in homemade excuses for uniforms, and Dutch burghers with important business appointments. There were women finishing up their shopping for the evening meal, rushing along with looks of sour distaste as they attempted to avoid physical contact with the dirty denizens of the street as they passed them by. And there was even an occasional Indian. To Thad, Albany seemed like the center of the universe.

Finally they stopped at a large store that seemed to sell just about everything. The place was full of men and women crushing against each other as they competed for the attention of the two young men in shirtsleeves and knee britches behind the counter. There was a balcony in the store with a plain wooden railing, and a stern older man draped over it, witnessing the transactions with a scowl that made all the features on his face seem to droop. He was plump in a

Dutch sort of way, thick-bodied from his bulky calves to his huge head and the curly wig that covered it. Nearly everything about him looked soft except his eyes, which were hard and shrewd as they stared down at his employees and customers. Big Oak imagined him recording every transaction he witnessed in his brain, to check against his clerks' receipt slips at the end of the day. His size and his station commanded authority.

Big Oak's demeanor and stature also commanded authority. Among the milling customers whining for service, he received response almost immediately. A new bullet mold was what he needed. He examined a number of them, comparing them with some of the bullets that remained in his pouch. Fine rifles like his demanded a custom-fitted bullet, and at times it was difficult to find the right-size mold. He finally found one he felt was close enough. His old one would go to Little Oak.

Also, he requested a couple of bars of lead and a small barrel of their very finest powder. And a skillet, some flour, and . . .

Little Oak's ears pricked up at the next things Big Oak purchased. These were city-man items, such as he had never before seen in his father's possession. When his father had finished, he paused for a moment, trying to decide if he had forgotten anything. A large, red-faced, perspiring man behind him demanded that he pay his bill and give somebody else a turn.

Big Oak turned and gave the man a look that froze him into silence. Then he smiled at the man and said, mildly, "I'm almost done," and paid his bill. The man turned redder, and shut his mouth out of fear or embarrassment.

The clerk was helping him carry out the goods, through the milling crowds to where the mule was waiting tied up in front of the inn where Big Oak had hoped to spend the night, but just as Thad was about to follow his father out the door, he caught a glimpse of a very familiar face standing on the balcony.

"Katherine!" he hollered above the din.

She looked for the voice and found Thad, standing near the door.

"You! You!" she shouted back in a happy soprano. "What *is* your name? Oh. Thad!"

"Father, look. That's Thad!" she said urgently, as if she had mentioned him before to the merchant, which she had, at times when his mind was on his balance sheets and he wasn't listening.

"So?" he said.

"Oh—come up the stairs!" she demanded.

"No, no," the grave authority figure started to say, but the machinery had been set in motion. In an instant Thad was up on the balcony with the authority figure and his beautiful daughter, whose ever-present smile was now twice as wide as the secret smile he had seen on the street.

Astonishment fought the scowl for possession of the man's face. "Who is this boy?" he asked. "This ruffian wit' a rifle in his hand. You have been hiding things from your papa?"

She ignored his questions. "I want you to meet Thad."

"So, hello, Thad. Demmit, who is he?"

"I'm Thad Watley and I am a fur trader," he said. Then he turned to Katherine, removed his deerskin cap and made a slight bow. "That is who I am, Miss Katherine—"

"Miss Katherine Wendel, Mr. Watley," she replied with a curtsy.

"I am confused," said the merchant, his sternness softened by the unaccustomed show of manners of his only daughter. "Do you or don't you know this boy?"

"Thad, what are you doing up there?" shouted his father above the din from the floor below. "Will you leave those people alone? We have to call on Warraghiyagey."

Thad looked at Katherine, then at his father, who for the moment he wished would disappear.

"Wait just a moment, Pa. Mr. Wendel I'm pleased to meet you. That's—Father down there, and we have to be somewhere else now, but may I call on your daughter tomorrow, sir?" he asked.

"Uh . . ." He was going to say no, emphatically, and in a normal year he would have done so, but this well-mannered boy in the animal skins looked pretty good next to the endless parade of rude, profane young soldiers and militia who had been gawking at his daughter since the verdammt war had begun—although the war had been an incredible boon for his mercantile and shipping business.

"If she wishes you to."

"Oh, yes, I—" She closed her mouth suddenly and tried to blush, but her huge twinkling blue eyes gave her away as she fastened them on her father.

The authority figure breathed a deep sigh and suddenly looked helpless. "Yes, yes," he said impatiently, and walked to the railing of the balcony to resume his calculations of the day's receipts.

"Where do you live?" Little Oak had almost forgotten to ask as he turned to leave.

"In the brick house next to the store," she said. "Come at four o'clock."

"I will," he said, and then like a flushed deer, he bounded down the stairs and out into the crowded street, past his surprised father.

Big Oak caught up to his son at the mule, just as the clerk finished up his chore of loading their supplies on the back of the animal.

"I thank you, sir," he told the clerk, and began to check the load as the clerk walked up the street back to the store.

"Now, I knew there was a girl in Albany, and I guess she must be it. Care to tell me about her?"

"Her name is Katherine Wendel and I met her the last time we were in Albany."

"Where did you meet her?"

"Well, I sort of met her, anyway. What do you think?"

"Very pretty girl," Big Oak said. "Of course, that's about

all I can tell. She might be a knife-tongued harridan, for all I know about her. I have only one question."

"What's that?"

"How in tarnation are you gonna know when it's four o'clock?"

Thad thought for a moment. "Easy. I saw a clock in the inn. I'll just hang around outside and look in until it's almost that time."

"I didn't even know you knew how to tell time."

"Pa, I think you forgot many things when Red Hawk clubbed you on the head last year. When I was young, you taught me how to read, right?"

"I remember that."

"And then you brought me a bunch of books that you got from the old dead dominie, right?"

"If you say so."

"And in the wintertime when the days were short and the men spent their time around the fire smoking, I read all the books."

"All of them?"

"So when you finally sent me to that church school, I had my letters and my reading, but they taught me numbers and they taught me manners—and they taught me to tell time.

"After my first year in school, I came back to the village, remember? And one day one of our braves comes back from a raid on the French and he brings back one of those little clocks."

"It's called a watch."

"What a time I had explaining what it was for. He couldn't understand why someone would need a clock to tell him what part of the day it was."

"They don't, do they?"

Little Oak understood that "they" meant the people of his mother, the people he used to live with but no longer did. It made him dizzy, this bustling city with all its white people and strange smells. But after the last horrible winter, he was seriously beginning to wonder on which side of the blanket he would live his life.

The sitting room of the house was the cleanest place he had ever seen, with a shiny floor of smooth, broad planks, big comfortable wooden chairs with cushions, plenty of light from the windows that looked out on the busy street, and a low table with two drinking glasses and a frosty pitcher of lemonade.

He stood in the doorway feeling like a bug at a bird convention.

"Please come in, Mr. Watley," said the woman, a light-colored black slave who was Mr. Wendel's housekeeper, cook, and general home secretary. "Mr. Wendel will be down in a moment."

Twisting his cap in his hands, Thad staked out a five-foot runway in the sitting room and began to pace it.

"You may sit down, if you wish," the woman said sympathetically.

"Thank you."

He detected a quick bit of muffled conversation on the second floor, so faint that even his acute hearing could not make it out, and then the figure of authority descended the stairs, ponderously, deliberately, as if the meeting were of solemn importance. Thad remembered himself enough to stand up.

"Sit down," Mr. Wendel said absently, as the housekeeper quietly left the room. "Is it really so, Mr. Watley, that until yesterday you and my daughter had never talked to each other?"

"We passed each other on the street twice, and she told me her name just before we marched off to Lake George last year," Thad replied.

"I see." Thad wished Katherine's father would sit down. He did not like having to look up at a man who loomed over him like a big old beech tree.

"She seems to . . . like you."

"I like her."

"You don't know her."

"I would like to."

At this point the merchant seated himself in the closest chair and leaned into Thad's face. Now Thad wished the man would stand up and loom over him again.

"How could you know whether you like her if you and the girl have never had a talk wit' each other?"

Thad recalled something his father said to him a long time before.

"Among the Seneca," he said, "we learn to read people's faces. The kind of person they are is written on their face." What he said was not exactly the truth, but neither was it a lie. He had read her face. He had read kindness and sweetness and adventure in her face. Get to know her? He couldn't wait.

"You were raised wit' the Indians?"

"My mother was a Seneca."

"You read people's faces?"

"I am too young to know much. But we do learn from the people we grow up with."

"Read my face, young man."

Thad sat silently, not liking the direction of the conversation, feeling hostility from a man whose friendship he desired.

The somber Dutch face curled into a smile. "I'm not trying to hurt you, young man. Just tell me what her papa is like. It is important, you know. Her mother died many years ago, like your mother, yes?"

Thad nodded.

"Katherine and I are very close. She is like me in many ways."

"I don't know what you are like. To me you look stern, and yesterday I thought you must think of money most of the time. But today is a business day and yet you are here thinking of Katherine."

The merchant laughed. "And I must get back to the store, but first you and Katherine may have your talk. Katherine!"

She must have been waiting at the top of the stairs. She came down immediately. Thad felt warm all over. The girl was bursting with the freshness that every day's new experiences brought to her. He was awed by how different she looked compared to the girls he had grown up with. The blond hair, the strong jaw, the sprinkling of freckles across the bridge of her tiny nose. Most of all the blue eyes that seemed to smile at him the way his heart smiled at her. She was a tall girl, big-boned, not delicate at all, the kind of girl to make a great partner. Thad stood up again and, he noticed, so did Mr. Wendel.

She seated herself in a chair next to her father. They were both facing Thad, but it was the father who continued the conversation.

"Are you a Christian, Mr. Watley, or do you worship the trees and rocks like your savages?"

"I spent several years at a Presbyterian school in western New York. I am a Christian." Thad was telling a half-truth. He was a Christian if Christian meant believing in Jesus Christ as his personal savior. He was not a Christian if Christian meant believing that Jesus Christ had to be everybody else's personal savior. The Caughnawaga, he believed, would be a less bloodthirsty bunch if they did not have the French priests telling them that they were killing for the glory of Jesus Christ.

"How do you plan on supporting my daughter?"

Thad nearly fell off his chair. In Tonowaugh he had never heard of any father asking such a question.

"For many years my father was a trapper, but since I have been with him, he does not trap. We trade with the Indians for furs. Business is business, my father tells me. He says my life will be different from his. Someday."

"How so?" Mr. Wendel asked.

"He says that in a very few years there will be no place for men like him in New York. He says that either I must find myself a place in the settlements or be a wanderer like him."

"Which do you think it will be?" the merchant asked with genuine interest.

"I don't know. But I was raised in a town. It may have been a Seneca town, but it was a place to come home to. I love the woods, but I love the home fire too. My father says that soon there will be no home fires left for the Iroquois in the valley of the Te-non—the Mohawk."

"I wish I could be believe that. Since the war started, everybody in Albany sleeps with their muskets in their beds."

"That is not the fault of the Mohawk. When did the Mohawk attack Albany?"

"Mohawk, Mohican, Kagnowaga, who can tell the difference? They are strange people. They run around the woods without their clothes on. We do not understand them. They do not understand us. We cannot live in the same place."

"And yet they were here first."

"So, you want us to give back the land? That is life. Back in Holland, the Spanish took land from my ancestors. It's a hard world out there, and we must survive, no?"

"Still, I wish that white men could tell their friends from their enemies."

"Are you certain you can tell your friends from your enemies?"

Little Oak thought of Tonowaugh, the town he would never come home to. "No, I am not certain," he said, feeling lonely as he said it.

Finally, Katherine, who had been listening to the conversation with a serious expression around her mouth but a sparkle in her eye, spoke.

"Father," she said, "I would like to talk to Mr. Watley for a while."

"Then talk," answered the father, giving no indication that he was about to quit his chair.

She sighed. "Thad is a nice name," she said.

"It belonged to my grandfather."

"Where did he come from?" the merchant asked.

"Father!" Her voice was mildly reproving.

"Connecticut. I never knew him. My father lost his parents in a house fire when he was ten."

"Thad." Katherine looked at her father with pleading eyes, and her father went silent. "The last time I saw you—before yesterday, that is—you were going off to fight the French. Will you be doing that again?"

"My father and I will be leaving for Fort Oswego later in the summer."

The merchant looked annoyed. "There are many others who can fight in this war and so many have died up there of disease, or so they tell me."

"My father says the same."

"Mr. Watley, I want my daughter to be happy. I want her to have a husband who stays home and does not go running around the countryside with stupid generals."

"My father agrees with that too. We hire on as scouts, and do not go with the soldiers. We are like the Indians. When our fight is over, we go home."

"Like the Indians, eh?"

"There are very many white men, and very few Indians. They cannot afford to throw away their lives in battle like the white generals do. They do not stand in rows to be mowed like wheat by enemy gunfire. They hide behind trees and use their own sense, and usually survive."

"But you do not plan to go running through the woods with the Indians for the rest of your life."

"Up until the last few moons, I did not plan anything. But now I believe that I will not live out my life in the forests."

"You don't sound very happy about it."

"The white cities are new to me. There is so much for me to understand."

"When you understand more, Mr. Watley, may be the time for you to pay us another visit."

"Father!" This time Katherine was visibly annoyed, but she loved her father, and she knew him.

As they both rose from their chairs to accompany Thad to the door, she finally had her conversation with him. He went out the door, followed by Katherine, who turned to her father and said, "I shall be right back," then softly closed the door behind her.

On the street, with the wagons, the horses, and the bustling people, she stood facing him and said, "I think he likes you. He does not like many young men."

"I haven't been seeing your *father* in my dreams all these many moons. Do *you* like me?"

"I thought I did, and even more so when I listened to you talk to my father. I got to know you much better than you know me. I like you very much."

"I learned a lot about you, watching you while we talked."

"Oh yes, I heard you tell my father. You can read faces."

"Not really. And yet you did tell me about yourself without having to say much."

"Tell me how."

At this point the door opened. "Katherine, I need you in the store now to help me. Business is good and we are falling behind on the books. Young man, I enjoyed our conversation and I hope to see you again when you come back from Oswego."

"We'll be finished in a minute," she said, gently pushing her father into the house and closing the door. "Thad, do you remember the first time you saw me?"

"On the street where that bakery—"

"Meet me there tomorrow at noon?"

Between the time he nodded and the time his mouth opened to say yes, her father opened the door again, took her hand and guided her down the street through the door to his establishment, but not before she was able to turn her head and smile back at him with her entire face.

* * *

He arrived a good fifteen minutes early, but he did not mind having to wait. Ever since the first day he had seen her, this part of town had taken on a magical quality to Thad. After that first time, he had returned again and again hoping to see her, and yet when she didn't appear, he was never disappointed. Thad was a natural optimist. It was enough for him to believe that she was interested in him, and that he was, at the very least, curious about her. Market Street was simply a place where he expected good things to happen to him.

He didn't loiter. There were too many things to see. He walked around one block and then another, gazing at the stores, the homes, and the people, some of whom stared back at him as if he were wearing feathers and a loincloth. He didn't care. He was proud of being a woodsman rather than a townsman.

He looked into the sky, noted the time of the year and the position of the sun, and sensed rather than calculated that noon had arrived. His pulse quickened and for the first time his nerves twitched. This time it would be him and her alone, with a chance to talk. What could the two of them possibly have to talk about? He stared hard at a man in a tricorner hat who had been gawking at him. The man averted his gaze and Thad chuckled, then almost jumped out of his skin as he felt a tap on the shoulder and turned around to face Katherine.

She laughed. "I hope you are more alert in the woods. Surely the Indians are more stealthy than I."

"Ah, but these are your woods," he said. "They're as strange to me as the tumbling waters of the Genesee are to you." He looked at her and enjoyed what he saw. There was something about her smile that instantly put him at ease and made him feel as if he were standing on familiar, comfortable ground.

"What's in the basket?" he asked.

"Some cold meat. Bread. Fruit. Wine."

"What for?"

"For us, silly."

"Us? That's very nice." He was touched. They were walking due east, in the direction of the Hudson River. For a time they were silent, and he found that he didn't mind the silence. These *were* her woods; she seemed willing to be his guide, and he was willing to be guided. It occurred to him that the basket might be heavy, and he reached toward her to take the handle.

"Thank you, sir," she said. Sir. He liked the sound of that, at least for the moment.

"Thad, we read faces too. You have an honest face. A kind face. A happy face. Other than that, I know so little about you. Do you mind if we talk about you?"

"If you don't mind telling me about you."

"Oh, you know about me. I'm like a hundred other girls in this town, but you are not like any boy I ever met."

He thought for a moment. "You know, I understand what you mean. The boys in the Seneca village where I grew up —Skoiyasi and John Thompson—they were my closest friends, and yet I was not like them. Now I don't think Skoiyasi cares much for me."

"And what about John Thompson? Was he part white too?"

"No. That's just the name they gave him. He's dead now." Thad decided that he did not want to ruin their afternoon with a detailed account of his death. "Earlier today, on my walk through town, a boy walked up to me, just like that, and asked me if I was a redskin. I told him yes, I was a redskin, and I would eat him for lunch but he didn't believe me. He just asked why I dressed like a white man if I was a redskin."

"What did you say to that?"

"I told him I dressed like my father, who was white. You know what he said?"

Her expression showed she certainly wanted to know.

"He said he didn't think a person could be both, that he had to be either one or the other."

Katherine laughed, but Thad's face displayed the frown

lines on his forehead that she loved so much because they made him look so earnest.

"What do you think?"

She stopped laughing, started to reach for his arm, then stopped. "I think he's right," she said.

They continued walking. He let out an audible sigh. "Me too," he agreed. "But I was a Seneca for many years. My pa always spoke English to me, so I learned it early, but until I went away to school I thought mostly in Seneca, and I always dreamed in Seneca."

She smiled. "How was school?"

"School was good. My pa had taught me to read by the time the Reverend Heflin got a hold of me, and I think he was so surprised that I knew a little that it made him think I was one pretty smart Injun. So he spent plenty of time on me and pounded enough learning into my thick head that some of what he taught me stuck."

"Can you do Latin?"

He shook his head. "The Reverend Heflin said that Latin was the tongue of the devil. And any Greek he taught me I lost a long time ago, but I kept about everything else. My pa taught me to keep accounts, and I still read when I get my hands on a book. Mostly the Bible. I guess I read it just to read, because if I forgot how to read . . ."

"You'd be back where you were before?"

He thought for a moment before he spoke. "The Indians I was close to are dead, or they don't care for me anymore. It is very hard to be an Indian. So if you have to be one or the other, I'm damned if I'm gonna be an Indian.

"I'm sorry about the profanity. I miss them. Every night I miss them. My mother, my grandfather, my uncle, John Thompson, Skoiyasi, Kawia."

"Who is Kawia?" she asked.

"A girl who was my friend."

"Your friend?" She had caught a nuance in his voice.

"We were too young to be anything but friends. Maybe

we could have been more than friends. Still, it hurts that she does not want my friendship."

"Is that all?"

He nodded. They had reached a hill that overlooked the river. Below, he could see ships and boats of various sizes plying their way north and south. He was surprised at the amount of traffic on the river, and he said so.

"My father says that soon there will be twice as much."

"I think I like your father. He doesn't mind that I am half a savage?"

She gave him a plate with a thick slice of meat, a thicker slice of bread, and some pieces of apple with honey. He waited to see how she would eat it. "It's an outing," she said. "Not like eating at table with your Reverend Heflin. You may use your fingers. And use this." She gave him a linen napkin.

"He thinks you are smarter than the other boys who come around. He calls them blockheads. But he says he doesn't know if you have gotten over scalping people."

"I think I have," he said, and began to laugh at the look of frank astonishment on her face. She saw him laughing and she began to laugh too, at his joke. He wanted to tell her that in battle people do evil things to each other, including scalping, but he didn't see why she had to know. But he wasn't going to lie about it either, so he let it pass.

They sat in the grass, eating and watching the ships and boats in silence. "This is good food," he said. "Thank you."

"Thad, the people here are afraid the Indians will attack Albany."

"Big town like this?"

"They are afraid of the Mohawks."

"They're afraid of what? I told your father yesterday that the whites could not tell their friends from their enemies? Would the French attack? Yes. Would the Caughnawaga attack? With the French, maybe; would the Abnaki attack? Maybe. But Katherine, the Mohawks will not attack Albany."

She looked at him through narrowed eyes. "How can you know that?"

"My father knows them well. He says they won't. And then, there just aren't enough Mohawks left to attack a big white man town like this. Don't the white men here know that? And I've been with the Mohawks. They don't like the English, and I don't blame them, but the English are still their allies, and they don't attack their allies. You can thank Warraghiyagey for that."

"Warraghi-who-gey?"

"William Johnson. Have you never heard of him?"

"Johnson, yes. That other name?" She shook her head. "I could never remember that." She leaned forward and looked hard at him.

"You have spent much time with the Mohawks?"

"Of course. They are our brothers."

"Whose brothers?"

"Ours, the Seneca."

". . . I keep forgetting. I feel so comfortable with you, I forget . . ." She looked at him carefully, in search of a hurt or offended expression, but he just laughed.

"Listen, so that you'll understand. I am half Iroquois, and yes, I have fought against the French, alongside Mohawks. A year ago I had never killed a man. The past year I've had enough killing to last me a lifetime. War is ugly, but my pa says the English have caused much of it."

"Will they come?"

"Who?"

"The Mohawks."

"I told you, not the Mohawks. The French."

"I'm not afraid of the French, I'm afraid of the Mohawks."

"You should be afraid of the French! They're the enemy, them and *their* Indians."

"But the French are so far away. And the Mohawks are so close." The fear on her face was clear.

He took both her hands in his. "Katherine, listen to me. You trust me to be alone with you. Do you think the Mohawk is a different kind of an animal than I am? Than you are? They are not demons."

"But the things they *do* to people. What I have heard about them."

"And you know what they have heard? That the English in Albany, their allies, plan to attack their castles and kill them in their longhouses. Who is afraid of who? How can we beat the French if we can't trust our own?"

"Is that what the Mohawks are, our own?"

"Katherine, do you know anybody that the Mohawks ever harmed?"

"Me? No."

"Please listen to me. We are fighting this war against the French, not the Iroquois."

"And if it turns out that we're fighting the Iroquois, then whose side will you be on?"

Suddenly Thad felt weary. His day, which had started so beautifully, had turned into a thunderstorm. "Why would you ask such a question? Suppose I said, 'Whichever side I think is right'? Suppose I said, 'Whichever side would have me'? Suppose I said, 'Why, I'll just go off and hide in the woods until you've finished killin' each other, cause neither one of you wants a thing to do with me!' Which would be the right thing to do?"

She had put away her food and looked away from him, back to the ships plying their way up and down the Hudson.

"On one of those ships," he said, "may be the furs we brought from the west, bound for New York." They both watched the ships, as if they might be able to pick out the fur-bearing vessel.

"I am sorry, Thad. I am frightened. The Indian in front of me, the one I know, looks like the man I could love. But the Indians out there, the ones I do not know, they frighten me. Am I an awful person?"

"Pa says that's what war does to people, makes 'em afraid of each other. But from what I've seen, I'm not afraid of what's gonna happen to the Iroquois during this war. I'm afraid of what's gonna happen to them after the peace."

She thought about that, but not for long. "I must be a selfish girl," she replied. "What I really want to know is, what's going to happen to us?"

"What do you want to happen to us?"

"I want you to stay here. I don't want you to leave."

"If I go, and I promise to be back, will you wait?"

"I will, but I'll be very frightened for you."

"I don't blame you. Waiting is much worse than fighting. But Pa ānd I don't run out and do the kinds of crazy things that get people killed. We don't charge cannons and we don't go flappin' around in the open where people can get a good shot at us. We keep our heads down and our hind ends down and we blend into the trees. Most of all, as I told you and your father, we stay clear of stupid generals. I was born and raised in the woods. The woods will protect us. They always have."

"Oh, I hope you are right. I will pray for you."

"Pray for us. Katherine." He wanted to add more but the words of endearment were strange to his lips, even if the feelings were familiar to his heart.

That night he dreamed that he was being chased in the dead of night by a band of screeching Caughnawagas. Before him his trail ended at a jump off point that may have been five feet, ten feet or a thousand feet, he could not tell in the dark.

He heard the screeches come so close that he had no choice but to jump, either to safety or to his death. Knowing he had no choice, he felt no fear, only a reckless exhilaration as he stepped off into eternity.

## ⊰22⊱

THE RUMORS THAT WARS BRING FLEW BACK
and forth along the Mohawk Valley in the summer of 1756.
Lord Loudoun was taking over from General Shirley. The
French were coming down from Canada with five thousand
Indians to burn every white settlement, scalp all the men,
rape all the women, and carry off all the children. The English were abandoning the entire line of forts from Oswego
to Lake George. General Johnson was sick and dying. General Johnson was sick of all the politics and was quitting and
going home to Mount Johnson. The Six Nations were all
going over to the French; their Mohawk neighbors would
soon be descending on Albany and bloodying their hatchets
on the local burghers.

Some of the rumors were all true, some slightly true, but
most of them were complete nonsense. In June, Sam and
Thad visited the Mohawks in what they still called
Gingego's village. As a present they brought a welcome gift
of Herr Wendel's excellent powder, a quantity of lead, and
some flints. Sam revealed to the warriors that he was a pass-
able repairer of muskets and rifles, and set about doing what
he could to put their weapons in shape for what he hoped
would be their summer campaign.

In gratitude for his help, they invited him to sit at the
council fire and let him speak. As he had several times be-

fore, he directed his remarks toward Louis and those who looked to Louis for leadership.

"I know you do not like the English. I don't like them so well either. They treat all colonials like fools."

Here he was interrupted by Louis.

"Hah—English, colonials, they are just different names for the same kind of skunk," he said, and from the firelight and the shadows came many sounds of agreement. "The truth, my brother, is that we like the king much better than we like his people that we must live with."

"There are good and bad in every race," Big Oak said.

"Too greedy, all Englishmen," Tall Bear said. "We do not want to fight for them."

"I am asking you to fight for yourselves. I promised Colonel Bradstreet I would bring scouts."

"Colonel Bradstreet is a good man," Tall Bear said to a mixed chorus of agreement and disagreement. There then ensued an argument among the braves as to whether Colonel John Bradstreet was a primping popinjay or one of the few good officers the English had in America.

Big Oak listened to the debate for a while before he finally decided to interrupt in order to steer the discussion back on track. "Never mind Bradstreet. Whether he is a good officer or a bad officer, we will not have to face cannon. We will not have to fight beside the soldiers. It will be our job to find the enemy, lay an ambush or bring the news, and then we will disappear."

"I have heard that before," said an older warrior, whose body was bent and scarred. "In the last big war they told us that, and then they made us go into the fort and fight behind wooden walls. They made me stay near a cannon. Big noise nearly drove me crazy. I sneaked away as far from that cannon as I could get, and the cannon blew up. Everybody near it in too many little pieces for spirit world. I tell you I will not fight side by side with those people. They have no sense."

"If they try to bring you to the fort, I will lead you home

myself. If they try to force us into the fort, I will fight, on your side, against them, for they have no right to order us into the fort. We are their allies, not their subjects, no matter what they think. But we must fight on their side. I tell you, if the French win, they will come down from Canada with your brothers the Caughnawaga. I don't have to let you know you what a fine bunch the Caughnawaga have become." Here Big Oak made such a scornful, funny face, as if to show the expression of a Caughnawaga brave speaking French, that most of the braves began to laugh, even as they turned red with passion.

He knew he had them. All he had to do was mention the Caughnawaga to jerk them into a frenzy. There is no hate that comes close to that enjoyed by close relations who have had a bad falling out.

"I'll tell you what I will do," Louis said. "I will go and I will scout, but mostly I will keep a sharp eye for our brother Red Hawk, who loves nothing more than drinking the blood of his own Ganiengehaka. I will not drink his blood, for it is full of poison, but I will gladly let it run into the earth, then watch it until the earth is again dry and Red Hawk is forgotten."

Gingego's widow spoke then. "To any who would disagree, I will tell you that the day our men were killed on Lake George, Red Hawk was there, killing his own people. How could someone hate himself so much that he would kill his own people?" Big Oak caught Louis's eye, and the two stared at each other for a moment.

The rest of the evening was devoted to solemn assurances from each brave present that the blood of their Caughnawaga brothers would flow, and that the blood of the hated French would pour in torrents, just as long as they did not have to charge the cannon, or fight behind the walls of the fort, alongside the English soldiers.

And yet it took forever for Big Oak to get the Mohawks to move. On this day, when they were supposed to start out, there wasn't enough food. Or the medicine wasn't just right.

Or someone wasn't back from a visit to a sick uncle who lived near Johnson Mountain. Little Oak watched his father get more and more restless, until one day he thought Big Oak would herd them onto the trail like a flock of goats. Finally, at the beginning of August, Big Oak announced that he and his son were leaving and that the brave ones could go with him now and leave the cowards behind.

Louis announced that he was ready to go, but Little Oak couldn't help noticing that Louis's younger brother, George —named by Gingego when he wished to send a message to the French—was staying behind. He was certain that this was the decision of White Bird, who was not about to risk the loss of all her family's protectors in one big uncertain battle.

Once Louis declared for the warpath, eleven other warriors signed up, so to speak, and the following morning, to Little Oak's surprise, the war party actually took their first steps along the trail to Fort Oswego.

Big Oak was not surprised that the warriors had been reluctant to fight.

All spring and summer, warriors had been coming and going in ones, twos, and threes. Instead of hunting deer, they were out prowling the woods, hunting information to sell to the English, the French, or, in some cases, to both. When they returned to their village, they would supply that information gratis to their friends and relatives. The information was generally gloomy from an English point of view, and at this time, liking neither side very much, the Mohawks longed to be on the side of the winners, whoever they were.

Slinking along the Mohawk, bypassing any of the scattered settlements along the way, the little group approached that stretch known as the Great Carrying Place, where in peaceful times Indians would bear their canoes from the Mohawk to Wood Creek, which poured into Lake Oneida, then to the Onondaga River, and finally Lake Ontario.

The English had chosen to defend this critical piece of territory by building two brand new bulwarks known as Fort

Williams and Fort Bull. The Indians didn't know any of the
officers in those forts so they bypassed them in the night
and the soldiers never were the wiser.

Quietly they ran the remaining sixty-five miles in under
two days. During that time Little Oak did not think much
about what had happened lately to him. He gloried in the
feeling of power that comes from having a strong, well-
working machine for a body. He appreciated the greasy,
painted, shaven-headed, mostly naked men who shared their
trail with him and were his brothers under the roof of the
Longhouse. Perhaps the hostility of his home Seneca village
had brought home to him the fragility of the Iroquois future
on the banks of the Te-non-an-at-che.

And when at last they had made it to the shores of Lake
Ontario, they found signs of the French and their allies all
around the three English forts that guarded the entrance
from the lake to the Onondaga River. Quickly, they vanished into the woods and made their way inland until they
could find a height from which to witness the proceedings.
It was obvious that the French were putting together a large
force, either to besiege the forts or to attack them.

"We are late to help our allies," Big Oak said to Louis.
"The French are here and they are very strong."

"Maybe better that we did not come earlier," Louis responded without emotion. "We might be stuck in there with
them." Louis pointed into old Fort Oswego.

"We should go to the English and report what we see,"
Little Oak suggested.

"No need," returned his father, pointing to a canoe that
was moving along the shore of the lake.

"English scouts," Big Oak said, indicating a spot well
down the lakefront. "They've spotted all those, and that's
why they're hightailing it back to the fort. Those are French
bateaux, and if you look beyond those trees, you'll see there
must be a hundred of them."

Little Oak peered into the dim dawn light. They were
there, all right, scores of bateaux of all sizes, about a mile

east of the fort. "They mean to attack," Big Oak said. "Not long from now."

"That's a strong-looking fort," Little Oak replied, studying the stone walls standing tall on what looked to his inexperienced eye like a staunch position.

"Sometimes what you see is not what there is," his father replied as Louis moved close to them.

"I don't like the look of this," he said, pointing out areas where he thought the French and their Indians might have hidden themselves.

"Mmm," Big Oak agreed.

The scouts from the canoe had hustled on into the fort, and almost immediately the witnesses from the hill could detect a swift flurry of activity. The drums rolled and men streamed from their quarters to help man the parapets. Two civilians paddled madly across the Onondaga River and leaped from their canoe, one heading for nearby Fort Ontario and one for useless Fort George. Their messages must have been inspiring, for both forts turned out their entire garrisons in minutes.

Faintly, in ghostly monotones that would echo through Little Oak's memory for the rest of his life, he could hear the commands that directed the preparations of the defense. Then, for a moment only, there was such complete silence within the forts that those on the scene could hear the waters of the great lake lapping at its shores.

From the woods to the east, not far from where the French boats lay, came the crackling of small-arms fire. Later the English would learn that the gunfire came from Caughnawagas accidentally firing on their French allies in the dark woods. Hearing the firing, and thinking their comrades were attacking the fort, the French and their allies began rushing out of the edge of the woods toward the fort, firing as they ran.

Very often battles begin not when the commanders command them to begin, but when the first itchy troops open fire. So it was here. The French commander, Montcalm, had not yet given the order, but the fight had begun without him, so he did the only thing he could do, he ordered the rest of his troops into the attack and hoped for the best. At first they fired at a distance, from the tree line, and the fort's defenders fired back, all at ranges too great for their muskets to be of much use.

So went the entire morning, with bullets splintering into the trees or pinging off the stonework of the fort, and little, very little, damage being done. The Mohawk group up on the hill sat back and enjoyed a cold lunch while they witnessed the contest. Occasionally they would see a figure keel over or hear the faint shout of a curse in French or English. A breeze blew off the lake, rippling the long grass along the banks of the river. The sun moved across the sky, and still the French and English fired their weapons at each other, with very little effect except that every once in a great while somebody would die.

"The French have some plans, I'm sure of that," Big Oak told Louis. "They aren't about to sit still till kingdom come banging away. Those mud walls might not be good for much, but they *can* turn away bullets."

Late in the afternoon more French troops arrived. "Ah, that's what they were waiting for," Big Oak commented as the French wheeled about two dozen artillery pieces out of the woods. From across the river the soldiers at Fort Ontario continued to keep up their innocuous fire at the well-protected French. The steady breeze from the lake blew a heavy pall of gray powder smoke toward the spectators on the hill.

Only the darkness put an end to the exchange of musket fire, and once the gunfire had died down and the last trace of daylight had faded from the midsummer sky, a new sound came to the eyewitnesses on the hill, the sound of digging, digging, all night, digging.

Several of the braves came to Louis and Big Oak in the dark and suggested that the battle was already lost and that it would be a good thing to go home. To Little Oak's surprise, Louis bristled at the idea.

"We are here," he told them. "They do not know we are here. Later, when they have had their fill of battle and grow careless, then we will strike a blow."

They were not impressed with Louis's reasoning. They would leave for home in the morning, they told him.

They pulled their blankets around them and slept in shifts, and whenever one woke up, the first thing he heard was the sound of shovels scraping dirt. Throughout the night the digging sounds continued, and when dawn came, there was a siege trench outside the fort with all sorts of junk piled up in front of it as protection. In the fort the cannon were hurriedly being moved from the west side to the east side, where the trenches were uncomfortably close. The shooting started up again and continued all day, with very little damage to either side. Those who had announced that they intended to leave decided to stay and watch for a while, but they insisted that they would not fight this battle, no matter what.

There were different sounds that night on the other side of the river—banging sounds, rolling sounds, strange sounds that made two of Louis's men curious. They decided to investigate, and nobody stopped them.

While they were gone, Big Oak and Louis discussed the prospects of Fort Oswego, with Thad as an anxious spectator. Both were concerned that the fort was doomed, and neither felt there was much they could do to help. Soon the talk died out. Most of the party, including Big Oak, were tired, and ready to grab as much sleep as they could.

Two hours later the young scouts were back. They had information, and more important to them, each returned with a scalp, one definitely Indian—"Abnaki," said its possessor with satisfaction—and one European.

"What is happening across the river?" Big Oak asked, ignoring the scalps even though he knew the braves were dying to talk about them.

"Ah," said the larger of the two, an Oneida named Left Hand, whose scouting report had its own priorities. "Red woman and white man together in the woods. White man was French officer in white uniform. We let them finish first."

"Almost," disagreed the other one, fingering the dripping scalp he had taken so recently that it was still warm from the body heat of the wearer.

"What is the noise across the river?"

"We crept up and found one of the English scouts, a warrior from my village," the Oneida said. "He told me that inside the fort they were throwing the powder down the well to keep it from the French, and breaking the cannon. Then they would cross the river to Fort Oswego."

They stopped their conversation and listened. Instead of metallic banging from across the river, they heard more digging sounds at the trenches. They were about to grab another hour or two of sleep when one of their braves came running into their little camp.

"The French are coming!" he hissed. "And the Caughnawaga."

"Do you think they know we're here?"

"I don't think so. It sounds like half their army."

"Should we warn the fort?" Little Oak asked.

"We don't know any passwords," replied his father. "They'd probably shoot at us if we tried. And we don't really know what the French are trying to do. Maybe they're attacking from another direction. Maybe they're moving south because more English are coming from that direction. If they're attacking, they won't matter all that much. It's the artillery that's gonna win it for somebody."

Almost immediately the Mohawks and the two white scouts had snatched up their packs and rifles. Those who were asleep awakened silently and moved with the rest, down the reverse slope.

They found a deep hollow by a creek and hid in it, listening while the attackers moved along the hillside, trying to

be quiet, but noisy nevertheless with the rattling and clank-
ing of packs and guns, powder horns and canteens. One of
the Mohawk braves, jealous of his friends' success with the
lovemaking couple, wanted to find a stray Frenchman to kill,
but Louis convinced him that he'd probably be detected and
then the Caughnawaga would make it very hot for all of
them.

The attacking army turned out to be a diverse lot, French
whitecoats, Caughnawagas, Abnakis, a few Nipissings, some
Iroquoian schismatics and Canadian bush lopers, but they
moved together quickly past the position of the hidden
Mohawks. Though the Frenchmen clinked and clanked as
they marched, the Indians and the Canadians were noiseless.
Nobody spoke, and neither Big Oak nor Louis doubted that
wherever this army turned up, it would be a startling surprise to the defenders of Fort Oswego. There were hundreds
of them, so the Mohawks had to wait endless minutes for
the entire attacking contingent to make their way along the
hillside. The Mohawks held their breath in the shadows of
their hiding place, for they knew that if they were discovered, the Abnakis would cut each of them into little pieces,
slowly, one piece at a time, over a period of days.

Among the warriors that nearly crossed the path of the
tiny Mohawk party was Red Hawk, who was having the
finest year of his life. After years of passive hatred of the
British, he had received the blessings of the French to wreak
havoc on the enemy and their allies to his heart's content.
That most of his victims happened to have been Indians did
not trouble him. They were "English" Indians, and as such
they were whetstones for his tomahawk.

In the months since he and Owaiskah's Caughnawaga had
left their village under command of the Canadian LeJeune,
they had murdered fifteen people in addition to the massacre of the farmer and his entire family and the debacle at
Tonowaugh. Tonowaugh had been his idea, because his hatred had focused on Little Oak and his father, men who
knew how to seduce the Ganonsyoni into trusting them.

The other deaths were quick and sudden pounces upon small groups of civilians who had been unlucky enough to find themselves in the same stretch of woods at the same time as the bloodthirsty raiding party: a couple of white trappers here, an old Onondaga hunter there, even a pair of English army deserters. The deserters had provided a particularly enjoyable afternoon of entertainment by the time their bodies had stopped twitching in forks of the two supple young saplings from which they'd been spread-eagled, upside down.

Someday, Red Hawk thought, he would have children, and when he did, he would have stories to tell them, year after year, around the longhouse hearth fires, of his wonderful exploits in his years as a mighty warrior.

He couldn't say that he liked the French, but they were useful, and their armies were good enough to make him wonder why, when every war between them and the English was over, it was always the English who triumphed. This time he knew it would be different. They had slaughtered the great warrior chief Braddock, down on the Monongahela. They had won a great victory at Lake George, only to throw it away in that stupid attack on the barricade, and now, he was certain, they were about to give the English a whipping they would never forget.

By this time they were beginning to find their way into the woods behind the fort. When the English awoke in the morning, they would find themselves surrounded by a relentless enemy. How would they cover four walls with a couple of pitiful cannon? Red Hawk wondered, especially with the big French guns blazing away up front. LeJeune had boasted that the French had pulled those guns all the way up from the Monongahela. They had been Braddock's guns.

They were now in position at the edge of the woods behind the fort. There were still several hours of darkness left, and Red Hawk was determined to be ready for the next day's activities. Gently, he laid his head on his pack, and his body immediately found sleep. The coming morning held no terrors for him.

Once the army had completely passed the Mohawks, Louis and Big Oak continued to wait until they were entirely certain there were no stragglers left who could discover them. Then they scrambled back up the hill to their former observation post, followed by Thad and the rest of the Mohawks.

"They're getting into position to attack from the west," Big Oak explained to Louis. "Remember yesterday when the English moved their cannon to the other side? The French saw that too."

"Pa, let's *try* to warn them," Little Oak said.

He nodded. "Stay close to me. It could get rough out there."

They prepared themselves for their foray, dropping their packs and tying down anything that might clank in the night. Then, leaving Louis behind, they moved down the hill silently and as quickly as they dared, toward the fort, circling around so as to approach from the gate side. When they were close, they huddled against the wall and in a loud whisper caught the attention of the sentry.

"Who in hell are you, and what the hell are you doin' out there?" was the sentry's response.

"Get an officer. We've got information for you."

"Give us the password then, mate."

"How should we know the password?" Big Oak was annoyed, but he kept cool. "Hurry and get an officer."

They waited and waited, their heads still and tilted to catch any outside sound that might indicate the beginning of an attack that could catch them in a cross fire between their allies and their enemies. As determined as Thad and Big Oak were to pass on their intelligence, the long delay unnerved them so that they were about to head back to the hills when a voice from the parapet finally said, "I'm Lieutenant Quinn. Who are you?"

"Sam Watley, known to the Seneca as Big Oak."

Little Oak was astonished to hear a guffaw from atop the wall.

"Never heard of you, Watley. What do you want?"

"I've got some information for you."

"We'll open the gate and let you in. We'll take your information where we can look at you."

"Sorry, Lieutenant. We ain't goin' in there."

"Then take your information and put it you know where. We are not paying you a cent for information thrown over a wall."

"I don't want your money, damn it. I want to help you save your lives." But Big Oak could already hear the lieutenant assembling a detachment to come out and collect them.

"They're sending men against your south and east walls," he shouted, and then he and Little Oak broke into a quick run that put more than a hundred yards of night between them and the gate by the time they heard it squeak open. They could hear the running footsteps of a small group of pursuers, so they put on a burst of speed and easily made it to the woods before they were spotted.

Once in the woods, they slowed down to a fast walk, knowing that no small English detachment would follow them into the wilderness. Carefully, silently, beneath the dark canopy, they moved almost by feel until they were close to the clearing on the hill where the Mohawks were ensconced.

"Louis!" Big Oak whispered.

"I am here," came the reply. "They were not interested in what you had to say, eh?"

"I tried."

"Why didn't we go inside the fort when they asked us to?" Little Oak asked.

"Because they would not have let us out," Big Oak responded. "And, my son, there are a lot of dead men in that fort tonight."

"How do such fools win wars?" Louis wondered out loud.

Big Oak shrugged his shoulders. "They are not all fools,"

he said. "Just most of them. Speaking of fools, when are your warriors going home?"

"When the battle is over, I believe. They are not much interested in fighting, but they would enjoy seeing what happens. They don't like any of the people who are fighting, so they don't much care who wins and who loses."

"They should care. The future of the Ganonsyoni may depend on who wins and who loses here."

"That might be so," Louis said, "but can you truly tell me which outcome would be better for us?"

Big Oak sat in silence. Both he and Louis recalled the arguments he had used for siding with the English, and both knew that his reasoning was not perfect. The silence lengthened.

"I thought so," said Louis.

"Are you going home, then?" Big Oak asked.

Louis's eyes gleamed in the moonlight. "Oh no. My eyes have seen much on this day. My days as a warrior are short. I will have one more battle. And the enemy will be Red Hawk."

# ❖23❖

**T**HEY AWOKE IN THE GRASP OF THE FIRST faint pink fingers of dawn, but before they finished their quick breakfast, they heard shouted French commands, followed by the sound of the guns.

Twelve and twenty pounders opened up nearly point-blank from the edge of the woods on the star-shaped wooden walls of Fort Ontario and splintered some mighty gaps in them before they realized that there was nobody home. So they manhandled their cannon to the fort and turned them across the river to bear on the east wall of Fort Oswego.

Now all hell broke loose. The artillery pounded the rock and clay walls of Fort Oswego, and pieces of the walls flew in all directions. Little Oak saw a figure up on the parapet of the east wall directing the defense of the fort, and then suddenly he wasn't there anymore, his body and life carried away by a cannonball. Again and again cannoneers served their pieces with swab, powder, and ball. Again and again the cannon belched smoke and recoiled on their carriages, and again and again precious portions of wall crashed to the ground. Before their eyes the sick and malnourished defenders of the fort watched their protection vanish as piece by piece the walls disintegrated. The French were in no hurry to form a direct attack. Their artillery was doing the job at no cost to their own troops, and considerable cost to the English. The cannon fired. Pieces of wall came down. Sometimes war gets very simple and direct.

Then, from the west and the south, Indians and Canadians swarmed out of the woods and directed their fire upon the fort. The cannon boomed and the walls of Fort Oswego continued to come apart, large segments crashing into the interior in some places.

The defenders of the fort were dismayed not only by the noise of the cannon and the incoming balls, but by the horrifying impact that brought home to them the fort's vulnerability, and the incredible bloody things that cannonballs can do to the human body.

There were dozens of women in the fort, laundresses, refugees, and providers of entertainment for the soldiers, and now their screams of horror were added to the wails of terror and pain from the wounded and dazed troops, many of whom had never before faced the ghastly effectiveness of an artillery barrage.

Big Oak watched the battle calmly, but not without feeling. The fire from the fort was not what it should have been, given the number of men stationed there. It meant that key officers were already dead, and that many soldiers were so terrified that they were more interested in taking cover than in returning fire.

It was clear to the defenders that the fort's location allowed the enemy to fire down from hills into the fort. Several gallant souls were attempting to raise the walls higher by placing a row of pork barrels on top, and some stalwarts stood their ground and fired back at the French, but months of sickness and too little experience made many of the soldiers useless, and had they not been useless, the position and makeup of the fort would have doomed them anyway.

Little Oak watched the course of the battle with a sickening feeling in the pit of his stomach. He was glad that he wasn't inside the fort sharing the pain and terror of the inhabitants, but his heart went out to them. Even from a distance their helpless fright was apparent. Men were appearing over the wall, firing quickly at nothing, and then disappearing. Others were huddled against the walls, doing nothing, not wishing to draw any attention to themselves by firing their muskets. Here and there officers could be seen attempting to kick their men into action, but among them was not one inspired commander who could ignite the mortified defenders.

Still, there were defenders who stood by their posts and kept up a steady rate of fire as if they were professionals, and Big Oak appreciated them. It was terribly hard, he knew, for a man to keep his courage when the resolve of those around him was crumbling like the stone and clay walls of old Fort Oswego itself.

As the morning wore on, the French commander was able to bring even more thundering firepower to bear on the fort, while the return fire from the fort became ever more meager. It was the brave ones, the ones who kept up a steady aimed fire at the enemy, who took the casualties, and as each of these was wounded or killed by the terrible firepower concentrated upon them by their enemies, there was no one else to take their place upon the parapets.

And then, suddenly, a white rag at the end of a long pole appeared, waved wildly above the stone wall by a defender who kept himself well below the top of the stonework. A command in French rose above the battlefield, followed by echoes of the command from subordinate officers. The cannon ceased immediately, but the command had to be repeated several times before the musket fire ended.

The relative silence rode across the plain like a long sigh of relief. Within the fort could be heard the screams and groans of the injured, and the cries of frightened or horrified women. The minutes of battle silence stretched out while the French officers held a conference and the combatants stood at their posts, staring at one another. More minutes passed, and finally, out of the knot of white-coated officers, walked a single tall, erect officer, flanked by several junior officers.

The gate was opened and the senior surviving English officer walked out to greet the French party. Two of the men with him were bloody and one walked with a heavy limp.

"What will happen now?" Thad asked.

"The French commander," Big Oak said with certainty, "will tell the English captain that he has fought a gallant fight and that no one could have stood up to such a fierce attack any better than he had. The French commander will tell him that surrender here and now will save many lives and that if the English captain does not surrender, then the French commander will not be able to guarantee them another chance of surrender."

"Does that mean either surrender now or get massacred later?"

"I think that's what the French commander will mean."

"Will the English captain surrender?"

"I believe that he must," Big Oak said sadly.

The men on the hill watched as the officers below parleyed. The parley did not last long. The French talked, and the interpreter talked, and mostly the English listened and nodded. One of the French enlisted men ran to the edge of the river and shouted something, at which time several boatloads of French troops landed on the riverbank in front of the fort, including one in a uniform so splendid that his general's status was apparent even to those on the hill. Then the officers and men outside the fort walked through the front gate.

The English captain was seen talking to lesser officers, who in turn talked to other groups of men standing by the walls of the fort.

Soon the soldiers inside could be seen surrendering their rifles and other weapons, at which point the Iroquois on the hill noticed the Indians and Canadians coming across the open field south of the fort and heading for the open gate facing the river, in order to be in on the surrender. Big Oak

pointed to them, then, particularly, at one figure who kept
itself somewhat separated from the rest. "Could that be our
brother Red Hawk?" he asked Louis.

The son of Gingego grunted with distaste, a form of
agreement.

The Mohawks were indifferent to white men's flags, but
Big Oak and his son watched sullenly as the English flag
came down and the fleur-de-lis went up to flap victoriously
in the brisk Ontario breeze. Little Oak's father had raised
his son to think of himself as sort of an Englishman, not one
such as might live in London or Canterbury, but a new
world Englishman, a colonial, maybe a New Yorker. That
made him different from all the other Senecas, but a Seneca
nevertheless. Over the years, he had spent a lot of time
trying to sort out just what he was.

Watching the men in Fort Oswego, their heads bowed in
defeat, laying down their arms, he shared their sense of
defeat. And at that moment he knew exactly who he was.

In the fort, the disarmed defenders stood disconsolately in
ranks, waiting helplessly to find out what the French would
do with them. Would they be dispatched to Montreal immediately as prisoners of war, or would they be held at Oswego
for a time? Perhaps a few of the braver souls were already
considering the odds of escape, but a surprising number regarded their surrender with a definite feeling of relief, especially relief from having to face the roar and destruction of
French artillery.

The sound of the war cry, bloodcurdling even from a
distance, grabbed Little Oak's wandering attention like a
rifleshot. The Caughnawaga and Canadians had made a sudden rush for the gates of Fort Oswego, apparently in a cele-
bratory mood.

But they were celebrating with knives and tomahawks
held high and crashing down upon the heads of defenseless
captives. Immediately the war cries were eclipsed by the
inhuman sounds of anguished screaming as unarmed English

soldiers by the dozen went down under the onslaught of their attackers.

"Oh my God," Big Oak whispered, strangling his rifle with the frustration of having to witness a massacre without the power to do something about it. The Mohawks around them watched impassively. For most warlike tribes like the Mohawk, this kind of event wasn't considered unduly awful unless their own tribe was the victim. Nevertheless, they were not entirely indifferent to the sudden and terrible slaughter of defenseless men who had trusted the word of the "civilized" French.

Caught by surprise, the French officers were slow to act, and maybe a couple of them were not sorry to witness the bloodletting as tomahawk smashed skull and knife circled scalp. The pleas for mercy were piteous enough to wring remorse from the heart of the cruelest priests in Quebec. The British had naturally broken ranks and attempted to rush to safety, but their French captors, with the rigidity not uncommon to the trained European soldier, used their rifle butts to drive them back within reach of the tomahawks of the Caughnawagas and *coureurs de bois*. It did not seem to dawn on these soldiers that they were duty bound to protect their prisoners from the treacherous onslaught that was decimating them.

The Indians and Canadians continued to swing their tomahawks and war clubs, and the helpless, panicked English militiamen fell dying and screaming. After what seemed like a lifetime, the French officers finally reacted properly and began to wade into the melee, hollering French curses and demanding an end to the slaughter.

The Indians and bush lopers slowly cooled their blood lust, some of them continuing long enough to dispatch one last prisoner with a well-aimed downward swing of the tomahawk. Nearly insane with panic, several English soldiers had made a dash for the gate. A handful of Caughnawagas gave chase, and the French officers let them go, apparently believing that since the English hadn't the discipline to remain in ranks helpless while their friends were getting their heads crushed, why, they deserved to be run down like dogs by the swiftly pursuing Caughnawagas.

Of the four soldiers who made it outside the gate, two were immediately overtaken, and, on their knees, begged for mercy. What they received were ferocious blows that broke their skulls open, poured blood all over them and killed them quickly and competently.

The third one went down from a tackle by his pursuer, who jumped on the poor man's back, stunned him with a quick blow from the blunt end of his tomahawk, placed his knee on the back of his neck and cut a deep circle around the top of his head. The colonial screamed and kicked and tried to fight his way out from under his tormentor, but the Indian inserted his fingers into the incision from the front, yanked, and tore the scalp free from the head of his victim.

The shriek from the scalped soldier was the most horrible sound Little Oak had ever heard. While the Indian leaped up and flourished the scalp for the approval of comrades who had spilled out of the fort to witness the fun, the scalped soldier was so maddened by the pain and fear that he was unable to take advantage of his respite to run for his life. He remained on the ground, facedown, his hands to the sides of his head as if he couldn't bear to touch his own gore-covered skull; he was thrashing around, kicking the ground insanely, and from his throat issued a long, hoarse, inhuman cry of agony and despair.

His Indian was not through with him yet. Quickly he grabbed the man around the shoulders and lifted him into a sitting position. The man stopped kicking and his scream turned to a terrorized gurgle. The Caughnawaga replaced the scalp on the soldier's head, comically askew. His audience of Indians and *couriers de bois* laughed and clapped their hands in appreciation. Then the Caughnawaga shook his head, as if in disapproval of the soldier's haircut, pulled the scalp off and showed it to his victim, who shook *his* head and mumbled something incoherent.

The Indian took his blood-coated tomahawk, waved it in the soldier's face, and appeared to say something to him. The soldier nodded, and the Indian struck with it, not on top of the soldier's head, but into the soldier's mouth and nose. When that blow failed to earn any worthwhile response from the soldier, who was, mercifully, nearly comatose by now, the Indian finally delivered the coup de grace by smashing his tomahawk deep into the brain of the unfortunate colonial. The audience of Indians and Canadians again reacted with appreciation at the Caughnawaga's showmanship.

Breathless and in tears from witnessing the merciless cruelty of the execution, only then, as the Caughnawaga did an improvised scalp dance, did Little Oak realize that the Indian was no Caughnawaga at all, but a Mohawk. The Indian, in fact, was Red Hawk.

Little Oak glanced over at Louis and saw a look of hatred in the eyes of the son of Gingégo. A smile curled around Louis's lean, dark features as he saw the effect of the event on the face of young Little Oak. "Would you like to see him dead?" he asked.

"I wish to see him begging us for his death," Little Oak replied. His father listened to the conversation.

"Maybe the time is near," Louis remarked.

One of the escapees had made it to the woods, with two Indians a good fifty yards behind him. The white man was young and swift, and with a little luck, Big Oak and Louis thought he might have a chance. Three of Louis's warriors slipped out of sight down the hill, hoping to save the white man, but mostly to gain a pair of Caughnawaga scalps. Before they had been gone more than half a minute, an appalling scream rose from the woods below. A short while later the three Mohawks returned, disappointed, to their hilltop vigil.

Gradually the screeching and tumult subsided, as the French officers restored order among friend and foe alike.

For the next several hours Big Oak, Little Oak, and the

Mohawks watched as the French took surrender of the tiny English fleet, assembled all the English supplies, and burned the wooden buildings inside the fort. Prisoners were digging a mass grave for those who had died in the battle and the massacre that followed. Some hot words were exchanged between the French commander and one of the Caughnawaga. "They want some prisoners to take with them back to their village to torture," Louis informed Big Oak.

"He won't give them any prisoners, will he?" Little Oak asked his father.

"Doesn't look like it," was the response, and indeed, the Caughnawaga was turned away disgruntled and empty-handed.

The watchers on the hill were curious as to the fate of the surviving prisoners, but they had no time to waste. Louis, who had made Red Hawk his personal responsibility, noted that he and nearly two dozen of his Caughnawaga comrades were preparing to leave, along with a pair of Canadians.

"Are you still heading home?" Louis asked his dissident braves.

Several of them smiled grimly. They too had picked out Red Hawk from among the players below, and like Louis, they wanted above all to have him in their hands. The Mohawks quickly gathered their few belongings, and when the praying Indians entered the woods, heading in an eastern direction close to the lakeshore, the Mohawks circled around the battlefield, picking up the trail of the Caughnawaga about three miles east of Fort Oswego.

They spent most of the afternoon traveling at a leisurely pace, keeping a mile of woodland between themselves and their quarry. They all knew in grim detail the story of the destruction of the Seneca village. Whether or not they loved the Guardians of the Western Door, they each understood that unity was the basis of their success as a nation. An atrocity committed upon the Seneca by an outsider was therefore an atrocity committed upon them. The Caughnawaga, who had many years before broken the unity of the Iroquois confederacy, were special outsiders, and when they perpetrated violence against the Longhouse, they were a special enemy.

There was no horseplay, no joking among the Mohawks as they clung to the trail of the Caughnawagas, which led east, roughly parallel to the Mohawk River valley. This was a hot August, and the trail led uphill into the foothills of the Adirondack Mountains. The flies and mosquitoes were thick and vicious, but the pace seldom slackened. Occasionally they would hear a whoop or a loud guffaw from the high-spirited, victorious gang ahead of them, and then they would slacken their pace to avoid stepping on the heels of the men they were following.

The second night, Big Oak and Louis held council together and decided that the Caughnawagas were making their way to Lake George, where the French and English had continued to peck at each other.

Little Oak's thoughts as he traveled through the forest veered wildly from dreams of Katherine, which were sometimes idealized, sometimes carnal, to haunting recollections of the massacre he had just witnessed and the winter massacre that he had just missed.

He longed for Red Hawk as hungrily as he longed for Katherine. He had been raised with Iroquois, albeit in a village that had spent many quiet, inoffensive years fishing along the Genesee River. Iroquois were aggressive and warlike, and he took pride in the belief that he was one of them, but Red Hawk had a thirst for blood that knew no lasting satisfaction. Little Oak would not rest peacefully until Red Hawk was Dead Hawk.

He looked at his big, strong hands, remembered the compact, muscular frame of Red Hawk, and wondered if he could take the renegade in man-to-man battle.

The following morning, Louis announced to his band that today was the day they would try to pass the Caughnawagas and set up an ambush where the trail was both steep and exposed. Almost all the Mohawks were familiar with the trail, as was Big Oak, and they did not need to be told where the general area of the ambush site would be.

They began a wide swing around the Caughnawagas through the woods, in a determined fast trot, so wide a swing that they managed to put an entire hill between themselves and the enemy. Strong though he was, by the time they had run through their third mile, Little Oak could feel the late morning heat as they made their way over the difficult terrain, dodging trees, rocks, underbrush, and an occasional snake. The Indians traveled lighter. His heavy rifle, his powder horn, bullet pouch and his backpack were becoming a bouncing burden. He gritted his teeth, got his second wind, and continued to watch the trees bounce by in rapid succession.

They crossed a narrow stream, then another, and veered up the steep side of a rocky hill, now climbing more than running. It occurred to Little Oak that this might be the day when he could finally satisfy the sharp, deep-cutting longing he had lived with since the day Red Hawk had nearly turned his father into an idiot for life.

They found an old remnant of a trail and took it as long as it took them where they wanted to go. The old elms and maples witnessed their passage in silence. They each leaped a tiny stream and then again headed upward, this time in a northerly direction that would intersect the trail at a spot where, Louis knew, ambush would be possible.

They climbed over the crest of a hill, then slid halfway down a steep slope and found themselves looking down on the trail where the Caughnawagas were due to pass within a half hour or so. The trail was sunk nearly four feet below the surrounding woodland, which was rocky and thinly populated with scrubby trees. The place was perfect. The Caughnawagas would be fatally exposed if they tried to climb off the trail into the woods, but the wooded hills that rose above the trail were high enough to provide excellent fields of fire even if the Caughnawagas attempted to use the sloping sides of the trail for cover.

They deployed their men on the hillsides perhaps twenty yards back and above the trail, five sharpshooters on each side, concealed in the brush. The four who were the worst shots, or had the worst firearms, they provided with buckshot loads, stationing two on the trail in front, and two closing in on the trail behind, to present a surprise to any Caughnawagas who would attempt to escape by running up or down the trail. Big Oak and Little Oak lay side by side to the right. Their mission, as the best shooters, was to pick off the leaders.

The Mohawks stripped themselves down to their breechclouts and took their time getting their paint just right. Louis and Tall Bear approached the two white men and applied red and white pigments to their faces, a first for Little Oak, save for when as a child he had played at war in Tonowaugh a lifetime ago. Then came the long wait in the brush, sweating and swatting silently at the voracious mosquitoes, who, Little Oak thought, might have been the blood brothers of Red Hawk.

Big Oak studied the site. The hills rose sharply over the trail on either side, magnificently wooded in a way that the English seemed to resent when they took in new territory. Like a tomcat staking its territory, they had this endless need to clear land and burn the fallen timber, as if the forests themselves were poisonous to their existence. Big Oak lay with his finger on the trigger guard, sweating under his deerskin, awed by his own sense that an era was closing and that he would have to be ready to survive in the midst of changes he would not like.

With discipline borne of experience, he forced himself to concentrate on the trail below and on the hills around it.

One very stealthy, very cautious Mohawk had been detailed to scout the back trail to make certain that the Caughnawagas were conforming to the plan. Just as Little Oak was beginning to consider the pleasant expedient of scratching his limbs on the sharp thorns of a nearby bush, the brave returned with the news that the enemy was approaching.

He need not have bothered. The ambushers could hear them from nearly half a mile away. Two of them were apparently arguing over either a squaw that one had punished or a prisoner one had murdered, Little Oak couldn't tell which. The waiting Mohawks froze and waited.

A painted face appeared along the trail, and then two more. Good, they were bunched up much more closely than they would have been if months of bloody success hadn't made them overconfident. They might as well have been taking a stroll in the park.

In the midst of this single-file mob were LeJeune and Moreau, entirely at ease among the Caughnawagas who had been their deadly associates for many months now. Like the Indians, the two Canadians strolled along without haste and in fine humor.

Many of them were loaded down with booty taken from the forts, and in any case they were so sated with their gory accomplishments throughout the killing season that they were in no hurry to face more battle at Lake George.

They should have been more wary, Big Oak thought, watching the lead Caughnawaga warrior framed in his rear sight. This, he thought in the final silence, was going to be one of life's simple pleasures.

When the first three Indians reached the agreed upon spot, nine rifles belched fire. Five Caughnawagas fell dead and four severely wounded. Stunned, the survivors dropped to the ground, tried to take cover against the trailside slopes, and looked for targets, but the shooters had pulled back behind big trees to reload. In the meantime, one late shooter, who had experienced a misfire, recocked his weapon, fired, and sent a .70-caliber ball through the knee of a tenth Indian.

What happened next sealed the fate of the Caughnawagas. As they finally began returning fire, and there were still more than a dozen of them who could do so, the four

Mohawks guarding the trail swung into action. Realizing that none of the Caughnawagas were fleeing in their direction, they quietly crept along the trail until they could see the enemy before them, shooting into the hills. The four let loose a crippling barrage of shot on the exposed Caughnawagas, killing none but inflicting painful, bloody wounds upon half of the remainder.

Shocked and frightened, the Caughnawagas clung tightly to the slope by the trail and fired into the hills. Their targets lay well concealed in the brush on the hillsides, but the Caughnawagas were all exposed to those who lay concealed on the hill opposite the slope to which they clung.

The utterly confused foe turned in all directions now, in fatal hesitation, but the shotgunners had vanished, and now from the hills came another volley that drove lead into nearly every surviving Indian on the trail. Immediately on the heels of the second deadly volley from the hillsides came a chorus of whoops, and the ambushers leaped down from the hill upon the stunned and demoralized enemy, brandishing an intimidating assortment of tomahawks, war clubs, and knives, their screeching, horrifying war cries echoing off the hills, further paralyzing the will of the already panicked and decimated Caughnawagas. Bravely the Caughnawagas tried to shriek their own war cries and fight back, but there were so many of them already dead and wounded, and the remainder were so stunned by the surprise attack, that the best they could do was extend their lives by a matter of a few minutes.

Little Oak rose from his hidden position with the Mohawks, but as he began his run down the hill, his foot caught a tree root and pitched him headlong down the slope into the midst of the Caughnawagas. Alone for a moment among the enemy, he expected instant death, but all the Caughnawagas close to where he landed were either dead or badly wounded. He looked up in time to see Red Hawk and two Caughnawagas converging on him with knives and tomahawks.

Their blades were still red from the Oswego massacre and
maybe a few previous massacres. Inhuman screeching
whoops erupted from their throats. No strangers to death,
they were fixing to renew their acquaintance yet again.

Little Oak felt choking fear leap to his throat, but the
generations of his mother's heritage stayed true to their
seed. He pulled his hatchet from his belt, screamed defiance
in their faces, and swung his powerful right arm.

As quickly as they had appeared, two of his three adversaries vanished beneath the deadly assaults of the attacking
Mohawks. The third closed with him, his tomahawk raised,
but even as he began its deadly arc, the blade of Little Oak's
hatchet cut to the big bone in Red Hawk's forearm. His
tomahawk flew wildly into the brush, and Little Oak had
started his knife forward into the renegade's belly when his
legs were taken out from under him by a tumbling, falling
Caughnawaga who was reeling from a fatal blow to the side
of his head.

Little Oak rolled quickly to his feet and looked for Red
Hawk, but somehow he had vanished, and the fighting was
still too intense for him to make Red Hawk his special proj-
ect. The Mohawks had quickly closed with the survivors of
the deadly gunfire, most of whom were severely wounded,
and the rest in such shock and terror from the sudden onslaught that they were virtually defenseless.

In the meantime, Big Oak had his own mission, which
took him far from the site of the ambush. After the shotgun
volley from both ends of the trail, none of the Caughnawagas had given a thought to using the trail as a means of
escape, and so they had no option but to fight and die
where they were. The two Canadians, however, were more
determined to find a way out. Even as the Mohawks on the
ends of the trail joined their brothers from the hillsides, the
two Canadians sprinted through the smoke and the screeching war, jumping over bloody bodies and finding a clear
path down the trail from where they had arrived. The ambushers were too intent on their descent down the hillside

into the battle pit to divert their chase. Only Big Oak noticed their exit, and his blood boiled like a bubbling caldron.

These were the vile ones, he thought. He would not let them escape.

Once he had put the ambush site behind him, his keen eyes searched the trail below and picked out the two figures desperately leaping over rocks and falling limbs as they sought to put distance between themselves and the sharpshooting Mohawks who, they knew, would take no prisoners on this day. Their fear was so great that even when the trail grew steep, they refused to slacken their stride. Moreau lost his footing and went sprawling in a rolling heap that tripped up LeJeune. Both slid headlong down the trail. Without coming to a halt to check their bodies for injury, they somehow got their feet back under them and continued their flight down the mountain. They did not even know that anyone was on their trail. They knew only blind, wild panic, panic so great that they ignored their agonized, inflamed lungs, and their bruised and scraped bodies.

Big Oak was not worried about being followed. He knew that the Caughnawagas were all headed for their spirit world, and so he concentrated on keeping his terrified quarry in sight. They were working too hard, he knew, and like a horse that was being overridden, sooner or later their muscles would refuse to do their bidding.

The trail was a familiar one to Big Oak. Eventually the sharp downhill angle of the slope diminished and he remembered that here the trail made a wide, U-shaped bow along the side of a hill. If he could cut across the bow, he could quickly cut the distance between them. By now they had seen him, and in their panic had taken him for a pursuing army. With all their might they strove to extract their final reserves of energy, but they were done. Their bodies rocked up and down as they entered the wide bow in the trail, and their legs moved heavily, as if they were running through deep water.

Big Oak left the trail and ran through the woods, dodging

trees, heading for a point that would intersect the trail close enough to the Canadians to allow him to overtake them and bring them to ground, one way or another.

For a while the denseness of the ancient forest hid the hunter from the hunted. Big Oak continued to run, swiftly but well under control, legs high to avoid roots and rocks, easily sidestepping the trees and rapidly closing in on the point where he expected to intercept the trail. And then, between trunks, he could make them out, still trying to run, their bodies heaving desperately for oxygen.

He hit the trail only eighty yards behind them and gaining so rapidly that the two Canadians decided that they must stand, then and there. Both men pulled their rifles into firing position, but their chests were heaving so that they could not bring their rifles to bear. Quickly Big Oak pulled his rifle into firing position. Moreau fired then, so wildly that Big Oak heard neither the buzzing bullet nor any foliage that the bullet might have clipped. Coldly, precisely, Big Oak squeezed the trigger and Moreau toppled like a felled hemlock, and lay just as still.

That left LeJeune and his unfired rifle. Surely, as frightened as he was, he should have fired his rifle by now, unless in the panic of his flight he had either neglected to load his rifle properly, or load it at all. He had tried to aim it at Big Oak. He must have tried to fire it.

Ah, there he goes . . . tilts his powder horn toward the barrel—by now Big Oak is within fifty yards—and pours Lord knows how much powder into the barrel. He thrusts his hand down into his bullet pouch, spilling balls right and left before his fingers finally close around one—Big Oak has dropped his rifle and pulled his hatchet. LeJeune pulls his ramrod and rams the ball home—just a few more yards and Big Oak will be there—with shaking hand he pours powder all over the rifle mechanism trying to charge the pan, then brings the rifle to his shoulder and jerks the trigger.

A spark but no shot. The old veteran of a dozen battles, LeJeune has failed to prime the pan, his last conscious thought as he brings the rifle up in a vain effort to prevent the keen-bladed hatchet of Big Oak from chopping through the side of his skull with a sickening, splintering sound.

Like a fire in a pile of dry brush, the bright blaze of furious hand-to-hand combat quickly died down to the feebly glowing coals of the final thrashings, and then, suddenly, stunned themselves, the Mohawk raiding party stood in awed witness of their legendary victory.

Within three minutes of the first shot, the soul of every Caughnawaga brave on the trail had departed, and so had their scalps and other assorted parts of their bodies.

Every brave but one.

In the very first volley, a bullet from the hills had exploded the skull of Red Hawk's Caughnawaga friend Owaiskah, splattering his blood and brains over the shoulders and chest of Red Hawk. During his brief combat with Little Oak, Red Hawk's nimble mind had perceived that the plight of his comrades was hopeless. When Little Oak went down in front of him, Red Hawk looked for a means of escape, and spotted a place on the side of the trail where a tree had been uprooted, leaving a sizable hole in the side of the hill. He had dragged a bloody body to the hole, ducked into the hole, and then covered the hole with the body.

The Mohawks stood around studying what they had wrought. They were extremely satisfied, like carpenters admiring the clean lines and smooth finish on the fine piece of furniture they had just completed.

"Did anybody get past you?" Louis asked each warrior separately, and each warrior responded in the negative.

"I saw Big Oak running down the hill," Tall Bear said, pointing down the trail. "The Canadians are not here. He must be after them." The Mohawks all stood quietly, ears cocked, waiting, and soon they were rewarded by two gunshots. They looked at each other questioningly, but Little Oak smiled.

The second shot, he insisted, came from Big Oak's rifle,

which sounded like no other. Louis and Little Oak decided
to take a little run down the trail. The remaining Mohawks
meanwhile looted the bodies of their late enemies and contemplated the awful perfection of their deed. On this day
their *orenda* must have been incredibly powerful.

They stood in reverent silence while each gave thanks to
the Master of Life for the victory he had so effortlessly
handed them.

One warrior had suffered a deep knife cut in his left arm
that would not be serious if it did not become infected, and
another was a little woozy from a glancing blow to his tem-
ple from a thrown tomahawk. There were a few fingernail
scratches and bruises from the last desperate struggles of one
or two of the deceased, but not a single Mohawk had sustained a serious injury in the course of their deadly ambush.

The sun glowed hotly through the thin shade of oaks and
hemlocks that stood back from the trail. A soft breeze blew
in and rippled a feather or a hair here and there. Slowly the
rage of battle receded, leaving behind the sweet, comforting
glow of triumph. The mighty warriors who lay so still
around them had but a few short days before wreaked death
and havoc among the men and women of Fort Oswego.
Even the mightiest of braves are only mortal and soon become dust. Perhaps even now, another enemy war party in
the area had heard the commotion and was preparing to do
the same to the victorious Mohawks. A single poplar leaf
slowly floated down in front of Tall Bear. It settled softly to
the earth in front of his feet.

Now Louis, Big Oak, and Little Oak appeared on the trail.
The scalps of the two dead Canadians were with them.
They were hanging from Big Oak's belt. The warriors received the return of Big Oak with his trophies in apprecia-
tive silence.

"Too bad they're all dead," Tall Bear said, craving the solemn ceremony of torture that so often followed such a victory. Quietly, the Mohawks continued to move from body
to body, relieving each of his weapons, his personal effects,

and his scalp. One of the Caughnawagas was not quite dead when the scalping knife entered his head; the knife finished what the rifle had started.

Tall Bear found a body lying on its back beside a fallen tree, but when he lifted the dead man's head, he suddenly stopped.

"Come on out there, you," he said, reaching behind the body and fetching out Red Hawk by the scalp lock. He smiled. "My old friend. Come out into the sun so we may take a look at you."

His fellow braves, their eyes drawn to the sudden movement, responded with sounds of amazement and admiration, as if they had just seen a magician pull a rabbit out of a hat.

For just a moment Red Hawk stood before them, covered with the gore of his friend Owaiskah, his useless right arm dangling by his side, trembling in anticipation of his appalling future. Then, before Little Oak's wondering, admiring eyes, the Mohawk renegade gathered himself and stood tall to his tormentors.

"Cowardly dogs," he spat. "Did you follow us all the way from Oswego? Did you hide in the brush while we slew your shaking, helpless English friends as if they were so many children? They who boast that they rule over the mighty Iroquois?

"Did you see how easily they died and surrendered and died again for the pleasure of the French and their mighty allies, the Iroquois of the Canadas?"

"Haughhh!" Tall Bear cried. "You dare compare the Ganiengehaka to the English, you filthy traitor?" Forgetting for a moment his hunger for the torture, he angrily raised his tomahawk, but Louis grabbed his arm in mid-flight.

"We will see how high this goose flies while his feathers are being pulled," Louis told his friend. Already several braves were chopping down a young, straight hemlock tree and stripping it of its branches, while another was digging a hole in the middle of the trail, and three more were piling dead brush and branches ten feet away from the hole.

Watching the preparations for a party at which he was to be the unwilling guest of honor, Red Hawk made one last sudden attempt to escape, tearing himself from the grasp of Tall Bear and taking a leap toward the downhill trail. He might have led his enemies a fair chase had not the youngest of the braves, Toolah, reached out with his rifle and sent the renegade sprawling.

Two other Mohawks immediately leaped on him, and a third bound his hands tightly behind his back, leaving a long thong dangling to serve as a leash. The rest of them laughed contemptuously at their prisoner.

"Red Hawk," said one, "are your legs made of water that they pour out from underneath you?"

"Not made of water. He is just very frightened," Tall Bear said. "Let's check his breechclout and see if he has soiled it."

"Filthy cowards," Red Hawk spat. "Very brave when I am helpless."

"Like you with the English prisoners?" Little Oak asked, standing nose to nose with him. "Like you with the Seneca women? Like you with my grandfather Kendee who was so old he could barely walk when you and your bold Caughnawagas stole the gentle evening of his life? Like you when my father was defenseless?" Furious, he hawked up a mouthful of mucus and spat it in Red Hawk's face, making the warrior so angry that he nearly burst his bonds trying to get his hands on Little Oak. To be tortured by his fellow warriors was one thing, but to be spat upon in front of them and then tormented in his own tongue by this half-white devil was too much for him to bear.

An animal growl escaped from his throat and he lunged at Little Oak, but Tall Bear pulled him back with a hard jerk on the leash and Red Hawk stumbled over a rock, landing upon his posterior. The Mohawks again laughed derisively.

"He will scream and wail at the stake like a woman," Louis lamented. "I had hoped we had captured a man."

Red Hawk looked up and saw the bright white summer sun suspended in the noonday sky. It was a good time, he thought, to make ready to die. Slowly he climbed to his feet and collected his dignity. Silently, he stepped out of his moccasins and allowed Toolah to remove his breechclout. Naked, he walked slowly to the stake and put his back against it.

"I will do you honor now," he said. "And you will honor me after my death."

## ᐊ24ᐅ

**T**HEY KNOTTED HIS HANDS TIGHTLY TO HIS sides and tied him to the stake with thongs around his waist, his ankles, and his neck.

Eyes narrowed with contempt, he gazed at them and waited. "I lived with you my whole life. You are women like your English masters. The French and the Caughnawaga will soon have you on your knees," he predicted. "And if the English win, *they* will have you on your knees. And you will enjoy being on your knees. You were born to be slaves. You are the lowest of the low."

Quietly, Big Oak had been a mighty warrior in the ambush. His rifle had quickly dispatched two of the hated enemy, and his hatchet had finished off another. Typical of his efficiency, none of his three victims had felt the shadow of their death approach before they died. And then, of course, he had by himself claimed the scalps of the two Frenchmen.

Now he stood before the hated renegade. "Red Hawk," he said, "these are the scalps of your Canadian friends. I do not usually take scalps, but your friends gave them to me as a present, and it is rude to refuse a present. But since I do not take scalps, I show them to you for your inspection"—here he held the two head coverings before the eyes of Red Hawk—"and I give them to my friends Louis and Tall Bear to add to their collection.

"Look around you, at your Caughnawaga friends. What do you see? Victorious allies or just dead men? Are these the mighty warriors who would conquer the Ganonsyoni? Look at them. For the sake of a bunch of dead men, you betrayed your brothers. And there *is* nobody lower than a man who would war against his brothers."

The breeze that blew east from Lake Ontario stirred the pale green leaves of late summer. The living warriors followed Big Oak's gaze from the furious blazing eyes of Red Hawk to the dead unfocused stares of the late Caughnawagas.

"Ah, the Seneca, our famous guardians of the Western Door," Red Hawk hissed. "You saw their village? Did you see how easy they went down before the might of a few real warriors? What is more disgusting than the *smell* of a Seneca village?" He laughed a hideous, evil laugh that echoed off the nearby hills.

"Why do you think we chose *your* village, great slayer of red men? *I* chose your village, *because* it was your village. Yours and the village of that one"—he turned his eyes toward Little Oak"—the white boy who thinks he is a red man. The betrayer of the Ganonsyoni."

"Aiii!" Little Oak screamed, thinking of his old friend John Thompson, burned so slowly and painfully, and of Swerusse, the Seneca brave who died in agony staring at the severed head of his wife. He thought of his grandfather, kind, peaceful, gentle, with a bullet through his head and his body scorched like a stick of firewood. And he thought of his friend Skoiyasi, and the promise they had made each other months over the ruins of Tonowaugh. "It is you who are the betrayer! My rifle has never slain my brother, you filthy—" His emotions so tightened the muscles of his face that for a moment his mouth clamped shut and the words died in his throat. He seized his hatchet, raced up to Red Hawk and took a mighty swing at his head before the horrified faces of the Mohawks, who were afraid that this foolhardy young half-white man would deprive them of a pleasure they had been contemplating for months.

The hatchet did not bury itself in the renegade's skull, but whizzed past the front of his face, carrying with it most of his nose.

"Uhh," the surprised prisoner grunted as the blood flowed from the middle of his face.

"Ahhh," responded several of the Mohawks in appreciation of Little Oak's skillful surgery.

"You will never again have to *smell* a Seneca village." Little Oak recovered quickly from fury. "I am sorry for my anger, my brothers," he said, and he turned his back on Red Hawk and walked away.

Big Oak peered at his son's handiwork and waited until Red Hawk had recovered from his surprise. The blood gurgled in what was left of his nostrils.

"Think of it, you villainous dog," Big Oak said. "If you were rescued now, and you mended, no woman would ever look at you again, and wherever you went, children would say, 'There goes that ugly man who has no nose.'" Red Hawk, who was as vain as the next, maybe a little more so, felt his heart fall in spite of his resolve to be a great man at the hour of his death.

The pile of brush and deadwood was now a fiery furnace. Three of the Mohawks laid their gun barrels in the flames.

"No wonder they can't shoot worth a toot," Big Oak quietly told his son in English.

Now young Toolah grabbed Red Hawk's right arm, the wounded one. When Red Hawk resisted, the brave clubbed him on the side of his head with the handle of his knife, then employed the blade end and, one at a time, severed each finger from Red Hawk's hand. After he had finished with the right hand, he began on the left. Red Hawk absolutely refused to grimace or cry out, but he did cast a quick look at the ground where his fingers lay.

"You see too much!" Louis declared through a clenched jaw. He walked over to the stake, grabbed Red Hawk by the tuft of hair at the top of his head, now done up in the Caughnawaga manner. Holding Red Hawk's head firmly by the hair, Louis used his knife to pop out an eyeball. He picked it up and stood before Red Hawk, throwing the eyeball in the air and catching it again and again. "Now you see half as much," he said, and the other Mohawks laughed. "But I will not cut out the other eye yet, because I want you to see what is coming before it arrives. You will beg."

"I do not beg women and half men," he gasped. Then, realizing the pain was showing through his voice, he went silent and spat a thick red stream of blood at his tormentors.

Louis approached Red Hawk. "When I was last home, my mother said that only the very lowest would hunt and slay his brothers as you did at Lac St. Sacrement. All the Ganonsyoni know what you did. They curse your name, and teach their children to curse your name."

"The Ganonsyoni warriors lay down for Englishmen. The English will ravish them at their pleasure and then extinguish them, then forget them as if they had never been."

"You were a Ganonsyoni warrior. Your father was a Ganonsyoni warrior. All the other tribes fear the Ganonsyoni. When one Mohawk appears in the villages to the east, all the Indians run back to town screaming, 'A Mobawk is coming!' But you think we are weak. That must be because you are a Mohawk, and *you* are weak. My mother also said that a man who hates his own people the way you do, must—"

"Your *mother* lays down for the English. All the English."

Calmly Louis gazed into Red Hawk's one remaining eye. "You *are* weak. I can see your legs begin to tremble. We must bind you tighter to the post so you will not fall to the ground when fear makes your legs fail you." Tall Bear came forward with a long leather thong and wrapped it round and round Red Hawk's midsection and the post, pulling it as tight as he could. Red Hawk could not help but grunt once or twice as Tall Bear, muscles bulging, tugged at the thong.

"Before the sun moves this much farther," Louis said, raising his hand, with an inch between his thumb and forefinger, "your spirit will be searching for its pieces. During *this* time," he raised his thumb and forefinger close to the renegade's eye, "you will wish a thousand times that you were seated in front of your lodge fire in our village. This I promise you."

The Mohawks now decided to pause in their tortures. They had special torments planned and they wanted Red Hawk to recover enough to feel each one without any blessed numbness to stand between their prisoner and his exquisite agony. Toolah came forward with a water-soaked rag of old blanket and tenderly wiped the blood off Red Hawk's face, and even washed the blood and brains of Owaiskah from his chest and shoulders.

As he came to terms with the shock of his disfigurement, and as long years of discipline helped him bear his pain, Red Hawk took hold of himself, stared at the assemblage with his remaining eye, and he began to speak.

"My onetime brothers. You who have made me ashamed to be Ganiengehaka and forced me to go north to the land of the *real* Iroquois, I speak to you for the last time.

"There is the clear water of our mountain streams, and there is the burning rum of the evil twin's brew. One is red and one is white.

"There is the honorable hand-to-hand battle of the stone knife and the stone arrowhead, and there is massacre by fire from far away by the enemy you barely can see. One is red and one is white.

"There is the longhouse where families live together, and there is the cabin where the single family cringes behind the clear rock that does not let in the wind. One is red and one is white.

"There are the woods of the west, where a man can still be free, and the fields of the east, where men think they can own land. One is red and one is white.

"You drink the rum and not the water. You shoot the far fire and not the stone arrowhead. You live in cabins, not the longhouse, and you live closer and closer to the fields every

year. You are not red, you are white. But you make a bad
white. They will not have you. Your men are fit only for
them to use as scouts. Your women are fit only for them to
mount. I have talked of this so many times, and what do I
hear? We *need* their blankets! We *need* their beads! We *need*
their guns!

"What else of theirs do you need? Their disease? Their
rum? Their Jesus?

"Why do you not understand that even as you conquered
the tribes around you, the English were conquering you?
Even as you became the most powerful of all nations, your
numbers were growing fewer and fewer?

"You think these Caughnawaga who lay still with their
eyes staring but not seeing, you think they are the dead
men, but you're wrong!" he shouted. "*You, my man-eating brothers,* YOU *are the dead men!*"

His last words escaped him in shrill, chilling syllables.
They bounced off the hills like a bullet ricochet, but when
they returned to the clearing on the trail, no ears were listening.

Toolah threw a few large pieces of wood on the crackling
fire. The barrels of the rifles glowed red in the flames. Louis
advanced to within three feet of the twisted face of the
renegade.

"Your tongue never could move hearts at the counsel fire,
Face Without a Nose," the son of Gingego said. "We know
about the English. Tiyanoga knew about the English. Our
friend Big Oak has never lied about the English. So we take
a little from the English, take a little from the French, and
hope they remain enemies to each other forever.

"But fools like you, and your Caughnawaga friends—your
. . . dead . . . Caughnawaga friends," Louis added with
satisfaction, "you would massacre your own people just so
you could boast that you killed *somebody*.

"The lives of the warriors of the Ganiengehaka are precious. We are so few, and they are so many. But your life is a
waste. We will all be pleased when you are no more." Louis

stepped back and nodded to the warriors whose rifles were glowing like the stones of hell itself in the superheated flaming coals of the fire.

One of the Indians removed his rifle from the fire and showed Red Hawk the red hot barrel. Casually he placed it across the renegade's chest and held it there while the flesh sizzled. Red Hawk sucked in his breath with a soft groan but did not cry out.

"Ah," commented one of the warriors. "He does not like the heat very much. See the tears. Like my little daughter when she hurts her finger."

"I will soon die," Red Hawk groaned through his agony, "but you will not outlive me by much—" He wanted to say more, but then a second Mohawk approached the tormented prisoner, presented his glowing barrel, and quickly shoved it between Red Hawk's legs, laying it hard against his genitals.

"Ah . . . ahhh!" he gasped. "Ahhhhggg." Not a full cry, but a weakening. The third watched as Red Hawk began to twist, trying desperately to rid his body of the searing agony that was turning his manhood into a cooked mass of fleshy pain. The second Mohawk removed his rifle, and the third carried his weapon with its hot, glowing barrel from the fire to a spot immediately in front of Red Hawk's face. Red Hawk had recovered enough to grunt a few syllables of painful articulate defiance:

"Filthy diseased scum will all be in hell before the passing of the season—"

His brief tirade was interrupted by a loud, prolonged, agonized, terrified scream, for the third Mohawk had jammed his red hot gun barrel deep into Red Hawk's empty eye socket and was now twisting it around, cooking the interior of his head closest to his brain.

The long, pathetic scream seemed to reach to Hell itself, and return to earth as an evil, shrill call from a thousand tormented demons. Then he fainted.

The way the Mohawks stared, silently, at the unconscious

rebel hanging forward on the stake, it was impossible to tell how much or even if they had been moved by his sufferings, or by his defiance in the face of those sufferings. He had done no more than what a warrior was supposed to do at the stake, but it wasn't clear whether they intended to judge him as a warrior to be respected, or simply a bitter enemy to be reviled without remorse.

It became clearer when Tall Bear reached into Red Hawk's mouth and cut out his tongue. Several minutes passed. The Mohawks watched their prisoner as he hung from his stake. They waited until his breathing had slowed down, then one of the braves splashed some water on his face and slapped his cheeks until he regained consciousness. They waited some more, while his one good eye cleared and he recovered his senses. He tried to speak to his tormentors, but all that came out was garbled, inarticulate noise.

"Red Hawk, my brother," Louis, son of Gingego, said patiently and slowly, so the tormented traitor could understand. "You are not the hero you think you are. When the torture came, you screamed like a woman and not like a Mohawk man. Do you understand me?"

Red Hawk nodded.

"We were embarrassed for you," Louis continued. "We took pity on you and we cut your tongue out so you could not scream bad words. Can you hear me?"

Another nod. His defiance had fled. They had at last reduced him to where he was ready to wish for compassion from his torturers. But compassion was the furthest thing from their minds.

Louis showed Red Hawk his knife.

"It has a good blade, does it not?" Red Hawk stared at Louis through his one good eye and gave no expression of opinion.

"It has a good blade. You helped to kill my father. Your scalp is mine." Now Red Hawk's one eye showed fear and his body began to shake. Quickly, with practiced hand, Louis made the incision and yanked the scalp from the head of Red Hawk. His body and his will weakened from the horrible torment he had experienced, Red Hawk screamed again as his face muscles sagged into the sadly inexpressive puddle common among scalped persons.

Again they all ceased their activities to stare at him and give him a last opportunity to view life through the eye of a living man. The mild summer wind had intensified, and roaring up the trail, begun to blow around the ashes of the nearly expired fire. Red Hawk strained forward from the post, breathing heavily, blood bubbling afresh from the cavity in the middle of his face. A lone whimper of despair escaped from his throat.

Three or four Mohawks who had stood back now came forward and began cutting chunks of flesh from his arms, legs, and buttocks. His body shook and he drummed his feet maniacally on the ground, as if a primitive part of his brain was telling him to run away.

Somebody cut open his abdomen and let his bowels slither to the ground. Somebody else picked them up and wrapped them round and round his neck. When he opened his mouth to scream, they tried to stuff intestine down his throat, but now his teeth were so tightly clenched together that they could not even smash his mouth open with the butt of a rifle. As he wriggled and he thrashed, they carved him and they cuffed them and they cut him and they cursed him and they took no pity on him for his screams and tears, but they didn't kill him. Not yet.

Then they stepped back. Consciousness remained, but all his dignity was gone. His legs no longer held him up. Only the thongs that bound him kept him from sinking to the ground. His body continued to tremble, and from his throat came a continuous keening sound.

"You're ready to die?" Louis asked.

Red Oak stared back blankly.

"You want to die now?" Louis nodded his head to prompt Red Hawk, and Red Hawk managed to nod.

"You would kiss our feet if only we would kill you now."

Red Hawk nodded again, without prompting. The keening continued, without him even knowing it.

"Your half-white Turtle Clan brother, you would kiss his feet if he would but end your life." Now the nodding was involuntary, continuous.

"Little Oak, he is yours."

"Louis," Little Oak said with affection. "I loved your father like my own. I love him still. My father lives. Yours died at the hands of him and others like him. If you kill him, I will be satisfied."

Louis nodded, looked around at his Mohawks, swung his Tomahawk around and made a great gash in Red Hawk's chest cavity. He reached his hand in, grasped the heart, jerked it out and cut it free with three quick cuts of his knife. While his warriors howled, he raised it high over his head and let the blood run down his arm, over his shoulder, and across his chest. He lowered the bloody organ and held it in front of his face, contemplating it for a moment. All eyes were on Louis as he brought it close to his mouth.

Then, suddenly, with a great grunt of disgust, Louis, son of Gingego, brought his arm back and flung Red Hawk's heart deep into the woods, where it fell to earth with a damp *squapp*.

By the time Red Hawk's heart had departed from his body, Little Oak had made his way up the side of the hill opposite the one by which they had arrived on the scene. He was not sickened by the sight. On the contrary, he was deadened to it. What was so important to his Mohawk brothers no longer mattered much to him. Red Hawk was dead, and that mattered. He would have been quite prepared to do the killing himself, but having gladly relinquished the honor, he did not feel deprived.

At the top of the hill he found a clearing that looked northeast toward the Adirondacks, and far beyond them, the country of the Caughnawaga. He wondered what was so powerful about the Catholic faith that its priests could have been able to seduce hundreds of Mohawks away from the powerful Longhouse to settle in the frigid country north of the St. Lawrence River.

Suddenly his father stood beside him. Little Oak studied him and wondered if he really knew him. His father read his expression and smiled.

"You're wonderin' why I scalped those two bush lopers, aren't you?" he asked.

Little Oak nodded.

"I'll tell you. You live with the Iroquois long enough, that's what you are. I just did it, that's all. I just did it."

"I was *born* a Seneca, yet you would not let me take a scalp down on Lake George."

Big Oak put his face close to Little Oak and let their eyes bore into each other. "Do you hate that I didn't let you take a scalp?" he asked, "Up on Lac St. Sacrement, I mean?"

"Hell no," his son spat.

Big Oak's smile grew wider. "I didn't think so," he answered.

The Mohawks stood in silent awe and stared at the tableau: Caughnawaga braves up and down the trail stretched out in various grotesque positions of death, many of them covered with blood, all of them devoid of any kind of skull covering; and most pleasing, the butchered, mutilated body of the hated Red Hawk, sagging against the stake, bound tightly by leather thongs.

They had done it all, and they were indescribably proud. But the time had come for them to make their departure.

The Mohawks carted off all the loot they could carry, with some bearing two or three extra firearms. In three hours they managed to put seven miles between them and the grim butchered corpses. These they had abandoned where they had fallen in battle. Red Hawk they left—what was left of him—hanging from his stake, silhouetted against the summer blue skyline.

More than two centuries later, somewhere in the foothills of the Adirondacks, there is a long forgotten Indian trail, overgrown with trees and brush until only an archaeologist could tell that it had ever been a highway for men.

In the center of that forgotten trail, seventy-five miles west of Lake George but not too far from the nearest ribbon of asphalt, where the sweet-smelling berries grow wild and the trees lay a new coat of leaves upon the ground every autumn, is a circle of discolored earth, all that remains of a young hemlock tree cut down and replanted to support the final agonies of a Mohawk who had gone over to the enemy.

## ❖25❖

IF THE MOHAWKS HAD HAD ANY RESERVATIONS about the legendary Big Oak and his son, their part in the perfect ambush had removed them. Their cool, deadly skill with rifle and hatchet marked them as dependable comrades in arms. Toolah, in fact, was spattered with the blood of a Caughnawaga brave who had had one big hand around his neck and the other about to plunge his knife into Toolah's belly when Big Oak's hatchet struck open the side of the Canadian warrior's face.

So it was with genuine regret that, while the Mohawks looked forward to further glory in battle at Lake George, they heard their Seneca companions announce that they would be heading southeast for Albany. Around nightfall they came to a fork in the trail, the place of their parting. There they decided to camp for the night. While Big Oak went from brave to brave, carefully checking their rifles and muskets, and making minor repairs on the spot, Little Oak sat with Louis and Tall Bear, listening to them speak in a language that he had learned to understand if not speak.

"A good day for us all," Tall Bear said. "We should return to the village and celebrate."

"I have been thinking of that," Louis answered. "How often does a nation win such a complete victory over its enemy? We will go home and show our people the scalps, and the guns, and all the things we have taken this day. Our braves will come forward, strong and untouched by their bullets. Our people will know that the Ganiengehaka are still the mightiest of nations. When the braves of the north fail to return to Caughnawaga, there will be great mourning in their villages, and when the word comes to them that the bodies of their mightiest warriors lie scalped and rotting on the trail, they will tremble even as did Red Hawk before he died."

Big Oak sat nearby, his back against a tree, quiet but attentive. Except for Louis and Tall Bear, the whole camp was quiet. No dancing, no rum. No celebration. That could wait until they arrived home. Fatigued from their run through the woods, the tension, the attack and the events that followed, they all rested. Some were already asleep.

And when they returned to the village, what would they celebrate? A brutal victory over their own at a time when they needed to unite? Big Oak shrugged his shoulders. He supposed that sooner or later he would be forced to make *his* choice, for his own survival. Perhaps the Senecas in Tonowaugh had made his choice for him.

In the morning it was time to say good-bye. Instead of taking the trail east to help Warraghiyagey continue the war against the French, the Mohawks would find their way back south to the valley that bore their name. Big Oak could not preach to them that General Johnson needed them, because he and Little Oak were going to tarry awhile in Albany, resupplying themselves, relaxing, and snooping around to find out if English incompetence and snobbery would put them in too much peril if they went north to join the forces on Lake George.

The twelve Mohawks and the two Senecas parted with much affection and many requests for the father and son to visit the village again before too long. Big Oak especially had a lump in his throat. He had come to like these young men very much, and he wanted to tell them again of his worries about the future of their people. But he knew that, fresh from their overwhelming victory, they would resent his worry. To them, at this moment, the Mohawks were invincible.

Two of them tried to present Big Oak with gifts from their store of captured loot, but Big Oak thanked them and refused the gifts so graciously that they could not be insulted. How could he tell them that he had cash in his pack worth much more than the value of the goods they had stripped from their dead enemies?

One last time Little Oak and his father said good-bye to their Mohawk comrades. Big Oak told Louis to please take care, that the lives of the Ganiengehaka were precious and that the perilous times required that they be on their guard at all times. Louis nodded, and the men turned away from each other to head for their respective destinations.

Yet one more time, before their trails took them out of sight of each other, both men turned for a last look. "Do not trust an Englishman," Louis said, and laughed.

Big Oak smiled back and started to reply, but something inside of him had a hold on his tongue. Instead he just nodded. Then the two woodsmen cradled their weapons and continued along the southeastern trail in the direction of Albany.

For the longest time they walked on in silence, brooding over the events of the past two weeks. The English were losing the war, and yet there was no doubt in either one's mind who would claim the final victory. The English colonies, after all, had people, English people, Dutch people, German people, hundreds of thousands of them. The French Canadas, on the other hand, were mostly an endless wilderness of wolves, moose, and Indians who could not fight like the Iroquois.

When the sun was directly overhead, the two stopped to appease their raging appetites, the usual parched corn and dried deer meat. They sat, chewing, and Big Oak had a few things to say.

"The time has come," he began, "to choose a new name for yourself. Little Oak is a child's name. Over the past year you have cast your childhood over your shoulder. You will never again be what you were."

Little Oak nodded. "I have been thinking the same."

"And have you been thinking of what your new name should be?"

"I have."

They chewed in silence for a while. Then, just as Big Oak was stretching his limbs, readying himself to get back on the trail, Little Oak spoke.

"Thad Watley."

The sounds hung in the air, but Big Oak did not reach out for them.

"That's the name I want. I don't want an Indian name anymore."

"That is your right," Big Oak said.

"That's how I feel," Thad said, staring at his father as if he expected an argument. But Big Oak gave no opinion. Without further comment, he picked up his rifle, checked the priming in the pan, stood up and slung his pack over his shoulder.

Thad was in the lead on this day. From behind, Big Oak watched him as his boy's long strides matched his own. When Thad looked back for a moment, Big Oak saw a dark look on his face that he hadn't seen since they had found Tonowaugh in ruins so many months ago.

"Your thoughts are of Red Hawk," Big Oak said.

"I hated him so, yet at the end, when he finally gave in, I did not feel triumph. With every scream, I thought of John Thompson, and Kendee, and Kawia and Skoiyasi, and how he caused us to lose them all, and I hated him even more. And I wanted to see him suffer. I was so glad to see him suffer. But still, it pained me to see him suffer. It pains me yet. He was always my enemy, and yet I wished it different. I wished he could have been my friend."

"Why?" his surprised father asked. "He was an evil man, was he not?"

"He was the cruelest man I have known, but he could see the truth. Just as you can see the truth. You told me the English will win. Do you still believe they will?"

"It will be a hard fight. Death will have a long party in the valley of the Mohawk, and many will come. But the English will win."

"Red Hawk believed that when the English win they will take all the land, and when they own the land, then you and I will be white men again. He told the truth. I know it now," Thad told his father.

"Even a clock that has stopped is right twice a day," Big Oak said. "Red Hawk was so full of hate that he could not think, he could only feel. I believe he stumbled over the truth by accident." He stopped and thought for a moment. "But you're right, son. Red Hawk knew the truth."

"Why did he hate *us* so?" Thad asked. "And why did Olida back at Tonowaugh hate us so that she had the people throw us away? And why did our friend Skoiyasi want to set us apart from him? These are things I do not understand. I grew up with the People of the Great Hill. They were my family. And yet, in the end, they treated me like a stranger. No, they treated me as if I were their enemy. Why? What did I do to them?"

Thad continued his strong, easy walk over the trail. Since they had left Tonowaugh, he had tried not to think of his last days there. Only now, with Red Hawk dead and gallons of Caughnawaga blood to wash away the pain of losing so many of those he loved, could he confront his Seneca past. He stopped, turned around and took a swig from his military-issue canteen. "Can you help me understand?" he asked.

"Maybe I can. They are helpless. We are not. We are free. They are not. They know we have been good friends to the Ganonsyoni, but they know that no matter how bad their life gets, they must remain what they are, but we can get out."

"Would they be white if they could?" Thad asked.

"They could no more be white than I could be a Canadian goose. We have lived with them. They have seen us as Indians. They have seen us as whites. Did any of them care to learn about how whites live and think?"

"John Thompson tried to learn English from you—and writing, remember?"

"But not for long," Big Oak replied. "They like their way of life. To them it is a far better life than the one the white man leads. At least that is what I think."

"You're not sure?"

Big Oak stopped walking for a moment, lost in thought. "Not sure? Son, now that you ask me, I haven't a notion. Fact is, I've lived with the Seneca for near twenty year now, and I no more know how an Indian thinks than how a bumblebee flies."

Thad turned to face his father. Big Oak put his hands on the boy's shoulders.

"I don't know how you turned out like you did. You must have spent too much time around me all these years. Most boys raised in the villages, white boys that they adopt, never leave the blanket."

This was one subject Thad did not want to discuss. It made him think of Kawia and Skoiyasi, and thinking of them still put a sick feeling in the pit of his stomach. And he realized that in spite of all the years, all the friends, in spite even of his mother and grandfather, he did not think any more like an Indian than his father did.

The thought made the earth feel unsteady under his moccasins. If he did not think like an Indian, who did he think like? The Dutch tradesmen in Albany? The stupid English generals who would rather see their men die in the ranks than hide behind a tree? The colonial farmers between the lakes, following behind a metal plow and raising huge families to plow up more land? If he did not belong in Tonowaugh, where did he belong? Running the wilderness trails with a pack on his back for the rest of his life?

"When you were near death," he said to his father, "when they were carrying you to the village, at a council fire in front of the whole village, he called me a betrayer."

Big Oak nodded. "He meant that you were free to turn your back on your people if you so chose."

"Ah, and *his* way of getting free was to turn his back on *his* people."

Thad trudged through much of the day imagining the silhouette of that twisted, tormented man still held erect by the thongs that bound his body and his neck to his stake, and eventually the sorrow went away.

The hate remained.

# ❧26❧

**H**E COULD FEEL A TUGGING UNDER HIS HEAD, and even in his sleep he knew what that meant. He could hear a knee move on the ground next to him, feel the pull on the rifle his head slept over every night.

He calculated where the face was.

And he hit it. Caught enough of it with his big fist to draw an "Augh!" from the thief. He then threw his body into the stranger, knocked him down, and drew a knife to the man's throat.

"Sweet God of mercy, don't kill me," pleaded a voice from the dark.

Thad was now fully awake. The low flames of a dying campfire flickered in the night. They were at the edge of the rapidly receding woods line, within sight of the walls of Fort Albany, and some scoundrel had attempted to relieve him of the Friedrich Deutschmann long rifle that his father had bought for him long before he was old enough to carry it.

"An investment," his father had told him, laughing while the ten-year-old struggled in vain to pull the hammer back. And the five-foot-long weapon was too heavy for him to lift into firing position when he was ten.

Over the past four years, he had killed many deer with it, as well as other edible bearers of fur and feathers. He had fed and clothed himself and other people with the rifle, and this year it had dealt death to a number of full-grown men of war, red and white. And now some no-good villain had coveted it and tried to take it out from under him in the middle of the night.

He could smell the fumes of rum, like an evil cloud, settling about his head. He reached for his rifle, pointed it at the tall, gaunt, desperate shell of a thief who had made such a foolish attempt to gain a weapon and instead had gained an enemy.

"Don't kill me. I n-needed a musket fer the army or they won't have me," jibbered the frightened man.

"Oh well, then," said Big Oak, who had awakened in a flash and was poised to crack the man's head open with his rifle butt if he had proved to be any threat to Thad. "We'll just march you on over to General Johnson's secretary and he'll see to it that you get a musket and some ball and powder and"—Big Oak looked into the man's face in the dim glow of the dying campfire—"a shave and a bath."

"Good," said the man, backing away. "Tomorrow. That's it. I'll look you boys up tomorrow, and you can show me the way to General Johnson, yes sir." And his long legs erupted into a frantic, clumsy run across the open field, past the myriad tents and sheds that continued to occupy the grounds around Fort Albany.

"I wonder how you think we can win this war with so many ol' boys like that fightin' on our side?" Thad asked.

" 'Cuz they've got arms and legs and eyes, and you'd be amazed what a bit of instruction and experience can do for even a poor piece of goods like that."

It was already tomorrow, with streaks of red coloring the dawn like fire arrows. They took out the last of their trail food and set it cooking in a pot for the first time in weeks. Then, as they always did at the end of a trail, Thad and Big Oak cleaned their weapons thoroughly and greased every moving part.

By the time they were finished eating, the sun had risen

high enough to cast the shadow of a man over the ground between them. They both looked up.

"Watley, is it?" came the voice from a man dressed like them, but with the air of a professional soldier about him.

" 'Tenant Jamison—you—how'd you get to live this long?" Sam rose to his feet.

" 'Major,' if you can believe that, Sam. That's what ten years and another war can do for you."

"Why—damn—John, this here's my pup Thad. He wants to know what you're doing skulkin' around the camps before officers are even up out of their lavender-scented beds."

"Ah, well, if you want to know, this is sort of a recruiting run. I've got this Colonel Robert Rogers looking for men to join his rangers, but they've got to be men like you, not like most of them." He pointed with his thumb over his shoulder at the pathetic collection of nervous and half-starved civilians camped out around Fort Albany.

Father and son looked at each other.

"You are the kind of men we need to beat the French. The Canadians don't have many men, but seems like most of them live their lives in the woods, marchin' and killin'. We've got farmers"—he pointed again at the campers outside the fort—"and tradesmen." This time he pointed toward the fort itself. "What we need is woodsmen who can march fifty miles in a day and fight a war at sundown. You're one of the best. What do you say?"

"Well I—" Sam began.

"We just come out of an Indian massacre," Thad said.

The major turned suddenly red. "Who'd they massacre?" he demanded.

"They didn't massacre. They *got* massacred," was Thad's response. "By us and some Mohawks."

"We've been out in it the past year," Sam said. "We're tired."

"We need you now," Jamison persisted.

"He needs to see his girl first," Sam said.

"There's a war on!"

"We know, damn it. We been fightin' it!"

"Then come with us and help us finish it. I know you. You like to have good men around you, and we have nothing but good men in Rogers's Rangers. Better that than fight a war with a bunch of redcoats, with captains that bang you on the arse with the flat of their sword and say 'Get back in ranks' anytime you dare to look for some cover. Those men are crazy. They'll get you killed. Come with us."

Sam looked at Thad, who stuck out his jaw. "When do we head off for the war?" he asked.

"This afternoon."

"I'm sorry, John. He's got a girl he ain't even kissed yet. He aims to do such a thing soon. And I have a few business things to wind up, by the way. When we've done what we came here to do, we'll find you, okay?"

"It's bad recruiting," Jamison said, "but I can't force you to *do* anything, and I know that you'll find us. I'd trust your word over a Dutchman's paper, that's for sure." Again he pointed toward the walls of Fort Albany. "Then I'll see you soon?"

They shook hands and Jamison walked off.

They watched him disappear, and Thad cast a worried look at his father. "Pa, I've always thought you were the smartest man alive."

"I never said I was, did I?"

"No, but I thought it anyway. Now you keep telling me the English are gonna win this war. I've seen two battles. One of them we won—"

"That we should of lost," Big Oak interrupted, "except the French were dumber than we were."

Thad nodded. "And the other one they just plain kicked our tails, now, didn't they?"

Big Oak agreed, as he stared out at the camp beyond them, watching men stir from their tents in various stages of undress, shivering in the cool morning air.

"Our home village got slaughtered by a small bunch of French and Indians, and there was no one to help them. An old friend of yours with a big rich farm and enough sons to have his own army says he ain't gonna support the war; and the Mohawks, who are the best red friends that the English have, don't really like the English or want to fight for the English, right?"

"Right."

"And these ragtag misfits roostin' in the mud out here, smellin' like the inside of a cow barn on a hot summer afternoon, are these the men that are gonna lick the French?"

Big Oak laughed. "They'll lick the French, all right, and when they're done, the English better watch out for them. They may be dirty and they may be wild and ignorant and maybe even a little crazy, but they don't like to take their hat off to any man, and the English gentlemen are big on bein' better than them."

"Then what are you saying?"

"I'm sayin' that once we've licked the French, we still better keep our powder dry, our flints sparkin', and our priming proper, because this country will not have peace until the redcoats are back on their side of the ocean."

"And what about the Ganonsyoni?"

"When the English have been kicked out, God help the Ganonsyoni. The New Yorkers sure won't."

Thad let it all sink in, but said nothing.

"Come on, son. Let's head for town. I'll leave you at the store and come back for you later in the afternoon."

"You think that ol' man'll let me see her?"

"See her? If you give him a business proposition that'll get him deep into the fur trade, why, I'll bet he'll let you carry her off."

The two rangy woodsmen entered the fort through the front gate and made their way to the store. The door was open, but when they walked in, there were no clerks and no thick cluster of customers crowding the counters. There was only Herr Wendel with a huge book cradled in the crook of his left arm and a quill pen in his right hand. He was check-

ing a shelf and making marks in his book. Balanced precari-
ously on the edge of the shelf was a container full of ink.

While Big Oak checked on some carpenter tools he
thought might be of use to the Mohawks, Thad walked over
to where Mr. Wendel was taking inventory.

"The shop is closed," the merchant said without looking
behind him. "I thought I had locked the door when I came
in dis morning. We will open in an hour."

He reached down to dip his quill and found Thad holding
the ink container.

"Ah, it is Katherine's trapper. How are you, Mr. Watley?
You come to take my daughter from me, yah? It is right that
a girl should leave her father's home and start her own family."

Thad was stunned into silence. He had only intended to
ask for permission to call on her again and had expected an
argument. Thad was hoping for a long, leisurely courtship
during which time a light from above would descend and
tell him that the time had come to ask for her hand.

The merchant dipped his quill and scratched an entry in
his ledger.

"Thank you, Mr. Watley. I must be truthful with you. The
way Katherine looks at you, I know you must think that she
would follow you into the heart of the woods, but you must
know that she is a practical girl. She would rather be happy
than miserable. She would rather be warm by a fireplace
when the snow is up to your shoulders, rather than shivering
in some dreadful forest.

"Do not think that you can bend her to your will. She
would have you only if you are a practical man."

He climbed down from his step stool, put his ledger on
the counter, and suddenly Thad knew exactly what he
wanted to say to this blunt but decent father.

"I too am practical, Mr. Wendel. I am not here to marry
your daughter. Not yet. I feel that I have one more battle I
must fight, and when I'm through with it, I'm gonna leave
the rest of the war to my father and *then* I'm gonna come

back and marry your daughter. And I am not going to carry her off into the woods as my grandfather Kendee might have done. My father is a businessman whose business is in the woods. My business will be in the towns, in the Indian villages, and on the big rivers. I believe that I would like a real home to come home to, not a longhouse with a fire in the middle that fills the room with smoke.

"I don't like the idea of killin' or of bein' killed. I don't like the idea of scalpin' or bein' scalped. I don't like sleeping with one eye open and one ear open all the time, watching for a bad shadow or listening for a new sound."

The older man listened with grave dignity to Thad's proclamation, but his eyes gave off a bit of a twinkle. "So Katherine should wait for you a little longer, yes? Why don't you just go off and kill your Frenchmen and then come back and ask her to marry you and we'll see then what happens?"

"Why? because I want to carry a little piece of her off with me. I want her to know how much I . . ." What he really wanted to do, what he needed to do, was hold her in his arms before he went away. The need was a hunger he felt in every muscle, every nerve of his body. "There are words and there are promises," he said. "In my village a promise was real."

"In my business too!" Wendel said defensively.

"I would like to see Katherine."

"You shall!" came a voice from the balcony above the counter, where Katherine Wendel had been listening to every word. Thad began to climb the stairs, and her father followed him.

"Father?" she said firmly. "I believe that the gentleman has something he wishes to tell me in private. If you will finish the inventory, then later in the day I will write up the orders for new goods."

The older man nodded and turned with an absent wave back to the shelves and the goods they held.

At the top of the stairs she took his hand and led him deep into the shadows at the rear of the balcony. He held both her hands and stared at her for the longest time but he did not speak.

"I heard every word you said downstairs," she told him softly. "If you truly feel that way, you need not say any more."

He nodded, then suddenly reached out for her and pulled her to him, but gently. He heard the breath leave her with a sigh and felt her hands on his shoulders and then touching the back of his neck. His lips found hers and held them in a long, tenderly searching kiss. He could feel her body tight against him, and for a moment he thought that his legs would no longer support him.

Then they both stepped back and took a new look at each other and loved what they saw. Thad saw more. In his mind he saw himself taking her with him to the woods, his woods, for just a few days of freedom, before the time came for him to leave those days behind forever.

It was just a dream, and he knew it, but the thought of carrying Katherine off stirred his imagination and warmed him from his cap to his moccasins. A girl like Katherine, why, he'd carry her to Niagara and back on his head, and kiss the whole Seneca nation good-bye in the bargain. His mind drifted off the balcony, through the gates of the stockade, and back up the trail that led from Albany to the mountains. In his mind he pictured the strong, stocky figure of an angry, hostile Mohawk, his belt awash with scalps, running through the woods on his way to his next furious encounter. Well, Red Hawk, he silently told the apparition, I won't be there. Little Oak smiled a secret smile that made Katherine want to discover what was on his mind. But this thought was his alone. Red Hawk, you murdering devil, you were right, he thought. But can you blame me?